STALEMATE

STALEMATE

a novel

Gary Briley

STALEMATE

By

Gary Briley

ISBN 978-0-578-10316-7

Printed in the United States of America

First Edition

Stalemate is a work of fiction. Any resemblance to
an actual person or persons living or dead is
coincidental and not intended.
References to locale, or naming of specific locations
is not intended to be precise or represent
actual conditions and exist only in the mind of the author.

Acknowledgements

I would like to thank the members of the 6Meet writing group
for their valuable comments, insight and patience.
In particular I am beholden to
Clidean Dunn, Neil McCabe, Mike Sajben, and Jim Smith, and
especially to Willa Perrine for her unflagging support, patience
and editing skills.

And thanks to my wife Kay for her patience
with my neglect of her and the many home duties
I set aside during the production of Stalemate.

Cover photograph by,

Aaron LaCluyze
http://mrbook2.smugmug.com

STALEMATE

2:00 PM Wednesday
20 May 2009

Diversions. Give them something outlandish to catch their attention, something you can change or abandon in an instant—a tactic she had garnered from Alonso the impersonator, a friend of her dead father. It had served her well for eight years.

She adjusted the rear view mirror, studied her reflection for a moment, fluffed the bangs of her black hairpiece, and pushed a stray reddish-brown lock under the wig. She opened a small cosmetics kit, applied a top coat of black lipstick that matched her eyebrow makeup, mascara and eyeliner.

Satisfied with the image, she removed a pair of dark-rimmed glasses, gaudy bracelets and earrings from her purse and put them on. When she ditched the wig, jewelry and makeup and put on the light beige slacks, the simple matching blouse and low-heel pumps secreted in her purse, she would create a new persona within minutes. Alonso would be pleased.

She slid back in the seat of her SUV and stared at the doorway leading into the Lancaster Mall. She had planned to melt into a swarm of shoppers, hoping that if someone took note of her as she purchased her supplies, they would remember only the black hair, heavy makeup, thick-soled boots, dangling earrings and the dark clothing beneath her black knee-length coat, but the nearly empty parking lot told her there were few people in the stores. If she waited for the evening crowd, her Lincoln City bank, a two-hour drive to the

Oregon coast, would close and deny access to her safe deposit box in which she had sequestered her escape package—$60,000 cash, passports, driver's licenses, and birth certificates to provide an identity for another life, her fifth.

She shivered, remembering when in Borders Books and Music in downtown Salem she had first noticed the middle-aged man, ordinary except for his ashen skin and hollow cheeks. She became aware of him not because of his bleak appearance, but for the furtive glances he threw her way, not the usual macho assessment, but penetrating to her core.

She had felt his presence for a week—a fleeting image reflected in a store window, in the mirror of a parked car, a shadow in the recess of the bookstore storefront—phantoms that were not there when she turned to confront them. She thought she had seen him in a car parked near the art gallery—there one minute, gone the next.

There was only one explanation—*The Wolf.*

What did he want? Why hadn't she detected his hired goon sooner? Surely he would not harm her—The Wolf knew if she were dead or incapacitated his life would soon be over. Their standoff had been in place for nearly eight years. Had something changed? Had the family life that had been thrust upon her blunted her instincts? Would he assault or threaten her husband? Her son? How far would he go to force her to give up the tapes and journals?

Her mind shut down as cold fear gripped her, terror she had not experienced before. Her body shook, her breath came in shallow gasps, her stomach cramped. She gripped the steering wheel and rocked back and forth for a few moments before her composure returned. She could not allow the Wolf to control her life or harm her husband—or her son.

Why had she married? It changed *everything.*

She had spent the past week agonizing over her alternatives. Her associates thought her life idyllic—a workaholic but considerate husband who provided more than ample financial resources, a son who was a joy, and success beyond expectations in her profession.

Idyllic? Yes, were it not for the asphyxiating routine that filled her daily life. She had to break free. Despite her meticulous preparations, doubt still plagued her. Should she stay with her original program to leave her husband—to become less involved and fade away gradually—a plan she had been working for a year before The Wolf's ghoul surfaced? Delaying her departure for six weeks could place her husband and son in grave danger. If she was to escape and return to her nomadic lifestyle, she had to disappear now.

She exited the SUV and walked across the blacktop toward the mall entry doors, head down, wondering if the heavy make-up and bizarre clothes were sufficient diversion. Well known in her art world, she seldom appeared in public without someone stopping her for a chat, but today she needed anonymity in order to collect some items missing from her getaway supplies.

Dread festered during the hour of shopping. Her previous relocations had provided the adventure and challenge she craved, and she expected this move would present fresh opportunities, but she wondered if she could tolerate the hole in her life that abandoning her son would surely create. She knew he'd be all right; his father and family would love and care for him.

She exited the mall, hoping nervous perspiration had not transformed her overload of cheap makeup into rivers of black goo. As she pushed her cart down the parking aisle, she was vaguely aware of a vehicle behind her, a car length away when she opened the rear hatch of her SUV. Its red finish and polished chrome grille and bumpers glistened in the afternoon sun. The ragged coughs of the powerful engine at idle stirred a vague familiarity. A reflection from the windshield blurred her view of the driver.

She placed her acquisitions in the rear of her Nissan, slammed the hatchback closed, and hiked the strap of her purse higher on her shoulder. As she herded her empty cart across the asphalt toward the collection stall, she wondered; does this guy want my spot? There's plenty of parking. She drifted to the edge of the lane hoping the driver of the classic would move on by. She slammed the cart into the nest, looked up, stared across the sparsely populated lot, her eyes wide.

He doesn't want my parking space—*he's after me!*

She whirled and faced the vehicle that was now less than twenty feet away and moving toward her. Her uncertainty about the car vanished. As if watching a slow motion video, she took in the disarray of the driver's dirty blonde hair, his grubby beard, his bulging biceps that stretched the arms of a black tee shirt. She didn't know him. She saw his smirk, heard the engine roar, the tires squeal. In the brief second their eyes locked she felt the malevolence she'd thought purged from her life.   The red and chrome behemoth accelerating toward her was no phantom. She made a diving leap. Too late.

The metal hood of the right headlamp smashed into her hip, threw her down the parking aisle. The wheels bounced over her body.

The car raced across the parking lot, merged into southbound traffic on Lancaster.

1:00 PM Wednesday
20 May 2009

    Nicholas Storey, President of Storey Construction Inc., swiveled his new office chair sideways to his new desk, stretched his legs, laced his fingers behind his neck and stared out the window in the sidewall of his freshly decorated office. A breeze stirred the leaves of the oak tree silhouetted against scattered white clouds in the sky. He wanted to be outside, to smell sawdust, to hear the whine of a Skilsaw.

    For years, he had urged his father to convert their partnership to a corporation. It was the thing to do: the tax benefits, limited liability—oh, he'd had a long list. Before the Inc. appeared on the company letterhead their projects moved to completion with minimal hassles. He, his grandfather Walter, his father Victor, and Valerie Price, Victor's secretary and alter ego, had been a team—in his father's words, a well-oiled machine.

    Nicholas had managed the field operations—the actual construction work. "Where the rubber meets the road," he liked to say. Victor handled their customers, subcontractors and suppliers. Valerie, when she was not backfilling for Victor or Nicholas, sorted out and dealt with administrative matters. Walter, Gramps, managed the cabinet shop and mother-henned the finish carpenters.

Now there were titles, job descriptions, a procedures manual, enhanced internal documentation, and new reports to the State and other authorities.

Nicholas turned toward the trophy wall behind his credenza and focused on a frame holding the yellowed original license for Storey's Cabinets, issued on May 10, 1949, to Walter Storey. Walter had started his shop after an apprenticeship provided by the GI Bill for his service in WWII. Walter had insisted that Victor and then Nicholas as teenagers and young men work in the shop. You won't understand the building business, he would say, unless you feel sawdust in your hair, splinters in your fingers, and your hands are rough with calluses. Then you will know the meaning of a day's work, and your understanding will begin.

Walter died in the fall of 2008. Nicholas hoped he could keep his grandfather's legacy alive.

In January 2009, Victor, then president of their new corporation, stepped aside to manage Walter's cabinet shop—the core from which Victor and Walter had grown Storey Construction into a contracting and engineering firm with a multi-million dollar yearly gross. It was time for Nicholas to take over operation of the company: Victor wanted to simplify his life, work fewer hours, and indulge his passions: fly-fishing and classic car restoration.

It was soon apparent to Nick that his father had not relinquished his right to schmooze customers, subcontractors and suppliers. If an issue or job piqued his interest, he elbowed in, full of energy and advice. Valerie, now administrative vice president, accused Nicholas of micromanaging, not focusing on the big picture—he spent too much time "in the field." Caught between Victor's and Valerie's concepts of the company operation, Nicholas wondered if he was president or a puppet with a title.

He walked to the window, crossed his arms over his chest and looked at the oak his grandfather had planted sixty years ago. He let his eyes wander from its base up along its sturdy trunk to patches of sunlit cumulus surrounding its upper branches. "Gramps, what would you do now?" he muttered.

His desk phone rang. He let it ring three times before he lifted the instrument from its cradle.

"Storey."

"Is this Nicholas Storey?"

"Yes. Who's this?"

"My name is Bill Stevens."

"What can I do for you?"

"I would like a moment of your time, ah. I want to build a house."

"I can have our design department contact you . . . or do you have plans?"

"I do not, but please bear with me for a moment. I've seen your work and am impressed, but my problem is, well . . . unique. That's why I called you directly."

"Okay, Bill Stevens right?" Storey grabbed one of his business cards from the stack on his desk, wrote the name on the back.

"Yes. Mr. Storey, I'm—"

"Nick. Everyone calls me Nick."

"Nick, I'm very short on time . . . a little break from my conference. Let me explain my predicament, then you can decide to help me or not. *Please.*"

"Okay."

"Thank you. My wife and I want to build a house on our lot up on Eola Drive."

"We've built several homes up there."

"I know, top-end, high quality."

"Thank you. We try."

"Nick, I've been very busy lately and, truth be told, I've neglected my wife."

"I know the feeling."

"Good. Sorry. I don't mean it's good, just that you might understand my situation better. I'm rambling. I'll get on with it. We have tickets for a vacation in Hawaii. Plane leaves at five this afternoon. My wife has given me an ultimatum. She's going with or without me. I have to—I want to go."

Storey pushed fingers through his hair. "How can I help with that?" he said, suppressing an urge to say they were builders, not marriage counselors.

"Here's my problem. I planned to surprise her with a design contract and preliminary drawings for our new house when we return from Hawaii. My work has been insane lately and I haven't had time to arrange it. Long story short . . . I'll be finished here in about twenty minutes. I'd like to meet you at the lot with our back-of-the-envelope sketches and magazine tear-outs and spend about an hour with you."

"I have made plans for my afternoon, Bill. If you had called sooner—"

"You could bring a preliminary contract—whatever you need to have something for us to review when we return. Nick, please say you'll come."

Storey rocked back in his chair. Steven's story was so strange it had to be real. Did he want to get involved with someone so harried? Customers who were generally unavailable meant delays and constant changes that ate into profits.

He had planned to visit the Harrison project today. Stevens's lot was just a few minutes out of the way. He could squeeze in an hour. Not much to lose. Contracts were scarce these days.

"Nick, you still there?"

"Uh, yes. I can make it."

"I'll bring my checkbook. How much would you need to get started?"

"How much do you plan to spend?" Storey rolled the business card through the fingers of his left hand.

"Mil, mil and a half."

Storey's instinct tugged at him. *Cover your ass with this oddball.* "We usually get one percent deposit for a concept layout and initial consultations," he said. "Call it ten thousand."

"Great. I'll see you there about 1:30?"

"Bill, I'll need to know where."

"Oh . . . wow, sorry. Of course. It's in the 3400 block, south side. Only vacant lot."

"Okay."

"Nick, I forgot, geez, my brain is fried. Can I get your cell number in case I get hung up?"

Storey gave it to him. "Bill, can I get yours?"

"Sure."

Storey wrote it on the card under the name.

"Man, I really appreciate this. Thanks. Gotta go." The phone went dead.

Storey resumed his stance at the window. Stevens' comment about neglecting his wife amplified an uneasiness that had been gnawing at him. Was his bond with his wife crumbling? Julia said she understood that the reorganization of Storey Construction required that he devote extra time to his work, that his leaving early and staying late was not a permanent thing. Despite her affirmation, Julia was spending more and more time away from home—asserting that without free time to wander the beaches, forests or backcountry, her work would go stale. She claimed she needed to recharge her creative batteries, that her "inspirational tours" allowed her to gather ideas and make sketches for new paintings and, perhaps, liberated from the demands of everyday life, she could find time to craft a canvas or two.

Julia had been upset, suppressing tears, when he left the house, but when he asked her if she was okay, she patted his arm, said "I'm fine," and kissed him goodbye. Feeling guilty that he had not questioned her further, he had called home, hoping to meet her for lunch, but Suzume, their part-time nanny and housekeeper, informed him Julia was not home.

Was his work taking too much from relationships with his wife and son Eric? Had he become oblivious to their needs and moods? Had he let work trivia divert him? Should he delegate more? Would it help?

Storey shook off his dark thoughts, walked into the reception area and entered Valerie's office. She held a phone to her ear, her lips set in a firm line. She worried a stray lock of fox-red hair between a thumb and forefinger. She raised a hand to squelch Storey's question. He guessed she was listening to "press one for . . . press two . . ." He tilted his head; rolled his eyes toward his office. She nodded, raised her hand, fingers splayed. "Five minutes," she mouthed.

Valerie's grasp of the subtleties of company operations matched or exceeded that of his father, and was superior to his. Despite their differences concerning his management style, if Storey needed information about some obscure issue or advice on how to best interface with someone or something unfamiliar to him, he sought her counsel.

Storey did a quick survey of her office and felt ripples of envy and inadequacy nibble at him. Her office could be the front cover of Architectural Digest.   Her desk had no more than three or four documents on its polished top at any moment. His — well, he knew the approximate location of everything, and he cleared it every month or six weeks. Perhaps, in time, he would adapt to his new status—or not.

He returned to his office, leaned against the side of the door, stared at the outsized common area, Victor's room, more commonly called "Victor's," and listened to the drone of voices punctuated by the occasional buzz of a telephone. Victor had toiled in the Oregon mists for several years before he was able to convert his ideas to actual brick and mortar. Nicholas was in elementary school when his father began sketching his new building, a sophomore at South Salem High when they occupied the first phase of the Storey Construction complex.

The offices of Storey Construction resembled a warehouse for desks and bookcases. *No walls or barriers will block the exchange of ideas at my company.* Storey smiled; his father's words as fresh as they were twenty-plus years ago. Valarie and Storey occasionally retreated behind the sliding glass doors that separated their offices from the common area, the two spaces Victor had conceded to individual privacy.

Storey forced his thoughts back to the present, to the conversation with Stevens. "Weird," he muttered.

Valerie strode past him and perched her five-two elegance on the sofa to his left. She sighed. "Talking to a computer raises my blood pressure." She took a sip from her water bottle, looked up at him. "What's weird?"

The Stevens saga could wait. "Oh, I just finished a quick look at the cost data you gave me about the Harrison job," he said. "I need to study it some more, but like you thought, something is screwed up. It's behind schedule and costs are excessive. You gave me last week's summary. Do you have an update? I'm going to the job site this afternoon."

"You have the latest." Another gulp of water. "Nicholas, have you reviewed the applications for a Field Operations Manager?"

He pressed his back against the doorframe, crossed his arms over his chest. He had heard her arguments before, ending with, "You spend too much time at the job sites." He was not in the mood to encourage her just now. "Yes, I have, but this thing with Harrison needs resolution now."

"You've been saying that for weeks. Every time there's a problem."

Storey grinned. "You left out, 'You can't put this off forever.'"

She stiffened her back, glared at him. "It seems a waste of breath."

"Do you know how sexy you are when you're miffed?"

She threw her empty plastic bottle at him. He caught it easily, chuckled, placed it on the sofa end table. "I'm leaving now—be gone a couple of hours. I'd like to have a chat about our esteemed insurance agent when I return. Were you able to arrange a visit with George?"

"George Rainey, at six tonight." She pointed at the floor. "Here."

"Wow. Here? That's a first. Little George never meets outside his lair, or after hours. How'd you manage that?"

She looked up at him, her lips pursed, said, "Nicholas, there are some things you don't want to know."

Storey stroked his mustache and stared at her for a long moment. Why did his father and Valerie become circumspect when their discussions centered on insurance—and Rainey in particular?

He shrugged, turned, and walked out the door. He stopped; stuck his head and shoulders back inside. "I like your new suit." He waggled his eyebrows. "Blue is definitely your color." He was not quick enough to dodge the sofa throw pillow.

1:45 PM Wednesday
20 May 2009

Storey made a u-turn and parked his Ford Crown Victoria in front of the only vacant lot along the stretch of Eola Drive Stevens had described. The property separated a three-story stucco with a red tile roof and a clapboard wood frame that seemed to flaunt its turrets, dormers and outsized glass windows.

Storey removed his camera from the glove box, exited the car, leaned against the fender, and studied the panorama spread below him. The sprawl of South Salem filled the quadrant to his left. The I-5 sliced north just past the airport, dividing the city like the spine of a book laid open. To the south, he could see the slate-gray Willamette snaking across the countryside. Stevens had chosen a prime location.

He took photos looking down slope from the corners and center of the property, then scrambled down the incline and repeated the process facing up from the street below. Back in the car, he made a sketch of the lot indicating his estimate of the contour of the land, a thirty-foot drop front to rear, the slope steep in the center, shallow at the top and bottom. Confident that his map and photos coupled with Stevens' ideas would suffice to produce a preliminary design, Storey set his clipboard aside.

He opened Valerie's report on the Harrison project, and studied the summary chart comparing the current status with the original cost estimates and schedules. The work was behind schedule and over budget. He retrieved the clipboard, pulled a fresh sheet to the top, and made notes as he flipped the pages of the document.

Forty-five minutes later he closed the report and stared at his notes.   Material costs were within limits.   Subcontractor extras exceeded the allowances, mostly charges due to schedule delays. All the labor costs for the work performed by Storey Construction employees were excessive and had taken longer to complete than estimated.   The problem, as he expected, was internal and the job superintendent, Joe Orland, was his first choice for investigation. Who else would have authorized a forklift rental and kept it on site for a month?

Storey had used Orland as a project manager off and on for several years.   Orland had performed adequately if the project was clear-cut, but he often required supervision to coordinate the subcontractors and maintain schedules, a task Storey had not found time for in recent months.

He looked at his watch.   2:50. Nearly an hour waiting for Stevens. He started the engine, reversed his u-turn, and drove down the hill.   He wanted to eyeball the Harrison job site to add some specifics to Valerie's report, details that he could use to implement actions to bring the project in line.

He parked on a street adjacent to the Harrison project at a spot that gave him a clear view of the site and the rear of the job office; a twelve-foot trailer. He hoped his venerable Crown Vic would not draw the attention that his red crew-cab truck would surely command.   He opened the glove compartment, removed his binoculars, and focused them on the trailer's rear window. The mini-blinds were closed. Three pickup trucks were parked nearby.

He shifted his view to the first floor of the building; saw no activity.   The framers had moved up to the second floor.   He wondered why the carpenter's debris still littered the slab if they were finished with the first level and why the plumbers and electricians were not present. Why had the mounds of earth from the footing excavation not been spread and smoothed? He picked his logbook from his briefcase and made some notes.

He fought an urge to walk across the street and see what was happening in the office. Was Orland in there? Who else? He rolled down his window, heard hammering, and a Skilsaw's growl. Lars and his crew of carpenters were hard at it. He closed the window, decided to wait for a few minutes.

His wait was short. The trailer door opened. Orland and two men came out, laughing and exchanging high fives. Orland locked the door and walked unsteadily to his truck. From his position a block away, Storey suspected they had been drinking. He grabbed his camera and snapped several pictures. Each man jumped into a pickup and left.

Storey followed the convoy at a respectable distance. Five minutes later, they turned into a parking lot of a downtown bar, McGuire's, a hangout for construction workers. He parked across the street and took pictures of them getting out of their trucks and going into the bar.

He opened the Ford's door, stopped short of stepping out of the car. He wanted to confront Orland and his cronies while they were off the job during working hours, but what could he say after *You're fired?* He didn't know what was and what wasn't happening at the job site. He needed to talk with the carpenter foreman and inspect the interior of the trailer. It was a safe bet the trio would be in the bar for an hour or more. He shut the door, and headed back to Harrison's.

Storey skidded the Ford to a stop in front of the job office, jumped out, slammed the door, and ran to the trailer. He fumbled with the combination lock. Inside he saw the desk was clear except for three empty glasses. He grabbed one of them, sniffed it.

Scotch.

He sat in the desk chair, opened drawers. In the bottom left, he found a nearly empty bottle of Bushmill's, set it on the desk. *Nothing but the best for these sleaze balls.*

He rummaged through the papers on the plan table, found two change orders still in unopened envelopes buried under a copy of the architectural plans. He grabbed the envelopes, slammed them onto the desk, and ran outside.

"Lars!"

A tall thin man appeared at the edge of the second floor.

"Ya. What you want. Ah . . . Nicholas." He unbuckled his tool belt, dropped it to the floor. "I be right down."

Storey returned to the trailer. He picked up a jacket, a raincoat, a baseball cap, a shirt and a pair of shoes, folded the clothes over the shoes, tied the roll with the shirtsleeves. He jumped down the steps of the office and tossed the bundle and the Scotch bottle into the Ford's trunk.

Lars Swenson trotted from the building. "Ah, Nicholas, I am so glad to see you. Tomorrow morning I was coming to your office."

"This place is a total mess. Why the hell didn't you call me?"

"Ya, I should have. You always come by every two, three days. I was wanting for you to see for yourself."

"Sorry. Didn't mean to yell at you. Not your fault. I've been busy with . . . stuff."

"Orland, he say—"

"Don't worry about him. You won't see him again."

"He was a decent job super until booze demon hook him."

"Yeah, well, we can't tolerate this." Storey waved his hand indicating the whole of the site. "How do you get anything done with these piles of dirt and junk everywhere? The backfill and rough grading should have been done before you started the framing."

"Ya. That woulda been nice."

"And the plumber and electrician should be working their rough-out on the first floor."

Lars nodded, shrugged.

"I'd like you to take over running this job—a promotion long overdue."

Lars looked at Storey for a long moment. "Nicholas, I thank you for your trust. You are in a bind. I will do this job. Then we talk."

Storey extended his hand. They shook.

"You'll find everything you need inside the trailer; the plans, change orders, list of subcontractors and suppliers, and schedules—if they are of any use by now. Oh . . ." Storey pointed across the lot. "Call the rental company and get rid of that damn forklift." He looked around the site again, pulled the camera strap over his head, handed the camera to Lars. "To make sure Orland and the Union know I saw it, I need some photos of me inspecting this mess."

Lars snapped several pictures as he followed Storey around the site. Storey knelt by the forklift, pointed at the flat tire. "Just one more."

He rose, reclaimed his camera. "Thanks Lars. That should do it. I've got to go dump some trash. Call me if you need something." He jumped into the Ford.

The rear tires spit a cloud of dirt as he accelerated away.

2:30 PM Wednesday
20 May 2009

Storey parked in McGuire's parking lot next to a tan Camry. He opened the Ford's trunk and retrieved the bundle of clothes. He hesitated at the door, picturing the layout of the bar in his mind then pushed the door open and stood to the side as his eyes accustomed to the dim interior. He laid the collection of clothing on a nearby table. Orland and his two companions were sitting at the L-shaped bar, their backs to the door, Orland in the seat at the corner, and next to him, an empty seat with a drink positioned on a bar napkin. Storey recognized the small dark-haired man in the third seat—Miguel Sanchez, then, in fourth position, a large well-muscled man with a thick neck and long dirty blond hair sat with his back to the wall. Storey guessed he, like Miguel, was a union laborer that Orland had hired.

Red McGuire, the owner, was tending bar. Four men sat near the far end of the polished mahogany.

Storey slid onto the seat around the corner from Orland where he had a good view of all three men. "Hi, Joe."

Orland looked at Storey, eyebrows up.

Red placed a napkin in front of Storey. "Hi, Nick. Been a while. "What'll you have. I still have Killian's on tap."

"Joe, are you buying?" Storey said.

Orland chuckled. "Shure."

"Thanks, Red, but I won't be drinking just now."

McGuire shrugged, resumed washing glasses.

"Too high and mighty ta drink with the help?"

"Joe, I'd be glad to after quitting time. I have the remains of your Scotch in the trunk of my car. Should be enough for one drink."

Miguel pushed his beer to the back of the bar. "I gotta be goin'." He stepped away from his seat.

"Miguel, you can pick up your final check at the office at 9:00 tomorrow morning."

The small man's shoulders slumped. He sighed, turned to Orland. "I shoulda known not to listen to you. Joe, you're scum. Don't be callin' me no more." He walked to the door and left.

"You firin' him?" Orland pushed back, glared at Storey.

"Yeah, I am," Storey said. "And you." He pointed at the hulk sitting next to the wall. "And your buddy. I collected your stuff. It's on the table by the door. Don't come back to the site ever."

The big man scowled, straightened his back. "Who's this clown?"

"You're looking at the big man hisself."

"Vic Storey?"

"Nah. This here's Junior. Nick-ole-ass. He's tryin' ta' push his ole man out and take over."

"He's firin' us?"

"So he says."

"What fur?"

"You were drinking on the job," Storey said. "You were drunk."

"Who says?"

"I do. I saw you."

"You been spyin' on us?"

"Supervising the work is my job."

"I'll file a grievance."

"Be my guest. So I'll know it's you when I get it, what's your full name?"

The man looked at Orland, then back to Storey. "Russell Bowie. Double S, double L."

"Got it. Like double S in dismissed."

"Ya got no right," Orland growled, slid from his stool, his fists clenched. "Gotta follow union rules."

Storey moved away from his barstool, faced Orland. "I don't know of a rule that says I have to tolerate drunks on a job site."

"N' I don't have to take yer bullshit." Orland raised his fists. "C'mon Storey. Show me what you got."

"Joe, don't be ridiculous. I don't want to fight with you."

"Don't want? More like you're fraid you'll get yer ass whupped. I bet you're all soft and squishy from sittin' on your butt all day. I'm thinkin' you never been in a real fight." He stepped closer.

"I don't want to fight with you."

"Ya got no choice, asshole." Orland cocked his arm, drew his fist back.

Storey moved closer, raised his left shoulder, snapped his left arm forward, his fist grazing Orland's ear. Orland's punch landed, ineffective, on Storey's upper arm. Storey made a fist with his right hand, index knuckle slightly extended, slammed it into Orland's solar plexus. Orland staggered back, bent forward gasping for breath.

Bowie pushed off his seat. "You sumbitch. Try me."

McQuire stepped between Storey and Bowie, slapping the business end of a baseball bat into his palm. "Sit! And shut up while Nick and Joe finish their business."

The big man stared at McGuire and the bat, and sank slowly onto his seat, chin quivering, face flushed.

"Thanks, Red," Storey said.

"Been lookin' for an excuse to kick these low-lifes outta here. They'll have to find a new watering hole. They just wore out their welcome here."

Orland straightened, sucked several deep breaths. He stared at Storey for a moment, lowered his head and charged. Storey sidestepped, dropped low, swung a leg parallel to the floor and swept Orland's feet from under him. Orland fell face first, rolled onto his back, cradled his nose in his hands. Blood oozed between his fingers.

A man of average height, thin, not skinny, ordinary except for his shock of bushy brown hair, rushed from the back of the bar and knelt next to Orland. "Dammit Joe, I can't leave you alone long enough to take a piss without you doin' something stupid." He looked up. "What in hell have you done to . . . ?" The man stood, his forehead furrowed. "Storey?"

"Loukas." Storey glanced toward the vacant second stool and the drink he'd thought abandoned. "Oscar, are you part of this august group?"

"What if I am?"

"Well, nothing, I suppose. Just seems strange."

Orland moaned, pushed up to a sitting position. "Sonabitch broke m' nose, I'll sue him for assault."

"Not a chance, Joe," said McGuire. "You attacked him. Storey was just defendin' himself. I'll testify to that. He should be the one doin' the suin'."

"I'll go along with that," said a man at the bar. "It was unbelievable. Joe never touched him."

"Red," said Oscar. "We need some ice and a towel."

McGuire pointed his Louisville Slugger at Bowie. "You stay put. Start somethin', you answer to me." He waved the bat. "And Big Bertha."

Storey moved to a table at the far side of the room and sat watching Loukas administer aid to Orland.

"Your nose is not broke," said Loukas.

"It sure feels like it was." said Orland.

"You're lucky. Could'a been worse. Storey's got a Karate black belt." Loukas released his nose pinch and lifted the towel from Orland's face. "Bleedin's stopped." He removed the ice pack from the back of Orland's neck, laid it and the towel on the bar. "I'll drive you home,"

"What about m' truck?"

"Later. We'll get it later."

"Where's Russ?"

"He left." Oscar grabbed Orland's arm. "Let's go."

Orland slid off the barstool, followed Loukas out the door.

Storey jumped up, grabbed the roll of clothes, and ran after them. Outside, he saw Loukas loading Orland into the passenger seat of the tan Camry. He tossed the package to Oscar. "You forgot this. There's no reason for him to go back to the job site. His check will be at the office about 9:00 tomorrow."

Loukas walked around the front of the Camry, opened the driver's door, tossed the clothes into the back seat. "Storey, this isn't over."

"Last time, you said I should watch my back."

"Didn't think I'd have to repeat myself." Oscar got into his car and left.

Storey walked back into the bar, sat on Russ's stool by the wall, motioned for McGuire to join him. "I'll have that Killian's, and I'd like to talk."

"It's on me." McGuire filled a glass from the tap. "Anybody need something, I'll be over there." He motioned to the spot by the far wall that Storey had vacated. He walked around the end of the bar. Storey joined him and they sat facing each other across the small table.

"That was quite a show. I'd forgotten you did Karate until I saw you punch him in the gut."

"I'm rusty; some might say I'm corroded. Don't practice much. If Joe had been sober, I might've been the one with the bloody nose."

"I doubt that."

"It's the first time I had to use it—in a real fight, I mean."

"Remind me to walk softly around you."

"While you carry Big Bertha?"

Both men chuckled.

"So, Nick, what can I do for you?"

"I don't want to impose on any confidences."

"As a bartender I listen, hear a lot of things, private stuff, but I'm not a priest. Ask away. If it makes sense, I'll give you my thoughts."

"I was surprised to see Oscar Loukas with Orland."

"They're cousins."

"Really. Not drinking buddies?"

"Well, that too until a few months ago. They still drink together, but since you banished Oscar from your jobs he's been doing the club soda thing."

"Interesting. I found him drunk on the job three times before I terminated our association. Now he's reformed?"

"Hasn't had a drop of booze in my bar for several months. Three times drunk, you say?"

"Yeah.   And I might've given him another chance, but he erupted with a rash of attitude.   I don't have to put up with that. Too bad. He did good work . . . was hard to replace."

"He tells a different story.   He claims you fired him for no reason.   Just suddenly, out-of-the-blue . . . gone. I didn't believe him, but a good bartender keeps his opinions to himself.   Oscar badmouths you a lot. He's carryin' a grudge, big time. Be careful."

Storey took a sip of beer remembering Loukas's obscure threats: *Watch your back, this isn't over.* "You think he's serious or just making noise?"

McGuire shrugged.   "Wish I could help. If I get a whiff of something, I'll call you."

"Thanks. What's with Orland? I've had no serious complaints with his work, but suddenly he's off the rails."

"His wife left him for another guy. Took his kid. Moved to Arizona."

"Bummer."

"Yeah. First degree bummer."

"So, he's trying to drown his troubles?"

"Seems like it."

"He's cost us a bundle. If he had said something, we could have given him some slack. Could Oscar have a finger in the pie?"

"Can't say, but Oscar, Orland, and their buddy, Russell, could mean big trouble if they team up. Now, they *all* think you did them wrong. Russell's a brawler, a street fighter. Orland is no slouch when he's sober, and Oscar has the brains. Don't turn your back on any of them."

"Sounds like I better hone my Karate skills." Storey looked at his watch. "I gotta go. I want to catch Valerie before she calls it a day."

They stood, shook hands. Storey pointed at his beer. "Thanks, but I don't feel like drinking it now."

McGuire lifted a shoulder.

"Red, I really appreciate your help."

"I'll call if I hear anything."

"Thanks." Storey walked toward the exit.

"Watch your back, Nicholas Storey."

4:15 PM Wednesday
20 May 2009

Storey set his camera and two pages of notes on Valerie's desk, flopped down in a client chair. "Tomorrow is Joe Orland's last day, and his two cronies, Russell Bowie and Miguel Sanchez he's worked for us before, Bowie is new. Have their paychecks ready by nine. It'll be my pleasure to hand them their final checks personally."

Valerie crossed hands on her desk, looked at him. "I take it you found the reasons for the overruns?"

"Yeah. It's all in my notes. Oh, I'd like hard copies of the photos for tomorrow."

Valerie cocked her head, widened her eyes.

"Please?" he said.

She chuckled. "Not necessary, but thank you. Aren't you going to tell me about it?"

"You really want to know?"

"You poked my curiosity button."

"I'm so pissed I'm afraid I'll just rant." Storey waved a hand at her. "It's all in my notes."

"I've listened to your tirades on occasion."

"Okay. First off; the Harrison project doesn't justify a full time superintendent. Lars Swenson, the carpenter foreman, can handle the job easily, and he's agreed to take over. You can adjust his pay. Right?"

Valerie nodded. "So, what happened?"

"Okay. I parked about a block away and just watched for a while. Except for Lars and his crew, nothing was happening. Bottom line, Orland, Bowie and Miguel left in the middle of the afternoon and went to McGuire's bar. I confronted them, fired them for being drunk on the job. Then, Orland and I had a bit of a tussle."

"You mean you had a fight? In a bar?"

Storey shrugged. "Had to give Orland an attitude adjustment."

Valerie put her elbows on the desk, leaned forward. "Will I have to deal with a union grievance?"

"Unlikely. Orland started it. McGuire and a couple of his customers will testify to that. Oh, Loukas was there; he and Orland are cousins."

"Oscar Loukas? You terminated his contracts—last January as I remember—also for being drunk on the job."

"Yeah. And he threatened me again. Same as before; said it wasn't over."

"Meaning?"

Storey shrugged, lifted his hands, palms up. "I didn't have a clue then; don't have one now. He said I should watch my back."

"Do you think he's serious or is it just talk.?"

Storey leaned back in his chair, sighed. "Don't know, but now I have three guys annoyed with me; two brawler types and one with some smarts."

"Perhaps you should take the 'watch your back' advice seriously."

"Okay. If I knew what to watch for."

They were silent for a moment. Storey put an ankle over a knee, crossed his arms over his chest.

"You said Rainey's coming to see me at six?"

"Yes."

"I'm going to tell him face-to-face that we will not renew our policies."

"One more to be annoyed with you?"

"Probably. Dad and I had an argument about the renewal. I compromised and agreed to meet with the little fucker. Dad said—"

Storey saw a cloud flicker across her face. She considered vulgarity an inability to express one's thoughts, but he knew she could silence the most experienced with her depth of vocabulary and years of exposure to masters of the expletive. "Sorry. George is the most pig-headed creature I ever dealt with. And, I think he's a thief."

"George is concerned only with George. He's a self-absorbed sonofabitch." Valerie smiled. "Sometimes there's just no decent word."

Storey grinned, continued. "Dad says we owe him a chance to reconsider, that his thirty years of service has to be taken into account. Actually he said, 'I won't let it be dumped in the crapper.'"

He leaned forward, arms on his thighs. "Did you finish the summary of how our re-organization affects our employees' exposure to high-risk jobs?"

She opened a drawer and handed him a manila folder. He flipped through its contents. "Good job. This could convince the little bas . . . uh, the little elf to give us a break on workers comp rates and the liability premiums."

"Thanks Nick. Do you think he will?"

"No. Maybe he'll throw us a little bone here and there."

"You believe that?"

"No. Do you?"

"I think you have a better chance of being struck by lightning and winning the lottery on the same day."

"That good?" They both laughed. "Tell me again," Storey said, "why we can't just forget Rainey's blackmail and find another broker? I want to be rid of him—whatever it takes."

Valerie turned, focused on the far wall for a moment. "Nick, you agreed with Victor to get together with George. Have your meeting, and try to be nice. We'll talk after."

"Val, that sounds, um . . . ominous."

Valerie leaned forward, crossed her arms, her elbows on the desk. She engaged her lasers. "Nicholas, Victor and George have a long history. There are things you don't know."

Storey returned her stare. Why do I continually find these secret corrals, he wondered. Don't go there . . . Stay away from that. How can I operate with a partial deck? Does Val think I can't handle the job? Does Dad?

"Have you completed the comparison of our rates to the industry—our premium history with George?" he said.

"Yes, I have the abstract. We went back ten years." She made no move to retrieve it.

"You aren't going to let me see it?"

"Not until Victor reviews it."

Another closed door. He felt his jaw tighten, his pulse jump. He stood, paced.

She slid back in her chair, chin on a palm, watched.

Storey sensed a change of subject. She did not disappoint.

"George says you assaulted him during your meet last week. Did—"

"Damn fool."

"He may be that . . . or worse. Nick, did you—?"

"Not really." He dropped into a chair.

"What does that mean?"

"I spent thirty minutes in his hermetically sealed, sound proof office listening to rambling lectures on why our reorganization was doomed."

"And you maintained your usual serenity?" She slid back in her chair.

"Of course," he said.   "Actually, I gave in to my curious contractor syndrome—I amused myself by inspecting the room. The air registers have fire dampers. The walls are at least two-inch thick concrete plaster, probably the ceiling too—and a heavy-duty fire door. The damn building could burn to cinders and his office wouldn't be singed. The guy is seriously paranoid.

"He wrapped up his tirade with a bunch of personal abuse: I didn't have enough experience, no business savvy, and a bunch of stuff I don't remember." Storey waved a hand to reject the thought. "He never once uttered the word 'insurance.' Then he told me our time was up. That's when I lost it."

"Lost it?" She dropped her arms to her lap, straightened in her seat.

"Yeah, well, I told him he should take a flying leap off a very high cliff and I used some language you might appreciate but wouldn't like. Then I pushed everything on his half-acre of walnut-burl desk onto the floor—shattered his antique desk lamp. He seemed a bit upset."

She smiled. "Sonofa . . .," she said. Her chin dropped. "Damn."

Storey thought he should mark his calendar—the day he broke her composure.

She gripped the edge of her desk, eyes wide. "You're pulling my leg . . . aren't you?"

"After I listened to George rant, I realized he was not interested in any facts but his own—he has an agenda of some kind. He's lucky I didn't throw him through the big window he uses to spy on his workers."

"No, *you're* lucky you didn't."

"I was steamed." Storey crossed his arms over his chest. "I don't understand how dad tolerated him all those years."

"Perhaps you should cultivate some of Victor's patience."

"So I've been told . . . and by you on a few occasions."

She took a chug from her omnipresent water bottle; looked at him, eyes squinted, lips pursed—to stifle a laugh Storey thought.

He stared into her green eyes for a long moment. He rubbed a hand across his face trying to calm his pique. "I suppose Rainey's bummed out?"

She chuckled. "You suppose . . .?"

Storey sighed. Whenever he let his temper overcome his reason he always lost something, paid a price. Truth was, it happened frequently of late.

"I think George has launched a vendetta against me. He won't listen to anything I say. Why?"

"You're a threat. You challenge his schemes."

Storey sucked a quick breath at Valerie's use of the word schemes. He hoped she would elaborate.

She returned his gaze for a long moment. "George has been the company's insurance agent since Victor started expanding the business beyond the cabinet shop." Another swig from her bottle. "George was obsessive then. He's much worse now, much. Janine thinks he's sick . . . dropped over the brink."

"Janine Green, his office manager?"

"Yes. You know her, of course."

"Yeah. You jog and go to the gym together." Storey knew they had been friends since elementary school, like Swanson and he and Jethroe.

"Normally, we don't share business confidences, but Janine is concerned for George's well-being."

"I'm supposed to care?"

Valerie paused. "Janine says he closes his office door, stays in most of the day shuffling his papers."

"Papers?"

"Some documents that he works on, keeps them in his big safe. She says he rarely talks to new clients anymore. They've been losing accounts every week or so."

"Well, you can tell her to add us to the list."

"According to Janine, he resists even the smallest change in office procedure. 'Stick with the devil you know,' he tells her, 'It's always safer.'" Valerie leaned back in her chair. "His personal life is a mystery. His brother Harold seems to be his only contact outside the office."

"Okay, then . . . talk to Harold."

"Well, we see him at the gym. He lifts his weights, runs on the treadmill and ignores everyone."

"No chance he would enlighten you about George's problem?"

"Unlikely."

"So, you and Janine have discussed this. What would you have me do?"

Valerie leaned forward, took a sip of water. "Nothing. Be calm. No violence."

"I should consider my dad and George's history?"

"You promised Victor."

"Yes. Not one of my smartest moves."

"When a deal turns sour . . ."

"I know. Make lemonade," he said, cocked his head and gave her a fake smile. He looked at his watch. Geez, 4:42. He stood, walked to the door, turned toward Valerie. "I skipped lunch. I need to get something to eat and organize my stuff for my meet with Rainey."

"Nicholas, be patient with him."

He shrugged. "I'll try, but no promises, Val, no promises."

5:59 PM Wednesday
20 May 2009

The front door burst open. George Rainey entered, strutted along the hallway, his lips squeezed into a thin line, brow rutted, head bobbing like a barnyard rooster surveying his territory. A large man in a Marine uniform followed in his wake.

Storey glanced at his watch: 5:59. He had expected Rainey to be late—anything to gain an advantage. He was a minute early.

Storey stepped from his office into the hall. He did not recognize the soldier. They stopped, Rainey only three feet away. He looked up at Storey. His companion assumed an at-ease position beside him.

"Good evening, George," Storey said, extended his hand.

Rainey ignored the greeting and the proffered hand.

Storey shifted his focus to the escort. Storey assessed him to be about his height, six-two, or three, but it was obvious that he spent considerable time in the weight-lifting section of the gym. Storey guessed his weight at 250 pounds, lots of muscle. Considering his attitude—someone to avoid in dark places. Service ribbons and medals on his chest included a purple heart. Insignia on his sleeve identified a Gunnery Sergeant.

"Harold, this is Nicholas Storey, the guy I've been telling you about. Nicholas, I brought my brother along to protect my interests." Rainey smirked, resumed his head bobbing.

"Oh . . . okay," Storey said. ~~Is he trying to intimidate me?~~

Storey smiled, extended his hand once more. "Harold."

Harold assumed a stiff parade rest posture. Storey rubbed his palm on his thigh, nodded toward his office. "George. Please, have a seat."

Rainey swaggered in, slipped into a client chair, hands crossed over the briefcase on his lap.

Harold grabbed a chair from a nearby conference table, slammed it down near the office door. The wood creaked as he straddled the back support, his biceps stretching his jacket as he crossed his arms over the top rail.

Rainey's remark puzzled Storey. *Protect his interests?* Was it a physical threat, or payback for making a mess of his paperwork and breaking his lamp? Perhaps it was simply narcissism—a "my dog is meaner than yours" thing.

He needed a prop. He snatched up a thick notebook from a nearby desk, put it under his arm, walked into his office, closed and locked the glass slider.

Harold stood when the lock clicked into place, but slowly resumed his seat, his brow furrowed.

Storey felt he had just prodded a bull. A part of him expected to see an enraged head shake. The openness of Victor's arena and the sense of camaraderie it encouraged had proved constructive, but this was one of those times Storey wished for a massive oak door in a sturdy wall.

The three-ring binder and its two-inch stack of paper made a loud thump when he tossed it onto his desk. Rainey flinched, raised his eyebrows, focused on the tattered book for a moment. He recovered composure, opened his tooled calfskin briefcase, yanked a single dog-eared page from a well-worn manila folder, flipped it alongside Storey's faux report.

"Here's your workers comp rates, old and new hourly premiums by job category . . ." He rummaged in his case, came up with a jumble of papers, tossed them alongside the rate sheet. "And the worker category descriptors . . . and your new liability policies, including your completed operations exposure."

He laced fingers across his narrow chest. "Study them carefully, Nicholas." His lips curled; the soles of his feet skimmed the carpet as he swung them like a happy child.

Storey sat, steepled his fingers and stared at Rainey for a moment. All their insurance policies and workers compensation would expire at midnight on Tuesday—five days and six hours. The concurrent termination was ridiculous. He understood having to gather up-to-the-minute information on employment, contracts past and present, and a myriad of other details including appraisals of buildings they occupied including their contents, and vehicle and equipment values and usage. To collect it all for presentation in one short meeting with George was a massive effort and expensive when not done in the normal flow of business activity.

He believed Rainey had consistently padded the premiums and pocketed the difference, but he could not prove it. If Rainey's stance prevailed, the additional costs could seriously impact profits from some existing contracts. Storey had to resolve the insurance issue soon. He had two other agents working up proposals; companies recommended by Stacy Coffman, the corporate attorney, a partner in the law firm of his friend, Mike Swanson.

He picked up Rainey's documents. He wished he had Valerie's summary of their history of insurance costs relative to the industry. Why did she refuse him access? Why did his father have to review it before exposing the data to Rainey? How did his dad always seem to know when to be unavailable? He had left messages on Victor's cell phone voice mail for the last two days to no avail.

Storey's desire to be free of the arrogant little man had grown each day. He thought it was simple enough. Not renew. Find another agent. Problem over. Straightforward—until Victor intervened, insisting that "little George" be given a chance to negotiate; that their thirty years of alliance not be ignored. His father had been evasive. Unusual.

Rainey stood, walked around the office, his head bobbing. He inspected the art, award plaques, photos of completed projects, Victor with community dignitaries, and yellowing pictures of Victor when he pitched in the minor leagues.

Rainey pointed at the aging baseball photos. "I saw every one of his games. Did you know that, Nicholas?"

Storey crossed his arms on his desk, leaned forward. He was familiar with the story, but decided to go along with Rainey's diversion for the moment. Perhaps it would make him overconfident.

"No, George, I didn't."

"Yes. Every one."

"Really."

"Victor was on his way to '*The Game.*'"

"The Majors?"

"Yes, until the Yankees took over the franchise and brought in their own. Arrogant bastards."

"That's when Dad started to expand the business beyond the cabinet shop. George, he gave up baseball."

"Yes. And, that's when I took over my uncle's insurance business."

Storey heard ~~the~~ bitterness in Rainey's voice, saw the slight droop of his shoulders.

Rainey straightened, the smirk returned to his face. "It was a long time ago." He strolled back to his chair, his head floating back and forth with each step. "Nice office, Nicholas. You've redecorated and added some paintings since you took over from Victor. Very nice. Did your wife—"

"George, we're here to discuss insurance, not reminisce. Let's get on with it."

"Nicholas, your reorganization of Storey Construction is idealistic, a foolish mistake."

"George, you expressed that opinion last week. It's old news. Can we get back to the business at hand?"

Rainey stared at Storey for a moment. "I can't believe Victor endorsed it. Time will tell if . . ."

Storey tuned out. Rainey waved an arm as if to set a cadence for his tirade. He yanked a handkerchief from the pocket of his custom-made suit, mopped sweat from his forehead.

Storey riffled the pages of his bulky tome, opened the stage prop. His charade slowed the torrent of words. Rainey was curious. Storey forced a smile trying to exhibit a composure he did not feel.

". . . and by requiring your staff to cross-train you expose more of your workforce to high-risk job-site activities, therefore . . ."

Storey raised a hand. "I apologize for the late hour. I know it's irresponsible of me to take you away from your usual evening pursuits—"

"I am surprised, but I appreciate that you acknowledge my inconvenience. I will assume your confession is genuine. However, I—"

"This workman's comp thing is complicated . . . well it is for me . . . insurance has always mystified me." Knowing the tiny man required regular ego stroking, Storey added, "Perhaps you can decipher it for me. Please, if you will tolerate my ignorance for a moment." His father had been loyal to George since they were kids—there must be some unseen value here.

A smile flicked across Rainey's lips. "I try to be of service," he said, placed an ankle across a knee. "Even under the most adverse of circumstances."

Storey continued. "One of the reasons for restructuring the company was to reduce risk—and costs," he said, trying for a neutral tone. "We have gathered some data concerning our new operating mode—" He ruffled the pages of the three-ring binder. "—data that I believe show that a reduction in premiums is in order." He flicked the notebook open with a thumb, ran a finger down a table that displayed the bending strength of Douglas fir beams. He raised an eyebrow.

Rainey squirmed.

"We have reduced the time our people are involved with high-risk tasks." He pulled Valerie's file from his center drawer, handed it to Rainey, "This is a summary. After you study it I think you'll agree."

He grabbed Rainey's "rate" sheet and pushed back as if to study it. His earlier scan reaffirmed there was no change from the original proposal. Storey stole a glance at his watch—6:45 p.m.—nearly an hour and no progress. If he could escape in the next few minutes, he could be home in time to read Eric his nighttime Dr. Seuss story, and enjoy a reheated dinner. He had missed too many family activities lately.

Rainey flipped past the title page of the summary document, sighed, took a moment to read the introductory paragraph. He threw the graphs and printouts aside without looking at them. They fell to the floor, a clutter of paper on the carpet.

"George! You . . .!" Storey clamped his jaw shut, attempted to bite off the rage rising inside him. He pushed his swivel chair back, rose from his chair.

Then, as if some elixir had cleansed him, the aggravation and resentment roiling inside him subsided. Why waste the energy? He would never put a dent in the little guy's opinions—and it didn't matter. He *would have* quotes from reputable insurance agents that negated the need for Rainey's services.

Storey saw brother Harold stand and try to open the sliding door, then pace, his eyes locked on Storey. Storey, thankful he had slid the lock into place, punched 0911 and his office number into his desk phone. Bob Abrams, the security chief, was staying late tonight. Abram's insistence on an emergency silent alarm system suddenly made sense—sometimes a little paranoia was healthy. Armed assistance should be at Victor's within minutes.

"Calling for help?"

"I forgot to clear my voice mail."

"I never talk to a machine. Real person or forget it."

Storey suppressed an urge to say that he had noticed.

Rainey nodded toward the remains of Storey's summary report. "Self-serving . . . irrelevant . . . exposure is exposure." He spread his twiggy arms palms up, cocked his head. "The new rates are mandatory. Nothing I can do—wish I could."

Storey focused on Harold who was still pacing, glowering.

Abrams, a retired special services marine, entered Victor's with a hand on his weapon.

Harold stopped in mid stride.

Storey turned to Rainey who had resumed his rant.

"—making the concept of your restructure ridiculous, childish at best. Surely it will fail within the year. It's essentially a co-op of independent contractors. It's blatantly foolhardy. Further—"

Storey slapped his palms on the desk, leaned forward. "Enough," he yelled. He pointed toward the office door. "Out. Now!"

Rainey flinched, turned toward brother Harold who had turned slightly away from Abrams; his shoulders slumped, his arms limp.

Storey moved around his desk, unlocked the glass door, pushed it open.

Abrams crossed his arms over his chest. "What's the trouble, Nick?"

"Bob, these gentlemen are leaving. Would you escort them?"

"Not a problem." Abrams pointed toward the exit. "I'm sure they know the way."

Rainey scrabbled to gather his papers, clutching them to his chest, gulping air as he tried to find his voice.

"Leave," Storey growled. "We will not renew any policies with you—now *or* in the future. Your prices are ludicrous, your attitude insulting."

Rainey's head bobbled furiously. He stuffed his paperwork into his soft leather briefcase and moved down the hall after his brother. He stopped, turned. "We will discuss this later . . . at my office."

"No more discussion. We're done. It's over, George."

"Nicholas, apparently there are things you do not understand, consequences you are not aware of."

"Are you threatening me?"

Rainey backed away, smiled. "It's not over quite yet."

"Is there something about *no* that you don't understand?" *That's two, It's not over, threats today. What's next?*   No (?)

Rainey followed Harold to the exit, slammed the door behind him.

Storey stared at the door for a moment. "Jerk."

"Nick, should I put them on the no access list?"

Storey's phone buzzed. He grabbed the instrument. Probably Julia, upset that he was late again.

"Storey."

"Mr. Nick, this is Suzume."

"Ah . . . I'll be with you in just a moment." He pushed the hold button, laid the phone in its cradle. Why was their part-time maid calling him at work at night?

Storey returned his attention to Abrams. "No access? I don't think we have to go that far. George is harmless. The brother was set up. He folded like a pussy when you showed."

Abrams inspected his boots, pursed his lips. He looked up. "The man was a Marine Gunney."

"Yeah, but I think he was just window dressing."

"I hope you're right; my gut tells me our pal George is dangerous."

"I'll give you treacherous, certainly corrupt."

Abrams smiled, tapped Storey's arm with a fist. "You know, Victor may give you more flack than George."

"Maybe," Storey said, shrugged. "Maybe."

"Better make sure our friends leave the property." Abrams turned, walked away.

Storey watched the security chief stride toward the exit, muttered, "You're right. I still have to deal with Dad."

7:15 PM Wednesday
20 May 2009

Storey returned to his desk, picked up the phone. "Yes, Suzume. What is it?"

"Mr. Nick, Miss Storey not home yet. I stay—"

"I'm on my way." He wondered what 'Miss Storey's' note would say this time. He wasn't sure how many more of her disappearances or inspirational trips he could tolerate.

"No. Mr. Nick, you must listen. The police come—"

"Police?"

"Yes. I tell them you working. They going to you. I think you best wait for them. I will stay. Watch Eric . . . okay?"

Storey crossed his office, flopped onto the couch. "What did they say . . . the police?"

"They ask for you. I tell me nothing. I say you working. Give your business card when they ask where. Mr. Nick, did I do wrong?"

"No, Suzume. You did fine."

"Mr. Nick, Me . . . Suzume . . . I maybe in trouble."

"Why?"

"The policeman . . . he say not call you."

"I won't tell. It will be our secret."

"Oh . . . thank you, Mr. Nick."

He heard her muffled sob. "You're welcome, Suzume. You did good."

"I will call sister. Tell her I stay all night . . . no problem . . . no charge."

"I'll see you soon. Don't worry."

"I try, Mr. Nick. But not rest until I see you."

"Goodbye, Suzume. Thanks."

Storey put his feet on the coffee table, crossed his arms over his chest. Police. What could they want? Another job-site break-in? Theft was not uncommon. A sign of the times, the slack in the economy, especially building.

Still, he reflected, cops don't appear for a job-site theft. You have to call them, file a report. Perhaps someone had been hurt . . . or killed. That had happened several years ago when a second-shift worker had taken a fatal fall. His father had been roused from his sleep.

The buzz of his desk phone shattered his ruminations. He leaped across the room to answer it.

"Storey."

"Nick, there are two detectives at the gate." It was Abrams. "They're asking for you."

"Detectives?" He pushed the fingers of his free hand through his hair.

"Yeah."

"What do they want?"

"To see you."

"I'll be right out."

"They want to come to your office."

"You're kidding."

"Hardly."

Storey paced, wondering what Swanson would advise. "Okay. Send them in. Bob, I want you to find Mike Swanson, get him over here—pronto."

"Will do."

He could hear Abrams giving instructions to the cops, then a few seconds of silence.

"They're on their way. Where can I find Mike?"

"Start at the Wooden Shoe, then his apartment—they're in the book."

"Consider it done."

Detectives. Detectives have agendas. What could detectives want from him? He felt his pulse throb in his temples, his stomach cramp. He dropped into the chair opposite the sofa, massaged the knot rising in a neck muscle.

"Relax," he mumbled. No need to panic. Wait until they tell me their problem. Be calm, neutral, stay in control. He rose, walked to his office door, leaned on the jamb, put one hand in a pants pocket.

Nonchalant.

The side door opened and a man in a dark blue suit entered the hallway. He was medium height, stocky, walked with a confident swagger. Storey recognized the burr cut, the gray-flecked black mustache—Sam Oliphant. He patronized the Wooden Shoe on occasion. Johnnie Walker Red.

A woman, tall, athletic, light-brown hair, wearing a gray blazer with matching slacks and running shoes, followed two steps behind. Olivia Barton. His mouth dropped open, but he recovered quickly, smiled at Olivia, his college roommate, his former lover. He knew she had gotten her gold badge. Why was she here?

Olivia stared into his eyes, placed a forefinger over pursed lips. It took a moment before he understood—they were to be strangers for now.

"Mr. Storey, we need to talk with you." Oliphant's voice was calm, soft.

Storey waved them into his office, pointed at the sofa. They settled in, he sat in the chair opposite, across the coffee table, leaned forward. "So, what can I do for you?"

Olivia placed her hands in her lap, studied them. Oliphant cleared his throat. "We have bad news."

"My day has been full of that, Sam."

"I have to tell you this." He paused for a second. "There's no easy way to say this. Your wife is dead."

"What? . . . Julia dead?"

"Sorry."

Storey stared at him for a long moment, turned, looked at Olivia. "*Dead?*"

She raised her head, nodded.

"How?" he whispered.

She lowered her gaze.

"Hit by a car," Oliphant said, his eyes fixed on Storey's.

"Where?"

"Lancaster Mall parking lot."

"When?"

"About two-fifteen this afternoon."

Storey felt his hands tremble. He clasped them together.
Oliphant's voice was familiar, but it seemed as though it came from
somewhere else, a place distant, metallic. A mantle of weariness
enveloped him. He shivered, cold from the inside out. Julia dead?
Not possible. He looked at Oliphant, but his eyes focused far away.
"Can I see her?" Had he spoken or thought it? He wasn't sure.

"We'll need you to identify the body. Tomorrow morning.
10:00 at the morgue."

Storey stood and walked to the door. He grasped the top casing,
leaned into it and stared across Victor's room.

Her light extinguished. Forever beyond his reach. Last night
they had made love. Julia intense, insatiable—as if . . .?

He shook his head, turned toward the detectives. "In the parking
lot? How could she get killed in a parking lot?"

"Hit and run." Oliphant scribbled in his notebook.

"Jesus. Why would anyone do that?"

"We don't know. Thought maybe you could help us."

"How could I help? You're sure it's Julia?"

Oliphant looked at Olivia. "My partner here says she knows
her . . . knew her."

"Did you catch the guy?'

"No, but we have a partial description of him and the car. How
did you know it was a guy?"

"Just assumed, I guess."

Oliphant was silent for a moment, staring at Storey. "Just a
couple of questions," he said.

Olivia interrupted. "Sam, shouldn't we—"

Oliphant silenced his partner with a glance and a wave of his
hand.

Storey returned to his chair, focused on Olivia. She averted her
eyes.

Oliphant glanced at her as if reinforcing his order of silence. He frowned, returned his attention to Storey. "Where were you this afternoon around two?"

Storey thought for a long moment. Two o'clock seemed like last month. "Got a call. Went to meet a new client. Then I visited a job site."

"You sure about that?"

"Uh . . . yes."

"Where did you meet this client?"

"He didn't show."

"Really. Where were you supposed to meet?'

"It was somewhere in the 3400 block of Bald Eagle, ah . . . no, Eola Drive."

"Which was it, Storey?"

"Eola."

"You don't seem very sure."

"I've got it written down." He fumbled in his pockets. "I wrote it on the back of a business card." He spread his hands. "It must have fallen out of my pocket."

"How convenient."

Olivia put her hand on Oliphant's arm. He brushed her hand away. "Don't ever . . ." His look left little unsaid. She rose, walked to the door, leaned against the jamb, crossed her arms, and looked at Oliphant, her eyes aflame.

The phone on Storey's desk rang. He moved to answer it.

Oliphant stood. "I'm not finished."

Storey looked at Olivia. Her eyes flicked toward the phone and back to him.

He removed the instrument from the cradle.

Oliphant stepped toward the desk. "Storey, I'm not . . ."

"Hello, Nick Storey."

"*Detectives*?" Mike Swanson.

"Yeah."

"What do they want?"

"Um. Mike, ah, they say Julia's dead." He brushed his hand over his eyes.

The phone was quiet for a long moment. "Julia is *dead*?"

"So they say."

"How?"

"Hit and run. Lancaster Mall parking lot."

"Oh, my God . . . Damn. Are you all right?"

"I need you here."

"I'll be right there. Twenty minutes. Shit. What am I thinking? Which detectives?"

"Sam Oliphant and—"

"Sonofabitch. Oliphant?"

"Yeah and, uh . . . Olivia Barton."

"Really! Olivia. Your Olivia?"

"Yes."

"Wow. Have they tried to question you?"

"Oliphant. Some."

"You got a speaker phone, right?"

"Yes."

"Put me on."

Storey punched the button, hung up the phone, turned the volume up. "You're on, Mike," he said, dropped into his chair and turned it so he faced the back wall.

"Sam?"

"Yeah. That you, Swanson?"

"You been quizzing my client?"

"Just routine stuff."

"I know all about your routine stuff."

"Just doin' my job."

"Well, Sam, It's over. You ask my client one more of your fucking questions, I'll have your badge."

"Swanson, you comin' here?"

"Yeah. Twenty minutes."

"We'll hang until then." He looked at Olivia. "To protect your client."

"Listen, you asshole. You don't touch or even exhale toward my client. You've already violated his rights."

"How's that?"

"Don't play your games with me. The answers to any questions you pose to someone under duress are illegal, inadmissible . . . not to mention unethical. I could sue your ass for harassment. Hell, you know that. I'm wasting my time . . . you've been forewarned."

"He didn't seem stressed to me."

"Right. I'll buy that when I see pigs flying by my window. You still there, Nick?"

"Yeah." Storey swiveled his chair toward the desk.

"Hang in there. Don't even breathe loud until I get there, you hear?"

"Okay." Storey shut down the phone, looked up at Olivia.

Her nod of approval was nearly imperceptible.

8:30 PM Wednesday
20 May 2009

To divert his thoughts until Swanson arrived, Storey busied himself clearing his desktop, credenza, and conference table, stuffing papers, plans, and documents into drawers and cabinets—some he shredded. In the reception area outside Storey's office, their angry words muffled by the sliding glass door, Olivia and Oliphant argued, waved their arms, Oliphant clamping his hands over his head and stomping in circles when Storey activated the shredder.

Storey rummaged in a desk drawer, found Valerie's gift of furniture polish and tackled the accumulation of stains and coffee-mug rings. The twenty minutes Mike had promised had become forty-five.

He eased into his chair, placed his elbows on his freshly burnished desktop, his thoughts centered on his son Eric. How could he tell a three-year-old that his mother was dead? What could he say? He shivered, tried to focus on work tasks, something familiar, structured, and logical. His construction business suddenly seemed unnatural, a blur.

He looked up at the figures in the foyer. They had stopped arguing and sat in a pair of secretary chairs, Olivia's pointed toward the center of Victor's. Oliphant, arms locked across his chest, looked at the floor.

Swanson and Abrams entered Victor's room; Swanson wearing his lawyer uniform; a charcoal-gray suit over a pastel maroon shirt, vest open, dark-red tie with black diagonal stripes, knot askew. Swanson's 6-foot 4-inch frame was forty pounds short of the Security chief's muscled two hundred thirty.   Storey waved them toward him.

They stopped for a brief exchange with Oliphant.   The detective took a half-step back, his head swiveling as he looked up at the two oversized men who had invaded his space.   Swanson pointed at the exit: *Leave . . . Now.*   Oliphant shrugged, followed Olivia to the exit.

Abrams slid the office door open, closed it behind him and Swanson.   Storey indicated a client chair.   Abrams sat, looked at Storey with his jaw set, his brow furrowed.

Swanson dashed around the desk, embraced his friend.   Storey's shoulders sagged.   Swanson patted his back.   Storey pushed away, brushed his eyes and cheeks.   "Sorry," he said, dropped into his chair.

"We will get through this," Swanson said.

"They say she was run over . . . hit and run."   He looked up at Swanson, his chin quivering.   "Who would do this?"

"We'll find out."

"Oliphant seems to think I had something to do with it."

"The spouse is usually the number one suspect.   Oliphant jumps in like a pit bull, pushes the limits.   He gets off flaunting his authority.   Don't worry about him, I'll handle his nonsense.   One thing you don't need is an aging police bulldog finding conspiracies lurking in every shadow.   Don't speak to him or anyone with a badge unless I'm there."

"Okay."

Abrams raised his gaze.   "Nick, I'm so sorry.   It's hard to comprehend.   What can I do?"

"Would you call Valerie?"

"I'll use the reception area phone."   Abrams left, closed the slider.

Swanson sat on a corner of the desk, looked down at Storey. "Sorry to leave you hanging for so long.   I called Roe.   I want his investigators ready if we need them."

Storey nodded.   Jethroe Washington, Roe to his friends, owned and operated Security Associates, a nationwide agency that provided executive protection and security systems to Fortune Five Hundred companies and other enterprises. Bob Abrams and his security team were employees of Jethroe's organization and provided Storey Construction's security needs. Storey knew that Jethroe would make the resources of his organization available to Swanson or himself as needed.

"Are you up to answering a few questions? It's important I know what happened with Oliphant while it's fresh in your mind."

"I'll try."

Swanson removed a miniature recorder from his pocket. "Should record this . . . okay? Make sure our memories don't play tricks later. We can add to it if you remember anything new."

"Sure."

"Feel free to say whatever you like; it's all covered by attorney-client privilege." Swanson read in the date, time, place, and their names. "Okay. What did Oliphant say—what questions did he ask?"

"Well . . . first he told me . . . told me Julia was dead."

"Then?"

"Then I asked the questions. Took me three or four tries before it came out that it was a hit and run in the Lancaster Mall parking lot."

"One snippet at a time?"

"Yeah."

"Typical."

"Typical?"

"Looking for tells—anything that would fit into his frame."

"Frame?"

"With him, you're guilty until proven otherwise. What happened next?"

"It's kind of fuzzy now. I think I remember most of what he said but the sequence . . . I'm not sure."

"That's okay."

"I have to go to the morgue at 10:00 tomorrow morning to identify Julia's body."

"We can deal with that later. For now, just focus on the questions he asked."

"Well . . . he wanted to know where I was at two. I assumed that's when it happened. I remember when I asked him how she could get killed in a parking lot; he seemed to think I could help him answer that.'"

"Now he's got you confused—wondering what the hell is happening?"

"Yeah."

"Where was Olivia? I mean, was she part of it?"

"No. He wouldn't let her talk. She walked over there." Storey nodded toward the door. "She just stood there looking like a volcano about to erupt. Oh, I forgot. When they first came in the door she gave me some sign language that said we didn't know each other."

"Smart move."

Storey shrugged.

"Did you tell Oliphant where you were?"

"Yeah. I was meeting a new client and visiting a job site. I'm afraid I screwed up."

"How?"

"When he asked me where, I gave him the wrong street. I fumbled around trying to find the card I wrote the address on." Storey reached in his back pocket, retrieved his wallet, pulled out a business card, and handed it to Swanson. "I was so upset I forgot I put it in my wallet. Right after that, you called. He didn't want me to answer the phone. Olivia nodded I should. After you finished with him, I asked them to wait outside."

Swanson held the card at arm's length, studied it. "This guy Bill Stevens. He can verify where you were?"

"He never showed."

"That's strange."

"His whole story was strange."

"How?"

Storey related the essence of Bill Stevens' phone call.

Swanson picked up the phone, punched in the number from the card. "Let's find out who this clown is." He drummed fingers on the desktop. "Ah . . . Zivo's Pizza?" He slid farther back onto the desk. "I . . . Is Bill Stevens there?" Swanson looked at the ceiling. "Thank you Mr. Zivo . . . no, not tonight. Some other time." He dropped the phone in its cradle. "Mr. Zivo the pizza man doesn't know a Bill Stevens."

"Stevens, or whoever he was, sounded so sincere."

"So, you went to the lot on Eola and waited for our mystery man. What time did you leave?"

"Around three."

"You just sat there for an hour or so, waiting?"

"No. I snapped some pictures of the lot. I studied some stuff Val had given me about the Harrison job. That's partly why I agreed to the meet. The lot was only ten minutes away from the Harrison project."

"Harrison, that's the job site you visited?"

"Yes."

"That three story office complex down by the river?"

"Yes."

"Did anyone see you—could they verify you were there, and when."

"Ah . . . yeah, Lars Swenson, the carpenter foreman. And there's McGuire and a couple of guys in his bar that saw me deck Joe Orland."

"You were in a fight at McGuire's?"

"Yeah."

"Whoa!" Swanson raised his hands, slid from his perch on the desk, and sat in a client chair. He opened a pack of Spearmint, stuffed a green stick into his mouth, chewed for a moment. "Okay. I think we'd better do this again. Tell me everything you can remember from the time you left your office until I walked in the door. Are you up to that?"

"I think so. I need to focus on something."

*****

Swanson picked up his recorder, turned it off. "You had a busy day. There were times I wanted to gut punch a judge or two. How'd it feel?"

"I'd never used our Karate stuff for real. Kinda scary. As if I took advantage of the poor slob."

Abrams knocked on the glass door, entered. He held a cell phone in his hand. "Nick, Valerie would like to speak with you for a moment if you feel up to it."

Storey reached for the instrument, swiveled his chair to face the rear wall. "Val."

"Nicholas, this is unbelievable . . . I can't imagine . . . how can I help?"

When he felt he could trust his voice, Storey said, "Business . . . take care of . . . business."

"Don't worry about it. How can I help *you*?"

"Mike is here . . . and Bob. I'm going home."

Swanson interrupted, "We'll take you,"

"I heard that," Valerie said. "Mike?"

"Yeah," Storey said.

"You'll have an escort. Good. I called your sister, Donna."

Storey sat upright. "Donna? I don't want to—"

"She's probably on her way to your place now."

"She's got her own problems . . . what about her son, Lee?" He stood, paced.

"I think Lee is going to visit his cousin Eric for a while, and you are going to have a live-in helper."

"But—"

"Nicholas, you need family and friends. You need their . . . our help. Let us."

"I suppose I don't have a choice."

"As it should be."

The conversation lagged. Storey sat.

"What am I going to do about Dad and Mom? They're off on one of their trips to nowhere. I've left messages on Dad's voice mail . . . nothing. Do you know how to contact them?"

"Sorry, I don't. I called Victor's cell, but only got his voice mail."

Storey knew when his parents took one of their nowhere jaunts, they vanished, their way of escaping everyday pressures, to rejuvenate. They had been doing it for years. They could be anywhere from Canada to Mexico to Colorado—or twenty miles away at a back-road bed and breakfast. If they had taken their fifth-wheel trailer they were in the wind. Somewhere near good fishing or a beach was a fair bet.

"Sometimes they're gone for a weekend," he said. "One time it was two weeks."

"Victor has called in on a rare occasion. Perhaps we'll get lucky. Maybe he'll check his messages."

"Unlikely.   Dad's interest in our day-to-day business has evaporated, and I think they turn their cell phones off."

"Go home. Get some rest."

"I'll try," he said, terminated the call.

Jethroe Washington burst through the door, jogged down the hallway, and into Storey's office.

"Bob called me," he said. "Julia is . . . *dead*? What can I do? Just name it."

9:30 PM Wednesday
20 May 2009

He was average height, thin, not skinny; ordinary except for his black Levis and shirt, black running shoes, latex gloves, and a dark billed cap pulled down to shield his face. The man looked to his left, then right, turned to survey the sidewalk and houses across the street, saw no one, walked briskly up the driveway to the rear of Victor Storey's home, opened the gate to the yard, stepped through onto the patio, approached the back door, removed a penlight from his pocket, grabbed it between his teeth and focused its narrow beam on the deadbolt as he removed his lock picks from a shirt pocket.

Within seconds he stepped inside, left the door slightly ajar, ~~aimed~~ pointed his light toward the keypad of the security alarm, punched in a six-digit code. A steady green replaced the blinking red LED.

He removed the light from his mouth, aimed it at the floor a few feet ahead as he walked through the laundry room, the kitchen, the family room, and down the hall to Victor's den. His chances of discovery were miniscule; Victor and Emily had gone on one of their "trips to nowhere" and would not return for several days.

He illuminated the bookcase near the desk, tilted back the fourth book from the right on the fourth tier and slid a key from the shelf. He turned to the gun cabinet on the opposite wall, unlocked the double doors, and swung them open.

He ignored the rifles and shotguns on the top shelf, opened the bottom drawer and removed a .32 caliber Colt automatic pistol and a magazine of cartridges. He verified that the magazine was full, slid it into the gun; put the weapon in a pocket of his Levis.

He closed and locked the cabinet, replaced the key, retraced his steps to the back door, reactivated the alarm, exited, relocked the deadbolt.

Before leaving the premises, he checked the street and sidewalks, and, satisfied no one was out for an evening constitutional or walking a dog, he sauntered down the driveway and to the next block where he had parked his tan Toyota Camry. He keyed the door open to avoid activating the chirp and flash of lights that the remote would generate.

He checked the dashboard clock. Twelve minutes round trip. He smiled, fastened his seat belt, started the engine and drove slowly away. He turned the headlights on at the next cross street.

9:30 PM Wednesday
20 May 2009

An accident—it had to be an accident. She's not dead. She's in a hospital somewhere fighting for life, thinking I deserted her. I have to find her.

The blare of a car's horn jolted him from his stupor. He had stopped on the shoulder with the left wheels of his truck partially in the traffic lane. He moved farther off the road, signaled the vehicle to pass, lowered his head until it rested on the steering wheel. Five minutes later, he drove on.

He parked in front of his garage, slid out of his truck, leaned against the fender. The ticks of the engine as it cooled and the occasional hoot of an owl were the only sounds to upset the hush of the countryside. He let his body go limp. The uproar in his mind gradually quieted.

He pushed wearily up the steps to the front deck where he saw Suzume and his sister Donna peering at him through the dining room glass door. When he entered the house, Suzume faced him with one hand on the back of a chair as if for support; her chin quivering, tears streaking her face. Donna embraced him.

"We heard your truck on the driveway. When you didn't come inside, we were worried."

"I'm okay, Sis. Just needed to relax a bit."

"It true, Mr. Nick? Miss Julia . . ."

Storey patted Suzume's shoulder, gave it a squeeze. "Yes," he said.

She buried her face in her hands, ran to the bathroom.

Donna pulled him toward the living room. "Let's sit; be comfortable." They sat on the couch. "How you doin', Bro?"

"Well, I've had better days."

"I'll stay until things settle down."

"What about your job—and Lee?"

"I've gobs of vacation built up. I'll start losing it if I don't use it soon. I can take care of Lee here just as well as at home. Besides. . . ." Her voice faltered, she wiped her eyes with a sodden tissue. "I need to spend some time with my little brother. We haven't seen much of each other lately."

She was right. In the past few months he had let his new job responsibilities push family obligations aside. It was time to get his priorities straight. "Okay, Sis. Thank you. Having you here will help a lot . . . but this is a hell of a way to make up for lost time."

She placed her other hand on his. "We're here now, Nick."

They sat, silent for a moment.

"Eric and Lee . . . they're asleep?"

"Yes. It took a while to calm then down. They get along amazingly well considering their age difference."

"Sometimes it seems Eric is three going on seven." Storey stood. "I'm going to take a peek."

In light that spilled from the hallway, Storey could see his son sleeping, lying on his side, his left arm extended over the side of the bed, the right curled behind his back under the blanket. Storey smiled. Like father, like son. The moment of Eric's birth was etched into Storey's mind and still seemed surreal—as if he had stepped through a portal into a new universe, his life forever changed. He stood for an extended moment watching Eric sleep, awed, as he always was, by the peaceful innocence. "It's just you and me now, son," he muttered, closed the door. He wiped a tear from his cheek as he returned to the living room.

Suzume, her eyes red, her face scrubbed and composed, was talking with Donna.

She turned toward Storey. "I leave now, Mr. Nick. I call sister. She coming." She paused, drew in a ragged breath. "So sorry about Miss Julia."

Donna embraced her, held her at arms length. "Suzume, you're such a good person. I will call you tomorrow. Okay?"

Suzume nodded.

Storey clutched her hand. "Good night, Suzume, and thanks."

"You welcome, Mr. Nick."

Donna accompanied her to the door and returned to the couch. "The news at six had a short minute about the incident at the mall."

"What did they say?"

"Not much. Hit and run, woman killed. Name withheld pending notification of family. Bunch of drivel from the reporter on site . . .usual stuff. Lots of police cars, ambulance . . . yellow tape everywhere. Cameras couldn't get close. Details at eleven."

"They'll have her name by then, probably sooner." Storey stretched his arms across the back of the sofa, silent for a moment thinking about what would happen after the media identified Julia. They would connect her to him—to Storey Construction. "After they identify Julia, the media feeding frenzy will begin. I should disconnect the phones."

"Good idea. But you don't want to block out everyone."

"Anyone that counts has my cell number." Thankful for a task to occupy him, Storey pushed up from his seat.

"You want some coffee? I made a fresh pot."

"That would be great, Sis."

He disconnected the base unit in the family room, shutting off all the portable phones, their personal line. He silenced the ringer of the business line in the den. The voice mail would pick up any calls. He could screen them later. He unplugged the fax machine.

In the kitchen, Donna was setting cups on the counter.

"You still take cream?"

"Yeah, or milk's fine."

He sat on a stool on the family room side twirling his mug between his palms, staring at the brown liquid. "I need to be alone for a while."

"After Joey died, I would go for long walks, just to think. I'll go into the bedroom."

"No, no. I'll sit outside on the deck."

*****

The breeze had grown from a soft whisper in the pines to a chilly wind. Storey hunched low in the Adirondack near the end of the deck. He looked up at the clear night sky, focused on Ursa Major, the Big Dipper, and traced from the pointer stars, Merak and Dubhe, to Polaris, the North Star, the end of the handle of Ursa Minor, the Little Dipper. A few minutes search and, despite the light pollution from Salem, he located Draco, the Dragon, and Cepheus, The King. He flashed to a night camping in an alpine meadow in the Three Sisters Wilderness, the night Charlie Mills and he had completed the requirements for the astronomy merit badge, the one that culminated his quest for Eagle Scout.

Charlie Mills. He had not thought of Charlie for . . . a year? Two? Charlie had married Anita the day after high school graduation—the stereotypical childhood sweethearts. Two years into their marriage, Anita was killed in a collision on I-5. Charlie had made their house a shrine to Anita, living with her virtual presence, making no attempt to start a new life. He spiraled into depression and eventually hanged himself from a beam in his vaulted ceiling living room.

Spurred by Charlie's death, Storey and Julia had made a mutual promise—should something happen to either of them the other would clear the house of memorabilia and move on with life. Making the move-on pact with Julia had been easy, a logical thing to do; but now he'd have to put action to the words.

What to do first? He'd have to make funeral arrangements—perhaps a Memorial service? Eventually he'd have go into their bedroom and . . . and what? What would he do? The bedroom had been his before Julia. Could it ever be his again? It shouldn't be difficult to dispose of her clothes; she had only a few jeans, sweats, tees and a pantsuit or two and a limited supply of undergarments. He groaned when he thought about the paraphernalia in her studio: the brushes, canvases, paints, sponges, her books, the unfinished works . . .

"Nick?"

Startled by Donna's voice, he bolted upright.

"Sorry, I didn't mean to scare you."

"It's okay, Sis. My thoughts were far away."
"The news will be on shortly."

11:15 PM Wednesday
20 May 2009

Storey paced in front of the now silent TV, punched numbers on the keypad of his cell phone, listened to three rings.

"Swanson."

When he heard his friend's voice, Storey felt the tightness in his chest relax a bit. "Did you watch the eleven o'clock news?"

"I did."

"They didn't identify Julia—withheld by the police pending notification of next of kin."

"I'm guessing the cops are playing it ultra safe until you confirm it's Julia."

"Maybe it's a maneuver by Oliphant?"

"Could be. I don't think it's too important. At least they kept the media vultures away. The video didn't disclose much, just the gurney being loaded into the coroner's van. You heard the witness the reporter found, the gray-haired lady who described the car?"

"Yeah, when she said it reminded her of the car that her husband had fifty years ago, that it was red with a black hard top and had two cannons in front for headlights, I almost spilled my coffee."

"Sounds like the '57 T-Bird you and Victor restored."

"This is beginning to feel like an episode from The Twilight Zone."

"We can't be sure about the car. When the reporter questioned her, the lady was confused and rambling. There has to be a rational explanation."

"I'm sure there is, but it is strange."

"Where is your T Bird?"

"In the garage next to the cabinet shop . . . I'm going to see if it's there."

"Roe and I are at the Shoe playing nine-ball."

"I'll come by after." Storey deactivated his cell.

"You're leaving?" Donna set her coffee cup on the counter. "It's late. You should rest."

"I have to go."

"There are probably hundreds of cars that fit the old lady's description. Half of what she said was probably memories rather than observation. She seemed a bit . . . well, to be kind . . . confused."

Storey paused, looked at his sister for a moment. Her advice was sound, her observations reasonable, but he needed to verify the T-Bird was in the garage. "Sis, I have to go. I'll rest if . . . after I see it."

*****

Storey drove north on Liberty with all windows open. The chill in the night air bit at him but he relished it; it recharged him, cleared his mind. Clutching the steering wheel near the top, his arms stiff, he filled his lungs several times. He turned at Kuebler, drove east, passed under the freeway, and, a few minutes later, turned north. He passed a car parked at the curb a block from the entrance to Storey Construction property.

He stopped facing the gate, got out of his truck, keyed the padlock open, and slid the chain link gate aside. Inside, he stopped his truck in front of the garage, the headlights illuminating the garage's roll-up door. He turned the engine off, left the lights on, walked to the padlock side, verified it was secure, moved to the pedestrian entrance, punched the keypad, and pushed the door open.

He stood transfixed for a long moment staring into the dark interior. He reached inside, found the light switches, but hesitated, wondering what he would find, hoping the Ford was still there. He pushed the toggles up, activating all four banks of fluorescents. He held his breath as the tubes flickered to life, washing the area with blue-tinted light.

The space between the '31 Chevy and the '64 Buick, the space allotted to the '57 Ford Thunderbird, was vacant.

He ran to his right, through the door in the wall separating the car wash area and paint booth from the main garage. He reached for and activated the light switch. Before the lights came on full, he knew there were no cars there. He pushed the switches to off, shut the door, leaned against it, his heart galloping.

He gulped a few deep breaths, opened his cell phone, activated a number, walked along the wall to the back of the garage and across to the workbench and tool storage chests.

"Victor Storey is not available. Wait for the beep . . . you know what to do."

"Dad, it's your son Nicholas. Remember me? I'm the one that's left you a half dozen messages already. Enough is enough. What the hell is going on with you? Your trips to nowhere I understand, but dropping off the planet is ridiculous. The T-Bird is missing, and . . . the family emergency I mentioned . . . Julia has been killed. Hit and run by a car matching the description of the Bird. For God's sake, if you took it on your trip, call me."

Storey closed the phone, stuffed it back into its belt holster. He leaned against the bench and looked at the area where the car should have been. The floor glistened. He, Victor, and Jack, their mechanic, had acid-etched the garage floor and applied an epoxy coating last year. Jack kept the cars, the space, and tools spotless. Usually, there was no trace of oil, grease, or dirt anywhere, but Storey saw muddy footprints tracking from the roll-up door to the spot where the driver's door of the Ford would have been. The cream-colored canvas car cover lay crumpled in the rear of the parking space.

"Dad didn't take the Ford," he murmured.

He looked at the trail of mud for a few moments, turned and retraced his steps along the back of the garage to the walk-in door, locked it, climbed into his truck and left, locking the perimeter gate behind him. As he drove away, he noticed the light colored car was still there. In his rearview he saw a brief flash of its brake lights.

12:05 AM Thursday
21 May 2009

Storey opened the heavy oak door of The Wooden Shoe; the favored hangout for him, Jethroe, and Swanson. The Shoe's tap dispensed teeth-cracking-cold Killian Red, Storey's drink of choice. The lunch crowd stood in line for the barbeque sandwiches, Cajun fries, and salad bar. Baked potatoes with a glut of toppings supplemented the BBQ menu after 5 p.m. The patrons were a mix of college students, lawyers from the nearby offices of the district attorney, police officers, and active and retired detective associates of Kevin Brown, KB, the owner, and bartender. Some blue-collars mixed in for happy hour.

A few die-hard regulars along with a half-dozen boisterous partiers populated the bar. Four couples occupied the dozen four-tops scattered about the front of the Shoe. A mellow jazz piano floated from the old Wurlitzer. A single couple moved slowly on the dance floor, a fifteen-foot square of polished oak that occupied the rear thirty feet of the room.

A loud crack pulled Storey's gaze up and to the left of the stairs that dominated the center of the tavern. He saw Jethroe leaning on his thousand-dollar pool cue watching the balls roll after his explosive break of a fresh rack of nine ball.

KB was bartending solo. A grin lit the black face, exposing a gap between his glossy white incisors.

Storey nodded.

KB pointed a stubby forefinger, cocked his thumb. "You got it." He pulled the tap and filled a mug, slid a twelve-ounce Killian down the bar. The heavy glass stopped directly in front of Storey. The head slopped over the top and oozed down the side of the thick frosty glass. Storey grabbed his beer, dropped some bills on the shiny mahogany, turned and walked up the stairs.

Swanson was sitting on a stool by the sidewall; his jacket, and tie draped over the back of his tall chair. "Park yourself," he said, patted the adjacent seat.

Jethroe walked around the pool table and faced them as he disassembled his McDermott cue stick. "So, was it there?"

"No."

"Shit," said Swanson.

"Nothing. Some muddy footprints and the canvas car cover on the floor between the '31 Chevy and '64 Buick. No T-Bird."

"You said Victor and Emily are off on one of their nowhere excursions." Swanson grabbed his jacket, slipped into it. "The T-bird is Victor's favorite. Could he have taken it?"

"Maybe, but I don't think so. The Bird's canvas cover is in a heap in the back of the parking space. Dad wouldn't do that. He'd fold it and put it on a shelf."

Jethroe put his cue in its case and snapped the latch closed. "I agree. It probably wasn't Victor. Muddy footprints? No way."

Swanson brushed a trace of chalk from his coat. "Maybe he was in a hurry?"

"They've been gone for four days." Storey looked at his watch, shrugged. "Five days. Typically, they use the T-Bird for short trips."

"So they could be anywhere?" said Swanson.

"Could they have gone to your condo in Newport?" Jethroe leaned against the pool table, crossed his arms.

"I called the manager. They haven't seen them."

Swanson put his cue in its rack. "Who else has access? To the garage."

"Several people. But, only Dad and I . . . and Jack, have keys to the cars."

"Jack Evans . . . your mechanic?" said Jethroe.

"Yeah. The cars are like his kids. He wouldn't—"

"Probably not, but this doesn't feel right. There's too much coincidence. The garage was locked? The padlock was intact, not cut, or sawed open?"

"Yeah. "And, the perimeter fence gate lock was fine."

"That means someone had keys or the padlocks were picked."

"You're saying it could be an inside job; someone attached to Storey construction?" Storey said. "Only a few people have keys.

"Unless the perpetrator stole or copied them."

"The way things are going, nothing would surprise me," Storey said.

They were silent as they descended the stairs and sat in a booth opposite the bar.

"Can't you tell if the locks have been picked?" said Swanson.

"Yeah, usually we can," said Jethroe. "Picks leave scratches in places a key doesn't. With a magnifying glass or microscope you can see the traces."

"If they were picked, it would tend to would eliminate those who have access to keys," said Swanson.

"Unless the guilty party is trying to divert our attention." Jethroe opened his cell, activated a number, leaned against the back wall. "Bob. Jethroe." He stretched his legs across the seat. "Yeah. Nick seems to be okay . . . considering. Listen, there's been a new development. Did you watch 'News at Eleven'?" He listened for a moment, nodding. "The lady's story rattled our antennae, too. Nick went to the garage. . . . the T-Bird is not there. . . . Our thoughts exactly . . . No. the locks are intact. How soon can you get a forensics team out there—you have keys, right?" Jethroe rotated his legs under the table, sat upright. "Okay, do it. Check if the locks were picked. Nick says there's muddy footprints. Maybe that will tell us something . . . Yeah, fingerprints, fibers, anything that seems appropriate. Call me when you know something . . . Yeah, expedited . . . Bye."

"Abrams?" said Mike.

"Yeah A team should be at the warehouse in a couple of hours." Jethroe pushed back in his seat.

"Good," said Swanson. "Nick, you should report the T-Bird stolen."

"Okay. When we're done here. Anything else?" Storey said.

"Just practice our poker face for Oliphant. I think he's withholding information," said Swanson.

Jethroe chuckled. "Really! You think Oliphant is devious?"

"He's a wily old fox. Never underestimate him."

"Let's worry about him later," said Jethroe. "We all need some sleep. Nick, go home. I'll pick you up at your house at quarter to eight. We can get some breakfast and talk before you meet Oliphant."

"Okay, but I'll drive myself."

"It's not a request, my friend."

Storey opened his mouth to object, saw Jethroe's extended chin, the squint of his eyes—the defiant expression that hadn't changed since elementary school. Storey felt his pulse accelerate, his fists clench. He dropped his gaze. To resist would be futile. "Okay, Roe. I don't feel like arguing."

"I think it's a good idea," Swanson said. "Tomorrow will be a rough day. We'll take you wherever you need to go—and we won't have to find a way to get your truck home if you don't feel like driving after . . ." He punched Storey's shoulder.

Valerie's counsel from the earlier evening echoed in Storey's thoughts . . . *family and friends* . . . "Okay. Tomorrow, you're my shepherds."

1:10 AM Thursday
21 May 2009

After Jethroe and Swanson left, Storey lingered in The Shoe to report the T-Bird stolen. He explained the circumstances of the break-in, identified Victor as co-owner, described the unique hubcaps and upholstery, the black hardtop and the red body paint, and affirmed that he would file a written report later. The dispatcher said she would broadcast a BOLO and alert the Auto Theft unit.

At home, Storey found Donna stretched out on the couch in the living room.

She threw off her afghan cover, rubbed her eyes, yawned. "Was the T-Bird there?"

"No."

"What?" She jumped to her feet. "Where could it be?"

"I haven't a clue."

"Could Dad have taken it on their trip?"

"Not likely. I saw some muddy footprints—"

"Mud? On the floor? Dad wouldn't allow that."

"Exactly. Someone made off with it."

"Do you think the thief used the T-Bird to kill Julia?"

Storey shrugged. "Can't say for sure. I stopped by the Shoe, kicked some thoughts around with Mike and Roe. They're as baffled as I am."

"This is scary."

Storey took a deep breath, released it slowly. "And weird. Jethroe has a forensics team on the way."

"What can they do?"

"Maybe get some impressions or photos of the footprints for comparison if a suspect is turned up. Dust for fingerprints? I really don't know."

"So, what's next?"

"Roe is picking me up a 7:45. I expect he'll know something by then. We'll join Mike for breakfast and review the situation before Mike and I go to the morgue."

"You're not driving?"

"Mike and Roe don't think I can handle the viewing at the morgue by myself. I'm going to have an escort tomorrow."

"Good."

"I suppose. I'd rather have my own wheels."

"They want to help. Don't shut them out."

Storey patted his sister's shoulder. "I get it."

She touched his hand, nodded. "It's been a long day. Unless you need something, I'm going to bed."

*****

Storey stood in front of the door to the master bedroom/studio for a long moment before he twisted the knob and stepped inside. A trace of lavender fragrance lingered in the air—Julia's body lotion.

He strode across the bedroom to her studio. To accommodate her art, he had broken out the east wall of the master bedroom, moved it out twenty feet, more than doubling the size of the room. With windows on the east, and clerestory glass in the north roof, the space provided the perfect workspace for Julia, or so she had said.

He stared at the empty stool in front of a blank canvas on her easel, *saw* her sitting there—the early morning sun in her auburn hair, a brush clenched between her teeth, another poised above the canvas, palette drooping from her left hand, her brows knitted—*Portrait of the Artist at Her Work*—the picture that most often came to him when he thought of her.

He sat on the bed, his arms splayed back, looking into her space. It seemed alien, as if he didn't belong. He slid up the bed, leaned on the headboard. What had happened to them? There were moments when he understood; flashes that evaporated like a dream. How long had it been since their silly argument? Two days? A week?

They had been sitting at the breakfast table with cups of coffee, she in her robe, he wearing sweat pants and hooded top. He had just returned from his morning run. Julia had said that she and Eric needed him, wanted him with them more. He had responded with something stupid about how she, and Eric, had to understand that the re-organization of the company was demanding more time and effort than he had expected, that important problems had to be resolved, issues that had to take priority for a while.

She had thought about his pronouncement for a beat, said, "I know. You're right, but things have changed with us. We're different. I hope you're still committed—"

Storey cringed, remembering his response. "What makes you think I'm not committed? Would I be sitting here listening to all this if I weren't?"

She had looked at him, her face a mask of anguish and confusion. "Okay, you're dedicated. But how about us . . . the romance?"

He knew where she was going. He missed it too, and there had been a lot. He would never forget the joy, the excitement and mystery of discovering each other or the quiet contentment of talking about nothing, everything. They had let everyday demands and the commitments of parenthood smother them.

"I know we're not the same" she said, "Not like we were. Parts of our lives are decaying from neglect, big chunks that we don't have time for . . . or energy."

Storey rubbed his eyes with the heel of his hands, tried to push the memories aside.

Everything Julia said was true, their lives had changed, but he had refused to think about it. He had thought marriage and fatherhood would add diversity to his life. But having a family didn't just change things—it ended his earlier existence. She needed something he had not given her. That chance was now and forever gone.

He rose from the bed and stood looking into Julia's quiet studio. "I'm sorry," was all he could think to say.

He walked into the bathroom. A hot shower would relax him.

He adjusted the stream to a few degrees below tolerable, scrubbed his body with his back brush, let the water cascade over his head and down his body until he felt the water grow cold. He stepped out of the enclosure and toweled himself dry, lifted his bathrobe from its hook, held it for a long moment before he shrugged into it. Hanging next to his was Julia's white terry cloth.

He flashed to images of her wearing it, brushing her hair, at her easel, in the kitchen, at the breakfast table, lounging on the back patio—opening the robe and pulling him inside. He could feel her silky skin, her lips on his. His eyes welled as the pictures flooded his mind. Forget Victoria Secret's frilliest, the G-strings, thongs and baby dolls; Julia in her threadbare terry cloth outclassed them all.

She had tenacity, a stubbornness combined with innate curiosity. She acknowledged societal mores selectively; was loyal to a select group of friends with whom she shared ideas and found inspiration. She asserted that being a mother and an artist were indistinguishable; that feeling insecure and phony was a natural state.

He steered clear when she was deep into a project or preparing for a gallery showing. At those times, she was brusque, nonconforming, sometimes rude. She complained about inadequate supplies, improper lighting, and lack of inspiration. He knew it was insecurity; fear that her paintings, her babies, were inadequate.

There was a part of her beyond his reach. She buried it in the unfocused stare that, on rare occasions, he observed when she sat in her terry cloth at the breakfast table, unmoving except for an occasional wince, a coffee cup cradled in her rigid fingers. She appeared to be looking into a distant filmstrip. If he approached she would recover, but never discuss her behavior. Her infrequent trances did not seem to affect their relationship. He had tried to ignore them.

He left the bathroom, tried to push his thoughts of Julia aside. He needed to sleep. He stared at their bed. Multiple images of her flooded his mind again, vivid, overwhelming. He covered his face with his hands, turned away. There were too many emotional triggers in the bedroom. He would crash on the den sofa bed. He pulled sweats, running shoes, a shirt and jeans from the closet, socks and undergarments from the bureau.

As he closed the drawer, he saw an envelope on the top of the chest. Julia's stationery, her handwriting. He stared at it for a long moment before he touched it. He stared at it as he walked to the den and dumped his clothes on the coffee table. He sat in his desk chair and stared at it, a scent of lavender stirring his senses. He thumbed the flap up and removed the note.

> *Nick,*
>
> *I feel that our recent divergence has grown beyond repair. We have become strangers living in the same house. My freedom is gone, replaced by demands of household, caring for Eric and a constant demand from the gallery for more of my time, more paintings, more autograph sessions . . . the list is endless. I regret taking on teaching at the college. I hate explaining the obvious and having to encourage those with little or no talent to persevere. What a farce.*
>
> *I have tried to live a structured life to no avail. My existence is nothing but a day-by-day struggle to maintain my sanity; to deal with nonstop routine, boring people and their inane demands.*
>
> *Evil forces from my life before I met you have reappeared, a malice that I believed—I felt certain and still do—that I had neutralized. You know nothing of them, and it is best you don't lest you do something that could place you and Eric in harms way. There is no reason to believe they pose a threat to you, Eric, or me—the risk to them is too great should any of us be harmed. I must resolve this myself. Believe me; it is useless to try to find me.*
>
> *My leaving you was inevitable: The reappearance of unpleasant individuals from my past life provides the impetus for my departure now rather than later.*
>
> *Your life is filled with work, Eric, your family and your friends, Jethroe and Mike. There is no*

way to explain my sorrow for leaving Eric, but I am confident you and your family will make sure he will want for nothing.

Looking back, my choices were selfish.   I hope you can forgive me.

Julia

Storey crumpled the letter, dropped it on the desktop.

5:42 AM Thursday
21 May 2009

Storey rolled his feet to the floor and sat on the edge of the couch. The digital clock on the end table flicked to 5:42. He blinked to clear his focus. He had slept in his clothes. He did not remember moving from the desk to the couch or removing his boots. He rose, groaned, rubbed his lower back, padded to the desk. The letter was there, crumpled but intact. He flattened it, returned it to the lavender-scented envelope, and centered it on the top of his desk. He stared at it for a moment, turned and walked to the kitchen.

While coffee was brewing, he showered in the hall bath, let hot water stream over his head and down his body until the twitches in his back moderated. He turned the water to cold momentarily. Shivering, he grabbed a large beach towel, scrubbed his body dry, pulled on a pair of boxers and threadbare Raider sweat pants, squirmed into a hooded red sweatshirt.

He sat at the breakfast area table absently munching a banana, sipping coffee. He sat for several moments watching the brittle yellow of first light spill through the windows. He was rinsing his cup in the sink when Donna came into the kitchen.

"You're up early." She went to the glass doors overlooking the patio and the fir trees that covered the steep slope behind the house. "I love to watch the sunrise."

From their early years he remembered her as a nocturnal wanderer who communicated with single syllables for the first half-hour of a new day; not as the cheerful up-with-the-sun personality standing by the window marveling at the crisp morning.

"Actually I'm a half-hour late," he said, put the cup into the washer, returned to his seat.

"You sleep any?" Donna poured a cup of coffee.

"Some."

"I'll take that to mean very little. I'm sorry, Bro." She put a hand on his shoulder, gently massaged it.

"I'll survive." He pulled on his socks, and pushed into his Nike running shoes. He patted her cheek. "I'm going for a run," He moved toward the front door.

"Roe will be here at quarter-to-eight?"

"So he said."

"Should I fix him some breakfast?"

"We probably won't have time . . . uh, thanks anyway, Sis." He opened the door and left. She was right. Roe, if invited, would probably eat two breakfasts. He was always ingesting something and never lost or gained an ounce. Friends of the wiry black man chalked it up to an overactive metabolism or to his workouts with his personal karate instructor.

Donna ran outside after him. "What about Eric?"

He stopped halfway down the deck stairs. He had hoped to delay this conversation until he returned from his run. How to tell his three-year-old son his mother was dead? He had to get it right.

"Eric will wake up soon. What do I say to him?"

He turned toward her "Nothing. That's my job."

"When . . . when will you tell him?"

"Not sure. Maybe tonight. I have a bunch of stuff that I have to deal with today."

"You want me to keep him in a bubble until you get around to it? You know he's going to ask where his mommy is."

"I need an hour or so to clear my head. I promise we will talk . . . when I get back."

"Okay. I'll hold you to that. What's happening? I feel there's more going on than—"

"There's a letter on my desk you should read. I'll tell you all I know, which isn't much, *after* I finish my run."

Storey jumped down the deck steps and jogged the length of the driveway, turned west on Bunker Hill for his usual three-mile circuit through the hilly back roads. He gradually increased speed until he was running full out. Soon, his legs burned and he struggled to breathe. He slowed to a gentle trot.

The gravel road weaved through the gentle slope of hills now lush with spring growth, crested between two hummocks, then looped down to Skyline Road, a major thoroughfare into downtown Salem.

Trying to clear the dark images in his head, he concentrated on the new green on the trees, the occasional wild azalea, listened to the birdsong. He saw a battered red Nissan parked off the road about twenty yards ahead. The car stirred a vague memory.

A tall woman with long legs and the sinewy build of a distance runner stepped out of the car. She was wearing dark green skin-tight spandex and a long-billed baseball cap. She stepped into the road, waited for him. He stopped. "Olivia?"

She put her arms around his waist, rested her head on his shoulder. "I'm so sorry."

They embraced for a long moment. He gripped her tight.

"It's been a long time," she said.

Storey pushed her to arm's length, hands on her shoulders. His gaze flicked from her black Reeboks to the brown cap. "Yeah . . . three, maybe four years if I don't count last night or a couple of beers at the Shoe. What are you doing here? *Should* you be here?"

"It's good to see you, too." Her eyes locked with his.

"Is this an official visit?" Unprepared for the hypnotic pull of her dark eyes, he looked away.

She stepped back, spread her arms. "Do you see anyplace I could conceal my gun or badge?"

"Do you need your Batgirl utility belt to make it official? . . . I don't think so."

"I just happened to meet an old friend while I was out jogging this morning."

"Liar."

"That's my story and I'm sticking with it."

"Does your buddy Oliphant know you're here? Can you get in trouble? Talking with me, I mean."

"He's my partner, not my buddy."

"Ahh . . . okay. Your partner. He thinks I had something to do with Julia's death?"

"Usual assumption."

"The spouse is always at the top of the suspect list?"

Olivia shrugged.

"Does he have evidence that points at me?"

"Let's run," she said.

They began a slow jog. Storey thought about her dismissive demeanor. Maybe she didn't know what Oliphant had. "I thought partners . . . ah, does he keep you in the loop?"

"He's old school."

"Close to the vest?'

"That too."

"Umm . . . oh . . . women don't measure up?"

She waved a hand. "We all should be behind a desk shuffling paper."

"Let me guess. You can outrun him, and with your karate skills you can whip his ass. It's obvious you're in better physical condition. I'll bet you score higher with your sidearm."

"That's a stretch, but I can type and know how to use a computer."

"But, he has better instincts?"

"So I've heard. I'm not here to—."

"I know."

They moved along in silence for a moment. Storey wondered what motivated her to arrange their "accidental" meeting. A card with a note or a phone call expressing her sympathy would have sufficed for now. She was involved in an investigation of Julia's death. She wouldn't risk alienating her partner or rile her superiors just to express her concern. She was obviously at odds with Oliphant. That was apparent from her reaction today and his observations of them as they argued outside of his office last night. She wouldn't seek him out to vent about her partner . . . not her style.

It had been years since they were together, but he felt he could still read her body language; interpret her clipped speech. She had something to say; information she wanted him aware of, but he would have to dig for it.

"Do you think I was involved with Julia's death?"

She slowed her pace. They stopped. She looked at him with her brow furrowed. "Nicholas, I believe I know you better than anyone. I didn't think you would have to ask."

"You're a cop, too . . . and caught up in an inquiry involving me, and—"

"Caught up . . . a good choice of words." She turned from him, resumed jogging.

He ran to catch up. "I know you can't directly reveal info from an ongoing investigation."

She said nothing.

"Mike thinks Oliphant will interrogate me after I identify the body."

"Mike is a smart guy."

"Will you be there?"

"Probably."

"I want you there."

She looked at him. "Okay."

"Mike says I should say nothing . . . let Oliphant take the lead."

"Following your lawyer's advice is usually a good thing."

"I know he'll ask me where I was yesterday afternoon, what I was doing, who saw me . . . that kind of thing. Can we expect something, ah . . . out of the ordinary?"

"Sam is not ordinary."

Storey thought about "not ordinary" for a moment.

"Totally unexpected? Peculiar? Outrageous?"

"Good adjectives."

"Will I be surprised?"

She gave him a wry smile. "You're getting smarter by the minute. I've got to go. Race me back to the car like we used to do?"

"You're on. But first . . . you've had your gold badge for about three years now?"

"Closer to four."

"Um. What happened to your other partner. Neil . . . ?" He shrugged.

"Neil Walker. We were reassigned about eight months ago."

"Problems?"

"Never."

"You and Oliphant, well, oil and water come to mind."

"Long story. Someday, soon I hope, I'll be able to explain. C'mon, let's go. One . . . two . . ."

She leaned on the fender of her car with her arms crossed over her chest and watched Storey labor through the last few yards. He stopped near her, bent down, panting, hands on his knees.

"I could never beat you," he gasped. "But ten yards? . . . Ridiculous."

"You've let your new job warp your priorities."

He looked at her agape. They were Julia's words . . . from their last clash.

"What?" she said.

"Nothing."

"Umm . . ."

"Liv, it's good seeing you. I needed a lift. Thanks."

"You're welcome . . . my pleasure. I wanted to see you . . ., and . . . well, enough said. I hope you understand."

"Stay alert, let Mike do most of the talking. Expect the unusual."

"Good thoughts." She focused on his eyes again. In the shade under the bill of her cap her dark brown iris melded with the pupil. The black pools pulled at him, but he severed the link.

"Oh," he said. "you didn't have to buy a new outfit. What happened to your baggy gray sweats?"

"You don't like my jump suit?"

"Whoa. I didn't say that. It's just not you . . . the Liv I remember."

"I didn't want anyone to recognize me. I just bought this last . . . how did you know it was new?"

"The tag is missing but the little plastic thingy is still there." He reached behind her neck and tugged the thin filament.

She shrugged, jumped off the fender. "I've got to go." She stepped to him, pulled his head down, and grazed his cheek with her lips. "Take care, Nicholas."

He opened her car door.

She slid in, fastened her belt and started the engine. "Practice your poker face."

She turned left—the long way to town. He watched until the red Nissan disappeared over the rise.

7:45 AM Thursday
21 May 2009

Eric abandoned his cereal, jumped down from his seat and ran toward Jethroe. "Uncle Roe!" He stopped in the center of the family room, knees flexed, fists clenched near his hips. He shuffled side to side on the balls of his feet. "Eeyaa," he yelled.

"Eric, my man," Jethroe said, dropped to his haunches, swept Eric into his arms and hugged him. "You been practicing our moves?"

Eric nodded vigorously. "Uh uh."

Jethroe chuckled, patted the boy's head. "Super." He set Eric on the floor, turned to Lee and tousled his hair—the five-year-old had slipped from his chair and approached Jethroe.

"Have you been practicing?"

Lee beamed, nodded. "Yeah. Everyday."

Jethroe sat on his heels, drew the boys to him, one in each arm, looked from one to the other. "What is Karate for?" he said.

"Defense!" they chorused.

"And never for . . . ?"

"Attack!"

"That's right. Never, ever forget." He pushed them toward the table. "Finish your breakfast, guys. Nicholas and I have to leave."

They ran back to their seats.

Storey waved at the boys. "See you later."

"Bye, Daddy. Bye Uncle Roe. You teach me kicks?"

Jethroe smiled. "Sure . . . sometime soon."

"Bye," Lee mumbled through a mouthful of cereal

Donna left her seat at the table, hugged her brother, looked up at him, nodded toward Eric. "Tonight?"

"Yes . . . or tomorrow morning."

Donna raised her eyebrows, locked her eyes on his for a moment. She grabbed his hand, pulled him outside onto the deck.

"Sis, I *will* be here later today." he said. "I can't say when. If it works tonight, I *will* have the talk with him." He grimaced. "I just want to do it right. I've been thinking since we discussed it. Mornings are his best times."

Donna nodded her head slowly. "You're right. What if he asks where his mommy is?"

"I'll have to tell him."

"I mean if he asks me today . . . while you're gone?"

"He's used to her being gone for several days at a time. Divert him until I get home."

"I'll try. I hope he doesn't ask." She turned to Jethroe, hugged him. "See you later, old friend."

He patted her cheek. "We'll get through this," he said.

*****

Storey braked Jethroe's BMW for the light at Kuebler. "Did Abrams find anything at the garage?"

"He thinks the locks were picked. They're still working it."

"Anything else? Finger prints?"

"It would take days, if ever, to separate strangers from everyday users. Bob is looking at the security camera recordings for the last few nights."

"The security camera! I forgot about it. That should show what happened."

"Hopefully."

"Hopefully? I'm overwhelmed by your optimism."

"Sorry. The area is not well lit. If the thief or thieves knew about or saw the camera, they could cover up. Don't get your hopes up."

"When will we know?"

"Bob was up all night. His guys are looking while he takes forty winks. He should have the results later in the day. I'll let you know as soon as we have something."

The light changed. Storey accelerated through the intersection. He removed the lavender-scented envelope from his jacket pocket. "I want you to read this before we get to Mike's office."

Jethroe examined the envelope, raised it to his nose. He lifted his eyebrows, turned to Storey. "A note from Julia?"

"Yeah."

Jethroe's lips pursed, his brow wrinkled as he read. His light chocolate face was clean-shaven, his head shaved. He claimed a height five-ten if he stretched his lanky frame. A skin-tight black tee with a long sleeved turtleneck accented the sinew in his arms and chest. Black jeans emphasized his thin but muscled legs. His fingers absently traced a scar that ran from beneath his ear along his jaw and curled up to the corner of his mouth.

Storey was familiar with the habit, a leftover from their teenage years. Jethroe had dropped out of school after his freshman year at North Salem High and immersed himself in the activities of an assortment of hard-bitten toughs. Two years later he returned to school determined to escape his life on the streets. Shortly after, the gang assaulted him as an example to those who would reject their dominion. The scar was a remnant of the fight.

After he recovered, Jethroe immersed himself in Shotokan Karate. He received the first level black belt, a Sho Dan, a few months before graduating school with honors. During those high school years, Jethroe reconnected with Storey and Swanson, his elementary school friends. They joined Washington in his training, and earned their black belts during their college years.

Jethroe, now a seventh level black belt, or Kyoshi, a knowledgeable person, was well on his way to Hanshi, a master. By focusing his life on the Karate disciplines, he not only reacted instinctively to physical situations but met life crises objectively, his faculties fully engaged.

Swanson and Storey practiced sporadically but never achieved Jethroe's capability and elegance or acquired the mental discipline.

Continuing north on Liberty, Storey glanced at his friend. He was anxious to hear Jethroe's reaction to the note. After what seemed an eternity, Jethroe looked up and stared straight ahead for a long moment.

"When did you get this?" he said.

"Last night. I found it on top of our chest of drawers in the bedroom."

"Why show it to me now, before we meet Mike?"

"Something doesn't seem right. I want your reaction first, without Mike's legalese sprinkled over it. You see through the fog."

Jethroe turned toward Nick "Last time you saw Julia was . . .?"

"Yesterday morning. She fixed breakfast and I left for work."

"That was unusual, the breakfast? Right?"

"Very."

Jethroe raised an eyebrow. "Anything else seem strange?"

"Well . . . when she kissed me goodbye yesterday morning, she hugged me. She was, ah, intense." And, he thought, her passion, when they had made love the night before, and in the morning, though not unique, had been absent from their intimacy for the past year.

"Intense?"

"She was . . . um, she was distressed."

"Distressed?"

"There were tears in her eyes. She stood on the deck watching my car until I was out of sight."

"You left knowing she was upset?"

"Lately, I have been so engrossed with my own stuff that I haven't thought about much else. The company reorganization has consumed me. This thing with Rainey and the insurance really bugs me. Something is going on there that's not right, and Dad and Val won't discuss it.

"A couple of days ago, Julia and I had a fight. She thought I needed to spend more time at home; said my priorities were warped. When I left for work, I thought she was frustrated about that. Now I know she was sad about leaving." Storey waved a hand. "Nicholas Storey, the self-centered ass."

"Hindsight is not always productive."

"Maybe, but I was so consumed by my own needs it makes me wonder if I'm the man I thought I was."

Jethroe pointed toward a mini-mall parking lot. "Pull in here," he said.

Storey picked a remote spot.

Jethroe put a hand on Storey's shoulder. "Our past is a book full of lessons. We can't live there or change it. The present, this moment, is where we exist, where we make plans and decisions."

Storey had heard versions of the homily on rare occasions when Jethroe would exposit his philosophy, the mind-set that had lifted him from denizen of the brutal streets to multi-millionaire linchpin of his own nation-wide security firm.

Jethroe was silent for a moment. He dropped his hand. "I know your head is filled with grief and guilt. You need to put it aside for a moment—focus on now."

"Yes, Obi-Wan. I get it. I'll try," Storey said. "Where do we start?"

"Yesterday morning . . . that was the last time you saw or talked to her?"

"Yeah, but I called home around ten. I thought about it and realized there was something more going on than our disagreement. Actually, that was later. When I picked up the phone I was feeling guilty about being such a shit. I hoped we could have lunch and talk, but Suzume answered. She said Julia had gone shopping. I asked her to have Julia call me."

Jethroe tapped the letter. "What do you think Julia was trying to tell you?"

Storey shrugged. "What do you mean?"

"You said something wasn't right. What?'

Storey compressed his lips, stared across the lot. "I don't know. It nags at the back of my brain, but I can't pin it down. The harder I try, the more elusive it gets. It's just a feeling."

Jethroe's brow furrowed as he read aloud from the letter.

"Evil forces from my life before I met you have reappeared, a malice that I believed—I felt certain and still do—that I had neutralized. You know nothing of them and it is best you don't, lest you do something that could place you and Eric in harms way. There is no reason to believe they pose a threat to you, Eric, or me—the risk to them is too great."

He looked at Storey. "Do you have any idea what that is about?"

"Julia never discussed her past in any detail . . . before us, I mean. Sometimes she would drop into a . . . well, it was like a trance, as if she went somewhere else for a little while. She said it had nothing to do with us, that she would tell me about it some day; when it made sense."

"Made sense?"

"That's what she said. I took that to mean when she was ready."

"You have no clue? I mean about the situation she had to deal with, confront, whatever."

"None."

Jethroe returned to Julia's note.

"I must resolve this myself. Believe me—it is useless to try to find me."

Jethroe folded the paper, returned it to the envelope. "What do you get from that?"

"That frightens me. Something really bad is going on. That's obvious now after what happened; the hit-and-run. Julia killed."

"You think you and Eric are at risk?"

"I don't know. The letter said that it, whatever *it* is, had nothing to do with us."

"Well, the odds don't favor an accident, and—"

"Apparently, that's what has Oliphant's shorts in a twist. Mike and Olivia both said the spouse is usually the first suspect."

"Olivia? You talked with Olivia?"

Storey related their early morning encounter.

"Why would she risk her status, maybe her career, to have a clandestine meet with you?"

"If you add up our time as college roommates and when we lived together, it's longer than I've known Julia. She's a concerned friend, a good friend. She was telling me that Oliphant has something. He intends to question me after the morgue visit this morning and that I . . . we, should be prepared, keep our guard up."

"Wow. She said all that?"

"Not directly. Sort of between the lines, making me ask questions. After our years together we, well, we don't need to be totally literal. It's like you, Mike, and me, only more so."

"She really put herself on the line."

"I'd do the same for her."

"Well, forewarned is good. If Oliphant does question you, they won't let me in."

"You think Julia's death was planned?"

"Yeah. It's doubtful there's a nut-job out there running down people in parking lots for the thrill of it. If there were such a psycho on the loose, it's not likely he would steal your classic car to do the deed."

"We don't know it was the T Bird."

"It's a fair assumption. It's missing. The lady on TV, the witness . . . her description matches your car. I'd say it's more than fair, it's highly probable it was the T Bird."

"Okay. If you're right, where does that take us?"

"Well, suppose Julia knew something that got her killed."

"Suppose? Roe, isn't it a bit more than a supposition?"

"Well, yeah, almost a given. They may think you know what that something is."

The short hairs on Storey's neck rose, his grip on the steering wheel tightened. "Do you think it's more than one guy, maybe a conspiracy?"

"Well, this Bill Stevens guy got you away from the office and out of sight so no one can vouch for your whereabouts at the time Julia was killed. They seemed to know where Julia was going to be and when."

Storey raised an eyebrow. "You said *they*. You're buying into my conspiracy idea, that there is more than one person involved?"

"As I was going to say, if you stand back and look at the big picture including the Stevens phone call, it makes me think the whole thing was deliberate. They're trying to put you in a frame."

"This is bizarre. Are you sure we're not being paranoid?"

"Paranoia is my business. It's more than coincidence. Too many things happened at the same time. Anyway, I don't believe in coincidence. If they had a plan it means they had to gather information and organize . . ." Jethroe sat upright, his eyes widened. *"They had to . . . Shit, I didn't see it!* Nick, we have to go back to your place. Call Mike. Tell him to meet us there ASAP."

Jethroe opened his cell phone, punched a number. He looked at Storey. "Nick, move it. Call Mike . . . *now!*"

Storey frowned, pulled his cell from its belt holster and flipped it open as he backed out of their parking space.

Jethroe drummed fingers on his thigh. "Pick up . . . pick up. Ah, Cal, it's Jethroe. Get security to Nick Storey's house. Two of our best. Code thirty-three . . . yes, Cal, it's urgent. And send a van with a crew. We need to sweep and secure the premises."

8:10 AM Thursday
21 April 2009

Goaded by Jethroe, Storey kept the horn blaring as he raced south on Liberty. He swerved to the right, passed an SUV. The woman driver honked her horn, gave them the finger.

"So many rude people nowadays," Jethroe said.

"Rude? Every cop in South Salem will be on our ass in a minute or two. They're trained in rude."

"If they show up, I'll wave my deputy badge. They can escort us."

"Before or after they arrest us?"

Storey slowed for a school zone; accelerated through the yellow at Kuebler.

"What's the plan?"

"Well, first, we have to make sure Donna and the kids are safe. I think there's a good chance your house is bugged. Your office too."

"Bugged? You mean wire tap kinda thing?"

"Yeah, but the technology today isn't hard wired."

Storey traversed the three miles to his home on Bunker Hill in record time despite slowing for two neighborhood schools. As he turned into his driveway, Jethroe pointed left.

"Park in front of your shop. We need space by the house for the equipment van."

Jethroe jumped from the car before it came to a full stop and jogged across the yard toward the house. Storey fumbled his door open and ran after him.

Donna came through the sliding door and walked across the deck. "Jethroe! Did you forget something?"

"Where are the boys?"

"In the living room watching TV. Cartoons. Why?"

Jethroe took the steps in two bounds, marched across the deck to Donna. "Have you seen anything or anybody out of the ordinary since we left?"

"Like what? You're scaring me."

Storey leaped up the stairs and joined them.

"Does it have something to do with Julia's letter?" said Donna.

Jethroe swiveled his head toward the door. "Check on the kids while I bring Donna up to date."

"Can do."

*****

Storey closed the dining room slider and dropped into the Adirondack next to Donna. Jethroe sat on the deck rail facing them.

"I hear the TV in your den," Donna said. "How did you talk them into giving up the plasma?"

"I bribed them with ice cream and cookies."

"Sort of early for that, isn't it?"

"Nothing else was working. I was desperate."

"Did Eric ask about his mommy?"

Storey shook his head. "No."

The tuned exhaust ports of Swanson's Corvette growled as it slowed and turned into the driveway. Jethroe waved him toward his BMW. Swanson parked the red machine and crawled out.

"Nick, if you'll give me the letter I'll show it to Mike." Storey handed him Julia's letter. Jethroe jumped down the steps and loped across the lawn to meet Swanson.

"Hi," Swanson yelled, waved at Nick and Donna. "What happened? Nick said you needed me here."

Jethroe pointed to a pair of lawn chairs by a bed of azalea. "Sit," he said, gave Swanson the letter. "Read."

"He did that for me," Donna said quietly.

"Who . . . what?" Storey said.

"Roe. He intercepted Mike, kept him down there."

"Oh. You and Mike . . . ah, you're not—what are you now?"

"We've hardly spoken since Joey's funeral." She crossed her arms on the table, looked down at Swanson as he read Julia's letter. "Then, only a few words. Well, we say hi, maybe wave at each other if we happen to meet somewhere."

"Joey was killed two years ago. I thought maybe . . ."

"You thought what?"

"Forget it. None of my business."

She lifted her gaze to the distant hillside, her eyes unfocused. "Best we keep it that way."

"Okay."

They sat mute, listening to snippets of conversation as Jethroe explained his interpretation of the letter and the actions he had initiated.

A black SUV turned from the street, rolled up the driveway and parked in front of the garage. The driver, an Oriental woman, and a large black man exited the vehicle. They wore no identifying patches or badges on their immaculate blue business suits. At the edge of the concrete pad they waited for Jethroe and Swanson to join them. Their movements exhibited a catlike ease—an elegance that Storey knew veiled a well-honed marshal-arts power. He noted the almost imperceptible swivel of their heads as their eyes flicked across the front of the house and around the yard— memorizing the layout of the property, he supposed. He saw slight bulges under the left armpits of their jackets. They were armed. Two of Jethroe's best, as he had promised.

Jethroe introduced them to Swanson, led them up to the deck "Nick, Donna, this is Kim Ng, and John Johnson."

Ng locked eyes with each in turn and shook their hands. Storey felt Kim's dark eyes scanning his as if she were vacuuming up his thoughts. He had difficulty breaking away from her gaze. He guessed her to be five-nine or ten. The sinewy muscle that stretched her tight-fitting garments over her lanky frame told him she spent considerable time toning her physique. Her smile seemed genuine, her grip firm. "Please, call me Kim," she said.

Storey speculated John would push a scale into the mid two hundreds. Storey expected a crushing grip from Kim's large partner, but John folded Storey's hand in both of his and held it softly for a moment.   John's eyes widened to match his grin as he studied Storey's face.

"Glad to finally meet you, Mr. Storey. Jethroe has told me a lot about you."

"Don't believe everything you hear." Storey smiled, looked up at the happy black face. "And, John, please, I'm Nick, Mr. Storey is my father."

John chuckled. "Okay, Nick it is."

Storey was impressed. Donna and the boys would be safe with Kim Ng and John Johnson.

"Donna, Nick, we need to chat."   Jethroe walked toward Swanson, who had been watching the introductions from his perch on the deck rail near the stairs.

Swanson slid down and stood facing them. His eyes focused on Donna as the trio approached. "Donna," he said as she stopped in front of him. He extended his hand, touched her upper arm. "It's been a while."

"Yes, Michael, it has." She laid her hand over his for a long moment.

Swanson removed his hand, cleared his throat, and turned toward Jethroe and Storey. "What's the plan?"

"Ah, yeah, well," Jethroe said, "if the house is wired for sound, I think it best we evacuate and let the techs find the bugs."

"Nick and I need some time to strategize before we go downtown," Swanson said.

"Donna," Jethroe said. "Can you take the boys somewhere for a couple of hours?"

"We could go to my house . . . or maybe the park. They like to play on the slides and climb the monkey bars. The park probably is best. Keep them busy."

"That should work. Kim and John will be with you."

"What do I . . ." She looked at Storey. "What do *we* tell Lee and Eric? Two complete strangers suddenly appear and we ride off with them. That will take some explaining, especially to these kids."

Storey shrugged. "If you go to your place—"

"Let me handle it," Jethroe said. "I promised to teach them some new karate moves." He spread his arms, cocked his head, smiled. "Kim and John are their private instructors. The park is a perfect place."

Storey and Donna looked at each other. Storey nodded.

A few moments later, Storey, Swanson, and Jethroe leaned on the deck rail watching the SUV depart. "The boys will remember this forever," Storey said. "But they wanted Uncle Roe to come with them."

"Kim and John can handle it. They're pros. They give it all they got, whatever the assignment. How could they not enjoy those little guys?"

"Their nannies were assassins, something the kids can tell their grandkids."

"They are not assassins. I'm not aware that either of them has had to terminate anyone."

"Sorry. Bad choice of words. What do you call someone who can kill you with their bare hands in a dozen or so different ways?"

Jethroe smiled. "Well-trained?"

9:10 AM Thursday
21 May 2009

"Nick, we have to go," Swanson said.

Jethroe looked at Swanson. "You've been quiet as a graveyard and bleak as a cloudy night since Donna and the kids left. What pushed your gloomy button?"

Swanson looked askance at Jethroe. "Nick," he said, "let's go. We can talk in the car about dealing with Oliphant."

"I'm driving by myself."

"What . . . why? Jethroe, explain to this idiot why that's a bad idea."

Jethroe locked his fingers behind his neck and rolled his head back. "I think Nick will be safe."

"You think?"

Jethroe dropped his hands, turned and looked at Nick. "Do you remember that locksmith guy . . . what was his name, ah . . ."

"Oscar Loukas?"

"Yeah. You thought he was stalking you after you terminated his contracts." Jethroe jumped up, sat on the broad top of the deck rail, raising his line of vision to that of his companions.

"You put me through your training sessions—taught me to spot and shake a tail."

"You can still do it?"

"Yeah. It's instinctive now, but no one ever follows me."

"You'll be fine," Jethroe said.

"They killed Julia," Swanson said. "You've got two of your best security operatives guarding Donna and the kids. Why not Nick?"

"This thing is too well organized. They have made a big move executing Julia. Assuming it's not a revenge thing, I expect their next move is to demand Nick cough up whatever they're after; perhaps threaten to harm his family if he doesn't. Hurting him at this point is counter-productive."

"So," Swanson said, "Nick is the bait?"

"Not really. It's their game, and, the next move is theirs. We need to make it easy. When we know something, what they want, who or where they are—anything—then we can mount an offense and stop playing by their rules."

"So we wait," said Swanson.

"And play safe," said Jethroe. He rubbed his hand across his shaved head, looked at Storey. "You want a bodyguard? Just say the word; you got it."

"No," Storey said. "The sooner we can end this the better. I can take care of myself."

"We better go," said Swanson. "Don't want to be late for Oliphant's quiz."

"Nick, drive the BMW," Jethroe said. "It's more maneuverable than your big red monster."

"That leaves you without wheels," Storey said.

"A new set is only a phone call away. Go. The tech team should be here any second . . . Ah, here they are."

A dark blue slab-sided van turned into the drive and parked in front of the garage. Two young men, an Asian with a crew cut, and a short, thin white sporting a long ponytail jumped out. They were wearing blue business suits. Storey wondered if their high school had just released them for the day.

Ponytail yelled up at them. "Sorry we're late, Mr. Washington. Construction on Liberty."

Jethroe waved at them. "Jerry, your timing is perfect. No worries."

Swanson looked at Storey, grinned. "*Mister* Washington?"

Jethroe shrugged. He tapped Swanson's arm. "Keep me in the loop. Let me know what happens with the detectives." He turned toward his electronic technicians. "Time to go to work."

Swanson and Storey walked down the steps and across the lawn toward the cars. "If Oliphant starts his twenty question routine, you don't speak unless I say so.   Don't volunteer any information. Okay?"

"I understand," said Storey.

"You're like a brother to me.   No matter what, I'm going to worry.   But, when we walk into the courthouse, I'm your lawyer, not your friend, not your buddy."

"I got it. Where should we meet?" Storey said.

"At the coroner's . . . it's on Center Street near the freeway."

"I know the place. Where's the morgue?"

"Meet me in the parking lot. I'll show you."

"I hope I'm up to this."

"You'll do fine.

10:00 AM Thursday
21 May 2009

He thought his knees would buckle when Swanson opened the door under the sign that read: Medical Examiner – Coroner. Storey stopped momentarily and put his hand on the doorjamb to regain his equilibrium before he walked inside. Oliphant and Olivia were sitting on chairs against the wall to his right. They stood when he entered. He looked at Olivia briefly; saw her strained smile. He focused on the back of Mike's head. Swanson was saying something to a young man at the desk to his left. Storey heard the words but could not decipher their meaning. They seemed far away, a dull echo in his head—he was an observer; not part of the scene. He focused on the cherry-red mane of the clerk who was talking into a phone as Swanson bent over the desk and wrote in a book.

Swanson put a hand on his elbow. Storey flinched,

"Are you okay?"

"Ah . . . yeah. Fine."

"I signed the visitor register, we can go in now."

Swanson guided him down a hallway into a small room with a window covered by Venetian blinds. Oliphant walked past them and pulled up the blinds. Storey blinked. He had not been aware that the detective had followed them. He turned and saw Olivia standing close behind him, her face like chiseled granite. Oliphant stepped back and stood beside her.

Storey returned his attention to the window. A green cloth covered a form lying on a stainless steel gurney. A young woman wearing green scrubs and a surgical mask pulled the sheet down exposing Julia's head and neck.

Despite the hours he had spent steeling himself for this moment, Storey groaned and his eyes blurred. He leaned his forehead against the glass for a moment, and then straightened his back and sucked a deep breath. He turned away, sat on a nearby couch. Swanson sat beside him and placed a hand on his shoulder.

Oliphant paced slowly from the window to the door, his head swiveling to maintain focus on Storey. Olivia left the room and leaned against the wall of the hallway.

Swanson locked eyes with Oliphant. "Detective, you don't need to be here. Show some respect. Wait in the hall with your partner."

Oliphant stopped his march, crossed his arms over his chest. "I have some questions."

Swanson pointed toward the hallway. "Out," he muttered.

Oliphant rubbed his burr cut, frowned, executed a military style left face, picked up his briefcase and strode from the room. Olivia stepped to the door, kicked the stop into its retainer, let the closer ease the door shut.

*****

Storey rose from his seat, and swiped his face and eyes with the back of his hands. "I thought I was ready for this."

"Believe me, there is no way to prepare," said Swanson.

"She looked so, um . . . colorless. I didn't expect that. She was always so . . . so vital. Can we get out of here now?"

Oliphant accosted them as they exited the room. "Was that the body of Julia Storey?"

"Yes," said Swanson.

"I need Mr. Storey to verify that."

Swanson shrugged, looked at Nick.

Storey nodded. "Yes."

"I have some questions." Oliphant pointed to his right. "There's a conference room down the hall."

"Now is not a good time. Even you must understand the distress that comes with—"

"Counselor, it's here or we go downtown to interrogation." Oliphant raised his eyebrows, smiled. "I'm trying to do you a favor."

Storey, his gaze fixed on Olivia, saw her tilt her head to her right and nod.

"Now, that is a first," said Swanson. "I don't believe it, of course."

"Your client, at a minimum, is a material witness to the murder of his wife."

Swanson ran fingers through his hair, glared at Oliphant. "Material Witness? At a minimum? That's ridiculous. My client has no knowledge of why his wife was killed or who was involved. He can't give you a hint, or provide any evidence that will point you toward finding her killer—or killers.

"And, wipe that smirk off your face. Wednesday morning my client left for work watching his beautiful and talented wife wave goodbye from their porch. Then, Wednesday evening you jumped in with your usual tact and magnanimity and told him his Julia was dead. That was your job, your duty. Legally, it isn't required you show any form of compassion, or even a modicum of understanding, so I'm constrained from suing your ass for being a heartless bastard. Further, you implied he knew something about why she was killed or perhaps who did it. You produced nothing but severe mental distress for my client, which is probably not actionable, but certainly worthy of discussion in certain circles."

Swanson threw his hands up. "You're wasting time you should be spending searching for the perpetrators of this heinous act."

Oliphant grinned and slowly clapped his hands. "Good show, counselor. Save it for your opening statement. We talk here on neutral territory or downtown—your choice."

"Take your best shot—"

Storey gripped Swanson's arm. "We need to talk."

"Now?"

"Yes, now."

"You can use the conference room. We'll wait here," said Oliphant.

"No thanks," Swanson said. "We'll step outside where the air is fresh."

Oliphant looked at his watch. "Fifteen minutes max, old friend."

Swanson glowered at the detective.

As they walked past the desk of the redhead, Swanson paused. "Richard, someone—probably Mr. Storey's sister, Donna, will call you with the name of the mortuary for Julia Storey." He laid one of his business cards on the desk. "Please, write your phone number on the back. We're going outside for a breath of fresh air. Be back in a bit."

Out of earshot, Storey said, "Why agitate Oliphant? You're purposely punching the beehive."

"Did I tell him anything he didn't already know?"

"Ah . . . no."

"Did I seem out of control?"

"Well, yeah, you were, I thought."

"Good."

"I don't get it."

"Do I tell you how to craft a house?"

"No."

"Then let me handle our friend Oliphant."

"Friend? He's hardly—"

"An overconfident Oliphant *is* our friend." Swanson smiled, tapped Storey's upper arm with a fist.

Swanson sat on the rim of a brick planter, ankle over ankle, arms splayed. "So, I don't think you just wanted to chat about how to deal with Oliphant."

"No. But, I did wonder about that. You want him to think you've lost control."

Swanson cocked his head, smiled. He sobered, crossed his arms. "You seem to have recovered some equilibrium."

"After the dam broke in there," . . . Storey waved at the building . . . "some of the fog cleared. I'm mad. I want to find the bastard who did this. I could strangle the sonofabitch without a second thought. She was leaving me, but nobody deserves to die like that."

"A little adrenaline can do wonders sometimes. Nick, why are we out here?"

"I think we should talk to Oliphant now, not later."

"You haven't done anything. He has nothing. He's probing, trying to find something. Let him twist in the wind for awhile."

"I think he has something we need to know about."

"Why do you think that?"

"Olivia told me."

"During your early morning rendezvous?"

"Yes, and inside. Just now."

"She didn't say a word."

"Well, I pieced it together from what she implied during our morning meet and what she said here. We should hear him out."

"I always thought you and she were telepathic—or touched."

"After you've lived with someone for a long time, you—"

"Yeah, yeah . . . I remember, you just know. What did she do? Touch her nose three times after she pulled on an earlobe . . . oh, forget it." He looked up at the sky for a moment. "You really believe Oliphant will show us something; not just his usual litany of rambling questions?"

"Probably both."

Swanson stood, rubbed his hands together. "Okay, it's your decision. Let's go slay the dragon."

*****

Swanson and Storey sat on one side of the gray steel table, Oliphant and Olivia the other. Oliphant opened his briefcase and removed a manila folder.

"Thought you would want to see these." Oliphant's lips curled into a sardonic smile. He stared at Storey as he laid eight by ten glossy photos on the polished surface.

Storey's thoughts ratcheted back to his early morning jog with Olivia and her tacit confirmation of his musings that Oliphant would do something unexpected, or peculiar, even outrageous. Was this it? When he saw Olivia's blank stare, his heart jumped, his scalp tingled.

Swanson glanced at each print as the detective aligned them into two rows of six. "What is this?" He waved his hand over the array. "My client—"

"Have *your client* look close," Oliphant said. "Here . . . try this one." He picked a photo, handed it to Storey.

Storey held the picture with both hands and studied it—a full-face view of a woman lying on her back on asphalt pavement. She had black hair and eyebrows. Her lipstick was black. Her eyes closed, the lashes heavy with black mascara. Black eye shadow covered her eye sockets down to cheekbones highlighted with white. A stripe of red slashed the bridge under her eyebrows. A silver and black skull hung from her ears on a silver S-shaped hook. She wore a lace choker festooned with rhinestones. A low-cut black blouse barely covered her nipples. A tattoo of a heart dripping blood from an impaled dagger was embossed on her chest just above her cleavage.

Storey's jaw dropped, his eyes widened. "Julia? What the . . .?" He looked at Olivia. "Tell me it's not . . ."

"I'm sorry," she said.

He flicked his gaze across the array of pictures. He stood, picked them up and one by one, studied them, and passed them in turn to Swanson. In a full body view he saw wristbands that matched the choker, a short, pleated black skirt, knit black stockings and thick-soled mid-thigh black boots. He passed the last glossy to Swanson and slumped into his chair. He wanted to hit something or someone. His hands shook. He turned toward the end wall. His jaw muscles pulsed, his eyes closed as he tried to calm the storm rising inside him. After a few moments, he turned, looked at Olivia. Her face telegraphed her anguish. "I don't understand," he said.

"Me either," said Oliphant. "Mr. Storey, did your wife habitually participate in Goth rituals?"

Swanson gathered up the photos. "These are for us?"

Oliphant shrugged. "Knock yourself out," he said. "You'll get them sooner or later."

Swanson grabbed the folder, stuffed the twelve eight by ten glossies inside. "We're done here, Sam."

"You need to explain what all that means." Oliphant pointed at the folder.

"You're assuming my client knows."

"Well, counselor, maybe he can explain why she was carrying a Canadian passport and a driver's license that said she was Diane Beaumont."

"What?" Storey's chin dropped. He shook his head. He spread his hands. "I don't have a clue."

Oliphant pushed back in his chair, put an arm over the back. He squinted and stroked his mustache as he looked at Swanson. "Michael, it stretches my imagination to assume your client, the deceased's husband for four years, knows nothing about his wife having an alias."

Swanson jumped to his feet, placed his palms on the table and leaned forward. "Are you accusing my client of something?"

"No, not yet. Let me summarize the situation as I see it." He pointed at Storey. "His wife—"

"Julia. Her name was Julia." Swanson eased back into his seat.

Oliphant placed his hands on the tabletop, interlaced his fingers, and sucked a deep breath. He cleared his throat. "Okay. *Mrs. Storey* was a Jane Doe for the first few hours. We didn't identify her until the medical examiner cleaned her up." He waved toward Olivia. "Luckily, my new partner recognized her. We brought up her Oregon drivers license. In my opinion, the photo matched what I saw. We went to the Storey home. The babysitter said Storey was at his office. We went there."

"Suzume . . . she's our nanny," Storey said. "Diane Beaumont? Who's Diane Beaumont?

Swanson patted Storey's shoulder. "Why wait until now to cough up this Canadian connection?"

"We didn't know about it until we returned to the station from Storey's office. A patrolman helping with the crime scene inspection discovered her purse with the Canadian ID's inside. It was under some flowers in a nearby planter. Apparently it was thrown there when the car hit her." Olyphant waved his arm at Olivia. "Barton thought we needed a positive ID from Storey before—"

"She's right," Swanson said. "Before you did *anything*. Why didn't you arrange for my client to ID the body last night?" Swanson cocked his head. "That's what you two were arguing about last night in Nick's foyer . . . wasn't it?" He pointed at Olivia. "She wanted the ID last night and you just wanted time to simmer your witches' brew. You're a piece of work, Sam."

Oliphant looked away, rubbed his cheek, sighed. "If you recall, you denied us access to Mr. Storey. I believe I told you this was the soonest I could schedule a viewing."

"And, I thought that was not usual, but I let it pass. Now I know it was bullshit. You were buying time. Anything else you want to share—or allege?"

Oliphant stared at Swanson, then Storey. "Did you know she was driving a '96 Nissan SUV?"

Storey blinked. "A Nissan? Why would she . . . she loved her Mini Cooper."

Swanson put a hand on Storey's shoulder. "Nick, I'll handle this," he said. "Are you saying she bought a used car?"

"Yeah. We found the title in the glove box. The previous owner signed it the day before the hit and run."

"And how do you know it was Julia who bought the car?"

"Well, the keys were in her purse. When we find the seller, I'm confident he'll verify she bought it. A receipt in her purse matched the stuff in the car."

"Stuff? What kind of stuff?"

"Camping gear—backpack, sleeping bag, raingear, a pop-up tent. And, dried food, the kind backpackers use . . . you know, freeze dried, dehydrated . . . enough for a week or more."

"That's not unusual. She often hiked into the backcountry—and along the coast. She sketched, painted, took photos." Swanson lifted his shoulders, splayed his hands. "Many of her paintings are from her trips."

"Okay, but did she buy a car for each trip . . . and fresh gear? Did she always carry a big wad of cash in the lining of a brand new purse?"

"Cash?"

"Yeah. One hundred fifty Franklins."

Storey's eyes ratcheted from Oliphant to Olivia. Olivia sat unmoving and expressionless, her hands folded in her lap. He looked up at Swanson. "Fifteen thousand dollars? That's ludicrous. The whole thing is absurd. He has to be making this up."

Olivia caught Storey's gaze. She gave him a slight twist of her head and flicked her eyes.

It's not a fabrication? She's agreeing with Oliphant! She hasn't been shutting me out. Storey rocked back in his chair and stared at the ceiling tile. The implications of Oliphant's narrative struck like a full-body brain freeze. He dropped his arms into his lap, focused on the far wall, and hoped his shivers were not noticeable.

"Counselor, tell Mr. Storey the facts speak here, not me."

"Sam, what is your presumption regarding my client? You're obviously implying he was involved somehow, or has information that's relevant."

"I try not to presume. I just arrange facts and evidence to—"

"Yeah," said Swanson. "Align facts and evidence to fit your theories."

"There's a few missing pieces just now. You're a smart guy. Maybe you can figure it out."

"She had a Canadian—?"

Swanson touched Storey's arm. "Don't say another word. Sam, you haven't read my client his rights; he's not under arrest; you have no subpoena; so . . . we're outta here."

Nick rose unsteadily from his chair.

Olivia stood. "I'll escort them out."

Oliphant gave her a scathing look. "Counselor, we'll talk later," he said. "Maybe sooner than later."

Olivia opened the door.

 "Knock yourself out, Sam," Swanson said,

Olivia and Storey stood alongside Jethroe's BMW watching Swanson drive away. Olivia momentarily gripped Storey's arm. "Wiley's at three. Tell *no* one," she said, nodded toward the Corvette, turned, and walked back into the building.

12:10 PM Thursday
21 May 2009

In Swanson's small conference room, Swanson and Storey settled into a pair of hard-back chairs at the table. Swanson opened a white paper sack, removed napkins, two hamburgers, a tray of French fries, and ketchup and mustard in tiny plastic wrappers. "I'm starving," he said. "You?"

"Yeah, well, sort of."

"Eat. When Roe gets here we can review and strategize."

Storey squeezed ketchup into the tray of fries. "I wish you'd gone to the fish place." He swabbed a fry in the red puddle.

Swanson shrugged. "This was quicker." He pushed the folder containing the crime scene photographs aside.

Storey looked at the tan folder, thinking of the cliché "the elephant in the room." Since leaving the morgue, they had not mentioned the file or its contents. Now the images flooded his mind. He knew every inch of her body, was sure she had no tattoos. Was Julia a Goth? Whatever that was. It made no sense. He had heard the—what was it—a cult? A lifestyle? A religion? Why the black wig? Why the disguise? Was it part of her plan? *My leaving was inevitable.*

He walked to the window overlooking the parking lot and stared out.

Swanson finished his sandwich and stuffed the wrappings into the sack. He sipped his coffee, turned and looked at Storey.

"Your burger is getting cold."

Storey didn't move or change focus. "I'll pass."

"I talked to Roe while I was in line for the food."

"And?"

"He found a bug."

"Somebody has been listening?"

"Yeah, but he didn't give me details. Said he would tell us when he got here."

Storey turned and faced Swanson, sucked a deep breath. He left the window and paced along the wall next to the table. The thought of someone capturing his private conversations caused chills to crawl up his arms. Were *They* listening to his conversation, or to Julia's, or was their private exchanges the target? His brow furrowed. Somewhere out there in the ether was a collection of electrons that could broadcast to the world their most intimate moments.

"About this time yesterday, I was uptight about renewing an insurance policy with that asshole, Rainey . . . and I was in a state about some stupid jerk and a flat tire on a forklift. Wanna talk about someone with their priorities screwed up? I was so engrossed in all my stuff I was blind to Julia's needs. I was selfish, insensitive, self-absorbed and, ah . . . shit." He waved a hand at Swanson. "You fill in the blanks."

"I know a gal who's into flagellation and all that weird stuff. I'm sure she would loan you her whip if it would help."

"Don't patronize me, Mike."

"You want to hear about misplaced priorities? I'll tell you my life story. Hey, buddy, all this shoulda, woulda, coulda shit . . . it don't help. Believe me."

Storey dropped onto a chair, sighed, and stared into the mid-distance. "In less than twenty-four hours my life is a disaster. Julia is dead; an obsessive detective thinks I'm involved. My family is under guard. My Mom and Dad are in the wind. I'm trying to find an anchor somewhere in this mess. I'm lost. I don't know where to go from here."

"Who's lost?" Jethroe walked into the room, grabbed a chair, turned it around, and straddled it. He crossed his arms over the back and studied their food choice. "Gourmet MacDonald's?"

"Yeah, " Swanson said. "Want some? Nick wasn't hungry."

"You're kidding." Roe shuddered. "I grabbed an apple and ham sandwich from Storey's fridge."

Swanson wiped his mustache with a napkin. "Enlighten us."

Storey ratcheted his chair closer to the table. "Yeah, what did you find?"

"There were three bugs. I'll describe the high tech ones first. There's one in the bedroom and one in the family room. They're buried in the phones and powered by the phone battery. They transmit to a receiver near the top of the hill behind the house. It records on a 4-gigabyte memory stick. Plug and replace. Also, if someone were nearby, they could record or listen real time."

Swanson dropped Storey's burger and fries into the sack, tossed the bundle into a wastebasket. "Any way to tell how long they been there?"

"Not really."

Storey frowned. "You said there were three?" .

"The third one was in your den—in the sofa end table. Powered from the lamp cord. Old tech. Probably bought over the internet. CD receiver on the backside of your shop building. Power tapped from one of the shop circuits."

Storey leaned back in his chair. "Did you remove them?"

"No. We turned the TV on to mask any noise as we did the sweep. We left them intact. Now that we know they're there, maybe we can use them to our advantage."

"As in, communicate with the bastards? Serve up sour information? I like it," said Swanson.

"You said the one in my den was old technology. Damn . . . does that mean we're dealing with two, ah, stalkers, spies . . . whatever, whoever they are?"

"Reasonable assumption. I believe the old stuff, the one in your den, has been there longer than the two upscale ones. Dust had collected on the receiver mike and the wiring."

"Dust? How could it collect dust inside a lamp?"

"The small amount of heat from the circuitry is enough to cause some air flow. Moving air . . . dust and lint collects."

"So, it could have been there for a long time."

"Yep. My guess . . . a year or two, maybe more"

1:15 PM Thursday
21 May 2009

Storey returned to the conference room window and stared at the distant mountains. *"Wiley's at three. Tell no one."* Wiley's was an upscale billiards parlor with a bar and restaurant a dozen miles from OSU in Corvallis, an upgrade from the smoky saloon with pool tables in the back that he and Olivia had frequented during their college years. Jethroe competed in Wiley's nine-ball tournaments and was the player to beat. If he did not win, he shook off condolences with a crooked smile, winked, said, "At least it keeps the marks coming back."

"What happened with Oliphant?" said Jethroe.

"Nick identified the body," said Swanson. "It was Julia. Oliphant and Olivia were there. Olivia left the room but Oliphant stayed until I kicked him out."

"Literally, I hope."

"I gave him the evil eye. He got the hint. Long story short, later, we met in a conference room. Oliphant is doing his best to tie Nick into the scene. I can tell Olivia is upset; she doesn't go along with her partner. I was *not* in favor of the meeting, but Nick insisted. I think he had a mind meld with Olivia and she told him it was a good idea. Oliphant did give us some new information." Swanson slid the folder across the table.

Jethroe opened the file and studied the photos, occasionally turning them ninety degrees, or bringing them closer to his face to focus on a detail. As he finished with and laid each one aside, Mike inscribed a number on the back with a black Sharpie and wrote a description of the image in his ubiquitous yellow tablet.

Storey moved his hand to his upper arm where she had touched him. Her voice had been soft, her touch gentle. Invitation or command? Olivia the cop or Olivia his friend? *"Tell no one."* Her emphasis on the no and her slight nod toward the retreating Corvette told him the nix included Mike and Jethroe. He did not want to exclude them, or, most of all, deceive them. Could he trust her? The Olivia he had known would understand without passing judgment or displaying a cloying over-the-top sympathy. He wanted to see her again. He could meet with her and tell Jethroe and Mike later—or not.

Storey looked at his watch. 1:30. An hour to Albany, fifteen minutes of side streets and diversions to assure he was not being followed . . . he had to leave in ten or fifteen minutes. He returned to his seat at the table

Jethroe, finished with the last picture, locked his hands behind his head and stared out the window.

Storey fidgeted in his chair, waiting for Swanson to complete his documentation. "Well, Roe, what do you think?" he said as Swanson closed the folder.

Jethroe placed his arms on the table and looked at Storey. "Goth," he said. "Julia was never into Goth."

"No. Whatever Goth is." Storey had taken Jethroe's statement as a question.

"You never heard of Goth?"

"Gothic architecture, yeah."

"Well, some of the Goth imagery and practices reflect the nineteenth century Gothic period. They are a subculture that began in the UK in the goth rock scene during the early eighties and grew from there. Their fashion is usually erotic and dark, sometimes morbid. A typical Goth has dyed black hair, dark eyeliner, and black fingernails."

Storey tapped the folder. "Like the pictures? What's the choker for?"

"The neckbands, dog collars if you like, can be a sign of the personality—submissive or dominant. The submissive may have a ring in front of the collar where the dominant can fasten a chain."

"Strange. How do you know all this stuff?"

"In my business, cultural awareness is mandatory. You never encountered a Goth?"

"I've seen people dressed that way once or twice. I thought they were going to a masquerade party or something."

"Sometimes I think you live in a convent."

Swanson rapped a knuckle on the table. "Hey. Guys. Enough culture bullshit. Back to the problem. You been studying the pictures for half an hour, so, elucidate."

"Well, I . . ." Jethroe looked at Storey.

"Don't hold back. I have to know. Better now than later. I've seen her in the morgue and looked at the pictures."

Jethroe sucked a breath and let it out slowly. "Okay." He folded his hands on the tabletop. "It's obvious that the car wheels rolled over her chest and crushed her rib cage, probably her heart too. We need to wait for confirmation from the coroner."

Storey's chin quivered. The images in the photos came to life in his mind—Julia struck by the car and flying through the air like a rag doll, the tires slamming into her as if she were a speed bump. He averted his gaze.

"We can take a break," said Swanson.

"No."

"Okay, if you say so." Swanson tapped the folder of photos, turned to Jethroe. "Any thoughts about why she made herself up like that?"

"I can speculate. Julia said in her note she had to confront something that had surfaced from her past life. She also said she had to do it alone and that it was useless to try to find her."

"We've all read the note," Swanson said.

Jethroe looked at Swanson. "Bear with me. Three relevant points from her letter." He held up an index finger. "She was trying to solve a problem." Another finger. "She needed or wanted to act alone." A third digit appeared. "It seems that she couldn't achieve her goal as Julia Storey."

"So, she assumed another identity?" Swanson said.

"Apparently." Jethroe leaned forward, elbows on the table.

"Why would she pick a Goth persona?" Storey said. "That's hardly covert . . . more like waving a flag. Here I am! Look at me! I would think she would choose something inconspicuous."

"I think it was a distraction while she gathered supplies and equipment before she melted into the Canadian identity. Much like a magician diverts your attention while he slips the coin into a pocket."

Storey raised an eyebrow. "Another personality?"

"Maybe more," said Jethroe.

"More?" said Swanson. "What's going on here? Julia had multiple identities? We just flew past speculation and crashed on weird."

Jethroe shrugged. "It seems the bread crumbs lead us there."

"Okay, smart ass," Swanson said. "If you're reading the road signs correctly, where are we?"

"Well, I think Julia's problem was more serious than a previous lover's blackmail attempt gone wrong. I—"

"I'm sure Julia had a life before me—other men," Storey said. He squinted at Jethroe. "You think she was having an affair, that she had a lover?"

"It's my crude attempt to illustrate a blackmail scheme. I'm confident it was not extortion. Killing her would eliminate their possibility of collection. I believe she knew something someone did not want revealed."

"That reinforces the conclusion we came to yesterday," Swanson said. "We should keep Donna and the boys' bodyguards in place."

"Yeah. Maybe we need some backup." Jethroe rose and walked toward the door. "I'll call Ng and have her update the team." He left the room.

Swanson pursed his lips, stared unfocused for a moment, then directed his attention to Storey. "We never discussed Julia's history in any detail. What do you know about her life before you met her?"

"Ah . . . like what?" Storey crossed his arms over his chest, frowned.

"I don't know. You once said she was from, ah, I think you said New York."

"I don't remember her identifying any specific location. It was somewhere in or near the metro area. We didn't chat about her past life. If I brought it up she changed the subject."

"Didn't that bother you, or raise more questions?"

"I'm not a lawyer. I don't need to dig out every little scrap of information to use for future entrapment or whatever. I thought we were happy, until recently . . . well, for the last year or so. What she was or did before us was not relevant. Was I curious? At first, yeah. Later, if she wanted to talk about her past, which was almost never, I listened. She had a philosophy that became part of us: Yesterday is over and done. Good or bad, we live today; it's a gift, make the most of it. Tomorrow is a mystery."

"Yeah, I remember her saying that."

"We've had this conversation before. Nothing's new. Julia was a very private person."

"Sorry. Sometimes we know things we don't know we know. Right now we are guessing. Roe may well be right; he's the bloodhound among us. He may have sniffed out the trail, but we're short on answers. I've had cases where unrelated tidbits or fragments pulled what we knew together, cleared away the rubble and exposed the big picture. So, it's possible, if we dig deeper, that we might find a clue."

"You want to probe our private lives? Put Julia and me in the spotlight?"

"That's not quite what I had in mind."

"Yeah. Right." Storey slid forward in his chair, put an ankle on a knee. "Okay, probe away."

"Julia was always gracious and warm with me. Since you are my best friend, it makes sense that she would try to get along. Our conversation covered everyday things: you, Eric, your family, nothing earth shaking. Did Julia have a lot of friends?"

"A few. Mostly within her art community. Do you mean someone she could bare her soul to—that sort of friend?"

"Was there someone?"

"Not that I knew of."

"Okay. Socially. From my personal observation, she wasn't the party type."

"Right. Large groups made her antsy. She was uptight for days before one of her gallery shows. She preferred small, intimate gatherings."

"No contact with outsiders, strangers; people you hadn't met?"

"Just her agent, the gallery folks from Portland, and an occasional painter or sculptor would visit her studio. To my knowledge, it was just business. I met most of them eventually. I remember a Larry Lawrence came by several times." Storey locked his fingers behind his neck, leaned against the chair back. This conservation was a waste of time. Mike was already familiar with most of it.

"The trips she took . . . when she gathered material for her art . . . her inspirational journeys. How often did she drop off the radar?"

"She would be gone for a week, maybe ten days every couple of months. Lately she was gone more than she was home."

"Where did she go?"

"She would say 'the mountains or north along the beaches and cliffs.' She wasn't specific. Said she would know when she saw something that was interesting, a place that inspired her. When she came home she showed me her sketches and photos and described where and how she got them. Usually they were pictures from the coast, people on the beach, fog rolling in over the shore, old houses, pastoral scenes. Sometimes she went to the mountains. Mike, this all seems redundant. You've seen sketches and photos from her trips."

"Does she see or visit anyone? Another artist perhaps?"

Storey sat upright in his chair, looked at Swanson, frowned. Did Mike know something about Julia's explorations that he didn't? In recent months, Storey had speculated that she was meeting someone. "There's no way for me to know. I thought she needed, ah . . . isolation, that it sparked her creativity."

"Did she behave differently when she returned? Was she inspired?"

"Most times she was moody and distant for a week or so. She jumped into her work as if she had to put it all on canvas before she forgot."

"Was she happy to be home again?"

"Not overtly, and not immediately. She was focused; worked in her studio night and day for a few days before she let the world in."

"Did this bother you?"

Storey settled against the back of his chair, his hands flat on the table. He stared at Swanson. The only significant arguments he and Julia had were about her secretive trips and his habit of working late. She had asserted more than once that he cared more for his job than family. He pursed his lips and frowned as he recalled his typical response—*well, I don't disappear for days at a time*—that would shut down their communication for a day or two.

He gritted his teeth, suppressing the *Damn you, Mike,* that flashed in his head. You're working me, he thought. Mike's uncanny ability to probe to the core of an issue was legendary. It was not the first time he had been at the focus of a Swanson probe. With just a few questions Mike could strike a nerve bundle. Storey knew that if he pretended her trips did not bother him Swanson would erupt with a glissando of questions. Best to face it now.

"Yes, it does, ah . . . did annoy me. It should be old news to you. We've talked about it once or twice."

"Was there a place she frequented more than others?"

"She did like the Cape Blanco area with its cliffs, the driftwood on the beach—you're an admirer of her paintings. You tell me."

"Okay, her paintings are mostly scenes on the coast, the beach, or waves breaking over rocks. She did an occasional mountain landscape, or a rustic old barn. So, she favored the coast?"

"The coastal environment, the ocean seemed to soothe her, stormy or calm, regardless of season."

"Did she favor a particular site? Visit one place more often?"

"I don't know."

"Was she always alone—"

Jethroe burst into the room, sat with his arms folded across the back of his chair.

Storey welcomed the interruption. His frustration with Swanson's interrogation had been building to an anger he was not sure he could contain.

"Everyone's on board now," Jethroe said. "I put a couple of people on call as backup to Ng and Johnson. We should sweep your offices for bugs. If they got your house, it seems likely your workplace is wired too."

"Okay, whatever." Storey threw his hands up. "This whole thing is totally fucking unbelievable."

"I think we need to do it like we did your house . . . so the buggor doesn't know we know. It's hard to be covert when guys with detectors are running around in an office full of people." He looked at Storey. "How can we clear out your staff without raising suspicion?"

"Have to be after hours. Call Valerie. She'll arrange something."

Jethroe opened his cell, closed it. "If your place is tapped, I can't explain our dilemma over the phone."

Swanson stared at Jethroe for a moment. "I'll handle it." He activated his cell, drummed his fingers on the table. "Ah, Valerie. Mike Swanson . . . I'm fine, thanks. We just came back from the coroner's office . . . Yes, it was difficult. That's why I'm calling. Valerie, I need your help with Nick, can you come to my office right away? . . . You'll understand when you get here . . . Good, see you soon." He closed the phone, turned to Jethroe and Nick. "She's on her way."

Storey shook his head, rose from his chair. "You don't need me here. Roe, can I still use your car? I want to go for a drive. Clear my head."

Swanson stood, grasped Storey's upper arm. "I think you should stay close. We just agreed that Julia may have been killed to shut her up. At the risk of repeating myself, *they, he*, or *she*, may think Julia confided in you and might come after you, too. I think you should stay close to us."

"I need some time alone. Relax. I'll be extra careful."

"I'm sure Julia was careful, probably paranoid. And, she probably knew what, or who, to watch for."

"Okay, if it'll make you feel better, I could go by Dad's place and get my .32 Colt. Anything happens; I'll just shoot the bastard and ask questions later."

Swanson rolled his eyes. "Yeah, now that's a winner." He dropped back into his chair, looked at Jethroe. "Help me out here. Shouldn't we keep Nick under our wing? He could be—"

"He'll be fine." Jethroe leaned back in his seat and looked at Swanson. "He knows what he's doing."

"I wish I had your confidence."

Jethroe raised his focus to Storey. "Stay alert, my friend. When and where can we expect to see you?"

"My house. Around six or seven."

*****

Swanson waited until the outer door closed behind Storey. "What are you thinking? The thought of Nick wandering around the city on his own gives me stomach cramps."

"Me, too—and shivers."

"Then why let him go?"

"You want to tell him he can't?"

"Good point. This whole business seems unreal. I'm having trouble wrapping my mind around it."

"Yeah." Jethroe walked to the window and stared down at the parking lot. "I can't imagine what Nick is thinking."

"I had a talk with him while you were gone."

"And . . ."

"He gets defensive if I mention Julia's trips."

"I've noticed."

"I think she has, ah . . . had a lover or old friend she visited during her outings."

"She always came back with ideas and sketches for new paintings."

"Visiting a lover and producing sketches and such are not mutually exclusive."

"True. Perhaps the inspiration bit was a ploy."

"Maybe." Swanson knit his fingers, thumbs under his chin. "It's hard to believe he tolerated Julia's expeditions without some serious doubts."

"Yeah. I've wondered why he put up with it."

The men sat silent for a moment.

"We have to do something," said Swanson. "Nick could be in serious jeopardy."

"Got it covered."

Swanson leaned forward, raised an eyebrow. "What have you done?"

"While I was gone," Jethroe waved a hand toward the door, "I assigned two of my best operatives to tail Nick. I had a feeling he would rabbit on us. They should have him in their sights before he climbs into the BMW."

"But Nick said, and you agreed, that you trained him to spot someone following him."

"Yeah, to detect an off the street civilian stalker. My guy David and his partner are pros. They'll be monitoring the GPS in the BMW. Nick will never know they're in the neighborhood."

"So, Nick can avoid Joe Six-pack, but not David who will discover if someone else is following him?"

"That's the assumption."

"I feel so much better." Swanson threw his hands up. "Shit."

3:30 PM Thursday
21 May 2009

He was late. His trip had taken longer than the hour and a half he had allotted. To confuse anyone following him, he'd planned a route through side streets and parking lots, but a maze of unfamiliar roads and dead ends delayed him, and bruised his pride in his Salem navigation skills. When he left Swanson's office the sky was clear, but the weather in Albany, where the wind whipped the rain nearly horizontal and miniature tornadoes filled with moisture, leaves, and bits of paper swirled around the corners of buildings and danced along the streets, added several minutes to the drive.

Not finding a spot on the street, he turned into a bank parking lot. He found Jethroe's umbrella under the passenger seat, and stepped out of the BMW. Within seconds, the wind blew the fragile canopy inside out. He ran the fifty yards to Wiley's Billiards and stepped into the lobby, water dripping from his clothing as he struggled to refold the umbrella.

Passing an elderly man and young woman tossing steel-tip darts, and a young couple playing pool at the front table, Storey moved through the billiard room. There, at a table in the back, Olivia, still wearing her blue skin-tight spandex and long-billed baseball cap, watched him approach.

"You're late," she said.

"Sorry."

"You look like a wet cat."

"In case you haven't noticed, it's raining buckets." He slid onto a stool nearby, watched her circle the green felt studying her next shot.

She banked the cue off the rail and tapped the seven ball into a side pocket; dispatched the eight, then the nine. She leaned on her cue stick. "How about a game?"

"Nine ball?"

"What else?"

"Want a beer?"

"No. Thanks."

Storey looked at her for a beat. "You're on duty?"

Olivia shrugged. "Sort of." She placed a pair of balls near the front rail. "Lag for break?"

Storey won by an inch, but his break did not sink a single ball.

"Why are we here?" he said.

"In the interest of justice."

Storey watched her make an easy shot on the one and roll the cue ball down the felt for a set-up on the two. "Does Oliphant know you're here?"

"Does it matter?"

"Depends."

"On what?"

"Olivia, we both know that a private meet with a suspect is not by the book. I don't want you to jeopardize your position, maybe your career, for me."

Olivia put the two in the corner pocket; the cue ball rolled behind the seven blocking her shot on the three. "Damn. Too much English." She squatted, sighted across the table assessing her next shot. "Did anyone say you're a suspect?"

"Not directly," Storey said. "I'll bet Oliphant has me in his crosshairs."

Olivia banked the cue ball down the table, ticked the three. "Damn . . . again." She retreated to a stool. "I'm sure you were not involved in Julia's death."

Storey grabbed a cube of chalk, rubbed the end of his cue. "How do you know I'm not part of it?"

"It's not who you are. You're not wired for murder."

"Thanks, but that's not very detective-like."

"It is what it is—truth."

Storey smiled, turned his focus to the game, aligned his shot at the three. The red sphere made a dull thump as it dropped into the leather corner pouch; the cue bounced off the rail and rolled to line up with the four and a side pocket. Within five minutes, he cleared the table.

"You've been practicing," said Olivia.

He sat on a stool adjacent to her, leaned on his stick. "Roe and I have been playing nine-ball for years. I suppose you could call it practice."

"Or masochism."

"Oh, I win on occasion."

"Really? You can actually win from a guy who attended college on a pool-hustling scholarship?"

Storey chuckled. "Yeah. Really." Same ironic wit and cut-to-the-chase demeanor. Classic Olivia. He looked into her eyes for a long moment. He had a bundle of respect for her, and, he had to admit, a soft spot. Could he be candid with her now? Could he trust her?

Olivia cocked her head, lifted her brows. She narrowed her eyes a bit. "Talk to me."

Could she still read him? "What do you want me to say?"

"Just the facts, man. Just the facts." She chuckled. "Always wanted to say that."

"I'm so happy to be your straight man."

"Seriously, we need to get to the truth . . . what happened and why."

"To quote Mike, 'Truth is hard to come by, proving it harder.'"

"Give me something to go with, anything. We'll work on the proof part later."

He scanned the room for eyes focused on him; found nothing unusual. The tightness in his chest eased; he could feel the knots in his gut unraveling. He had to find answers to his questions about Julia and their life together. Even though Olivia was part of the blue bureaucracy, he had to confide in her.

She tugged on his sleeve. "Hello. World to Storey."

He looked at his watch, returned his cue to the rack. "I'm starved. The restaurant should be open by now. I've only had a bite

of a greasy hamburger and a French fry since my banana with coffee
before our run this morning. How about we have an early dinner?"

"I skipped lunch. I'm ready."

"I'll buy."

"You'd bribe a police officer?" She slid from her seat, looked
up at him, smiled.

Storey hesitated for a beat. "Can't I take and old friend to dinner
without upsetting the establishment?"

She removed her cap, ran fingers through her short, tight curls.
"I'm already off the reservation." She replaced the hat, pulled the
bill low over her eyes. "Let's not compound the issue. I'll pay for
mine. I need to maintain some semblance of protocol."

She's cut her hair, Storey mused. Nice.

*****

They sat at a table at the rear of the restaurant and across from
the bar.

"I'm going to have a beer," Storey said. "You still drink white
wine?"

"For the record, you twisted my arm."

"A Killian Red from the tap, and a glass of chardonnay . . . Eola
Hills," he said to the waitress.

Olivia waited for the girl to leave. "You remembered," she said.

"Some things just stick in the mind."

She stared at him for a few seconds. "I'm listening."

"On or off the record?" He unfolded his napkin; put it on his
lap.

"I'm . . . oh, what the hell." She leaned forward, fingers
interlaced, elbows on the table. "Okay. Off the record . . . to a point.
I won't perjure myself. Detectives are officers of the court. I can't
withhold information or evidence concerning a crime or an
investigation."

"I understand."

"I need a starting point. Give me something that will provide, or
lead to, proof of what we both know . . . that you were not involved."

"I might have to go back a ways."

"Whatever it takes."

Storey stared at her, his mind churning. Where to begin? After a long moment, he said, "Maybe before I married Julia?"

"I'm not going anywhere."

The waitress placed their drinks on the table. "Would you like to order now?"

Storey hid behind the menu; welcomed the break in the awkward silence.

Olivia ordered a Cobb salad, ranch dressing on the side. Storey went for the small fillet, medium rare, with mixed vegetables and a side salad.

He looked up at their server's nametag. "Thanks, Sylvia."

Storey watched her walk away. "When I came in, there was a teenager vacuuming the floor. He was so engrossed in ogling her he tripped over a chair."

"You're having trouble finding a starting point for your story?"

"Yeah."

"How about you tell me about the last couple of days and fill in the back story as you go along?"

"Okay. So. Tuesday evening. Julia and I had a fight . . . well, not really a fight, a lively discussion. She planned to leave for a few days, and wouldn't say where she was going."

"One of her 'inspiration trips'?'"

"You know about them?"

"The information is out there."

Apparently, my *little secret* is not so secret.

"Okay," he said. "Fast forward to Wednesday morning. Nothing special happened, just routine stuff, except I couldn't stop wondering where Julia was going. She was teary when I left for work. The last time I saw her alive she was standing on the front deck waving goodbye. I called home later, but Suzume said she had gone shopping.

"Then, just after lunch, a guy called me. Said his name was Bill Stevens."

Olivia opened her purse, pulled out a small notebook and pen.

"Are we going on the record?"

"Just names, places, and the like. A memory jogger. If it seems to be important I'll fill in the blanks. Do you know Stevens?"

"No. The guy had a long tale about . . ." Storey described the Steven's call, and his going to Eola Drive.

"What time did you arrive at the property?"

"About 1:15."

Olivia made a note.

"Stevens didn't show. Val had given me a report that showed the labor costs on the Harrison project were out of control so I went to the site to have a look-see. I noted the time in my log: 2:28."

Olivia nodded, scribbled.

"I parked across the street and watched for a while. Joe Orland, the job super, and two of his buds took off; went to a bar. I followed them, snapped some pictures, documented the whole mess in my log."

"They abandoned the job in the middle of the afternoon?"

"Yep. All three of them."

"That must've ticked you off."

"You think? It never happened when I was in the field."

"I remember you liked to be on a job site. You would say, 'That's where the action is.'"

"I think I should demote myself to Operations Manager. This administrative shit is not fun."

"I'm told you pushed to reorganize the company. Now you're not so sure?"

"At the moment, I feel . . . Liv, I'm not sure what I feel—certainly not in control of my life."

"Understandable. Just hang on."

"Easy to say."

"I know, but you will. Where did you go after your stake-out?"

"Onto the Harrison job site. Lars Swenson agreed to run the job for now. Then I went back to the bar . . . McGuire's—."

"Downtown Salem?"

"That's it. I went inside, fired Orland and his two buddies. Orland came after me. I had to put him down. He—"

"You had a fight in a bar?"

Storey shrugged. "I defended myself. Oscar Loukas was there. McGuire tells me they're cousins."

"Loukas?"

"Oh, sorry. He was our security systems subcontractor and locksmith. I terminated his contacts about six months ago. Found him drunk on the job . . . third time. He turned surly, threatened me. He repeated his threat yesterday."

"He threatened you?"

"That's how I interpreted it. He said I should watch my back . . . that it wasn't over."

"Meaning?"

"Haven't a clue."

"Fascinating." She made some more notes. "Then you . . ."

"I chatted with McGuire for a bit and went back to the office around 4:00. I wrote up a summary describing what I saw at Harrison's, and left it and my camera with Valerie. I had a tête-à-tête with George Rainey and his brother Harold at six. I kicked him out just as Suzume called and said the police were coming to see me."

"Rainey? The insurance agent? You still deal with him?"

"Well, I don't think Dad will be happy, but I'm not renewing any insurance with Rainey and company."

"A friend in Frauds showed me a list of people they were looking at. Rainey was on the list. Interesting."

"I'm not surprised. He's an unethical schmuck at best."

"We can talk about that some other time. Suzume called you?"

"Yeah. She said Oliphant told her not to. Did I just get her in trouble?"

Olivia smiled. "No."

"When you and Oliphant showed, you made it clear that you didn't want Oliphant to know we knew each other. Won't he find out eventually?"

"When he does I want to have enough evidence to shoot down his suspicions. We need to focus on finding who really did this, and not waste our time and effort on dead-ends."

Sylvia brought their dinners. "Do you need anything else? Can I refill your drinks? Coffee perhaps?"

"We're fine. Thanks Sylvia. Maybe later," Olivia said.

"I'll check back when you've finished."

Olivia dipped her fork in her side of dressing and speared a lettuce leaf. "What happened after we left your offices?"

"Mike, Roe and I had a review session. Then I went home."

"What time was that?"

"Nine-thirty, ten maybe. I was in a fog."

"You were home all night?"

Storey sliced a piece of steak, chewed. "No. The description that the elderly lady gave the reporter on the 'news at eleven' fit the T Bird. I went to our garage to see if it was there. It wasn't."

Olivia put her fork down, stared at Storey, her eyes wide. "You think your Ford was the car that ran over Julia?"

"Don't know. At first, I thought Dad might have taken it, but the garage was a mess . . . He wouldn't have left it that way. He and Mom have disappeared."

"They still go off on their nowhere trips?"

"Yeah. But they didn't take it. I drove by their house on the way here to be sure. Their truck and fifth-wheel are gone. No T Bird there. We've called their cell phones. Just voice mail. After my visit to the garage, I met Mike and Roe at the Shoe."

"Why didn't you say something this morning?"

"Before I left the Shoe last night I filed a report that the T bird was missing, probably stolen. Mike advised me to answer Oliphant's questions and not volunteer information."

"You could have told me."

"I wasn't thinking very clearly this morning. I had filed the report. I take it you haven't seen it?"

"Sometimes information gets sidetracked or stuck in the system." She pushed her salad around her plate, was quiet for a moment. "Who would want to set you up?"

Storey shrugged.

"Well." She stared over Storey's head, focused on the far wall. "Let's recap. You get a phone call from a guy you don't know. He wants to meet with you, in a fairly isolated place, but he doesn't show." She paused. "At this point, you have no witness that can place you on Eola Drive during the time Julia was killed. Right?"

"None that I know of."

"Nick, it sounds like a set-up to me."

He recalled Swanson's comments about the grizzled detective's approach; assume the suspect is guilty and gather evidence until he proves it—with veracity not a big issue. Storey felt his neck and shoulder muscles tighten. If Olivia saw the possibility of a plot to frame him for Julia's killing . . .

He sawed off another bite of meat. "Lars can verify I was at the Harrison job site. There's plenty of witnesses at McQuire's."

Olivia's manner shifted to cop mode. "That still leaves a gap of an hour or more—*if* your man Lars can substantiate the time you met with him. Now you tell me one of your classic cars could be the murder weapon. Add in that you had an ongoing and escalating disagreement with your wife. It's all there, Nick. Motive, means, and opportunity."

"I don't know what to say, other that I didn't kill Julia. I haven't been to the Lancaster Mall for weeks."

"I believe you." She returned to her salad, chewing slowly and staring at the table centerpiece. "I'm not the one you have to convince,"

Storey reflected on his ongoing dispute with Julia over her "inspiration getaways." *Was* a dispute. He wondered how long it would be before he thought of her in past tense.

Were Julia's trips an elaborate ruse, a cover for an affair? He had been rejecting the thought as his own unruly paranoia. He reasoned that if her outings and the stimulation they provided was what she needed to function as an artist, who was he to question or deny her need? While they may have been constructive for her, he had refused to admit that her vacations were caustic for him.

"Sir, are you finished?"

Storey jumped, looked up to see Sylvia standing by the table. "Ah . . . yes, I am."

"Sorry sir. May I take your plate?"

He saw she was holding Olivia's partially empty salad bowl. "Certainly, thank you. I've had enough."

"Would you like your coffee now?"

"Yes. Black." He looked at Olivia. She nodded. "Two please, Sylvia," he said.

Olivia watched Sylvia walk away. "That's the second time tonight you dropped off the network. You do trances often?"

"Sorry."

"Something you'd care to share?"

Storey glanced into her dark eyes, felt their pull. He looked away, wiped his mouth and mustache with his napkin. "I was thinking about Julia . . . our life together." He caught her gaze again. "I feel you want to know a bit more than my history for the last couple of days. I'll tell you my story if you'll answer a question or two for me."

"Personal questions?"

"Yes."

"We're trying to save your ass, not mine." Olivia looked away, stretched her arms, hands clasped over the table. After a long moment she said, "You can ask."

Sylvia returned, refilled their coffee mugs.

Olivia handed her a few bills. "That should cover it. Keep the change."

"Thank you." Sylvia left.

Storey looked at Olivia. "Are you trying to bribe a suspect?"

"Just buying dinner for an old friend. Enough stalling, Nick. Speak to me."

Storey leaned forward, put his elbows on the table, and crossed his arms. "I first met Julia on the beach at Newport. She was—"

"Painting a picture of two young girls making sand castles with the harbor and bridge in the background. The painting is hanging in your living room. I've heard this part. This is relevant to our problem?"

Storey smiled. She had kept tabs on him. "Yes, it is. Bear with me."

Olivia crossed her arms over her chest, sighed.

"I asked if the painting was for sale. She said yes, but it wasn't finished. We chatted. I gave her the condo address, said I would be there for a few days. She showed, with the painting, a couple of days later. We had lunch at The Grotto. We married six months later. Julia was the most independent person I have ever known—"

"You always said I was independent."

Storey stared at Olivia for a moment. "Not the same, Liv. Perhaps I used the wrong word. Julia was private, mysterious, completely unfettered. To this day I don't know her background, or where she came from. Back east somewhere, I think. I do know that her parents died suddenly—victims of some sort of violence—but I don't know why or how. She would never talk about it. After they died, or were killed, she traveled the country and lived in a small trailer she pulled behind a Suburban. She did a lot of backpacking into wilderness areas, or just wandered the beaches."

"There was some camping gear in the Nissan SUV we found in the mall parking lot."

"Yeah. Makes me think that was her plan. She wanted her space, but somehow it was more than that. She needed, required, alone time. She would . . ."

Olivia leaned forward with her elbows on the table and her eyes searching Storey's face as he related his abstract of Julia's inspiration trips and the effect on their lives.

Storey pushed back in his chair, let his hands fall to his lap. "Now you know *the rest of the story.*"

"Nick . . .um, there's no easy way to say this. Was there someone else? An affair?"

Storey looked away. "I don't know. Fits with her behavior and moods. I've avoided thinking about it, but now . . ."

"You think she was leaving you?"

Storey stared into Olivia's dark eyes for a long moment. He'd told her things she most likely didn't want, or need, to know. Personal stuff. Dirty little secrets.

Olivia spread her hands. "What?"

Storey reached into his jacket pocket and placed Julia's letter on the table. "Read this."

4:45 PM Thursday
21 May 2009

Olivia folded the lavender-scented letter and looked up at
Storey. "Well, it's clear she intended to leave you. But it raises
more questions. You've shown this to Mike and Roe?"

"Yes. They think Julia was killed because she knew something"

"If true, you and your family could be next."

"Roe has assigned two of his best to guard Donna and the boys."

"And you? You're wandering about naked, dumb, and happy?"

"Hardly." Storey explained the precautions he took to avoid
surveillance. "And—I'm driving Roe's BMW. I'm sure there's a
GPS on board. He probably knows within a few inches where it's
parked. I'm not fooling myself. I probably couldn't detect, or shake,
a professional tail." Storey looked around the restaurant and bar, saw
that the evening crowd was gathering. "I'm confident that
somewhere in this gaggle; one or more of Roe's guys is watching us.
Between him, her, or them, and you, I feel perfectly safe . . . and
cared for."

Olivia didn't move, but her eyes scanned her surroundings.
"You think someone is watching us? Are you sure?"

"Well, when I left Mike's office to come here, neither Roe nor
Mike put up any objections worth mentioning. Under the
circumstances . . ." Storey raised his hands, shrugged.

"They would have insisted someone accompany you?"

"That's my assumption."

"Any thoughts who it is?"

"My money is on the father-son pair." He nodded his head toward their table. The two men had been arguing, but were now talking, gesturing and laughing occasionally.

"Nick, for now I think it's best for everyone that I stay incognito."

Storey smiled. "Officially, Roe is working for Mike. Anything they see is work product and falls under the attorney-client privilege."

Olivia sighed. "Should I feel better?"

"Sure. Why not?"

She sat with her arms crossed over her chest; her eyes focused somewhere above Storey's head. From time to time she sucked a deep breath and let it out slowly.

Storey leaned forward in his chair and aimed his gaze at her. "Liv, . . . my questions?"

Her back stiffened. "Nick, if my response to your queries relates to our investigation, I'll gladly answer now. If not . . .?"

Storey looked away.

"Nick, we need to keep the focus on you. I'm thinking that *our* first priority has to be to establish and verify your alibi for yesterday. As I said before, we need to get you out of the spotlight and focus on a productive investigation." She touched his hand. "My . . . our situation can wait."

Storey nodded, sighed. "You're right."

"When you're in the clear, I'll answer any questions you have."

"I'll hold you to that."

They sat silent for a moment.

"Other than Roe's keep-the-secret-in-the-closet motive, can you think of other reasons someone would want Julia dead?"

"No. But I'll bet Mike and Roe have a page-long list they haven't shared with me."

"Probably." Olivia put her elbows on the table, rested her chin on a palm. "Have you told Eric?"

"No, but if things work out tonight, I will. I'd prefer to tell him in the morning. I still don't know how to handle it. How do you tell your three-year-old his mommy is dead and he won't see her again?"

"Eric is three? Already?"

"Going on five."

"Sounds like my Sarah at that age. Were they close, he and Julia?"

"Julia was indirect in her relations with people, but connected easily if her art was involved. She isolated herself a lot, disliked structure. I hired Suzume, our part-time maid and nanny, to take charge on weekday afternoons and early evenings. The household function smoothed out if Julia didn't have to bother with everyday details."

"Was Eric close to Julia?"

Storey pulled at his mustache. "Well, they seemed to get along fine when Julia made herself available. When she was gone for the day or overnight, he always asked when she would be back. Was she going to 'bring me present, tell me story?' After one of her getaways, Julia always brought something for him and had a tale to tell him about her adventures . . . embellished of course. She was a good storyteller. Eric bugged her to tell them over and over."

"Typical. Sarah watched the tape of 'The Little Engine That Could' so many times that it broke. I had a hell of a time finding a replacement at seven PM."

"Yeah, sounds like Eric."

"Tell him the truth as simply as you can. Children blur fantasy and fact."

"I know. My plan is to say mommy is dead and she won't be back." Storey poked a finger skyward. "This business of her being up there somewhere and watching over us . . . I won't go there. But, I can't seem to come up with the words to fit his vocabulary and understanding."

"Nick, trust your instincts. Kids adapt. Almost certainly faster than you will."

"Probably. But, I can hear his questions now and I can't think of a response that won't generate more inquisition."

"Such as?"

"I'm sure you remember. I'll bet Sarah still does it. What, why, when, how . . . that sort of thing, and he'll expect easy quick answers."

"I think you are overdoing your what-ifs. As I remember, that was your—."

Storey threw a hand up. "Okay, Liv. I got the message. It'll come if I relax. As I remember, you regularly accused me of obsessing about stuff."

Olivia smiled. Her eyes went out of focus again. "I'm not sure I should be giving you advice about obsessing." She went silent, staring, unfocused.

Storey studied her for a long moment. Her trance-like state was familiar. Was she still driven by her father's unsolved murder? A person or persons unknown had shot and killed Anthony, her hero and confidant, when Olivia was fifteen, leaving her feeling angry and abandoned.

Storey had met her during their sophomore year of college. They began living together shortly after; an ideal couple some said, including his parents and her mother. He knew that she had studied criminology and psychology attempting to come to terms with the loss of her father. After graduation she attended the police academy, received academic honors, and won the class marksmanship award.

They gradually drifted apart, because, or so Storey thought at the time, they were so concentrated on their careers that they lost focus. He wondered if her fixation on finding her father's killer had contributed to their gradual disconnection, of if her fear of abandonment overcame their bond. Their relationship had ended suddenly. They argued over something, he had long forgotten what, and she had stormed out of their apartment and removed all her personal effects.

She moved in with John Stark, a bouncer at one of the downtown clubs. Olivia left John when her child, Sarah, was born and settled in with her mother permanently.

"You said you left your camera in your office."

Storey was so absorbed in his thoughts that it took moment for him to reply. "Ah , yeah. On Valerie's desk, with my log book."

"You think she could meet me there and give me the camera, and your notes? I'm presuming it's okay with you?"

"I'm sure she will, and it's fine with me. How long will you keep them?"

"Until this is over. I'll copy your camera chip onto a memory stick and photocopy your notes. Valerie will have the duplicates by tomorrow morning."

"When would you like to meet?"

"As soon as I can get there from here." She looked at her watch. "Seven-thirty?"

"I'll call her." He reached for his cell, stopped. "I've been avoiding using my phone; turned it off. I want to escape Donna, Roe, and Mike's mother-hen routines. I'm trying for a cone of silence for a while so I can think. May I use yours?"

Storey started to enter Valerie's home number, cancelled. "I forgot to tell you. Roe's technicians found bugs in my house."

"Wiretaps?"

"Remote transmitters, receivers."

Olivia's eyebrows rose. She whistled. "Wow. That puts a different twist on it."

"Yeah. And, Roe and crew are going to sweep my offices sometime tonight. Val is going to meet them there. I'm guessing you want to arrive first and be gone before they show up."

"That would be best."

Valerie answered after three rings.

"Val, It's Nick."

"Where are you?"

"I needed some alone time."

"Okay . . . I didn't recognize the caller ID . . . almost didn't answer."

"I'm using another phone."

"Why are you calling me? How can I help?"

"Hang on, there's someone you need to talk to."

Storey handed the instrument to Olivia. "Your show," he said.

*****

Olivia snapped her cell phone closed, looked at Storey, smiled. "I'd forgotten Valerie was such a take-charge lady. She's leaving for the office now to make sure the place is empty. She'll lock the doors and make sure no one enters until I get there. Roe was coming at seven with his crew, but she'll put them off until I'm gone."

"Val has a heart as big as outdoors, but beware if you cross her or a friend. With me she's the mamma grizzly and I'm her cub."

"I remember," Olivia said absently. She stared toward the TV in the bar, shoved her chair back. "Nick, follow me." She strode across the room. "They just replayed a shot from the scene at the mall yesterday. I think they're going to do a follow-up." She caught the attention of the bartender. "Would you please turn up the TV volume?"

The bartender looked at her for a moment.

"It's important we see this," she said.

The young woman shrugged, grabbed the remote, eased the sound up.

Storey stopped beside Olivia. She turned toward him for a second. "Nick, Julia's ID was released to the media this morning."

"I know. After I identified her body." Storey pointed at the TV. "Here it comes."

The big screen filled with a head shot of the male anchor, Ralph Andrews.

"The clip you just saw was the scene at the Lancaster Mall yesterday afternoon. The victim of the hit-and-run has been identified as Julia Storey, a prominent local artist."

A picture of Julia appeared in the right half of the screen. Storey sucked a quick breath.

"The police suspect her death was a hit-and-run; possibly a homicide. Mrs. Storey's paintings, prints, and sculptures beautify many galleries and homes in the Willamette Valley. Her husband, Nicholas Storey, is the President of Storey Construction, a building contractor firm in Salem."

"Great," Storey mumbled.

A picture of Storey replaced Julia's.

"Attempts to contact Mr. Storey or family members have not been successful."

"Right. And when you do, you'll try to dig up something nasty," Storey said.

Olivia elbowed him. "Cool it," she whispered.

"We have attempted to contact the police for clarification, but they will not comment on an ongoing investigation. We expect a news conference sometime tomorrow. KOIL will provide further updates on the Julia Storey hit-and-run as they become available. Stay tuned. After the break we will have . . ."

"Sonofabitch," Storey muttered.

Olivia threw a five on the bar, pointed at the bartender. "Thanks," she said.

The server smiled and pocketed the bill. She looked up at Storey. Her eyes widened. She glanced toward the TV.

Olivia pulled a card from a pocket, handed it to the woman. "Would you please write your name on the back?"

"You're a cop?"

"Yes. I might need you to verify that Mr. Storey and I were here at . . ." She looked at her watch. "At 6:10. Okay?"

"What . . . why?"

"You're not in trouble."

The woman looked from Storey to Olivia. "I'm Ruth, Ruth Bellamy."

Olivia extracted her note pad, wrote on it. "Keep the card. Call me if you have any questions." She grabbed Storey's arm, and pulled him toward the exit. "We have to get out of here now," she said.

Outside, the wind was calm; the rain had stopped.

6:45 PM Thursday
21 May 2009

Oscar Loukas left their shop in the Lancaster Mall to go for his customary run. His wife, Evelon, also a certified master locksmith and more proficient at handling customers and their issues than he, was watching the store.

Their business had suffered a serious downturn after Nicholas Storey terminated their contracts. Storey Construction had been a significant portion of their sales of locks and security systems. The humiliation Oscar suffered from Storey's action and the associated loss of income jarred him from his malaise. He cut back on his drinking, joined a gym, and began a routine of daily runs to restore his vigor. Three months into his recovery, he developed a plan to terminate his association with George Rainey, who, Oscar reasoned, was the root of his business and personal problems. After tonight he would be free of Rainey's manipulation. Thinking of it put a smile on his face, a spring in his step.

Loukas fast-walked past the Oregon State Hospital and entered the adjacent Salem Hospital. In a unisex restroom he locked the door, used a folded pad of paper towel to daub black food coloring from a small bottle onto his five-day stubble. He flushed the towel, washed the residual color from his fingers, rummaged in the pockets of his cargo shorts, and removed his Seattle Seahawks cap and a set of surgical scrubs he had lifted from a laundry cart during a previous run through. He pulled the hospital's garments over his cut-offs and plain gray tee-shirt and put the cap on his head, the bill shading his face.

He examined his transformation in the mirror—a middle-aged doctor or intern, dark beard, harried and sleep-deprived. He spread his arms wide, smiled.

Perfect.

He left the premises and jogged the quarter mile to MacRoy Park where hospital personnel sometimes went for a lunch break or respite. He picked a spot, sat, and puffed cigarettes as he watched one of the several office buildings on the west side of Twentieth Street. He had allotted three unfiltered Camels for this act of his charade. He drew in the blue smoke, coughed. Oscar had quit tobacco twenty years ago.

After the office manager, the clerks, and Rainey left the premises, Oscar walked across the street and entered the alley behind the row of businesses. He stopped facing the rear entry of Rainey's building, looked left, right, saw nothing but the usual collection of dumpsters, and the occasional scrap of paper and plastic grocery bag. Satisfied no one was there, he donned paper booties and latex gloves.

It took less than a minute to pick the lock and deadbolt, step inside, and ease the door closed. He waited for his eyes to adjust to the darkness of the musty hallway. A suggestion of light at the bottom of the door at the far end was the only illumination and did not suffice. He dropped to his knees, silently cursing himself for forgetting his penlight. He crawled along the corridor feeling his way, avoiding the mop and bucket, the broom and boxes of files that he knew were stored on the floor against the wall to his left. Kicking or tripping over an obstacle could alert anyone in the front offices and trash his weeks of preparation. He was sure no one was there, but was taking no chances now that his plan was underway.

He reached the door at the end of the twelve-foot corridor, stood, placed an ear to a panel. Satisfied that no one occupied the front offices, he felt for the deadbolt. Twenty seconds to pick it, open the door a few inches. He cringed when the hinges screeched, but squeezed through, closed it—another squeal. A single fluorescent and the remains of daylight leaking through the single front window cast shadows across the main office area, a collection of chest-high cubicles. To his left, Rainey's office, his target for the evening. He stepped into the hall on his right, which led to the restroom and file storage room. The storeroom was unlocked. He entered; shut the door behind him. Darkness beset him once more. The air was stale, oppressive, smelled of old paper.

Nothing to do now but wait for Rainey to reappear, a near certainty—it was Thursday. He would return after dinner to review information for his "special" clients and file their documents in his refrigerator-sized safe.

Oscar, one of the clientele, was familiar with the arrangement of the office, the placement of every table, couch, chair, desk, filing cabinet, and bookcase. He could envision the pictures on the walls, the sayings and comic strips employees had pasted on the sides of files and partitions by their desks. He had made sketches of the layout following his many visits. Filed in his memory, the drawings became ash in his fireplace.

He drew a sleeve across his forehead to wipe away beads of perspiration that, despite the chill permeating the building, had formed there. He extracted a flask from one of his many pockets, took a gulp of bourbon, wiped his lips with the back of a hand, sighed, and returned the silver container to its pouch. His need to bolster his resolve had overcome his vow of sobriety.

*****

An hour passed. Oscar paced a one-step track behind the door, massaged the back of his neck, rubbed his hands together to quell their shaking.

I could just leave now, return to the shop. No one would know.

He heard the back door open, the click of the light switch, footsteps moving along the hallway. A key slid into the door on his left. The now-familiar hinge squeak spoke to Oscar. *He* was here.

The lock to Rainey's office clicked open.

Okay. Do it. Can't back out now. Too much at stake . . .

Oscar waited a few minutes to calm his trembling and let George settle in. He shuddered. The moment had finally come, the apex of all his plans. Hoping the hinges would not object, he pulled the storeroom door open enough to squeeze through. He sucked a deep breath when he saw the door to Rainey's office ajar. Relieved he would not have to pick the lock and risk alerting Rainey, he exhaled slowly, reached back, lifted his shirt, and extracted the .32 caliber

Colt pistol from under his belt. Holding it behind him, he pushed the door open and stepped into the office.

"What the hell . . . ? Who are you?"

Oscar removed his cap, placed it on his chest, cocked his head.

". . . Loukas?"

"Yeah, George, it's me, Oscar Loukas, your friendly locksmith and whipping boy." He replaced the hat.

"Why the silly green giant outfit . . . and the black face?" Rainey slid his hand across his desktop toward the right side.

Oscar whipped his right arm around, gripped the pistol with both hands, pointed it at Rainey's chest. "Not your concern. Stand up . . . NOW!"

Rainey jumped to his feet, hands high, eyes bulging. "You . . . you have a . . . a *gun*."

"And I can shoot the eye out of a skunk like you at fifty yards, so don't give me any trouble. Now, back away, slow and easy . . . easy."

Oscar moved closer, opened the top right drawer, removed a handgun.

"A nine-millimeter Glock. Big gun for a shrimp like you." He ejected the magazine, threw it across the room, pulled the slide. A cartridge dropped to the floor. "Bullet in the chamber. Man, you're ready for instant action. Get many intruders?" He tossed the pistol back into the drawer.

"What . . . ah, what you want?"

"I think you know."

"Ah . . . there's no money here, Oscar."

"Don't play games, you little bastard. You know what I'm after." He sidestepped to the window overlooking the cubicles. He saw his faint reflection in the glass, grinned. He lowered the mini-blind, cranked it closed. "Don't need any sidewalk superintendents."

"Don't hurt me!"

"I've got two girls in college. Lost a major customer because of you.. Can't afford to pay your blackmail anymore. Rainey, it's over."

"I'll give you the pictures—and the camera chip. We can forget the whole thing. Just don't hurt me."

"Get 'em—now."

"They're in the safe."

"Open it."

Rainey twisted the dials, pushed the latch. Nothing.

"I told you no games," Oscar yelled. He pushed the gun into George's ear.

"I . . . I must've missed a number. I'll try again. Ca . . . ah, can you point that thing some . . . somewhere else?"

"Just open the damn safe, prick."

Rainey wiped both hands on his thighs, slowly rotated the knobs. He pulled the heavy door open, reached inside, rummaged a bit, removed a file, clutched it to his chest with trembling hands.

"You promise not to harm me if I give you this?"

"Put it on the desk." Oscar stepped back, kept the pistol leveled at Rainey's chest. "I'm not promisin' you anything."

Rainey dropped the manila folder on the desktop. Oscar opened it, glanced at the photos. "This all of them?"

"Yes."

"Better be. How many other clients are you playin' judge and jury with?"

"I . . . I don't understand."

"Sure you do. Those special fees you charge to assess your customer's insurance needs."

"Perfectly legitimate service."

"Bullshit. George, it's called extortion when you coerce your patrons to buy insurance through you *and* pay those ridiculous . . . ah, 'consultation premiums', in cash."

"I don't know what you're talking about." Rainey swiped his brow with the back of a quivering hand. "Can't you put the gun down?"

"I've seen the inside of your safe, George. Quite a collection of information you got there. So many people with secrets. What you call it . . . business insurance?"

"How—?"

"C'mon, no lock is safe, ah, that'd be safe from *me*. George, I could've cracked your safe anytime, but I didn't, ok? Your taping the combination to the inside of your desk . . . dumb, but a common mistake. So. I pull out three drawers, left side—and there it is, stuck to the inside panel!"

"Oscar, you . . . you don't need the gun. Besides, it's your word against mine. You have your photos—the chip. Let's . . . ah . . . just forget the whole thing."

"As simple as that?

"Sure. You have my word."

"*Your word*! George Rainey's pledge. Now *that's* reassuring. *Shit.*"

"Always keep my promises."

"I'd be free to buy insurance from anyone? No extra fees? No consequences? That's a truly unique concept."

"All my clients have free choice to pick any agent they want."

"Funny how almost everybody that pays your not-so-little extra either has shady business activities or a personal misadventure to keep under wraps."

"You're the one with the wandering dick. Did I ever say the pictures of you fucking your *friend*, my office clerk, would go public if you didn't place your business with me?"

"No. But, when your brother delivered my copies, he suggested it could happen. Really, more like a threat, almost a guarantee."

"Harold suffers from PTSD. Vietnam. He does strange things sometimes. His voyeurism is a real problem. Counseling, doctors, shrinks. All useless."

"Except to you, you sonofabitch." Oscar waved the pistol. "Over there. Put your back against the wall. Next to the door. Face me. Now, move your feet out a bit . . . a little more . . . good. Now lace your fingers behind your head. That's great. Stay put or a kneecap is history."

"You didn't need me to open the safe. Why have me—"

"To see you sweat, and so you'd know who did you in."

"Please, Oscar. I'm just keeping records for Harold. He'd . . . um, break most of the bones in my body if I crossed him. I—"

"Oh, you want me to believe Harold collected all the stuff about tax evasions, kickbacks, and such? He may be good with a camera and sound recording . . . and he's probably experienced in covert stuff. I don't think he's able to follow a complex paper trail. That's your thing, George."

"I just keep the records. Harold would—"

"Stuff a sock in it, George. You're such a liar."

Oscar reached behind the couch, came out with a paper bag. "Left you a present last time we palavered." He lifted a spray can from the sack. He moved a client chair, stood on it, activated the can's nozzle with his left hand, keeping the pistol directed toward Rainey with the other. The overhead sprinkler head near the front of the office disappeared in a mass of sticky foam insulation. He repeated the process for the rear sprinkler.

"What're you doing?"

"Installing a time delay for the sprinklers in your office."

"You're not—"

"Shut up, George." Oscar aimed the gun low. "Your knee . . . remember?"

Oscar pulled a plastic bottle from a pocket. "I bought me a new cigarette lighter today, and lots of fluid. Took a bunch of those little cans to fill this." He shook the quart-sized container, grinned, chuckled. He popped the top, splashed the liquid over the files in the safe.

"Don't!" Rainey trembled; his knees wobbled.

Oscar grabbed a paper from the desk, lit the corner with his lighter. "Just makin' sure other folks are free, too." He held the paper aloft, smiled at Rainey, waited for the flames to grow, threw the torch into the safe. Fire roared from the steel box.

"Stop!" Rainey's shoulders slumped, his hands fell limp at his sides.

Oscar opened his folder, and, one by one, tossed the camera chip and the pictures into the inferno. He wagged his gun again. "You stay right there. Gotta make sure there're all gone."

As he watched his photos curl and turn to ash, Oscar felt detached, as if he were viewing an old movie—in slow motion.

He raised his arm, aimed the Colt at Rainey's head. "Gettin' kinda smoky in here. Time I skedaddled. You've got about ten seconds to make peace with your maker if you're so inclined."

"No . . . NO! Oh my god you can't —"

Oscar's hand trembled, the gun wavered, steadied, discharged twice. Bits of plaster sprayed Rainey's head as the bullets slammed into the wall not more than an inch from each ear.

George's eyes closed, the front of his pants darkened, the stain flowed down a pant leg.

To Oscar, his every move was protracted, deliberate—sound muted, a tape played on slow speed, each gunshot far-off thunder. He lowered his aim, shot another hole in the wall just below Rainey's crotch, let his arm drop.

It seemed several minutes passed before time revved up to full speed and sounds returned to normal. He shook his head to dispel the feeling.

"You're right, George. I can't," he said.

He stared at the lump of flesh sliding down the wall and rolling into a ball on the floor.

"George, you're such an asshole."

Oscar's eyes watered from the smoke. He turned, walked to the door, stopped. His shoulders slumped, his chin dropped to his chest. "Oh, hell," he muttered.

He stuffed the Colt under his belt, grabbed Rainey by the collar, and dragged him out of the office into the vestibule. He slammed the office door and pulled Rainey's dead weight into the back hallway, flicked the light switch and closed the door. He seized the front of the elf-sized shirt, lifted the little man to a sitting position against the wall. "George are you hearin' me? Wake up."

Rainey slumped to his side like a loosely stuffed rag doll. Oscar sat on his haunches looking at the figure collapsed on the floor.

"You thought your office fire-proofing was protecting your safe and its dirty secrets if the building caught fire," Oscar murmured. "Didn't expect a fire *in* your office, did you? Dumb shit.

"You deserved killin', but it don't matter. You identify me and you'll have to come clean about your dirty blackmail schemes. You'd spend more time behind bars than I would." Oscar stood. "Goodbye, George."

Loukas left the building and locked the back door. He removed the booties and latex gloves, stuffed them into his cargos, and walked away. He trotted through the park and back to Salem hospital. The same restroom was available.

He removed his Seahawks hat, stuffed it into a pocket, and studied his image in the mirror. He scrubbed the food coloring from his face. "Time to disappear," he mumbled. On his way out of the hospital, Oscar dropped the latex gloves and booties into a medical waste disposal bin, the scrubs into a laundry basket.

Midway through his jog back to the Lancaster Mall, Oscar stopped, turned to face west—toward Twentieth Street. He lifted his flask high in salute. "To freedom," he whispered. He took a taste, poured the remaining whiskey into the gutter. He wiped the flagon clean on the tail of his shirt and threw it into a trash receptacle. He walked away, head high, whistling.

8:05 PM Thursday
21 May 2009

Storey was sprawled on his lounger in the family room holding a Killian.

At the bar, Swanson splashed some Scotch into a glass, moved to the sofa. "Roe is late."

Storey sipped his beer, nodded. "Unusual."

They were silent for a moment.

"Are your phones still bugged?"

"Yeah. In the den and bedroom. I put a pillow over them and shut the doors so they can't hear us from here."

The three-note door chime sounded. Storey looked at Swanson. "Who could that be? Roe wouldn't punch the doorbell." He set his beer on the coffee table, walked to the entry hall and peered through the side glass. "What the . . .?"

He opened the door. "Liv. What are you doing here?"

She stepped inside, chuckled, said, "Come in, Olivia. I'm so glad to see you."

"I didn't expect you."

"Roe didn't tell you?"

"No, but . . . yeah . . . well, come in. Nice . . . ah . . . can I take your jacket?"

Swanson approached. "Olivia. Great to see you."

"Come on in." Storey said. "We're in the family room. I've got some Eola in the fridge."

They settled in, Swanson on a bar stool, Storey and Olivia on the couch.

"I got your camera and the chip from Valerie all bagged and tagged," Olivia said. "I'll log them into evidence after we're finished here. Valerie agreed to go to the station tomorrow and give a statement. I met Jethroe at your offices. He said he had some security camera video he wanted me to see."

"You know as much as we do," Storey said, "Roe should be here by now—"

"Hello . . . anyone home?" Jethroe appeared in the doorway. "Sorry I'm late. Hi, Liv."

Storey jumped from his seat. "Did you find any bugs?"

"Abrams and the team are sweeping your office and Valerie's, and the reception area. We should know soon."

Jethroe set his laptop on the counter separating the kitchen and family room, took a memory stick from a shirt pocket, and plugged it into a slot. He turned to Olivia. "I wanted you to see the surveillance camera video. We reviewed several nights of records and boiled it down to five scenes and copied them onto this memory stick." He slid onto a stool and activated the computer.

"What are we looking at?" said Olivia.

"This is from a camera under the eave of the building near the front of the Storey Construction property. It covers the gate and the front of the garage where Victor and Nick store their classic cars."

Storey, Swanson and Olivia stood behind and on each side of Jethroe.

"This first clip is at 1:05 AM Wednesday." Jethroe activated the video. "The camera takes a picture about every second. So it's a bit jerky."

Peering close, Storey could see a man approach the perimeter fence gate, fiddle with the padlock for a few frames, slide the gate partially open, and step through carrying a small stepladder.

Jethroe froze the picture. The man was average height, thin, wearing black Levis and shirt, and a dark cap with the bill pulled down to shield his face. Jethroe magnified the picture, focusing in on the man's hand that held the ladder. "The guy knew what he was doing. He picked the lock in less than a minute. You can see he was wearing gloves. Looks like latex. That four-foot ladder is more than enough to reach the camera."

He reactivated the video. The man walked toward the camera, head down. He passed under the camera and disappeared from the field of view. A hand holding a can of spray paint appeared. The picture gradually turned dark.

Jethroe stopped the action again. "Look at the right side of the picture. The paint didn't completely cover a small sliver at the edge of the lens. He either missed that spot or there was some condensation on the side of the lens and the paint didn't stick. See the gate. It's blurred but recognizable. As the paint dries, the view at the edge clears a bit."

Jethroe let the video run. "Watch close now." A fuzzy form of a man approached the gate, stopped, turned toward the garage, and moved out of the picture. "See, he leans his ladder against the fence."

"What's he doing now? He disappeared," said Swanson.

"Just watch."

Shortly, the man reappeared, lifted the ladder, moved through the opening, and closed the gate.

"Okay," said Swanson. "Some guy picked the gate lock, painted the camera lens, putzed around for a minute, and left. He didn't take the Ford."

"Hold on. The next clip starts about five minutes later, at 1:12."

Olivia and Swanson leaned forward, stared at the screen. Storey crowded in behind Olivia.

A larger man appeared, pushed the gate fully open. Jethroe stopped the video. "If you look close, this guy's wearing a dark hoodie . . . not the same man as before."

"Yeah, but, I can only see his back," said Storey.

Jethroe clicked the video to life. The form moved toward the garage, disappeared behind the mask of paint.

"We cut out about ten minutes here," said Jethroe.

A large red object appeared, moved through the gate, and stopped.

"The T-Bird," said Storey.

The man came into view, walked toward the garage, disappeared for a few frames, returned, closed the gate, entered the vehicle, and drove away.

"The first guy opened the locks, so the big dude could steal the T-bird," said Swanson.

"The locks were picked," said Jethroe. "We disassembled the gate padlock and looked at the tumbler and pins under a microscope. They have scratch marks in places the key could never reach."

"You've contaminated the scene," Olivia said.

"We didn't touch the lock on the garage."

"Their planning and execution was flawless," said Swanson.

"Except for the partial paint job on the camera lens," said Storey. "We wouldn't have much otherwise."

"There's more," said Jethroe. "This starts just before midnight last night, at 11:49."

A large dark vehicle stopped near the fence and a blurry form moved to the gate, opened it.

"That's me," said Storey, "when I discovered the T-Bird missing."

"Right. Now we fast forward about 45 minutes to 12:33 AM, today."

Another person appeared at the gate, opened it enough to squeeze through, moved toward the garage and disappeared behind the paint mask. A few frames later, the man returned, closed the gate and left.

"That looks like the guy who sprayed the camera," said Storey.

"Probably," said Jethroe. "Now, like the first time, but about twenty minutes later, at 12:52."

A red car stopped outside the gate. A large man wearing a dark hood opened it, returned to the vehicle, and drove through.

"We took out about twenty minutes here. It's 1:15 now."

The man reappeared, closed the gate, and walked away.

"They returned the T-Bird," Storey said. "It's in the garage now?"

"Yes. When Bob and the forensics crew got there around 2:30—"

"You had people in the garage?" said Olivia.

"They wore paper booties and latex gloves. Your crime scene is pristine."

"How many guys?"

"Three. Bob Abrams and two techs."

"I hope they were extra careful."

Jethroe shrugged. "They're pros. They found the T-Bird sitting in its space with the car cover draped over it. The engine was still warm. Nick, the floor was spotless."

"The muddy footprints I saw are gone?"

"Yeah. The mop in the utility closet was damp. The guy scrubbed the floor."

"They *are* meticulous," said Olivia. "This operation was well organized."

"The Bird had been hot-wired, and . . ." Jethroe turned to Storey. "The rim of the right headlight is dented. We found traces of blood."

Storey sucked a breath, let it out slowly. "They used the Bird to kill Julia."

"Apparently they're trying to make it appear that Nick did it," said Swanson.

"It would seem so. We sent samples of the blood to a private lab for typing and DNA testing."

"You said you didn't—"

"Liv, just a couple of Q-tip swabs. Nick, we need something to compare . . . a hair brush, toothbrush."

Storey nodded. "I'll find something."

"Hold off on that," said Olivia. "Let Forensics search for it with you . . . to maintain the chain of evidence."

"Fingerprints. Did you find any?" Swanson said.

"No. We didn't look. When Bob saw the blood, they took the swabs, and he got everyone out of there. He knew the police would treat the area as a crime scene and he didn't want to contaminate their investigation. He left a man there to be sure no one went inside until the police showed. He did take the perimeter padlock for examination. The team entered through the pedestrian door. The garage lock is undisturbed."

"So," Swanson said, "they steal the Bird early Wednesday morning, run Julia down that afternoon, hide it somewhere, and return it Wednesday night . . . well, early Thursday morning."

"There's at least two of them," Storey said, "one guy to pick the padlocks, another to steal the car. He's probably the one that ran over Julia."

"Good bet," said Jethroe.

"Took a lot of planning," said Olivia. "They had to know where Julia was going to be, and when."

"My guess is they got their info from the wire taps of Nick's home," said Jethroe. "We've studied the security videos for hours and couldn't find anything that would help ID the lock picker or the hijacker."

"I need to get our forensics into the garage," said Olivia, "and here to search the house."

"You've got to search my house?"

"Chain of evidence . . . for the DNA and whatever else they may find. I'll have to assign someone to guard this place until the crew can get here. You'd best vacate until the techs arrive."

"Great. Can I take a change of clothes? My razor?"

"I'll log whatever you take."

"You can stay the night with me," said Swanson. "The couch folds out."

Storey rolled his eyes. "I'll find a motel."

"You should have search warrants," said Swanson, "to insure whatever evidence you find holds up in court."

"Yes. I'll start the paperwork as soon as I leave, and have a warrant tonight . . . unless Nick will agree to the searches now."

"Have at it," Storey said. "The sooner this is over the better."

"If I can use your computer, I'll go on line and print out the consent forms and you can sign them."

"No problem."

"Jethroe, you should have alerted us sooner," Olivia said.

He turned, looked up at her. "Probably."

Olivia raised an eyebrow. "Better to ask forgiveness than permission?"

Jethroe smiled. "When your crime scene crew is ready, Abrams will meet them. He has the DVD from the camera recorder. Maybe your people can have better luck identifying these guys."

"We need to withdraw the missing vehicle report," said Swanson.

"I'll take care of that," said Olivia, "and send a patrol to replace Jethroe's garage guard."

Storey looked from Swanson to Jethroe. "Why didn't you tell me this morning that the Bird was back? You knew Oliphant would question me. You didn't trust me?"

Jethroe locked eyes with Storey. "You might've been put in a position where you had to tell Oliphant—or lie. You had enough on your plate."

Storey turned to Swanson. "Did you know the Bird was back when we were with Oliphant?"

"Mike didn't know," said Jethroe. "No one knew. Just Bob Abrams, a couple of techs and I. I wanted to study the surveillance records . . . have a complete picture before any of us had to deal with Oliphant."

"I don't like being left out."

Jethroe shrugged. "You're in now."

"I still don't like it."

"Nor I," said Olivia. "You've pulled the tiger's tail. Sam will be livid. God knows what he'll impute from your delay."

"Well, we know what happened. Not much chance he can warp the facts."

"You don't know he would do that."

"True, but now we have the evidence, and the scene is pristine. Everything we know will be available. We proceeded with our internal investigation in good faith until we had evidence that a crime might have been committed. If Oliphant or anyone else wants to object or file a complaint, I made the decisions. Hold me accountable if it comes to that."

"We'll hope it doesn't go that far. Convincing Sam will be difficult."

"I know. Isn't that what they pay you the big bucks for?"

Olivia sighed, gave Jethroe a wry smile. "Lucky me."

10:00 AM Friday
22 May 2009

Had Julia been in contact with anyone from her life before you were married? Not to my knowledge. Any strange phone calls? Not to my knowledge. Any letters or other correspondence? Not to my knowledge. What do you really know about her inspiration trips? Nothing I haven't told you already. Anybody make threats or have a grudge? Have you . . .?

And so it had gone for nearly an hour—Swanson and Jethroe probing, jabbing; attempting to pry loose any scrap of Storey's memory that would help them in the search for motive to kill Julia.

Storey walked across Swanson's conference room and leaned on the side of the window. "Okay, what's next? Bright lights and rubber hoses?"

Swanson placed his head in his hands, elbows on the conference table. Jethroe slid down in his chair, and crossed his arms over his chest.

Storey watched the morning traffic on Commercial Street for a few moments. He looked west across the roofs of the buildings on Front Street, saw the Willamette River, its surface smooth, slate gray, mirrored the clouds concealing the sky. The air was clear, washed clean by the light rain that drifted down on the city like mist from a spray bottle. If only the drizzle could flush his mind of dark thoughts and expose a fragment of helpful memory.

He turned toward his friends. "Sorry. I did agree to this inquisition. Snapping at you won't help. I know you're just doing your job. I've tried my best to dredge up something." He tapped a forefinger on his temple. "Guys, if there's anything there, it's buried deep."

Jethroe looked toward Storey. "Maybe we're trying too hard. Let's drop it for now."

"Good idea," said Swanson. "Sometimes I remember things when I'm not trying—when I'm involved in something unrelated."

They were silent for a few moments. Storey returned to his seat. Swanson broke the hush. "Nick, why do you think Olivia has put her career on the line for you? She has, you know."

"I do. Didn't expect her to go that far."

Jethroe rolled his eyes, released a long breath.

"What?" Storey said.

"Subject for a later discussion. Nick, I've been thinking we should move your family to your condo in Newport . . . at least for the weekend."

Storey squinted. What did he mean, *subject for a later discussion?* "Newport is good," he said. "But, why?"

Jethroe pushed his chair closer to the table, focused on Storey. "Well, it's much easier to protect. It's carved into the hillside, so no rear to guard. And, the front faces the ocean which eliminates the worry about someone on top of the hill across the road from your house."

"You're worried about a spy, maybe a sniper?"

"Nick, considering what has happened, and our complete lack of intelligence, we have to consider every potential threat. The condo is an order of magnitude easier to protect than your house, and we can keep the media sharks away if they discover us."

"I like the media part," Storey said. "I came home the back way last night. There was only one car parked roadside about fifty yards from my driveway, but the street in front of the house was jammed with vans and equipment. I was able to zoom past them before they knew what was happening. I asked John to get rid of them. He did."

"How did he accomplish that?" Swanson asked.

"I can answer that," Jethroe said. "He advised them that were trespassing on a private road and that he'd call the tow trucks if they didn't vacate. People tend to believe Big John. Some left, some moved east to Liberty, others departed to the west. It's temporary at best."

"Roe, lots of boats go in and out of the harbor at Newport," said Storey. "What about the boats?"

"We have your telescope and some high-power binoculars. We can deal with that."

"The boys will want to go to the beach."

"Not prudent. That's a problem for you and Donna to solve."

"Easy to say, my friend."

"I like the Newport idea," Swanson said. "It's safer, and it gets you and the family out of Oliphant's jurisdiction . . . sort of. When would you make the move?"

"As soon as possible, if it's okay with Nick . . . and Donna."

"Fine with me. A change of scenery would be great."

"Okay. I'll call John and Ng." Jethroe opened his cell phone, punched a number. "They can drop the plan on Donna and help her get ready for the trip, assuming she agrees to go." He left the room.

"Nick, I should stay in town," Swanson said. "Watch the home front. And, I want to clear my desk so I can focus on your issues. I need to brief Stacy on some active cases so I can minimize my involvement."

Storey sucked a deep breath. "Mike, I hate to see you involve your partner. You've done enough . . . more than I could ask."

"Nick . . . shut up. We do what's necessary."

"I appreciate—"

"I can link up with you in Newport later."

Storey shrugged. "You know where to find us."

They sat silent for a few moments. Storey let his gaze wander over the paintings and prints hanging on the walls. He fixed his eyes on one of Julia's, an impressionistic oil depicting a frothy rock-strewn stream surrounded by pine forest and tall mountains. One from a backpack excursion shortly after Eric was born. Better times.

His phone vibrated. He flipped it open, looked at the screen, closed the instrument. "Damn lawyers. Sorry, Mike. Nothing personal."

"It's okay. Why would a lawyer be calling you now?"

"It's Barry Coleman, our estate planner.   You recommended him."

"He's a good man."

"And he's done a fine job. He called earlier, but I don't want to talk to him just now. All the trust and will stuff can wait."

Jethroe returned, grabbed a chair, and straddled the back, arms draped over the top rail. "It's all set. Donna loves the idea, even with the no beach caveat. We'll put together a caravan of cars and SUVs for the trip and go to Newport by the back roads. I'll have a cadre of plainclothes guards rotate 24/7."

"Sounds expensive."

"Nick, my allocation of resources is not open for discussion."

11:10 AM Friday
22 May 2009

Storey's phone vibrated. He flipped it open. "It's Valerie. I better take it. Hi, Val. What's up?"

"Rainey's dead."

"Rainey? Dead? Sonofabitch."

"What the hell . . .," Swanson muttered.

"I'm in Swanson's office with Mike and Roe. Hang on for a second. I'll put you on speaker." He returned to his seat, placed his cell phone on the table. "Okay, we're set. What happened?"

"What really happened is not resolved at the moment. Oh, Janine just walked in. I asked her to come to my office. I'll let her tell the story. I'll put you on the speaker in my office."

"Janine is Rainey's office manager," Storey said. Swanson and Jethroe nodded.

"Hello, this is Janine. Nick?"

"Yes. Hi. I'm with Mike Swanson and Jethroe Washington. George is dead?"

"Yes."

"Can you tell us what happened?"

"I'll try. George was not a nice man, but after twenty years . . . well, it's a shock." Janine sniffled, blew her nose.

"Take your time."

"Okay, I arrived at the office about 8:30. I try to get there early. When I came through the door I smelled what I thought was burnt paper.   The mini-blinds on the window to George's office were closed.   That was strange.   He's usually at his desk long before any of the office staff appears so he can keep tabs on who comes in early or late."

"Where did you find George?" said Jethroe.

"I didn't.   I knocked on his office door, but got no response.   I checked the file storage room and bathroom.   No George.   I peeked through a small gap in the window blind and saw that there had been a fire.   I called 911."

"You didn't go into the office?" Jethroe asked.

"George's office is like a vault.   He has the only key and he kept the door locked if someone else was in the building."

"Yeah," Storey said.   "I've been there."

"The fire, police and paramedics all showed up within five minutes.   A fireman took an axe to the window.   There were two panes and both of them exploded into a million little pieces."

"Double pane tempered glass," Storey mumbled.   "George *was* paranoid."

Janine continued.   "A fireman climbed inside and opened the door.   George was not in the office.   I sneaked a peek inside.   The safe door was open and the papers were charred.   The desk was blistered.   George's chair was destroyed.   The clock on the wall behind the safe was scorched and the hands pointed to 8:12.   I saw what looked like stalactites where the sprinkler heads were.

"The only place left to look was the back hallway.   George used it as his private entrance and kept it locked.   One swing of a fireman's axe smashed the door.   They found George slumped against the hallway wall.   He was dead."

"Killed?" Swanson asked.

"Don't know."

"Would you like to take a break?" Storey asked.

"No.   I'm okay."

"Then what happened?"

"The police escorted me outside into the back seat of a cruiser.   They called the coroner and detectives.   They strung the yellow crime scene tape.   The detectives showed up and went inside.   Eventually they came out and questioned me.   Ricardo Sanchez and his partner Louise Nelson. They were very nice. I told them what I knew, which wasn't much."

"I'm sure you did fine," Storey said.

"Well, they frowned at my answer to their last question."

Swanson, Jethroe, and Storey exchanged glances. The phone was dead air for a moment.

"The question was . . .," Storey said.

"They asked me if George had any enemies or had he been threatened by anyone."

Jethroe sighed, "Does a bear shit in the woods?"

"It's a stock question," said Swanson. "Jamie, how did you answer?"

"I told them I wasn't aware of any threats, that I managed the office and supervised the four other agents that dealt with our customer's insurance needs . . . except for George's special clients."

Swanson straightened in his chair, looked at Storey and Jethroe.

"George managed the accounts of several companies by himself. No one in the office was involved. Then, I screwed up. I said there were rumors that some of George's people were unhappy. They asked me for names. I didn't know what to do. I said I wasn't sure; that most everyone wrangled over the premiums; that it was part of doing business. Nick, if I started naming everyone who argued with George there would be no end. You're one of them."

"Yeah. Did they stop there?"

"Louise, the woman detective, stepped in. She said that was enough for now, that they might have questions later."

"Janine, it's Mike Swanson. If they come back and want more, tell them you have answered their questions to the best of your ability and that you need to talk to your attorney. Feel free to call me."

"Thanks. If they had pushed any further, I don't know what I would have done."

"You did great. Did they let you go then?"

"Yes."

"Janine, this is Jethroe. Did you hear anyone say what caused the fire?"

"No, but I heard one of the firemen talking to the Captain. He said the sprinklers were disabled and that was why there was no alarm. He believed the fire most likely ate all the oxygen in the sealed room and just died. I heard the Captain call for an arson investigation."

"The sealed room bit is believable," Storey said. "I was there last week and when he closed the door, the outside world ceased to exist." He shuddered. "I still feel claustrophobic."

"Janine, thank you for talking with us," Swanson said. "If you remember anything else, please call."

"I will. Nick I'm sorry about Julia. Is there anything I can do?"

"No, but, thank you."

"From what Val has told me, there's one more thing you might want to know. As I was leaving, a middle-aged man with a graying burr haircut walked up to the policeman that was checking ID's. The officer raised the tape and yelled, 'Hey, Sanchez, Oliphant is here.'"

Storey closed his cell phone, slid back in his chair and looked from Mike to Jethroe. "Oliphant? Is he taking over from Sanchez and Nelson?"

"Unlikely," Swanson said. "They were probably at the top of the list for the next case, so the investigation of Rainey's death belongs to Sanchez and Nelson. I'm sure Oliphant knows there is . . . was . . . bad blood between you and Rainey. He's likely looking for a connection to you, or he's trying to connect Rainey's death to Julia's. I've seen him work. Once he bites into a suspect he hangs on—Salem PD's Pit Bull."

Swanson's cell buzzed. He opened it, listened, put his hand over the mouthpiece. "Nick, it's Coleman."

"I don't feel like talking about wills and stuff. Tell him later . . . something. Tell him I'll call next week after things calm down."

"Barry. What can I do for you?" Swanson said. He leaned his chair back, looked at the ceiling. "Yeah. Well, Nick is a bit distracted just now. Julia's estate issues are not high on his priority list. Can't it wait until—?"

Swanson pursed his lips; frowned. After a moment he handed the phone to Storey. "Perhaps you should hear what he has to say."

Storey took the phone. "Barry."

"Nick. Finally. I left you several messages."

"Yeah, I saw your name on my voice mail list."

"I've been out of town and just returned early this morning. I read about Julia in the paper. I'm so sorry."

"Thanks. We're trying to deal with it. What's so urgent?"

"Nick, ah . . . I not sure how to put this. I—"

"Just say it, Barry." The phone was silent for a moment. Storey paced to the window and back.

"Okay. Julia left a package with me with instructions that I give it to you immediately after her death or incapacitation. She said any delay could be a matter of life or death. I hope my two-day sabbatical hasn't fouled the works. Her instructions were very clear—I should give it to you and only you, no one else."

"When did she do this?"

"Shortly after your wedding."

"For nearly four years you've had this, ah, package, and I'm just now made aware of it?"

"That was Julia's instructions. Nick, I was bound by—"

"Yeah, the attorney-client shit." Storey exhaled a long breath. "I'll have to come to your office?"

"That would be best."

"I'll be there shortly."

12:30 AM Friday
22 May 2009

Storey walked the three blocks to Barry's office. Coleman seemed more frayed than usual. Several tufts of his profuse gray hair poked out from his head at odd angles. A three-day stubble of beard covered his face and neck.

He removed a stack of files from a client chair. "Please have a seat."

Storey leaned back in the chair, crossed his arms over his chest.

Barry ran his fingers through his bushy hair. "I flew in from Phoenix last night and went directly to bed. I read about Julia in the paper this morning, called you and came straight to the office." He placed a legal-sized manila envelope on his desk. "We best get to it." He broke the seal and removed a small envelope. "Julia's instructions were specific; If she were to die, or be killed, she—"

"She actually said *killed*?"

"Yes. At the time it did seem implausible." Barry sighed. "But, here we are."

"Yeah. And it's getting more far-fetched by the minute."

"I can only imagine." Tapping the edge of the envelope on the leather desktop, he stared into the mid-distance for a moment. "Julia wanted me to give you this letter and have you read it before I give you the complete file. Nick, I want you to know I have no clue what's in this package. I hope whatever it is will give you solace and shed some light on some of the questions you must be grappling with." He slid the envelope across to Storey, picked up the file, and walked to the door. "I'm sure you'll want privacy. I'll be just outside. Call me when you're finished."

Storey stared at the envelope for a long moment. It was plain white, smudged with brown fingerprints, and crinkled as if it had once been wadded into a ball. Storey ripped it open and removed a rumpled letter. His hand trembled as he smoothed it on the surface of the desk.

January 9, 2006.

Nicholas,

Since you are reading this I'm dead, most likely from unnatural causes. My death was probably violent and sudden. For your and our child's safety I have purposely not disclosed anything about my life before we met. I cannot describe the pain that this deception causes me, but please believe me, it is necessary to protect you and the spark of life inside me that we created. I do not want him or her to grow up without a father.

I want to be with you, to make a new life with you. I admit a large part of my desire is selfish, perhaps more than I acknowledge.

When I discovered I was pregnant I packed my painting supplies and a few clothes in my old Suburban and started down Hwy. 1 thinking I needed to get away, to disappear from your life and resume my beachcomber existence; the life that served me well for years.

I stopped in Big Sur and walked the beaches for hours thinking about what my life had been and how it could be with you. When the sun was low in the sky, I stopped and sat on a piece of driftwood to watch the waves crashing over some rocks.

I saw a Condor floating on the thermals along the cliffs. As I watched the prehistoric creature soar, dip, and turn in the air, a feeling of stark loneliness overcame me. I realized my feelings of freedom that once gave me a connection to the giant bird were gone. I felt detached, as if suddenly set adrift, alone, abandoned. I lived a solitary life for several years, but I never felt lonely. I realized that my gypsy style of living could no longer be. The life growing inside me ended that, and I am surprised how good that makes me feel.

I do not want to lose you nor do I want to place you in harm's way by exposing you to the evil that haunts me. Complicating your life with the baggage from mine does not seem right, but if something were to happen to me, what would become of our child without your protection? A child needs a family, something I had once—sort of. Our son or daughter deserves something better than what I can offer—a day-to-day existence of wandering without purpose. I could not imagine our child without someone to care for her—him. I have no doubts you will love and care for our child with or without my presence.

You knew me as Julia Dee Williams, then as your wife Julia Dee Storey. I lived as Julia for six years, the last of several identities. I was born in New Jersey and christened Maria Imelda Fortunato, the only child of Marco and Arianna Fortunato. Their death launched me on my journey of deceit and impersonation trying to evade the evil that killed them.

I feel that I have made a deal with the devil. Deceiving you is not something I am proud of, particularly with your sense of fair play and honor.

In the package I have left with Barry, there are instructions showing how you can access my diaries and journals that explain my situation and how it came to be. I hope as you read them that you can understand the need for my secrecy, and that you will forgive me.

Read my journals before you contact any police authority. I am confident you will understand and *know what has to be done to protect yourself and our child.*

Nicholas, you must move on with your life.
Forgive me,
Julia

Storey read the letter a second time. He stared, unfocused, for several moments.

"Sonofabitch," he muttered. He crumpled the letter into a tight ball and threw it across the room.

He stood, his head bowed, his hands splayed on Barry's desk, wondering how to escape his shadows that he knew were waiting for him to exit the building. Earlier, as he studied the street from Swanson's office window, he had spotted Jethroe's man—the man playing the role of the father of the pair at Wiley's Billiards. On several occasions in the past two days, he had seen a silver mini-van driven by a balding middle-aged man with pallid skin and hollow cheeks. Was Jethroe's guy aware of the van?

He walked to the window overlooking the street and saw Jethroe's operative parked in a lot across the street, the van a block south around the corner at the next cross street—they were still following him. He leaned on the wall next to the windowpane for a long moment, his gaze shifting from the silver SUV to the black Honda.

Until he had seen the contents of the folder, and evaluated the risks involved, he wanted to stop Jethroe and Swanson from peppering him with suggestions and initiating plans before he could react. He needed to digest and interpret the papers in private, undisturbed by his well-intended friends—and Julia's letter stressed a need for secrecy.

When he thought of going underground and abandoning Jethroe's protection, his cramping gut and racing pulse propelled him back to the chair with sweat beads covering his forehead. Who was following him and did they intend to harm him? Perhaps they meant to kill him also. Why? Were they aware of Julia's package? Did they want access to it?

For a few moments he stared absently at pictures of Barry's Bonanza and other airplanes covering the office walls.

"It's time I take control," he muttered.

He needed a plan.   Jethroe's comments about Julia's Goth disguise flashed through his head: create a diversion; take the focus away from him and onto something odd or different.   Storey rose, walked into Barry's private bathroom, and opened the wardrobe and rummaged through the clothes on the bar. He quickly concluded that a suit was not sufficient change from his sport jacket and slacks. His eye caught a small pile of clothes on the top shelf—a nondescript ball cap and a pair of coveralls and a toiletry kit in a small leather bag. He opened it, removed a Gillette razor and a small mirror, and put them in his pocket.   He recovered the small notebook he always carried and wrote a note for Barry.

> *You can bill me for the razor, coveralls and ball cap. No disclosure. Atty. Client privilege.*

He tore the page from the notepad and inserted it into the wardrobe door pull. He opened his shirt, partially unfolded the coveralls and spread them across his belly and side, concealing the cap in the folds of cloth. He buttoned his shirt and jacket over them, and inspected the result in the mirror. *Hardly noticeable.*

He strode into the office, retrieved the crumpled letter, smoothed it, replaced it in its envelope, and put it into his inner jacket pocket. He selected a cigar and a matchbook from the humidor on the sideboard, stuffed them into his side pocket and walked out of the office. Barry was sitting at a small table in the foyer studying some documents.

"I'll take the package now. I'll open and study it somewhere else."

Coleman stood, looked at Storey for a moment.   "You're welcome here, Nick."

"It's best I leave now."

"Okay. Just a second." He walked to the secretary's desk, retrieved a sheet of paper, wrote on it, and motioned to Storey. "Just sign and date this for my file. It says you took the folder."

Storey scribbled his signature and the date. "I was not here."

"Does that include Swanson and Washington? They must be aware that you came to my office."

"Yeah, Especially them. Tell them you can't say; something—whatever you do when you have to protect attorney-client business."

"If that's what you want, you got it." Coleman gave Julia's package to Storey.

"I want. Oh, do you have something I could carry this stuff in? Wouldn't want to spill it all over the street."

Coleman opened the bottom drawer of the secretary desk, removed a brown cloth bag with sewn-in handles, and handed it to Storey. "Use this. Janice makes them by the dozens. She gives them away for grocery bags; it's her bit to remove plastic from the environment."

Storey dropped the packet into it. "Perfect. Thank Janice for me. Gotta go."

"Nick, I'll pray for you and your family."

"Thanks Barry. We'll need all the help we can get."

1:30 PM Friday
22 May 2009

On the first floor of Coleman's office building, Storey entered the men's room, pulled two paper towels from the dispenser, squirted a puddle of soap into one, dampened the other, stepped into a stall and closed the door. He removed the razor and mirror from his pocket.

Five minutes later he rinsed his face over the sink and inspected his image in the mirror thinking he looked a bit rotund with the coveralls over his clothes—probably a good thing. His mustache was gone, along with two inches of sideburn. He pulled the collar of the coverall up, pushed the cap low over his eyes, and gripped the cigar between his teeth at the side of his mouth. He looked into the mirror spread his hands, cocked his head. "Hi," he said, turned, and left, cradling the cloth bag under his arm.

Except for a stocky woman guiding a polisher over the lobby floor, the hall was clear. Storey turned his head so the bill of the cap hid his face and, affecting a slight limp, moved toward the rear entrance and left the building.

In the alley, he walked about a hundred yards north away from his stalkers, hoping they were still parked near Coleman's or Swanson's office. He entered through the back door of an office building, ducking his head when he met people in the hallways. He limped his way to the front door, stepped out onto the sidewalk, lit the cigar and shuffled north. He turned east toward the Salem center where he dropped the cigar in a receptacle, found the men's room, removed the coveralls, and deposited them under the paper towels in the trash can.

At an ATM, he withdrew the maximum. In Penney's, with the company credit card he bought a denim jacket, jeans, shirt and work boots, found a fitting room, changed into his new outfit, placed his old clothes and Julia's package into the sturdy Penney's bag. In an electronics store, he added a prepaid cell phone to the card, then walked the four blocks to Riverfront Park, trying not to look over his shoulder every thirty seconds.

To protect himself and the folder of documents from rain, he chose a shelter with a roof near the park edge. His heart thumping against his ribcage, his temples pulsing with each beat, he placed Julia's package beside him on the bench of a picnic table wondering if his strategy of hiding in plain sight was as clever as it had seemed. He stretched his legs under the table, and did a quick survey of the park.

Except for two couples walking by the river, and a man and woman jogging the periphery, the park was clear. Satisfied, he opened the blade of his miniature Swiss Army knife and slit the tape sealing the box. Inside he found an expandable folder tied with heavy cord. He undid the knot, stretched the accordion file so each compartment was visible, and saw each slot numbered in sequence. Typical Julia, he thought. Disciplined, organized; everything had its place.

He swiveled toward the sound of footsteps behind him. *They had found him! Run!* He reached for the file, stopped, turned and faced the man, squaring his shoulders and steeling himself for a confrontation. As the man approached, Storey realized the guy did resemble the silver van driver, but was bald with a fringe of brown hair, ponytail flopping from side to side as he jogged.

"Good afternoon," the man said, waved, and continued on his way.

Storey straddled the bench, his back against the shelter wall. Now he had a view of the park and the street. His eyes raked the area for anything out of place. He felt as if steel bands were compressing his chest. Roe was right. Eric and Donna were in danger. Where were Mom and Dad? Had they disappeared on one of their trips to nowhere, or . . .? Gooseflesh crept up his arms. He yanked his cell phone from his belt and punched a number.

"Nick! Where are you?"

He'd forgotten about caller ID.

"Roe, the danger is real. Protect my family. I'll contact you soon." He terminated the call, turned the phone off, vowed to use his new cell phone until he had a better grasp on his situation.

He laced his arms across his chest and stared at the river. He'd made two big mistakes so far. Sitting with his back to the street . . . *dumb*, and using his cell with GPS . . . *dumber*. You're a builder, not a spy. Can you do this? Get control. Think.

He retrieved the throwaway phone from his jacket pocket and dialed his father's cell phone. He had to know if they were okay—at least he could rail at his father's voice mail for not responding to his calls. The phone rang five, six, seven times. Odd. The voice mail was turned off.

"Hello." The echo told Storey his father was on speakerphone. Strange.

"Dad? Where are you?"

"Nice to hear from you, Nick."

"Dad, where are you?'

"Can't say."

"Don't play games with me."

"I don't play games. You know that."

"Well, if you can't tell me where, can you tell me what's going on?"

"I'm reading your mother's novels."

The speakerphone resonance stopped. A heavy male voice came on the line. "Mr. Storey. Have you finished studying the file?"

Storey held the phone at arms length, stared at it frowning. He rose, paced, returned the instrument to his ear.

"Who is this?"

"Not important. I know you have the file."

"What file?"

"Hey, don't be a smart ass. We know you left Coleman's office with Maria's file."

Storey sucked a breath. *Maria?* How does he know? Storey dropped to the bench, put a fist over his mouth and stared at the phone for a long moment. The guy said *we. They knew her before . . .*

"Who's Maria?" he said repositioning the cell.

"I've heard you're as mulish as your old man. Defiance won't help. Believe me."

"What do you want?"

"Maria's journals and the photos and the tapes."

Storey thumbed through the papers. He saw passports, driver's licenses, and other forms of identification, and another envelope. Should he admit he had the file? What would they do with Mom and Dad?

"Okay, I have the file," he said. "I see nothing that looks like a journal. There's no photographs. What kind of tape?"

"It seems you need some convincing, smart ass."

The phone went silent for a moment, and then Storey heard grunts and banging followed by a *thunk,* and a moan. "Okay, big guy. Your old man just lost his left pinkie at the first knuckle. Care to try for two? Mess with us and we move up each finger joint by joint. Got the picture?"

Storey leaned on the shelter wall, and slid down until he sat on his haunches. "Sonsabitches."

"Whatever," the voice said. "Now, tell us what's in the file."

Storey hesitated for a beat. "After I talk with my Dad."

"Not a chance."

"I haven't finished with the file. Perhaps what you want is in the envelope I haven't opened."

"Well, get to it, asshole."

"After I've talked to my father.'

"No way."

"Then you get nothing." Storey put his head back against the wall, closed his eyes. *I blew it.*

He heard rustling, some muffled conversation. After long moments he heard the speakerphone activate.

"Nick?"

"Dad." Storey expelled air, breathed again. "Are you okay?"

"Yeah. I've hurt worse smashing my thumb with a hammer. They gave me a towel. Didn't want me bleeding on the upholstery."

"Is Mom all right?"

"I can see her next door, sitting at the dining table of our fifth wheel with her escorts. She's good."

"They separated you?"

"Yeah. I'm in their big rig."

Storey paused, thinking about their previous conversation. "And you're reading Mom's books?"

"Always wanted to. They let me bring a couple. I guess they thought it would keep me quiet."

The speakerphone reverberation ended.

"Enough of the family blather, Storey," the voice said. "Just get on with it."

"When I've finished reading the file I'll call back. My Dad better answer the phone—"

"No way, dickhead."

"Hey, dickhead," Storey shouted. "My Father better answer the phone in robust good health or you will never see any journals, tapes or whatever. Believe me!" Storey turned the phone off.

2:30 PM Friday
22 May 2009

Storey opened the next compartment and pulled out an envelope, ripped it open.

> *January 2006*
> *Nicholas,*
> *The following describes how you can acquire my journals and diaries. The diaries are my ramblings spanning the time from when I was a young girl in boarding school until I finished art school in Paris and my father insisted I come home. My diaries may be of interest to you, but the journals are a day-by-day account of my activities since my parents were murdered (shortly after I returned to the U.S.) until we were married. The journals and some photos and tapes contain information that has kept us safe from my parents' killers (I thought forever, but since you are reading this . . .) You must recover the documents from a safe deposit box in the Oregon Beach Bank in Lincoln City, Oregon. The box is registered to Julia and/or Norman Storm.*
> *I have included a copy of the registration form and a key to the box. It takes two keys, the one in*

the small brown envelope and the bank's, to open the box. The driver's license I made in the name of Norman Storm should be sufficient identification. If not, I have included a passport. If you practice the signature a few times, you should have no trouble getting access.

Julia

P.S. April 2008
I have updated the IDs with new pictures.

Storey inspected the license and passport. The photo showed him with his mustache. Hoping his now bare upper lip would not cause problems at the bank, he folded the letters and put them, the key and IDs in an inner jacket pocket.

He activated his throwaway phone and dialed Jethroe.

"Washington."

"Roe, Dad, and Mom have been kidnapped."

"Nick? What? Where are you?"

"Just listen. I'm fine, but have to keep moving. Are Eric and Donna okay?"

"Yes. No problem—Victor and Emily have been kidnapped?"

"Yeah, and they've chopped part of Dad's little finger off as a warning and will do more If I don't give them what they want"

"Shit. What can we do?"

"Go get them."

"Where?"

"In the Deschutes National Forest there's a remote campground, the East Campground, at the O'Dell Creek outlet of Davis Lake.'

"I know the place. We've been there."

"Right. Mom is in their fifth wheel and Dad is next door in a motor home. There's four bad guys at least."

"You know this how?"

"Dad told me."

"What? You talked to him?"

"Long story. Later. Pull off your surveillance. Stop looking for me. Could lead them to me."

"Them? Nick—"

"Roe, just keep my family safe. I'll call later if I need more."
Storey terminated the call, punched in another number.

"Checker Cab."

"I need a ride at Riverfront Park, north end, ASAP."

"You got it."

Storey turned the phone off and pocketed it. He dropped the
empty envelope and the Penney's bag into a trashcan, grabbed the
cloth bag holding his clothes, and walked briskly to the north end of
the park.

As he waited for the cab, he entered another number in the cell.

"Barton."

"Olivia, Nick."

"Oh . . . yes. Just a moment."

Storey heard a jumble of voices, then silence.

"Nick. I had to get away from the squad room. Where are you?
Everyone is looking for you."

"For me?"

"Yeah, Oliphant—"

"Liv, you can tell me later. I've found some important
information. I need your help. Can you do that—I mean without
jeopardizing your job or assignment?"

"Nick your safety is . . . ah, where do I meet you?"

"You remember my hangar at the airport?"

"Of course."

"I'll be there in twenty or so. Meet me in the parking lot in
front of the restaurant."

"I'll be there."

"You still keep that sleeping bag in your trunk?"

"Yeah."

"You'll need it—and a change of clothes."

"Got that too. Are we taking a trip?"

"If you can."

"Probably."

A cab pulled to the curb. "My ride's here. Gotta go. Bye."

3:30 PM Friday
22 May 2009

As Storey paid the cab driver, Olivia exited her vehicle and leaned against the driver's door. He waited until the cab left the airport parking lot before approaching her.

"Liv, you sure about this?"

"Yes."

Storey activated his cell phone.

"Nick."

"Yeah. Dad, how are you?"

"Fine. They even bandaged my finger."

"And Mom?"

"Good."

The now familiar gruff voice broke the speakerphone echo. "Okay, Storey, enough games. We gave you a little rope for now. Where's the stuff. When do we get it?"

"The letter only gave me directions telling me where to get instructions to find the journals and tapes."

"Storey . . . I think your old man just lost another finger joint."

"*No*. Wait. Would I be playing roulette with the lives of two people I love?"

"Fuck, I really don't know. Would you?"

"No way. I'm telling you. The letter only told me where to go next. I'll be there in two, maybe three hours. Depends on traffic, and then however long it takes me to find the second package."

"Second package?"

"That's what the letter said."

"What is this shit? A scavenger hunt? Where are you? We're not playing fucking kid's games, Storey."

"I'm doing the best I can, ah, um—sorry, I don't know what to call you."

The voice laughed. "Nice try, Storey. I'm your worst nightmare."

"I'm well aware this is not a game, Mr. Nightmare. I'll call you when I find the first packet. If I could do more I would. Please believe me."

"Maybe I do, maybe I don't. Storey, you didn't tell me where you are."

"I don't need any help."

"Maybe. Do it again, Dom."

Storey heard a thunk and a muffled scream. He put a palm to his forehead, leaned on Olivia's car fender.

"Just so you know how committed we are, Storey. Only one joint left on the pinky. Three hours; another joint if you don't call. I'm being generous. We got lotsa towels." Nightmare terminated the call.

Storey closed his phone, kicked the front tire of Olivia's car. He could not stop the tears that oozed through his lashes.

Olivia leaned against him, put an arm around his waist, wiped his cheeks with a finger. "What's happening, Nick? Talk to me."

He raised his head and stared at the sky for a moment, shook his head. He put his hands on Olivia's shoulders and pushed her to arms length. "I will, but we have to get out of here now. When we're in the air I'll tell you everything."

She frowned. "Promise?"

Storey nodded. "Let's drive your car to the hangar. We can park it inside while we're gone."

*****

Storey dialed the lock combination, pushed the right half of the hangar's rolling door open; Olivia opened the left side.

He retrieved a sleeping bag and a small pop-up tent from a storage cabinet, unlocked the plane's baggage compartment, and tossed the equipment and his bag of garments inside. "Liv, you can put your things in here."

She wrapped her badge and gun in her change of clothes and stowed then with her sleeping bag. "A Skyhawk. When did you upgrade?"

"A couple of years ago." He removed the pitot tube cover. "I'll do the engine and fuel pre-flight if you'll do the rest."

"Same as the 172?"

"Yep."

In the cockpit, buckled in their seats, earphones on, Storey activated battery power.

"Okay. Checklist in the glove compartment?" Olivia opened it and removed a package of small laminated cards on a cord; waved them at him. "Me Read. You Check?"

He gave her a wry smile. "Works for me."

Storey completed the engine run-up and received clearance for departure to the north, runway 34. He removed the letters from his jacket and gave them to Olivia.

"Read these. Then I'll show you the rest of the stuff and we'll talk."

*****

He leveled at 4500 feet, leaned the engine, and set the prop for cruise. He adjusted the trim for level flight, released the yoke, and looked toward Olivia. She was staring at the horizon, the letters gripped firmly in both hands.

"The first letter was crumpled and ripped," she said.

"I got a bit carried away."

She looked into his eyes. "Really! Because you were deceived for four years?"

"Partly, and I was mad. The letter verified our suspicions—my family is in jeopardy. Me too. Maybe my friends."

"You married Julia . . . Maria . . . because she was pregnant?"

"That was part of it."

"The rest is based on lies."

"It would seem so."

"And I—"

"Moved in with Big Andy, the bouncer."

They sat in silence for a moment, staring through the windshield.

"Yeah. I did that," she said. "Show me the rest of the stuff before this turns into a soap opera."

Storey gave her the fake identification and the safe deposit receipt, showed her the small brown envelope.

"The safe deposit key is in here."

"Where are we going? Lincoln City is that way." She pointed southwest. "We're headed north."

"Right." He pointed down and to the right as he eased the plane into a slow turn. "There's McMinnville. We'll turn west to the ocean and then south to land at Glenenden Beach. Then we'll head up to Lincoln and get whatever is in the safe deposit box."

"As I recall, a straight line is the shortest distance."

"Call me paranoid, but these guys seem to know my every move. I'm trying to make it difficult . . . don't file a flight plan, take off to the north, fly a circle to the south."

"How are we getting from the airport to the bank?"

"While I was in the cab, I got online with my cell and dug out the number for the local taxi company. They'll have a ride waiting when we land. It's about a fifteen minute drive, probably less."

Olivia looked at her watch. "3:40. What time does the bank close?"

"Five."

"I'm so glad we have so much time." Olivia pulled the Flight Guide from the compartment and thumbed through it. "Glenenden Beach; Siletz Bay State, single runway, 17, 35, unmonitored, CTAF 122.7." She set the second radio to the frequency.

"We're camping overnight. Our next destination has no night lights."

"It's time you told me what's going on, Why were you upset talking to your Dad?"

"Dad and Mom have been kidnapped."

Olivia sucked a quick, deep breath. "Kidnapped?"

"Yeah. And they're being held hostage."

"Why? Who would do that?" She flopped back in her seat. "And you didn't tell me sooner because . . ."

"You just said our time is short. It's a long story. If I had started telling you before we left Salem, would you have let me stop in the middle . . . or want to call somebody? I'm sure your copliness would have kicked in somehow. Maybe you wouldn't have come with me. I wanted to get in the air ASAP."

Olivia sighed. "Okay. So tell me."

"Well, at first we thought they were off on one of their 'trips to nowhere', but . . . ." Storey described the conversations with Nightmare and Roe, and summarized the situation as he understood it.

Olivia grasped his hand to her cheek briefly. "God, Nick. I'm sorry. They cut his finger off? No wonder you are upset." She frowned. "You should contact the FBI."

"Roe will do whatever is necessary."

"You hope. Jethroe doesn't always follow the rules."

"He gets the job done."

"With a bunch of collateral damage on occasion."

Storey looked at her, brows arched. "Are you mad at me?"

She compressed her lips, looked away for a moment. "The jury is out." She returned her gaze to Storey. "There is no second package. That was your ruse to buy time?"

"Yeah. Hopefully, it will give Roe and his team time to corral the bastards. I figure if they get the journals, Mom and Dad's life expectancy will take a nosedive. Better Dad's finger than their lives."

"How do you know where they are?"

"Dad told me."

"You said that. How?"

"Well, a couple of years ago we were camping there. Fishing was not great, so one afternoon Dad picked up one of Mom's *love stories*." Storey made quotes with his fingers. "He spent the afternoon reading it. About four in the afternoon, he threw it on the table and said he would never open one of those damn things again, that he would have to stock up some of his books. They argued about it for a while, and Dad stomped out of the trailer."

"So. When he told you he was reading her books, you knew where he was."

"Immediately."

They were silent for a few moments.

Olivia looked up from studying the Seattle sectional chart. "You'll need to start our descent for Glenenden shortly after you turn south at the coast." She looked at her watch. "3:55. You said you had to make the next phone call to Nightmare at 5:45?"

"Or sooner."

"Our ETA is about 4:20. Leaves us about half an hour after we secure and tie down to get to the bank."

5:15 PM Friday
22 May 2009

Storey sat on a bench outside the bank, opened his personal cell phone.

Olivia slid in next to him. "Roe?" she said.

"Yeah. Maybe he knows someone who can get us into the bank after hours."

"Or his FBI friends can push some buttons."

"Whatever works" He activated a call to Jethroe's cell. "Thanks for being here, Liv."

Olivia smiled, placed her hand over his.

Jethroe answered on the second ring. "You're using your usual phone. No more cloak and dagger?"

"Roe, do you know anyone who can get us into the Oregon Beach Bank after hours?"

"Good evening to you. Which Oregon Beach Bank?"

"Lincoln City."

"Legally or otherwise?"

"Officially authorized entry would be nice."

"What's going on?"

"I have to pick up a package with some journals that Julia sequestered in a safe deposit box—a legacy from her previous life. Her notes imply that the information exposes who killed her parents—and why."

"Her parents? I thought they—"

"It's a long, long story and not germane at the moment."

"If you say so."

"Although he has never said it directly, it seems Nightmare wants the package in exchange for Dad and Mom."

"Nightmare?"

"Yeah, the guy holding Dad and Mom. So far we've agreed I call him Nightmare and he calls me dickhead, or big man or Storey—whatever."

"You talked to Victor again?"

"Yeah, and he lost another body part." Storey shuddered. "Just to clarify their position."

"Bastards."

"Can you help—get us into the bank?"

"Well . . . I know Bill Dawson, the Lincoln County Sheriff. We worked a missing person case together last year. You're after Julia's journals?"

"Yeah. I have to phone Nightmare in the next fifteen minutes or so. I'm hoping to set up another call to him at 10:00 tomorrow. I want to know what's in Julia's package before then. I hoped we could get the documents this afternoon and study them overnight, but the dim-witted cab driver took us to the wrong bank. By the time we got it sorted out, it was too late. The doors were locked, and the security person was by-the-book stubborn."

"Well, I can call Dawson. Maybe he knows someone."

"Good . . . oh. The safe deposit box is registered to Julia and Norman Storm. Julia made up ID's for me with that name—drivers license and passport."

"Great. Now we have to risk charges of deceiving an officer of the law, plus whatever goes with using a fake ID to empty a safe deposit box. You've come a long way, my friend."

"If it will get Dad and Mom released . . ."

"I know, Nick, and I understand. It might be better to call a judge off the golf course."

"No time. I . . . we need the stuff now."

"Uh . . . we?"

"Olivia came with me."

"Olivia? Our Olivia?"

"Yeah."

"Wow! Is she buying into all this?"

"You can ask her." Storey gave her the phone.

"Good evening, Jethroe." She stood. Paced.

"Yeah. Too late . . . by ten minutes." She looked at Storey, crinkled her forehead. "I can't think of an alternative." Olivia returned to her seat. "Sorry, I don't know Dawson. . . . Okay, but if he can't, or won't, help . . . Um, you could try the judge thing, but you'd likely have to explain the fake ID's . . . Yeah, really complicated, and time consuming. It's probably quicker to wait until the bank opens tomorrow morning. . . . Nice talking with you, too. Here's Nick."

"I want to pick up the documents and join you at East Davis Campground tomorrow morning—hopefully, before I have to call Nightmare. Somewhere in there we need to study the stuff."

"How are you going to get to the campsite?"

"Fly."

"Oh, you have the Skyhawk?"

"Yeah. We'll fly to Crescent Lake airport. That's, what . . . twenty minutes from the campground. You can pick us up?"

'Sure. No problem. We'll be there and set up by then."

"I see a restaurant just down the street from us. We'll get a drink and some dinner. I know this gets more bizarre by the moment, but we need those documents yesterday."

"I got the picture."

"Call me when you have something."

"Will do. You'll keep your cell active? You're through with the undercover stuff?"

"For you, Roe. Otherwise, no."

"I'll be in touch."

Storey closed the phone, stroked his non-existent mustache. "If we have to wait for the bank to open at 9:00 in the morning, we'll be stuck here till after I phone Nightmare—assuming I can finesse him into a 10:00 call."

"The bank opens at nine?"

"Yeah. That would give us only forty-five minutes or so to study the documents."

"That's not much time. Tell this clown the bank opens at 10:00. Try for an 11:00 contact."

Storey lifted his brows, pursed his lips, nodded. "Good idea."

For a moment, neither of them spoke.

"Liv, I'll call Nightmare now; then we can go have dinner, maybe a drink."

"Okay."

"I'd like you to listen in. Anything you can detect may help."

"Sure."

He punched in the number, hunched down so Olivia could place her head against his and hear the phone speaker.

"Nick?"

"Yeah, Dad. It's me. How you doing?"

"I'm fine, Nicholas."

Storey could hear a quaver in his father's voice and lack of his earlier vitality.

"What have they done to you?"

"Nothing. I'm just tired."

"Okay, Storey. Have you got the package?"

"Ah. Mr. Nightmare. I think I should call you Recurring."

"Always a smart remark, eh, Storey. You got your three hours for your little quest. Can you get our package now? If you can't—"

"Yes, I can. And stop the threats. You do anything more to either of my parents, I'll give the stuff to the cops, or maybe I'll just burn your stuff when I leave the bank." Remembering that his last threat precipitated the loss of a section of his father's finger, Storey bit his lip, wondered how far he could push before Nightmare would retaliate.

"Bank?" the voice asked.

"The journals and other info are stored in a bank safe deposit box."

"Can you get to it?"

"Yes."

"What's stopping you?"

"I uncovered the instructions not ten minutes ago. I called you right away."

"Well?"

"I guess you don't do business with banks. It's after hours now. I don't include in my array of meager talents the ability to break into a bank vault."

"Storey, you're stalling. I'm not sure I believe anything you say."

"Nightmare, you can believe what you want. Let's talk about an exchange."

The phone was silent. Minutes passed. Storey imagined he heard the now familiar thunk of another finger joint being severed.

"Talk's cheap," the voice said.

Storey rubbed perspiration from his face and neck, looked at his quivering hand, hoping it did not show in his voice.

"Put my father on."

The cell was silent again. Storey felt his gut clench, waiting for the scream.

"Nick. It's okay."

"Dad. You're sure?" Storey felt lightheaded.

"Yeah, I'm sure."

"Okay, big man. Talk." It was Nightmare.

Storey thought his knees would fold. "I'm the only one can access the safe deposit. I go after the stuff when the bank opens at 10:00 tomorrow. I get it. I call you around 11:00. I talk to my father. You send my parents, unharmed, to a place, at a time I designate, and you'll get your package."

More silence.

Finally, when Storey thought he could no longer breathe, the voice growled in his ear. "You pick five public and accessible places. I choose the one, maybe a different one. Storey, you make copies, or if this comes back to bite us, we know where you live. I'm sure you don't want your little boy, Eric, or big sister, Donna, to have an accident like your wife. Understand what I'm saying?"

Storey lowered the phone, looked at Olivia with raised eyebrows.

Olivia shrugged, but slowly nodded.

Storey returned the phone to his ear. "I get it. Deal."

5:30 PM Friday
22 May 2009

The waiter delivered Storey's Killian and Olivia's Eola. "Keep the change," Storey said, laid a ten on the table.

From the back corner booth of the restaurant, he watched Olivia in the bar talking on her cell phone, wondering why she needed privacy to check her voice mail, why she paced, why she gestured so vigorously, why as she closed her phone she threw her arm upward, stomped her foot and stared at the ceiling for a long moment. Storey sipped his beer, smiled as he always had when he witnessed, or was the focus of, Olivia's exasperation. Some things never change. He hoped that her pique dissipated before she returned to her seat in their booth.

Another stomp of her foot, wave of her arm. Olivia uttered an expletive that Storey did not have to hear to translate . . . *sonofabitch*. She punched a number into her phone, returned it to her ear.

When they had attended seminars or parties, he loved to look at her from across the room, watch her move and marvel at her feline grace—and the best part—when their eyes met, the rush, the knowing smile, the wink. He did not expect any such quiet and private interchange tonight. He remembered long walks, holding hands, not saying much, enjoying the feel, the presence of each other; times they would sit in the quad at the university, in a park, or in a mall, and conjure stories or make flippant remarks about people passing by. What had happened to them? Why had she left?

Olivia, distress muted, eased onto a bar stool, looked toward Storey, smiled. He grinned, lifted his glass in salute, sipped, held her gaze.

His cell vibrated. "Storey."

"You've given up screening your calls?"

"No. Roe, I was distracted for a moment."

"That's all it takes . . . a moment."

"You have something for me? When can I get into the bank?"

"The earliest possible time . . . 7:30 tomorrow morning."

"Why not tonight?"

"Time lock. The vault has a time lock set for 7:30 in the A.M."

"Damn!"

"I've convinced Sheriff Dawson to accompany you and drive you to the airport, sirens blaring. It's close, but you should be able to make the campground by 10:00."

"I've finessed Nightmare into an 11:00 call. The extra hour should give us time to get there. Roe, I really wanted to examine the documents tonight."

"We play the hand we're dealt, my friend."

"How and where do I contact Sheriff Dawson . . . Bill Dawson I think you said."

"He'll be at the Pig and Blanket at 6:15 tomorrow morning."

"Okay. I'll be there."

"You *and* Olivia have to meet him."

"Both of us?

"Yeah, he wouldn't budge until I told him you had a police escort."

"Does he know it's ransom for a kidnapping?"

"No. I didn't think it was wise to open that can of worms. Someone from the sheriff's office or the bank's staff . . . well, the word could leak out. Just a whisper about kidnap and the media go crazy."

"So. What's our story?"

"The package is new evidence—crucial evidence for the prosecution of a fraud case on the docket tomorrow morning in Salem."

"Suppose he checks."

"It's a real case. One of my agents is testifying. That's my hook with Dawson."

"What's my role in this?"

"You're turning State's evidence in exchange for a reduced sentence."

"And Olivia is making sure I deliver the goods?"

"Yep. And who said crooks weren't quick on the uptake?"

"Thanks a lot."

"Will Olivia go along?"

"I'll have to talk to her." Storey turned toward the bar, waved for Olivia to join him. She held up an index finger, slid from her perch on the barstool. "She's busy on the phone just now."

"Call me if there's a problem."

"Thanks, Roe. I owe you, again. Oh . . . Dawson . . . what does he want for his services?"

"At the moment he thinks it's part of his job. When I tell him the truth, I'll probably be doing him favors for life."

"Sorry."

"We play the hand we're dealt. Call me, Nick. Either way."

"Will do." Storey closed his phone, took a slug from his Killian.

Olivia slid into the booth. She tasted her wine, set the glass on the table, stared into it as she twirled the stem between her fingers.

Storey, seeing her pursed lips, furrowed forehead and lowered eyebrows, decided to wait her out.

After a moment of studying the wine slosh in her glass, she said, "You talked with Roe?"

"Yeah. We meet Dawson for breakfast at 6:15 tomorrow morning. He'll be our escort to the bank and take us back to the airport."

"Tomorrow? Not tonight?"

"There's a time lock on the vault."

"Great." She sipped her wine, frowned. "*We* need an escort? You did say we—*us*—like you and me? Right?"

"Yeah . . . well . . . assuming you go along with the program."

"Ah." Olivia leveled her gaze at Storey. "Why do I get the feeling I'm not going to like this?"

Storey shrugged. "You don't buy in, we wait for the bank to open and take our chances that we can get to the campground before I have to call Nightmare."

"Two hours to get Julia's stash, and back to the airport, and fly to . . . not likely."

"Okay, I'll call from here."

"The idea was to get the, um . . . the ransom . . . you, Victor and Emily, and the bad guys together—within shouting distance—to improve the chances of your parents coming out of this alive. It seems I don't have much choice here." She gulped half her wine.

"Sorry."

"What am I buying into?" She lifted her glass toward Storey. "Am I going to need something stronger?"

Storey raised a shoulder. "You," he aimed a finger at her, "an officer of the law, will be escorting a felon . . .," he tapped a thumb on his chest; ". . . to pick up crucial new evidence in a fraud case prosecution on the docket in Salem tomorrow." He smiled. "I get parole instead of jail time."

"What if Dawson checks it out?"

"It's a real case. One of Roe's guys is testifying."

"Typical Jethroe setup. Verifiable facts that are not necessarily related." Olivia finished her wine, raised her glass toward the waiter. "I could use another."

"Ditto," Storey said.

They sat quiet for a long moment.

Olivia broke the silence. "Do I get to handcuff you?"

"If I can choose when."

More silence. The waiter brought their drinks.

"Seriously," Storey said. "What—"

"Who said I wasn't serious?"

"Seriously, can you tell me what pulled your chain during your phone calls?"

"I can."

Silence

"Will you?"

Olivia touched her glass to her lips. Her eyes raked Storey's face. She sighed. "There's a warrant out on you."

"A warrant?" Storey set his beer down, shook his head. "For what?'

"They want to question you about Rainey's death and the fire in his office."

"What?" He blinked, sucked air. "I don't know anything about the fire or his demise."

"Your fingerprints were found on the arm of a chair in Rainey's office and—"

"I was there last Friday. Nothing unusual about that."

"And they were on his lamp base and the bottom of his pen holder."

"We had a—"

Olivia put her hand on his mouth. "Don't say anything."

"But—"

"Do you want me to tell you or not?"

"Yes, but—"

"Then shut up."

Storey slouched back in his seat, crossed his arms over his chest. "Whatever."

"Nick, they found three bullets in the wall."

"What does—"

Olivia held up her hand. "You want to hear . . . be quiet, don't say anything . . . *kapish*?"

Storey blew out a breath.

"They got a search warrant, found a gun in Victor's gun cabinet, a .32, recently fired, with three cartridges missing from the clip. Your prints were on the clip and all the remaining shells."

"I keep my Colt pistol at Dad's house. Don't want Eric to get hold of it. There's three missing—"

She held up a hand, took a sip of wine. "And how, you might ask, did they get the search warrant?" Before Storey could speak, she put a finger over her lips, cocked her head.

Storey listened, chin in his palms, fingers covering his mouth and nose.

"You had a violent encounter with Rainey last Friday, and another argument this week at your office. The animosity between the two of you is common knowledge. Your prints were in unusual places in his office. Your troubles with Rainey involved Storey

Construction. Victor has disappeared. Add it all up, some judge thought it sufficient to issue a search warrant for Victor's home."

Storey slumped. "Let's see if I understand. They know I've had arguments with Rainey, they found my fingerprints in his office, and three bullets in his wall, and three cartridges missing from my gun."

Olivia nodded.

"Now they want to quiz me under the bright lights?"

"They don't use lights anymore."

"The way it's going, the ballistics will match my gun. Then they can bypass the inquisition and send me directly to the slammer."

Olivia, quiet for a moment, finished her wine.

Storey stretched his arms across the table, took her hand in his. "Liv, I get it now . . . why you shut me up. You're a cop. If it comes to court, or a disposition . . . whatever . . . anything I say can be used against me, and you certainly can't perjure yourself. Even if you were so inclined, I wouldn't allow you to. I shouldn't have brought you into this."

She gripped his hand, looked into his eyes. "Nicholas, I wouldn't want it any other way." She stiffened her back and released his hand. "Enough with the mushies."

The waiter appeared. "Would you folks like an appetizer?"

Storey waved him off. "No, thanks. Later maybe."

"Nick, there's more. They found diaries at your place."

"More diaries? Julia's? At my house? Where?"

"In her closet, top shelf, under some art magazines."

"What did they say? Obviously, something incriminating."

"Julia was having an affair. Almost . . . um . . . almost from the beginning."

Storey pushed back in his seat, took a deep breath. "Her inspiration trips?"

Olivia nodded.

"I knew it! It's the only thing that makes sense. I didn't want to believe it. Was it the art dealer?"

Olivia placed a finger on his lips. "I don't know and I didn't hear any of this." She paused for a moment. "Nick, they want to question you about Julia's death, too."

"Because they think the diaries give me motive for killing Julia?"

"Yeah. And Oliphant thinks you made up the story about Stevens and the lot on Eola . . . and your visit to the Harrison project. He checked the tax roll. A guy that operates several Taco Bell restaurants owns the Eola lot—not a Bill Stevens."

"Great."

"There's even more."

Storey shuddered, imagining the clang of a cell door closing. "Okay." He sighed. "Tell me."

"They found the bugs on your phones."

"We expected that."

"And, the blood on the T-Bird headlight cover is Julia's."

"Jethroe's tests—"

"Oliphant thinks you bugged your own phones to find out what Julia was doing and when—that you planned it all and hired someone to steal the T-Bird and run Julia down."

7:15 PM Friday
22 May 2009

The taxi rolled to a stop. Storey put his hands over the back of the front seat. "Can you pick us up here at 5:30 tomorrow morning?"

"Um. 5:30? Here, at the airport?" The driver frowned, looked at Storey. "That's really early. I'm not sure. My wife—"

"It's okay, sweetheart." Olivia said, grabbed Storey's arm, pulled him back into his seat, raised a hand when he looked at her, incredulous. "I'll phone my mother. She'll pick us up."

Storey's eyebrows shot up. "Your mother?"

"You know how she is. She'd harp at us for days if we didn't call her." She waved Storey toward the door. "Just pay the man, honey."

"Okay, whatever." Storey looked at the meter, counted out some bills.

The driver directed a nod at Olivia, smiled. "Sounds just like my mother-in-law. Makes walking on eggs easy."

"You have no idea," Storey said, handed the money over the seat back. "Keep the change," he said as they exited the vehicle.

They headed for the plane, silent for a moment. Storey rolled his head toward the departing cab.

"What was that about? . . . Honey."

Olivia chuckled. "Just trying to keep a low profile . . . sweetheart. We don't need a guy spreading the word that there are two people, a man, and a woman, waiting at the airport that are going to give him a big tip for showing up."

"I didn't offer him a tip."

"You were about to."

"How did you know?"

"Why else would you palm a Franklin?"

"How do you propose we get into town tomorrow morning?"

"Call the cab company. Arrange it. Standard procedure. No red flags waving."

"Has my paranoia infected you, too?"

"After my phone calls to Salem PD—yeah, some paranoia may have oozed through my pores."

"The warrants?"

"Umm . . . yeah."

They walked, not speaking, until they reached the airplane.

"So, Liv, you're happy with sleeping bags in the tent?"

"I wouldn't say happy."

"As I recall, you liked camping."

"Still do—but, I don't have a toothbrush, soap, anything."

"I have my kitbag of stuff. It has most necessities, except for a spare toothbrush."

Olivia smiled.

"What?"

"Just remembering that time at Big Sur."

Storey unlocked the storage compartment. "We need to put up the tent."

"Okay."

"I'll phone Roe; get an update. Then the cab company . . . if the number is still in my call list."

"Find out if Roe contacted the FBI."

Storey opened his phone, punched the number, turned away from her.

"Nick. It's important."

"Liv, I know. We'll need the sleeping bags."

She turned toward the plane, muttered, "No problem." She shook her head, mumbled, "*We* need to put up the tent, *we* need the sleeping bags."

"Nick. Speak to me."

"Roe. What's happening?"

Olivia, tent poles in each hand, put her face next Storey's. "Roe, you need the FBI."

"Olivia?"

"Yeah," Storey said,

"That was a smart move, my man. How did you convince her to join you?"

"Asked her."

"Well, I can stop worrying about you. An official police escort."

Storey looked at her. "Not sure she's that official."

"I'm surprised she—does Oliphant know?

"Haven't asked her."

He turned, leaned a shoulder on the engine cowling. "Roe, there are at least five of them. Dad implied that there are others outside the motor home and fifth wheel."

"We've spotted them."

Storey sensed Olivia behind him. "Roe, I'll call you later."

"Be safe, my friend."

"Ditto." Storey closed the phone,

"Haven't asked what?" she said.

"If your partner knows you're here."

"Oh."

Storey watched Olivia assembling the tent supports. "I see you remember how it goes together."

Olivia looked up at him. "It's color coded."

"You want some help . . . with the tent?"

Olivia sighed. "Sure."

Within five minutes they had the two-person pop-up placed and staked on the grass under the left wing of the aircraft.

*****

They sat on the grass under the wing in front of the tent.

"Getting dark soon," Olivia said.

"Liv, is there a chance Sheriff Dawson will know about the warrant?"

"Possibly. Even if he does, the chances of his connecting it to you are remote. You'll be Norman Storm and you'll be with a law officer."

"You know they'll never release them. Dad and Mom can identify them. What did you get from the conversation—when you listened at the bank?"

"I'd bet Nightmare is from the East coast, New Jersey maybe . . . for what that's worth."

"Well, it's something."

"Nick, you realize he raised the ante to five sites to make it difficult for us to arrange adequate surveillance at any of them."

"Yeah. I was afraid he might do something like that. But *five* places? Liv, it's nearly impossible."

"And, he reserved the right to reject any of them."

"So. My task is to select five likely spots for an exchange that will probably never take place. It's an exercise in futility."

"Perhaps."

"Liv, I'm scared. Nightmare seems, well, desperate. I'm afraid he'll escalate."

"To what? You've put him in a bind. They harm your parents, he doesn't get the documents."

"That's a bluff. The more damage they do to Mom or Dad, the more I'm inclined to give in. You know that. And I'm sure Nightmare does, or will figure it out. I have visions of one of them lying in a ditch somewhere, mangled and bloody. Then, they threaten to do the same to the other and my options go up in smoke."

"Nick, I don't think it's that bleak. Roe, the FBI and locals will be there. I'm betting these clowns never make it out of the campground. I've listened to plenty of shitbags like Nightmare. I just don't feel he'll stray too far from his program."

"Cop intuition?"

"Could be."

"Can you intuit what to do next?"

"Well, you know where they are, and they don't know you know. Don't suggest an exchange place that's close to them. Maybe that will force them to pick a spot close by—if they haven't already. Then, Jethroe, the FBI, and whatever other authority they have marshaled will be able to position their teams to protect, or liberate, Emily and Victor."

"Liv, that might work. I best call Roe again and update him."

He opened his cell phone, punched the number, waited. "Roe, Olivia has an idea . . ."

With his hands on the front edge of the wing, Storey watched Olivia gathering the sleeping bags. "Between Roe and the FBI they have a motor home, a Ranger maintenance truck, and a car in the campground. They have people stationed on all the exit roads. A helicopter is on standby.

"Roe was concerned. Something about the FBI's involvement . . . said it might be a stretch, but if the perpetrators are from out of state . . . The phone was garbled. I didn't get it all."

"Well, technically, the FBI can be involved only if the kidnapping crosses state lines. Do they have a plan to rescue your mom and dad?"

"They don't want to attempt anything tonight. Too many things could go wrong. It's overcast there, and will be quite dark. They plan to use the cover of darkness to plant a bug on Nightmare's rig. Roe liked your plan. Unless something develops, they are going to wait until morning . . . until we appear on site with the ransom package."

"So there's nothing more for us to do but get what's in the safe deposit and go to the campsite."

"That's it."

"Nick, do you feel better?"

"Yeah. Finally, I think we have a little control over this mess."

He sat on the grass next to Olivia. They stared across the runway into the dark shadows, each with their hands locked over their knees.

After several moments, Storey turned toward her. "Liv, I'm asking."

"Does my partner know I'm with you? No."

"Can you get in trouble?"

"Hard to say. Maybe."

Storey leaned back on outstretched arms, extended his legs flat on the grass. "Why did you come?"

"You said you needed me."

"I did. I do."

"For what?"

"Well, I . . ." He extended a hand outside the aircraft wing protection. "Hey, it's misting. We should get inside the tent before it rains."

Olivia compressed her lips, turned toward Storey. "Nick . . ."

"What."

"Oh . . . nothing."

He stood, stooped to clear the wing. "I'm beat. Only had about one night's sleep in the last three days."

"Same story here. I'm ready. I'll go in first. I have to get out of my clothes before I zip myself into my mummy bag."

"Okay. I can undress inside my bag."

"It is a bit oversized."

"I like to be able to move around. Tried a mummy like yours once. Drove me crazy. Didn't sleep much."

Olivia ducked into the small tent, drew the entry closed. Storey pulled an LED miner's lamp from the plane's storage compartment and secured it to his forehead with the strap. He circled the aircraft checking the tie-downs.

8:30 PM Friday
22 May 2009

Storey placed the LED between them. "It's here if you need some light." He switched it off, rolled to his side.

Olivia squirmed, rolled away, turned several times. She unzipped the top few inches of her bag, fumbled for the light, activated it. She turned toward Storey, propped her head on her palm, her elbow on the tent floor.

"What's the matter?" Storey said.

"We need to talk."

"You said you wanted to snooze, not schmooze." After a moment of silence, he said. "Okay. What should we talk about?"

"Nick, what happened to us?"

"Ah . . . back then?"

"Of course, back then. There is nothing else."

"You're here now."

"Nicholas!"

"Okay, okay. Back then, you left, threw a book at me. A big one, as I remember."

"Obviously not big enough."

"You said you never wanted to see my face again. That I remember as if it were an hour ago."

"I was mad."

"About . . .?"

"You were acting like a pompous ass."

"About . . .?"

"The usual stuff. Telling me I should do this, not do that, or be like Christi. Always something."

"Liv, why didn't you tell me? We always talked things out. . . . Who's Christi?"

"Doesn't matter. How could I tell you? You didn't come after me."

"I didn't come after you? How was I to know you wanted me to come after you? You said you never . . . You could have—"

"Nick, if you cared, you . . ." She sighed. "Oh, just forget it. Water over the dam."

"If I cared? When I came home the next day and your stuff was—"

"Nick, I'm not doing this." She unzipped her sleeping bag, gathered it and her clothes under her arm, crawled toward the tent opening. "I'll sleep in the back seat of the plane."

"Liv. Don't be ridiculous. It's cold out there. You're not dressed for—"

"There you go again."

"But . . ." His words were lost in the sound of the tent flap zipper.

"Goodnight, Nicholas."

"Olivia. Come back." He heard the plane's door open and latch shut.

Thirty minutes later, he was still awake and could not find a comfortable position. His thoughts churned, centered on the night Olivia had stormed out of their apartment, his last viable memories of her. He had loved Olivia. When she stalked out of their apartment she had taken a piece of his heart with her. The next evening he had come home to an empty space—all evidence of her gone, as if she had not existed.

She had dumped him—but now he wondered if she had, or had he simply given up, intimidated by her anger? Or was he simply too traumatized, too ego-driven to search for her, to soothe and comfort her? Had he taken her for granted?

For a long time he had felt he would never be whole again. Then, when he was convinced he was destined to settle for someone lesser or be forever alone, he had met Julia. Julia, the free spirit who brought spring-like freshness and unlimited possibilities into his life, bound by nothing and no one—and she was his simply for the asking.

He recalled their first full night together, lying in bed after, in that front-to-back spoon position, soaking in warm feelings, when she pulled his hand over her breasts, squeezed, and said, "The past begins here." He had asked what she meant, but got no answer. He realized now that she was saying she wanted her past to end there. It had worked for a while.

Best case scenario. Julia had been lying to him; deceiving him—for years. Rather than letting go of her past, she had embraced it. Had he asked her to marry him? Had he just acquiesced, panicked by his loneliness?

"Shit," he said, sat upright, found and flicked the LED on, and strapped it to his forehead. He grabbed a blanket and crawled out of the tent. It had stopped raining but he felt the damp ocean air bite at him. Must be forty degrees, he thought, and I'm in skivvies and a tee shirt. "Storey, you *are* a doofus," he muttered.

He opened the pilot-side door. Olivia, in a fetal position on the rear seat, blinked, put a hand up to shield her eyes as the light hit her face. Storey saw she had been crying. He held the blanket out toward her.

"Come back, Liv. I want you to. Please."

She wiggled out of her bag, wrapped the blanket around her, got out of the plane, and walked to the tent, shivering. Storey gathered her clothes and sleeping bag and went to her, laid her things inside, held the tent flap open. He followed her in, turned the LED off, and slid into his sleeping bag. He heard the zipper on Olivia's mummy slowly ratchet closed. He was asleep within minutes.

5:00 AM Saturday
23 May 2009

Storey came awake when the first rays of morning sun flickered on the tent wall and before his watch alarm sounded. His right arm tingled. Asleep, he thought. He brushed at an itch on his nose, but it would not go away. He closed his fingers over it. What the . . .! Hair? He turned to his right. Olivia's head rested on his arm, her curls cascading over his shoulder and face. He rolled up onto his side and looked down at her.

"You're awake," she said, turning toward him.

"It would appear so. My arm is not." He pulled it from under her head, massaged it. "I was dreaming Eric crawled into bed with me. How did you get in here?" He lifted the cover, saw she had not dressed.

"Like Eric, I crawled in."

"Well, that's obvious, but why?"

"I was cold. I usually sleep in my sweats in that light bag, but I didn't bring them with me. I thought I'd creep in next to you for a bit to warm up. Nick, you were so sound asleep, you just cradled my head in your arm, mumbled something and, well . . . evidently we were both exhausted."

"I need to find a bathroom," Storey said.

"Me too."

*****

The waitress in the Pig and Blanket wrote on her pad, pushed her pencil into the hair over her ear. "Two orders of ham and eggs, over easy, sourdough, hash browns. How about a fruit plate?"

Olivia nodded.

"Sure," Storey said.

They sipped their coffee.

"At least this cab jockey brought us to the right place," Storey said. He let his gaze move from her golden-brown hair to her dark eyes to her full lips and firm chin, down to her brown turtleneck sweater flecked with hints of green and gold—to match her hair and dusky complexion, he thought. Earlier, he had noticed her dark green skin-tight jeans and marveled that she had kept her figure trim and firm, that she had always, seemingly without effort or plan, picked a wardrobe that flattered her figure and coloring.

"Do I pass?" Olivia pursed her lips.

Storey raised his focus to her eyes. "Liv, are we okay?"

She locked onto his gaze, smiled. "You came after me."

"Would it have mattered then . . . when you left?"

Olivia looked down at her cup. "Something we'll never know. A path not taken."

"You never returned my phone calls."

Olivia sighed, turned toward the window. "Yeah."

Another moment of silence.

"Liv, I—"

"Nick, there's bigger issues to deal with at the moment."

Storey stared at her over his coffee. "Yeah. You're right, but we have to. Sooner or later, I want to talk about us."

He removed the fake driver's license and passport from his jacket inner pocket. "I suppose it's time I became Norman Storm." His brow furrowed. "Am I doing something illegal?"

"Technically, assuming an alias is not. I'm not sure, but I think the bank could freeze your access if they knew Julia was dead, but falsifying a driver's license and a passport? Yeah."

"I didn't forge them."

"If you're going to use them, the point is moot."

Storey touched her hand, stared at her for a moment. "That makes you an accessory."

She shrugged. "Our first priority has to be to get Victor and Emily away from Nightmare and his cronies. We'll deal with all that later."

"I really appreciate this, Liv. My mind is mush thinking about what can happen to Mom and Dad, or Eric, or Donna."

"Donna and Eric are safe for the moment. Just concentrate on what we have to do for your parents."

"You're right of course." He pulled a pen from his shirt pocket. "Do you have something I can write on? If I'm going to be Norman Storm, I should practice signing his name."

"And we have to come up with places for a hostage exchange." She tore a page from her notepad. "Here. Practice."

Storey studied the license. "It's a composite of my handwriting." He penned a pair of signatures, pushed them across to her.

She compared his attempts with the license. "Good. They're almost too perfect . . . Norman."

Storey cocked his head. "Norman. Yeah. I need to focus on responding to Norman or Storm . . . at least for the next couple of hours."

"Storm. I'll call you Storm. It seems more appropriate if I'm your official escort."

"Okay. Whatever."

"We're not allowed any mistakes . . . Storm."

"You're right . . . Barton."

Olivia chuckled. "That seems so strange."

"What?"

"Hearing you say Barton. It's seems forever since you used my surname. Usually you were upset with me when you did. It's strange . . . the things we miss."

"Yeah. Weird."

Olivia waved her hand toward the window. "Suck it up, Storm. Our sheriff just arrived."

Storey stuffed the license and passport back into his jacket pocket. Olivia wadded his rehearsal signature paper into a ball, pushed it into a pants pocket.

"Storm, I think it's best I do most of the talking."

"Barton, my lips are sealed unless you give me the nod." Storey saluted her with his cup, took a drink, moved his elbows off the table as the waitress slid their plates of food across the Formica.

"Anything else I can bring you?"

"Maybe a refill?"   Olivia set her cup on the outer edge of the table.

The waitress nodded.   "Sure."   She turned to leave, saw the sheriff approaching, grinned.   "Bill Dawson.   Haven't seen you in a while."

"Been busy, Angie."

"Would you like your usual—"

"Just coffee—black. Thanks. I'm looking for—"

"Sheriff Dawson?"   Olivia stood.   "Detective Sergeant Olivia Barton, Salem PD."   She flashed her badge with her left hand, extended her right.

Dawson let his eyes drift to her face and down over her body. He grasped her hand with both of his, squeezed, his world-weary indifference evaporating.   "Jethroe didn't . . . ah, he didn't warn me. I wasn't expecting . . . well, a detective, and a beautiful female one at that.   How did you get tapped for this duty?"

"I just happened to be in the wrong place at the right time,"

"Well . . . it's my pleasure, ah, Detective, um, what do they call you?"

"Detective Barton will do just fine, Sheriff Dawson."

"Does Salem PD usually send their detectives out as escorts?"

"I have a pilot's license.   Time is critical here."

"Ah.   Yeah.   Jethroe made that clear . . . about the time element, I mean."

Olivia waved toward Storey's side of the booth.   "Have a seat. This is Norman Storm."

Dawson gave Storey's hand a perfunctory shake, slid into the booth.

Storey guessed Dawson was mid-thirties, six-two or -three, would weigh in at about one-ninety.   He wondered if the curly reddish-brown hair trailing below his cap, his easy smile, and rugged Marlborough-man guise had played a part in his election to the sheriff's office.

Dawson took his eyes from Olivia for a second to flick a glance toward Storey, who now occupied the far side of the seat. He tilted his head toward Storey. "He's your suspect?"

"Material witness," said Olivia.

"Oh. Yeah. Jethroe did say that. I'm not used to white collar types. My scumbags tend to be grubbier."

"More down to earth . . . gritty reality?" Olivia wiped her mouth with her napkin.

Dawson nodded, removed his cap, pushed his fingers through his bushy locks. "You got it." He placed the cap on the seat beside him. "Yeah, my days are filled with common folk doing dumb things or dumb people doing dumb things." He put his elbows on the table, leaned toward Olivia, focused deep into her eyes. "Nothing earth-shaking, but we do have our moments."

"Oh, I'm sure you do, Sheriff."

Storey recognized the beginnings of her whimsical smile, the lift of an eyebrow.

"I could give you the tour. Wouldn't take long. I know you're on a short schedule, but . . . is there a chance you could work in a half-hour or so?" He cocked his head, grinned.

Olivia returned his smile. "Sorry, not today, Sheriff."

"Too bad. I understand, duty calls. . . . Well, how about you visit our little town again someday soon?"

"Perhaps," Olivia said, forked some potato, pushed it into her mouth.

Dawson let his gaze float down Olivia's form fitting outfit. "Nice sweater," he said.

Olivia stared at him for a moment, laid her fork on her plate. "Sheriff Dawson, are we set to get into the bank?"

"Yeah. And, it took some doin' on my part. He didn't like it, but I convinced Ernie Slothower—he's the bank manager—and his assistant, Janet, to meet us at the bank a few minutes before 7:30."

"I really appreciate that, Sheriff . . . and your escorting us. Jethroe said you could take us to the airport after?"

"My pleasure, little lady, my pleasure."

Storey saw Olivia's face cloud; took a bite of toast to disguise his grin.

8:30 AM Saturday
23 May 2009

Frowning, arms folded across his chest, jaw clamped tight, eyes squinted, thoughts churning, Sheriff Bill Dawson leaned against the side of his patrol car watching the Cessna lift from the runway and turn to the east. Something is screwy here, he mused. You said you had a pilot's license but your perp is flying the plane. Detective Olivia Barton of the Salem PD, you led me down the garden path with your gorgeous smile and big brown eyes—and I followed along like some testosterone-charged teenager.

He pushed upright, turned and kicked the right front tire. "Damn." He fumbled for his cell phone, punched in the number for dispatch, marched around to the driver's side. "Ah, Adeline . . . Dawson. I'm on my way in. Find the number for the chief of the Salem PD detectives. I want to talk to him the minute I walk through the door."

He replaced the phone in his shirt pocket, looked up at the plane, now a speck in the eastern sky. The sun flashed from its wings as if to taunt him. He lifted his hand toward it, his middle finger extended. "To gorgeous, brainy women," he muttered. "Go to hell."

Dawson entered the cruiser, sat staring through the windshield for a long moment, his thoughts flooded with his final image of Olivia smiling sweetly from the right seat of the plane as she pulled the door closed. Her parting words echoed in his mind. *"Thank you for the invitation, sheriff. Don't hold your breath."*

He hammered the steering wheel with both fists.

"Bitch."

He started the engine and activated the light bar. The tires spat a shower of gravel as he accelerated away.

*****

Dawson shrugged out of his jacket, hung it and his hat on the coat rack in his office. "Adeline, what's happening with Salem PD?"

"The detective captain, Bob Soames, is not in the office today."

"Shit." Dawson dropped into his chair. It gave out a squawk as he swiveled toward his desk. "God damn it, Adeline, I been askin' you to get someone to grease this stupid chair. What's so difficult about that?"

"Did you pick up that can of WD 40?"

"No. Do I have to do everything myself? Jesus!" He waved a hand. "All I want at the moment is to talk to someone in charge about a Salem PD detective."

"A name would help."

"Oh. Yeah. Okay. Detective Sergeant Olivia Barton."

"Thank you." Adeline scribbled on her pad, left the office.

Dawson interlaced his fingers behind his head, turned to put his feet on the desktop, grimaced when the chair squealed.

Damn you, Olivia Barton. Well, win some lose some. Plenty a others out there. At least she could've been honest with me . . . said she was married . . . or engaged . . . something. *All* I did was ask her out to dinner and she comes up with, *Don't hold your breath . . .* Well, what can you expect from those intellectual types?

He flinched when Adeline appeared in his doorway.

"Jesus. Don't creep up on me like that." He sat upright, elbows on the desktop. "What is it?" he said.

"Salem PD is on line two."

"Okay." He reached for the phone, looked up at her, brows raised. "You got a name?"

She looked at her pad. "Detective Sam Oliphant."

8:45 AM Saturday
23 May 2009

Jethroe looked across the motor home at Dale Holiday, the Special Agent in charge, commonly known as Doc. "Doc, we got a couple of hours before Nick's call to Nightmare. I should leave soon to meet him and Olivia at the airport."

"Everything's in place, Roe. Just hope nothing changes in Nightmare's camp."

Jethroe had worked with Dale Holiday on two similar rescues of corporate executive kidnappings, and had sought his counsel for several years. Holiday ran well-coordinated and efficient operations. Unlike many agents, he did not display the heavy-handed-know-it-all arrogance that most local police authorities encountered from the FBI, but sought the knowledge and experience of the locals and made them part of the action.

Jethroe had urged Holiday to include him as part of the team. Holiday was reluctant to expose a civilian to risk, but had eventually agreed, knowing that Roe's unique martial arts skills could be invaluable in the confined space of the motor home.

Jethroe moved to the front of the vehicle and through the curtain separating the driver's compartment from the living area that, in this extraordinary motor home, was crammed with desks and shelves accommodating satellite links, radios, electronic listening equipment, and computer screens monitoring remote cameras. It was the communication control center for the agents and plain-clothed police scattered throughout the campground disguised as fishermen or owners working on their rigs.

He cleaned the inside of the windshield with a Windex spray bottle and a towel as he surveyed the area. Seventy-five yards across the center of the campground he could see Nightmare's motor home. There were two outside lookouts: Fish Line sat on a camp chair in front of the motor home trying to unsnarl a wad of fishing line; Tie Fly was twenty-five yards east with a fly-tying apparatus on a small bench in an unoccupied campsite.

Near the western end of the site, two agents wearing forest service garb were loading metal trashcans, each containing handfuls of rocks, onto a ranger service flatbed. Early on, Doc and Jethroe had had reservations about bringing Forest Service equipment and FBI personnel dressed as rangers into the non-hosted campground serviced by a single attendant, Nate Owens, who cleaned and made contact with the campers several times daily. It was obvious that Nightmare and his cohorts were neither experienced fishermen nor outdoorsmen, and were clueless how the camp operated. Their ignorance simplified the removal of the occupants of the half-dozen rigs that populated the camp and provided some flexibility to implement a rescue strategy.

In the trees, shrubs and grasses bordering the bare central part of the campground, Jethroe found, only because he knew they were there, Doc's three snipers hidden under bushes and behind trees situated to cover Victor's fifth wheel and Nightmare's motor home with crossfire. He marveled that the men could keep their positions, unmoving, for hours.

The plan to liberate Victor and Emily was simple, but Jethroe was worried. He'd played more than a few scenarios in his head trying to visualize where the attack could go awry. Precise timing of several agents' and supporting sheriff, police, and forest service actions was crucial to success.

To initiate the operation, two female agents in fly fisherman vests and hats with flies stuck into the wide brims and carrying fly rods would approach the lookouts and engage them in conversation. Simultaneously the service truck would approach and "accidentally" dump its load of trashcans in front of Nightmare's RV. The ruckus of the rocks rattling inside the metal cans would hopefully divert

Victor and Emily's captors sufficiently to allow the teams sequestered in some brush immediately behind Nightmare's rig and Victor's fifth wheel to break through the doors of the RV's and subdue, or take out, the inside guards. The instant the doors flew open, Holiday, with the outside speakers at full volume, would say, "This is the FBI . . . "

The weak link, as Jethroe saw it, was the time required to break the locks—they had to assume the doors were locked—and pull the doors open. Any misstep or delay at that point could prove disastrous. Jethroe discussed his concerns with Holiday, and they decided to split the teams, and attack the driver's door of the motor home, and break through the large rear window of the fifth wheel concurrent with the assault on the primary entrance doors. Jethroe could not think of a better plan.

He slid through the curtain and back into the control center. "Doc, it's a little early, but I'm going to leave for the airport. Its possible Nick and Olivia are ahead of schedule. And it'll give me a chance to check on how Nate is coping with operating the roadblock."

"It appears Nightmare and his cohorts are hunkered down waiting for Storey's 11:00 call," said Holiday. "See you later."

8:30 AM Saturday
23 May 2009

Storey checked the windsock, advanced the throttle to fast idle and eased the Skyhawk onto the taxiway leading to runway 35 as Olivia ripped the tape from the cardboard box they had retrieved from the bank safety deposit. "Don't hold your breath?" he said, grinning. "I think I saw steam rising from the big hole you just ripped in Dawson's ego."

"Arrogant bastard. He deserved it, and more."

"He is sort of full of himself."

"Sort of? He'd win chauvinist of the decade . . . no contest."

"Perhaps. I wonder what he'll do now?"

Olivia shrugged. "You still carry that pocket knife? There's more tape than box. I'll have to cut this thing open."

Storey found the small penknife in his pants pocket, handed it to her. "I thought the gal at the bank . . ."

"Janet."

Yeah, Janet. I thought she recognized me. I think she wanted to ask some questions, but her boss squelched her."

"The one good thing Dawson's presence did. The manager didn't want to be involved in official police business. He just wanted us out of there. While you and Slothower were in the vault getting this box, she said your face was familiar."

"Really."

Olivia suppressed a smile. "I told her it happens all the time, especially with people that have a face as common as yours."

"Thanks."

Storey braked short of the runway, completed the engine run-up.. "Glenenden traffic, Skyhawk five three one niner Hotel ready for take-off, runway 35, departing southeast."

Storey leveled off at 7500 feet, set the propeller pitch, throttle, and mixture for cruise, and adjusted the heading to 135 degrees. He fine-tuned the trim for level flight.

"What have you found in Julia's *gift?*"

Olivia showed him a brown metal box that Storey guessed at just short of a foot in length, six inches wide and tall.

"It's got a four number combination lock."

"Julia had a system. I can probably open it."

Olivia set the box on the floor. "We can work that later." She held up a black composition book. "There're eight of these. They have names penned on the front cover—and dates. The top two are labeled Julia Williams."

"Julia's maiden name . . . uh, well, that's what she told me."

Olivia shuffled the books. "They're stacked chronologically. The next one is labeled, Cheri Davis, then Annie Johnson, um, then we have one for Diane Beaumont, and three for Maria Emelda Fortunato with subtitles . . . France, College, High School. All eight are handwritten journals. And this one." She held a small book decorated with yellow and pink flowers. "I'm guessing it's her childhood diary. Apparently, we have the life story of Maria Fortunato and all of her other identities up to the time she married you as Julia Williams."

"Nothing beyond that?"

"No."

"She obviously didn't stop there. You said the search of my house turned up more."

"Two."

"She was big-time serious about her journals. I never knew . . . or didn't pay attention."

"I can fly the plane if you want to skim through them."

"No, I've had enough for the moment. Hey, you told Dawson you have a pilot's license."

"Yeah. I finished my training and soloed about three years ago."

"Something else I didn't know about. We haven't been communicating much since we split."

Olivia placed the journals in her lap, crossed her hands over them, and looked out the side window. "Nick?"

"What?"

"I'm sorry I didn't take your calls."

For perhaps the thousandth time, Storey heard the echo of her mother's voice—*Nicholas, Olivia doesn't want to talk with you.* He pursed his lips. stared through the windshield, scanning the sky for other aircraft. His gut clenched as he remembered his response, *Then I'll come to her*, and the comeback, *I don't think that would be wise just now.* The old desolation overcame him for a moment. He sucked a deep breath, exhaled slowly.

"Your mother said—"

"I know what she said. I was there. I told her what to say."

"Why? What did I do to drive you away?" A question he had asked himself for years.

"Do you really want to know?"

Storey brushed her cheek with his fingers. "Liv, I've wanted to hear it from you for a long time."

"I thought . . ." She looked away, blinking. "Well, back then I felt that you were patronizing me, taking me for granted . . . as if I were a possession, not a partner. When you wouldn't talk . . ."

Just above them, a Bonanza flashed across their flight path. Storey straightened, his heart pounding, his head swiveling. He swept the area with his eyes, settled back in his seat. "That was too close."

He placed his hand over hers. "Liv, I have to concentrate on flying the airplane. Please, can we talk later?"

"Sure."

"Promise?"

"Promise. Do you want me to . . . I mean, should I try to find something in the journals?"

"All we need is something that might help us free Mom and Dad. You'd do a much better job than I can."

"Well, I'm obviously not going to read some 800 pages of handwritten ramblings in the next half-hour. If these journals contain information worth killing for, where do you think I should start?"

"The big change in Julia's . . . Maria's life probably happened when she started the alias business."

"So if I concentrate on the latter parts of Maria's diaries and the beginning of the one following . . ." Olivia sorted through the books. "The Diane diaries—"

"You might find the key to crack this puzzle."

"Nick, when this is over, and your parents are safe, you should write a book about this. The plot is laid out. With a little embellishment you've got a best seller, The Diary of—"

"Liv, just read the damn journals."

*****

Storey throttled back, began their descent to Crescent Lake airport. "Crescent Lake Traffic, Skyhawk five three one niner Hotel, ten northwest, for landing."

Olivia closed the diary, wrote notes in her logbook. "I think I found what we need. I know why Maria bailed out of her life and became someone else."

"We got a crosswind. About 15 miles per hour."

"This plane can handle that."

"Sure. But in these mountains I'm betting on big gusts."

"Just keep your speed up."

"I'll do that, but the runway is only 30 feet wide."

Olivia removed binoculars from the glove box. "I'll look for the windsock. What's the traffic pattern?"

"Left. The flight guide shows the sock on the southeast end of the runway."

"Got it. You're right. Definitely a cross wind. Strong. I see an SUV in the tie-down area."

"I hope it's Roe or one of his guys." Storey touched the mike button. "Crescent Lake traffic, Skyhawk niner hotel downwind for three one, full stop." He adjusted the prop to full pitch, added carburetor heat, engaged partial flaps, throttled the speed back to 80, began his descent abreast the runway threshold, turned 90 degrees at the crosswind leg, made another 90 to line up with the runway, cranked in full flaps. He touched the mike button. "Crescent Lake traffic, Skyhawk niner hotel on final, three one." He banked left into the wind to align his flight path with the runway, started his dance on the rudder pedals to keep the nose of the plane pointed down the centerline.

"Aren't you a little above the glide path?"

"Yeah. In this wind I want all the margin I can get. I'd rather drop it in at the last minute than have the wind die and put us in the trees."

"I'll keep my fingers crossed."

At 50 feet above the asphalt the Skyhawk jumped left the width of the runway, and began to sink. Storey eased the throttle open, pushed the fuel mixture to full rich, and announced, "Crescent Lake, Skyhawk niner hotel, go around, three one."

"That was exciting," said Olivia.

Storey let the speed build, pulled the plane up, climbed to pattern altitude, entered the downwind leg again.

"We're burning time," he said. "We're marginal to get to the campground before I need to call Nightmare."

"Nick, can't you call from the airport, or the SUV."

"Perhaps. Jethroe's signal from the campground was ratty. It could be worse here closer to the mountains. We've got to get on the ground this time around or my call could be late."

Storey repeated his landing procedure and lined up on the runway again. "Let's hope the Wind Gods smile on us this time," he said, pointed the nose of the Skyhawk down the centerline. The plane crossed over the trees, dropped toward the ground, but veered left again at 50 feet above the runway. "Crescent Lake, Skyhawk niner hotel, go around three one."

"Damn. Now, my Nightmare call will be late." He pushed the plane to pattern altitude.

"Essentially, that was a duplicate of your first try," said Olivia. "The wind pattern must be fairly steady. I think when we drop below the treetops, the crosswind drops off in the lee of the trees and we slide hard left before you can react."

"You're probably right. I was busy trying to keep it lined up on the centerline." Storey banked into the downwind leg once more. "Maybe the third time is magic."

"If the wind is consistent, you need to do something different."

"You mean if I keep doing the same thing I shouldn't expect different results? Some wise guy said that a long time ago." Storey dropped flaps, began his descent routine. "I think I'll go in a tad faster."

"Why not line up to the right of the runway and—?"

"And let the wind, or sudden lack thereof, drift us back to centerline? It's worth a try. I still have the go-around option. I hope Nightmare doesn't do something nasty when my call is overdue."

"What option do we have?"

"When you're right, you're right. Here we go."

He aimed the plane thirty feet to the right of the runway edge. The Skyhawk descended below tree level, dropped and slid left. Storey fought to stay aligned with the center stripe. He eased off on the flaps, the left wheel bounced once three feet from the left of the runway. He cut power, let the right wheel settle in, his feet doing a salsa with the rudder to keep the plane pointed down the runway.

As the plane slowed, Olivia said, "Can I breathe now?"

10:20AM Saturday
23 May 2009

Storey taxied to the parking area, spun the plane around, and shut the engine down. "Well, that was fun," he said. They removed their headsets.

Jethroe ducked under the wing, opened the door for Olivia. "I was beginning to wonder if you were going to make it."

"Only two go-arounds. I thought Nick did a fantastic job. I wouldn't have made it."

"We've lost too much time," Storey said. "By the time we get to the campground, I'll be late contacting Nightmare."

"Nightmare—the name struck a chord, it's the official name of the operation."

"Well, it fits."

Jethroe looked at Storey. "What happened to your mustache?"

"Long story. Later. We have to tell you what we found in Julia's journals. . . . Liv read them. She'll fill us in on the way. Anything new? Mom and Dad okay?"

"All quiet on the eastern front," Jethroe said.

"How about Donna and Eric?"

"I talked with John and Ng before I left the camp. They're snug in the Newport condo. Mike is there too."

"Our Mike Swanson?"

"The very same. The boys play with their remote controlled cars while Mike and Donna sit on the couch, hold hands, talk, and look at each other like lovesick cows."

"You're kidding me."

"Hardly. I could almost see Big John's smile as he told me."

"It's about time. They've been circling each other like a pair of cats."

Jethroe nodded. "Let's get this baby tied down."

In the SUV Jethroe started the engine, accelerated toward the airport exit, wheels spinning. He glanced at Olivia. "Oliphant called me. He knows you're with Nick."

Olivia and Storey locked eyes. "Dawson," they said in unison.

"Right. He called, too."

"You should have warned us about your oversexed friend."

"Would it have made a difference?"

Olivia chuckled. "Probably not."

"What did Oliphant have to say?" Storey asked.

"I didn't talk to them. I let them go to voice mail. Dawson was hot. Said I set him up, which I did. Oliphant wanted to know where you were. There's a warrant out for you, Nick."

"We know. I called the station," Olivia said.

"He implied he could get a warrant for you," he pointed at Olivia, "for aiding and abetting a fugitive."

"I expected he'd do something like that. Oliphant may know I'm with Nick, but he doesn't know where we are. We'll deal with him after we rescue Emily and Victor."

"Tell us about Julia's diaries. And, what's in the box?"

"Don't know.   It's locked. Nick thinks he can work the combination."

"It'll take me a while to decipher Julia's code," Storey said from the back seat. He pulled a small notepad and pen from his shirt pocket.   "She had a system to assign numbers to all of her combination locks. I'll work at it while Olivia tells us about Julia's past. How long before we get to the campground?"

"About twenty minutes."

Storey glanced at his watch. "That puts us past 11:00. I said I'd call at eleven."

Jethroe looked at Nick's image in the rear view mirror. "I'm thinking it might be a good thing to let this Nightmare joker stew for a few minutes,"

"Let's hope so. Maybe I should call from the car. Can I get a signal?" Storey opened his cell phone.

"Pure luck if you do. It's better at the site, but still on the fringe. Also, my FBI friends can give us a status update before you dial."

Storey returned the phone to his pocket. "You're right. Talk to us, Liv."

"Okay." Olivia thumbed through her notebook. "I made some sketchy notes . . . memory joggers. I'll fill in details as I remember them.

"Julia's real name was Maria Emelda Fortunato. Her parents were Marco and Ariana Fortunato. They lived in a suburb of Newark, New Jersey. She went to Catholic schools through high school. After two years of college, she went to France to complete her studies and graduated with an art major. She spent two years in art school before her father called her home. She lived with a Larry Lawrence for most of those two years."

"I've seen paintings by a Larry Lawrence," said Jethroe.

"He's been to the house several times to look at Julia's paintings, or so he said." Storey remembered him as a lanky guy with delicate features, a dirty blonde ponytail and scruffy beard and usually wearing a threadbare denim jacket over tattered jeans and well-worn Nike running shoes. His edgy, overly polite demeanor suddenly made sense.

Olivia squinted at her notes. "I can barely read my writing. The plane was really bouncing around. . . . Her father, Marco, was accountant for Ernesto Lupo, commonly known as The Wolf."

"The Wolf?" said Jethroe.

"Yeah. English for Lupo . . . a predator."

"Sounds ominous."

"The diary says Marco was feeding information to the FBI that could convict Lupo of murder and take down his drug and protection rackets. Marco was afraid Lupo would harm Maria to stop him, so he brought his little girl home and he, the mother, and Maria went into the witness protection program."

"From an artist's carefree lifestyle to the confines of a protection program, I'd wager *Maria* wasn't happy with that," said Jethroe.

"She didn't make the transition."

"She jumped ship?"

"Do you want to play twenty questions or listen to the story?"

"Sorry. I'll shut up and drive."

"Good. Where was I? Oh . . . witness protection . . . the FBI had them all housed in a safe house, a residence in the outskirts of a village near Newark. The home had a garage that had been converted to sleeping quarters. A breezeway connected it to the house. One evening, Maria was napping in one of the garage bedrooms and Marco and Amelda were in the living room talking with two FBI agents when an explosion demolished the house and set it on fire.

"Later, she read in a newspaper that the explosion and blaze was caused by an accumulation of butane from a leaky pipe in the basement. The article implied that the gas leak was suspicious, perhaps arson. Maria believed The Wolf had arranged it."

"The Big Bad Wolf strikes again," said Jethroe. "What happened after the blow-up?"

"The garage was damaged but still standing. Maria was not injured. She grabbed her backpack and a briefcase her father had given her, and ran out a back door. She hid in a thick hedge at the back of the property."

"Her parents were killed?" Storey said.

"And the FBI agents. Her diary entries said the house was a ball of fire within seconds after she escaped."

Well, part of what she told me was true, Storey mused; she said her parents died in a fire. He looked up from working with the combination lock. "What was in the briefcase?"

"I'll get to that, *if* you guys will just listen. It's hard enough to read my notes without skipping back and forth.

"Okay. Her father had told her if something happened and she had to leave or run away, the briefcase was her lifeboat. She was to keep it with her always. She moved along the hedgerow, mingled with the crowd that gathered to watch the fire, and walked away. She hiked for an hour, found a gas station, locked herself in the restroom, and opened the case. There was a letter from her father, two complete sets of identification including social security card, birth certificate, driver's license, and passport. One set of papers was for Diane Beaumont, a Canadian from Quebec, the other for Annie Johnson from Miami, Florida. And—"

"And so began her journey into obscurity," Storey said. "And I stumbled into it."

Olivia stared at Storey for a moment. "As I was going to say, the briefcase had a false bottom hiding a hundred grand in hundred-dollar bills."

"Impressive," said Jethroe. "So . . . daddy Marco gave his little girl an option for a new life. It's an interesting tale, but I have yet to hear anything that might help Victor and Emily. Nothing Nightmare or *The Wolf* would be salivating after. More to the point, Maria and her AKA's have likely spent the money by now."

"Not quite," Storey said. He held up a small stack of bills bundled together with a rubber band. "There's more of these in this box. I'm guessing, fifty or sixty thousand bucks."

Jethroe whistled. "That's a sizeable sum, but from what Olivia has said about The Wolf, it would be pocket change for him, or his associates—probably not a motive for kidnapping."

Jethroe lowered his window and slowed for an orange-vested worker holding a stop sign. "Hi, Nate. Anything new?"

"Hi, Mr. Washington. Not much. We turned Chuck Rogers and his three kids away. They weren't happy. I told them to check in tomorrow. Maybe we would have the road cleared by then. Hector and Fernando, two old fishermen I've known for years, drove up; said they were going farther up the road to fish the upper lake, not to the campground. I radioed Holiday; he said I could let them through." He shrugged. "That's it." He leaned forward, looked inside the vehicle. "Oh. Hi, Nick. I wondered when you would show. Sorry about Victor and Emily. We're all workin' to get 'em outa there."

"Thanks." Storey pointed at Olivia. "Nate Owens . . . Olivia Barton."

Nate tipped his cap. "My pleasure."

"We're on a short schedule," said Jethroe. "We gotta go."

"Good luck, Mr. Washington. I'll call Vance, tell him he don't need to crank up his chain saw."

"And, tell Holiday we're on our way in."

"You got it."

Jethroe raised the window, accelerated away. "We set up this checkpoint to divert the good guys out of harm's way."

"How does Nate know the good guys from the bad?" said Olivia.

"Nate has managed the campground for years—it's a favorite place for lots of people. He knows them all, including the Storeys, Swanson, and me. Claims he can smell a real fisherman 100 yards away. We were fortunate he volunteered to be the front man for our roadblock."

"Something wrong with the road?" Storey asked.

"Around the next curve, we cut a fir tree, dropped it across the road. It's tricky, but you can drive around it. We put a guy there . . . Vance. He cranks up his chain saw if anyone shows."

"Who's Holiday?" Olivia said.

"My FBI buddy. He took over the operation at the campground."

"Liv, you need to finish. We're getting close to the site," Storey said. "What did Marco's letter say?"

"Four numbers, seven words, and a sketch: 'Food at Gina's cellar. Destroy this note.'"

Storey looked up from counting the money. "That's all? A sketch of what?"

"The drawing baffled her, but the note told her everything she needed to know. Her great grandparents had a cabin in the Catskills. The land is off any maintained roadway, and owned by a distant relative. Maria and her parents used to visit Granny Gina's old homestead for picnics and to hunt for relics.

"Long story short, the night of the fire, she found an old motel, paid cash for a room. The next day she bought some clothes, boots, dried food, and bottled water. She hiked and thumbed for two days to get to the property."

As they rounded a curve, Storey saw a fir tree lying across the road ahead blocking their progress. An orange-vested man was directing them to drive to the right and around the obstruction. The shoulder was rocky and sloped, but the SUV traversed it easily.

"I presume you had permission to chop that tree down," said Olivia.

Jethroe smiled. "It's better to ask for forgiveness than permission. In this case, it was certainly quicker. I presume Maria found her granny's land?"

"After a wrong turn or two. It had been ten years since she had been there. The cabin is long gone, but the fruit cellar they dug into the hillside is still there. She had to push her way through some vines and bushes to get to the entrance—a heavy oak door with rusty iron hardware. It was locked with a modern-day combo padlock."

"The numbers on the note?"

"Good guess, Roe," said Olivia. "Inside, there was another letter from her father, some dried food, a supply of water, sleeping bags, blankets and air mattresses."

"Marco built his own safe house?"

"Apparently. Considering the food, water, and sleeping gear, it's a reasonable assumption that he thought he might need a place to hide for a while."

"And the second letter?"

"It was a list of the evidence he intended to give to the FBI—letters, maps, accounting ledgers, photographs, VCR, and audio tapes. It took Maria a couple of days to realize the sketch from the first letter showed where her father had stashed the records."

"You're kidding me," said Jethroe. "Like a treasure map?"

"Yep. It even had an X to mark the spot. Marco had put it all in a box, wrapped it in plastic, and hid it in a hole he dug behind a rock in the back of the fruit cellar."

"She found it?"

"Yeah. And before you ask, I didn't find any detailed description of the evidence. Just the list and a statement that said it could convict Lupo of murder and take down his drug and protection rackets."

"How long did Maria/Julia stay in the cave?"

"About ten days, but I'm guessing. There's a blank period in the journals between the end of Maria's and the start of the Diane diary."

"What happened to the box of evidence?"

"I don't know. I didn't find anything that would point to it."

Jethroe sighed. "Nothing?"

"When she, now Diane, was in Quebec, she wrote that she had made the monthly call to L to tell him she was alive and well. I skimmed through several pages of her journal and found similar notes. She never said it directly, but it was obvious that if she didn't make contact with this L every month the evidence would go to the FBI."

"So, L has the evidence, or access to it . . . maybe it's still in the cave. No clues about L's identity?"

"I didn't find any. After a couple of months she simply wrote 'Call made' and stopped referring to L. I did find several entries that said, 'If I'm dead, Wolf is dead.' I'm guessing again, but it seemed she needed reassurance she was safe."

"Damn," said Jethroe. "We're back to square one. I still haven't heard anything that Nightmare and company would consider worthwhile. They're likely aware of everything you outlined and probably know what's in the evidence package. They just want to find it."

"Jethroe, I only skimmed about 50 pages of nearly 800."

"Whatever is in the other 750, we still have a leg up," Storey said.

"How's that?" said Olivia.

"Nightmare thinks Julia's package is, or leads to, the smoking gun."

"Yeah." Jethroe pounded the steering wheel. "We can still use the diaries for ransom."

11:05AM Saturday
23 May 2009

Jethroe slowed and stopped the SUV. "The campground is just around this curve. Our vehicle, the command center, is the only one next to the road. I'll park beside it. We can get out and go inside without being seen from Nightmare's rig. He's directly across the campground in a cream-colored Winnebago just to the right of Victor's fifth wheel." He glanced at Olivia and Storey in turn. "Ready?"

"Ready," said Storey.

"Go for it," said Olivia.

"No talking until we're inside." Jethroe moved ahead slowly. As they rounded the curve, Storey saw a man standing in the entry door of a motor home waving them toward him.

"That's Holiday," said Jethroe. "Looks like he wants us inside ASAP." He rolled alongside, stopped.

They left the SUV and quickly climbed the steps into the motor home.

"What's the rush?" said Jethroe.

"Just got a call from Nate," Holiday said. "Two oversize SUV's showed at the roadblock shortly after you left. There's two big guys in the front of each one and an old man in the back seat of one. Said they wanted to visit their cousins and join up for some fishing. Nate thought the only time any of them saw a fish, it was warm and they stuck a fork in it."

"You let them through?"

"Yeah. If they're part of this we can bag them all. We got the resources."

"I'm late with my phone call to Nightmare," Storey said.

Holiday extended his hand. "You have to be Nick Storey. "I'm Dale Holiday, call me Doc."

Storey stepped aside, placed his hand on Olivia's shoulder. "Doc, this is Olivia Barton, a Salem police detective and my friend."

"Jethroe has told me about you." He took her hand in his.

"Are we in trouble?" said Olivia.

Holiday chuckled. "Not yet." He sat on a swivel stool in front of a TV screen, placed a clip with microphone and earpiece over his head. "Jethroe, you're late."

"Yeah. Nick had trouble landing . . . nasty crosswinds."

Olivia studied the TV monitor. "How do you get such a clear picture?"

"Cameras hidden in the clearance lights along the top of our rig," said Holiday. "We got sound pickups with transmitters on the sides and under the Nightmare's motor home and the Storey fifth wheel. We creeped the place, stuck 'em on in the dark last night." He tapped his screen indicating the trash barrels. "Jethroe put a couple in the rubbish bins. We got good sound coverage.

"Everyone is in place for the rescue. Jethroe, you're off the assault team, Not enough time for you to get in position. Nick, we're ready to move in. We start the rescue shortly after you get Nightmare on the phone."

"What's the plan?"

"First," said Holiday, "we have to distract and neutralize the lookouts." He tapped his monitor. "Tie Fly and Fish Line."

"Doc, are you sure you can do this . . . without them doing who knows what to my Mom and Dad?"

"They don't know we're here. We have a good plan. Surprise is on our side. Should be over in a few seconds. Any distraction you can provide will help."

Storey looked at Jethroe.

"Nick, you know there's no guarantee. We think we've covered every scenario."

Storey turned to Olivia.

"Make the call." she said.

Storey opened his phone.. "Marginal signal."

"Use ours," said Holiday. "Dave . . . oh, Nick, Olivia . . . This is Dave, our electronic wizard."

A young man with brown curls and freckles gave them a two-finger salute, handed Storey a phone. "Here, use this one. I can record your conversation."

Storey looked at the instrument for a moment.

"Just punch the number and press enter."

Holiday closed his fingers over Storey's hand. "Sorry. I know you're anxious about being late with your call, but Nate's heads-up about the two vehicles is bothering me . . . um . . . If they're part of this and show up in the middle of our operation . . . well, it could get ugly. Hold off on your call for a bit. They should be here shortly."

"I go along with that," said Jethroe.

Storey stared at Jethroe, then Holiday. "I understand where you're coming from. You have the manpower, and a plan to carry out a rescue. But, you haven't talked with Nightmare. He's a real wild card . . . totally unpredictable." Storey waved his arm toward the RV's. "My parents are out there with a madman that gets his jollies by chopping fingers off. What'll he do next?"

"Nick," said Doc, adjusting his earpiece. "We haven't heard sound one from these guys in the last hour. I think it's safe to stall for—"

"I can't see how my talking with Nightmare can disrupt anything. You said I should distract him." Storey punched the keypad. "I'll distract the hell out of him . . . and, it might save Dad another body part." He activated the call, focused on the monitor.

Holiday sighed, motioned for Dave to route the audio to their earphones.

"That you, Storey?"

"Mr. Nightmare. What a pleasure."

"You're late. I was about to chop another joint off your old man. I'm thinkin' I should do it anyway, just to prove I'm serious."

"Hey, it was busy at the bank. Had to stand in line, sign a bunch of forms. I'm lucky I made it out of there this soon." Storey looked at Olivia, shrugged.

"You got the stuff?"

"I got it. Now what?

"What's in the package?"

"Don't know. Haven't opened it. I thought that's what you wanted."

"Storey, I don't trust you."

"Wow. Something we have in common. What do you want me to do with the package?"

"Where are you?"

"Lincoln City. Where are you?"

"Where in hell is Lincoln City?"

"On the ocean, southwest of Salem."

"How far from Salem?"

"Couple of hours. Same as yesterday."

"Storey, every time we talk you want more time."

"I didn't ask that. I asked what you wanted—"

"I know what you said. You think I'm fucking stupid. The drop-off is in Salem. If you're where you say you are, it's the same as asking for more time."

"Where in Salem?"

"Nice try, Storey. You go to Salem, stand at the corner of Liberty and Market with the package and call me. Maybe I'll tell you then. Two hours. One minute past and your pop loses a whole finger . . . maybe more. I'm fed up with your fucking games."

"You said I should pick five spots and—"

"You've got your head up your ass if you think I'm goin' to any place you . . . what the hell . . ."

The phone went silent. Dave waved his arms, pointed at his screen.

Storey looked at Holiday's monitor. He saw two large Suburbans, black and mud spattered, race across the campground and skid to a stop in front of Nightmare's motor home and the fifth wheel. Two large, muscle-bulked men stepped from each vehicle.

A fifth man, small, emaciated, with sparse steel-gray hair slid to the ground from the SUV parked in front of the motor home. Dragging his left leg and leaning on his cane with each step, he moved slowly toward the lookout with the tangle of fishing line. Fear etched Fish Lines' face as he stood to meet the diminutive figure.

"Storey?"

"I'm here. What's—"

"Call me back in twenty." The line went dead.

"He hung up," Storey said, gave the phone to Dave.

Holiday handed earphones to Storey and Olivia.

"Who is this guy, Doc?"

"It's Ernesto Lupo, commonly known as 'The Wolf.'"

"*The Wolf* . . . Oh shit." Storey leaned closer to the monitor, his brow furrowed.

Olivia sucked a breath, put a hand over her mouth. "Damn."

Jethroe adjusted his earpiece. "Fascinating."

"Doc, you've got to do something," Storey said. "This sonofabitch kills people for spitting on his sidewalk."

"I know, and we will."

Jethroe placed a hand on Storey's shoulder. "We need to think our way through this carefully before we jump in. Relax."

"Easy for you to say."

"Lupo's high on our wanted list," Holiday said. "We've been after him for years. Our kidnapping just jumped several levels in priority." He touched his microphone button. "Nightmare team. Hold your positions . . . hold your positions." He turned to the technician. "Dave, get on the satellite and call Special Agent Doug Martinez in Manassas. I need to talk with him ASAP." He swiveled his chair toward Storey. "Martinez is the agent in charge of the Lupo investigation."

Storey positioned himself to look over Holiday's shoulder at the monitor. He saw the Wolf stop three feet in front of Fish-Line and look up at him.

"Gavino, you Aunt Luigina, she not going to be happy."

Storey could see Gavino's knees buckle.

"Dino made me do it," he whined. "He said he'd hurt Luigina and her kids if I didn't help him."

The Wolf slapped the quaking man, who collapsed into his chair. "How many times I tell you. You got trouble, you . . ." Wolf punched Gavino's sternum with a knuckle, then slapped his own chest. "You call me." He pointed toward the group from the other car. Tie-Fly had joined the two men from the second SUV. They were smiling, and tapping fists as if it were a family reunion. "Like

Fredo. He loyal. He call me." Wolf tapped his chest with a thumb. "I come. We end this now, before it become greater tragedy."

Fredo and the two enforcers approached The Wolf and his pair of guards. Fredo and Wolf embraced. "You did good, Fredo."

"I'm sorry about Maria. Dino didn't call me till after his man in Salem heisted Storey's Thunderbird and run her over."

"Fredo. Already, you say that when you first call."

"Oh, yeah. There's been so much goin' on I—"

Wolf patted Fredo's arm, smiled. "You did good."

"Doc," said Jethroe, "those four big guys are carrying serious heat."

"Yeah. I see." Holiday keyed his mike. "Nightmare team. The four new guys are carrying. I don't want any nervous trigger fingers. I'll give the word. Affirm." One by one, the agents, sheriff, and police verified Holiday's message.

Wolf whacked Gavino's shoulder with his cane. "Get up. Put chair here." He tapped the ground behind him. "I want to sit." Gavino obeyed instantly. Wolf dropped into the canvas-draped seat, put both hands on his cane handle, looked up at the front of the large vehicle, and shouted, loud and shrill, "Dino, come out. Now."

No response came from the RV.

"Dino, I know you hear me. You not come; I send Danny and Rico in. I don't think you like that."

Two of the men stepped forward. The motor home door eased open and a stocky, dark-haired man stepped to the ground.

"Cover him," the Wolf barked, pointed.

Two long pistols appeared from under the jackets of the men and pointed at the man.

Holiday activated his mike. "Cool it. Their fight is not ours . . . yet."

"Dino, who inside with you?" Wolf growled.

"Dom."

"Dom . . . you use Dom?" Wolf pounded the ground with his cane and stood. "Dino, you disgusting." He stroked his small goatee with his free hand for a moment. "Dom, you can come out now," he said. A tall man, thin, with black hair cut close to his scalp ducked through the door and stepped to the ground. Wolf waved the man toward him, turned the chair to face away from Dino. "Come. Sit," he said. The man sat with his hands folded in his lap. Wolf put a hand on his shoulder. "You okay now, Dom."

He turned toward the now quaking Dino. "Put you Glock on ground . . . easy." Wolf leaned forward on his cane. "And you little pistol you strap to ankle."

Dino complied, moving slowly.

"Now knife."

Dino rolled his eyes, threw the stiletto down, stared at Wolf.

"So, that's Nightmare," Jethroe murmured.

"Yeah," Doc said. "Dino Bartalotti, The Wolf's nephew, his sister's kid. This is beginning to make some sense. Dave, any luck with Martinez?"

"He's out to lunch with a congressman. They're trying to locate him."

Holiday shook his head. "Congress. They seem to confound us wherever we go."

A yell from TheWolf pulled their attention back to the monitor.

"What in hell you do, Dino? You screw up whole thing. You put us all in jail, maybe worse."

Dino spread his hands wide. "Uncle Ernest, I'm trying to fix it so we don't have to worry about Maria's blackmail any more."

"You dumb as stump in field. Maria . . . not be threat if she alive. Now we all go down."

"Uncle, you would never try to fix it. I'm at least trying. I'm about to get my hands on the journals and tapes."

"No, nephew, I wrong. Stump smarter. It stay where it belong."

"You expect me to stay in my office, shuffling paper and money?"

"You got fine home on lake. Nice cars. Kids in good schools. Pretty wife. Sexy mistress—"

"How do you know about Gina?"

"Dino, you life open book. Shut up when I talk."

Dino crossed his arms over his chest, looked skyward.

"And don't be smart ass. You want Danny shoot ear off?"

Dino dropped his arms, looked at Wolf, his eyes wide as Danny raised his weapon.

"Now. Listen. You got respect in community. Run legit car dealers enterprises. Make our money clean. Important. All this and you not happy? Dino, you not just dumb, you stupid."

"It's boring; I want to be where the action is."

"Dino, you think you flash you guns and body guards and act like some Capone gangsta gonna make you big man? It only bring bad trouble."

"Well, when you showed, I was on the phone with Nick Storey. We were settin' up a place to trade Maria's records for his papa and mama. He's gonna call back in about twenty—"

"All wrong, nephew."

"But, Maria's gone. No more threats. You're free. What's wrong with that?"

"We not free now. Maria, dead. Before, we free. You not listen."

"But—"

"Shut up," Wolf yelled as he shook his cane at Dino. "I not finish. I deal with Maria. We have agreement. She alive, safe; journals, tapes stay buried and I . . . we all safe. Old history. Now you fuck up agreement. All stuff go FBI. Everything shit."

"But, Ernesto, I'm going to get all—"

"Come . . . here," Wolf thundered, stabbed his cane into the ground,

Wringing his hands, Dino shuffled across the space separating them and stopped four feet from Wolf.

"Closer."

Dino closed the space to two feet. Wolf stabbed him in the solar plexus with the tip of his cane. Dino, fighting for breath, staggered back two steps.

"How many time I say you not start operation without ask first?" Wolf moved forward, jabbed Dino again. "And you involve innocents."

"Innocents?" gasped Dino.

Wolf punched again. "You not listen. Thief, gangster, shoot, kill each other. No big deal. Police write report, *yawn*. Hurt, kill someone outside—innocent—all hell break loose."

"But . . . Uncle," Dino wheezed. "You –"

"Dino, you plan kill Storey's mom and pop?

"Well, they can identify us. You whacked lots of guys."

"You head real dense, Dino. No innocents. Cardinal rule. Never, no innocents. Only competition or traitor like you."

"Me? Traitor? But Uncle," Dino whimpered. "I'm getting it all for you in two hours . . . when Storey gets back to Salem from the coast."

"Nicholas Storey smart guy. I bet he figure you plan to kill parents anyway. All you get is copy."

"Copy? No way. He knows his mom and pop in deep shit if he copies the stuff. I got that covered."

"Dino, what Storey has *is* copy."

"What!"

"Maria call it her personal back-up. Real stuff, account ledgers, videos, cassette tapes . . . somewhere nobody know, we never can find. She dead, it get sent to FBI. Good chance it there now. Stuff you after mean nothing. You open gate to hell, Dino."

"How was I to know?"

"Ask me." The Wolf tapped his cane on the ground, stared at Dino.

"Nick," said Olivia, "he knows Maria's package didn't have any cassettes or VCR's, and—"

"Yeah. We just lost our advantage. If he believes, and It's probably true, that the original records are, or will be, in the hands of the FBI—"

"Our stuff is worthless to him."

Storey nodded. They returned their attention to the TV.

The Wolf waved his arm at the nearby SUV. "Danny, Angelo. Find back road away from here. . . four, five mile. Estinguere il parassiti. Via. Now."

The two large men grabbed Dino under his armpits and pulled him toward the SUV.

"No! You can't kill me. I'm family. Your sister Sophia's bambino," Dino wailed between sobs. *"Please, Uncle Ernie . . . I'll fix it,"*

Holiday opened his mike. "Nightmare team. One of the SUV's will be leaving. Let it go." He turned toward the console. "Dave, get me Martin at outpost one."

"Yeah. Got him Doc. Comin' on line . . . now."

"Doc. What's up?"

"Marty, you don't need to hide in the trees anymore. Block all the access roads. Nobody gets in or out. There's a black Suburban coming your way. Three guys. One will be happy to see you; consider the other two, the big ones, armed and very dangerous. Stop and arrest them all."

"What charge?"

"Accessory to the murder of Julia Storey will do for now."

Jethroe placed a hand on Holiday's shoulder, pointed at the monitor screen. "Look."

Wolf had moved toward the SUV and waved for Danny to return. When they met, Wolf pulled Danny's lapel compelling the big man to bow his head. Wolf whispered a few words in his ear. Danny nodded, returned to his vehicle.

"Anybody hear that?" Holiday asked as the SUV left.

"Too muffled," said Dave.

Wolf limped over to the spot where Dino had dropped his gun. He picked it up and threw it toward the camp chair. The Glock plopped into the dirt beside the canvas seat. He retrieved the dagger and snub-nose revolver and dropped them into his outer jacket pocket.

"Fredo," he yelled.

"I'm here."

"Who in there?" Wolf waved his cane at the fifth-wheel trailer.

"Ah . . . Vito and Bart. They're guardin' the old broad."

"Get em out here."

"Somebody gotta' watch—"

"Fredo, where she gonna go?"

Fredo shrugged, walked toward the trailer and disappeared from view as he traversed the far side to the rear door.

"Sergio, Jack, cover."

The remaining two black-suited men drew their guns and leveled them at the hitch end of the fifth wheel.

"Nightmare team. Still not our fight," Holiday said.

"Wolf is gathering them together. Makes our job easier," said Jethroe.

"Yeah. And Victor is alone in the motor home," Holiday said. "Nightmare team. Move in on my command."

Two men came into view at the front of the Storey RV; one small, lanky, with blond hair and a pocked face; the other portly with bushy steel gray hair and a full beard. They stopped, jaws slack, when they saw the guns pointed at them.

Wolf waved his cane. "Over by chair. Drop guns there. Jack. Frisk both."

Wolf shuffled over to the two men and stood, his gaze flipping between them. "Vito, you unfaithful turncoat. No can trust any more." He struck the portly man on the side of his head with his cane. Vito groaned, placed both hands over his cheek. Blood flowed between his fingers.

Holiday opened his mike. "Team behind the Storey fifth wheel."

"Pete here."

"While they're distracted, get Mrs. Storey. Move her to your van."

"Consider it done, Doc."

"Confirm when she's safe," Holiday said.

Storey could not see them, but knew they could easily slip, unseen, along the rear far side of trailer and enter the door.

"Vito," Wolf shouted. "Down on ground. Face in dirt," He turned toward the small man, who had dropped down without being told. "Bartholomew, you question mark in my mind from beginning." Wolf flailed the back of the small figure several times, then stood leaning on his cane staring at the prostrate men for a few moments.

"We should make our move now," Holiday muttered, "but until we know Mrs. Storey is out of harm's way . . ."

Wolf hobbled toward the motor home. "Sergio, Jack. They move. Shoot. Dom, you stay in chair," Wolf said. "Sergio, watch over him. I need talk with Victor Storey." He opened the door, climbed the steps, and disappeared inside.

"Dave. Is the sound from their motor home still garbled?"

"Yeah. Sorry, Doc. I'm workin' on it."

Holiday paced for a moment. "Can you use a sound dish?"

"Have to be outside with an unobstructed view."

A voice from the team channel interrupted. "Doc. Pete. We've secured Mrs. Storey."

"Good show, Pete," said Holiday.

"That's a relief," said Jethroe. "A few seconds earlier would have been nice. Now we got Wolf inside with Victor."

Holiday nodded his assent, returned his attention to Dave. "So, we're deaf inside the motor home."

"Sad, but true, Doc. I've tried to clean up the circuit, but the pickup is defective or the attachment to the RV skin is bad."

Holiday activated his mike. "Nightmare team. Hold your positions. Situation in the motor home is unknown."

11:30 AM Saturday
23 May 2009

The moment the small man with the shriveled leg stepped out of the black van, Victor Storey had noticed a shift in Dino's demeanor. The arrogance and bravado evident in his smirk and the cock of his head melted. His face blanched; his hands trembled. Sweat dribbled down his forehead and cheeks as he sat on the gaucho bench and watched and listened through the partially open side window to the exchange between the diminutive Italian and the men outside. The scene was so bizarre, Victor wondered if it was a melodrama played out for his benefit, but Dino wasn't applauding.

When he first heard the little man's raspy voice he thought he saw a smile flick across the face of the man who had twice wielded the cleaver and lopped off parts of his finger. The man, the one they called Dom, his face a blank, had made no sound or showed any emotion since Victor first set eyes on him two days ago.

When the gravelly voice commanded Dino to come out, he stood, shuddered, and wiped his face with his shirt. After the strident declaration, *". . . I know you hear me . . . ,"* Dino sighed, lifted his shoulders, strode to the door, and exited the motor home.

When the man summoned him, Dom left.

Alone, Victor pulled at the rope securing his ankle to the central column of the dining area table. He knew that if he could lift the tabletop and supporting chrome tube from the floor socket he would be free. With only one hand useable, the leverage was wrong, causing the tube to jam. It would not disengage. He tried pushing up with his knees to no avail.

He slid under the table and tried to untie the knots securing the rope to his ankle. Again, with only one set of fingers functional, he was unsuccessful. If he could reach the kitchen utensil drawer—there must be a knife there. Too far.

He sat back in his seat, stretched his arms across the table. He was probably safer inside the motor home than outside with the new bunch of thugs. If he were to go up through the escape hatch over the bed in the rear they would see him . . . if he could lift himself with one good hand. Leaving through the front or rear door was not an option.

He was confident that Jethroe and the FBI were outside. He wondered why they were waiting to launch a rescue.

He had assumed from listening to one-sided phone conversations between Nicholas and Dino that Julia had been killed—set up by Dino. The exchange between the man and Dino confirmed his suspicion. The man had called her Maria. Why? What documents could she have that they considered so dangerous to them? What kind of person could command that his own nephew be killed?

Victor's heart jumped when he realized the man was climbing the stair to enter the motor home. He pushed back in his seat, stiffened his spine, and waited as the old man struggled up the steps.

Inside, the man squared his shoulders, rocked his head back and stared at the ceiling. He took a deep breath, held it for a moment, then exhaled slowly. He turned to face Victor.

Victor thought the man who stood leaning on his cane in the entry seemed relaxed, more composed, less intense than the angry dynamo he had been observing.

"Victor Storey, I am Ernesto Lupo. We need to talk." He hobbled toward Victor and pushed the side window closed with the tip of his cane. "A little privacy seems appropriate. If you would slide over, I'll sit opposite."

"My leg is tied to the table support."

Lupo bent down and examined Victor's bindings, shook his head. He pulled Dino's knife from his pocket and laid it on the table. "Cut yourself loose." He patted his shriveled leg. "I don't think I could reach."

Victor severed the ropes, moved to the end of the dinette, laid the knife on the tabletop, slid it toward Lupo and crossed his arms on the Formica top. He nodded toward the men outside. "I'm not going to try anything stupid with your army outside."

Wolf returned the dagger to his pocket. "You are a smart man, Victor. You live up to the reports I get . . . thoughtful, level-headed." His brow furrowed. "What happened to your hand?"

"Your idiot nephew, Dino, had Dom whack part of my finger off."

Lupo flinched. "Sorry. It seems Dino always goes for the melodramatic."

"Well, your man Dom was quite efficient."

"Don't blame Dom." Lupo tapped his temple. "Dom is scrambled. Car accident killed my sister, Louisa, and left her son without reason. I'll never let him visit Dino again."

"You just ordered those two bruisers to kill him."

"Danny and Sergio will scare him until he loses control of his body functions; maybe break a thumb and a couple of fingers. Kill? No."

"Ah . . . that's what you whispered in Danny's ear before he left?"

"Umm."

"I thought assassination was a common thing you . . . ah, your society, did."

Lupo laughed. "Don't believe everything you see in the movies or read in the newspapers. Like it or not, he's family. However, Dino's career as a businessman is over. Want a job, Victor? You're good at organizing and managing enterprises."

"I'm not your type, Mr. Lupo."

"Ernesto."

"I'm not your type, Ernesto."

Lupo chuckled. "You're right, of course, Victor."

Victor cocked his head, his brow furrowed. "What happened to the loud-mouth Godfather with limited verbal skills that I saw outside?"

Lupo waved a hand toward the exterior. "I give them what they expect. Badass gangster. Lots of yelling and intimidation. Control them with fear. You, Victor, are educated, a businessman, a respected member of society.   I don't think you are easily manipulated.   A reasonable discussion with, as you put it, a Godfather type, is not probable."

"Why would I want to have a reasonable discussion with you? You kidnapped my wife and me."

"Well, Victor, technically I did not. I was not involved in any way."

Victor rolled his eyes. "You are now. My son's lawyer friend would call you an accessory after the fact or something. Lawyers always find some connection."

"You refer to Mike Swanson. A fine man and attorney."

"You seem to know a lot about my family and friends."

"Self preservation, Victor, self preservation. I had no choice. It was necessary that I be up to date concerning your Julia's life and associations."

Victor leaned back, crossed his arms over his chest, cradling his damaged hand.

Lupo pointed. "Does it hurt?"

"A bit."

"Nice bandage.   Dom's work, I suppose.   Dino couldn't, wouldn't bother."

"Dino was worried I would bleed on the upholstery. His words were, 'Dom, take care of it.' Lucky there was a first aid kit in the cupboard."

Lupo sighed, shrugged.

Victor stared at Lupo wondering which personality was real, the madcap mobster he had observed earlier, or the thoughtful, apparently reasonable man who sat across the table from him now, or, were they both characters portrayed by a master manipulator? I'll probably never know, he thought. "Ernesto," he said, "considering the resources you must have expended gathering information about my family, the documents, or whatever Julia had, must be a major threat to you."

"Devastating. But that's not really your concern."

Victor raised his bandaged hand. "Oh. Really?" His voice quavered as he attempted to suppress his rage. "And killing my daughter-in-law . . . and abducting Emily and me. Plus, my son is involved, and Jethroe and Mike. I wonder about their safety, and if my daughter and grandsons are in danger." His voice rose a few decibels. "Ernesto . . . I have multiple concerns."

Lupo placed his hands on the tabletop, interlaced his fingers and diverted his gaze. He pursed his lips and after a long moment said, "Victor, have I done anything but remove you, and your wife, from a dangerous situation? Think carefully now . . . as if you were testifying in court."

"Well . . . no."

Lupo refocused on Victor. "Have I, or any of my men, threatened you?"

"You mean Angelo or Jack or Danny or . . . um—"

"Sergio."

"Yeah, Sergio. They're big, scary guys, but, no, you . . . they, have not."

"Then, if I were to tell you to get in your vehicle and leave, your testimony would indicate I came to rescue you?"

"I suppose, but I'm not a lawyer. Is that your intention?"

Lupo slid back in his seat, trailed an arm across the top of the cushions. "It's a hypothetical for now, but we must decide what to do with you."

"We?"

"You and me, Victor."

Victors brows lifted. "Ernesto, you're implying that I can suggest a solution?"

"I am."

"Then my input is simple. We follow your suggestion. I walk out of here, hook my Explorer to my trailer, and my wife and I leave."

"Okay, but there's a condition."

"Why did I expect you to say that?"

Lupo smiled. "Victor, I need an hour before you contact the authorities . . . a small favor for rescuing you from a likely fatal accident."

Victor straightened, looked at his companion. Could he believe him? "Ernesto," he said. "I could do that, but it's too late. Wouldn't work now."

"Why not?"

"Haven't you wondered why the campsites are vacant? That there are no curious bystanders wondering what the shouting and gun waving is about?"

"The thought crossed my mind, but I haven't worried about it. Sergio has DEA ID to flash as if it were an arrest of drug dealers or whatever. It's worked before."

"Ernesto, Nate Owens has operated this campground, by himself, for years. He makes rounds of the sites three or four times a day with his old Ford truck to pick up trash and offer assistance. The same people come here every year. They're family to him. Except for an occasional game warden, the Forest Service never sets foot here. In the last day and a half I've seen lots of Forest service Green, but no Nate."

Lupo's eyes widened and his jaw set as he listened to Victor's revelation. He moved across the aisle and sat in the seat next to the side window. "Why should I believe you? I don't see anything."

Victor smiled. "Exactly. Usually, the campground is full of wives gossiping or busy with crafts or card games, and kids playing. No one is in the tents or RVs. Yesterday, I saw Jethroe, in a green uniform, collecting garbage bags. Ernesto, they're out there."

Lupo absently tapped the carpet with his cane, his lips a thin line. He stared at Victor and sighed; his eyes lost focus, his shoulders slumped, his head drooped.

11:45 AM Saturday
23 May 2009

The chorus of "Take Me Out to the Ball Game" streamed from Victor's cell phone.

"That should be my son."

Lupo struggled to his feet, snatched the device from the tabletop and flipped it open. "Nicholas Storey. Finally we meet."

"Ah . . . who's this?"

Victor, hearing his son's voice from the speakerphone, rubbed his hand over his face and mouth to mask his reaction. He wondered if Lupo was aware the speaker was active. Perhaps he wants me to hear the conversation?

"Nicholas, I believe you know, but to preserve the niceties, I will introduce myself. I am Ernesto Lupo, aka, The Wolf, a label your FBI friends and my envious associates have burdened me with. Both are names you are familiar with if you have read your Julia's documents, which I am sure you have, as I would in your circumstances."

"Is my father there?"

"Victor and I just finished an interesting discussion. He is a good man, and quite clever. His coded message to you that exposed this location was quite ingenious."

Lupo extended his arm, holding the cell near Victor. "Say hello to your son."

"Nicholas, I'm fine. I—"

"You can chat later." Lupo returned the phone to his ear.

"Where's Nightmare?"

"You're referring to my nephew, Dino? At the moment, he is indisposed. Nightmare. I like that. Original. Describes him quite well."

"Nightmare, ah, Dino, is your nephew?"

"Nicholas, if we are going to be friends, we need to be honest with each other."

"Friends?"

"Yes. Friends talk. Have productive interaction."

"Mr. Lupo, I've done nothing but ask questions."

"Ernesto."

"Ernesto, I've done nothing but ask questions."

Lupo chuckled. "Like father, like son. Nicholas, we need to be *more* honest."

"Okay, Ernesto. Honestly, I'm trying to find a way to free my parents. I thought I had an arrangement with Nightm . . . uh, Dino, but now, I'm confused."

"Nicholas, you are not confused. We both know that when Victor hoodwinked Dino and told you he was at this campground, you called your friend, Jethroe, who rallied the FBI and anyone who would pay attention to him. They are here now and are probably listening to our conversation. Pardon the cliché, but it is time you put your cards on the table. You need to stop the act."

"If, for the moment and just for discussion, I accept your view of the situation, what benefit would I get?"

"Then, Nicholas, you would no longer have to be circumspect. We could speak directly to the issues."

"Such as?"

"We could chat about your Julia's documents, and what can be done to save your parents further distress."

"My first priority is to liberate my parents."

"Victor and I have a gentlemen's agreement about that, but the presence of the FBI and others, including your friend Jethroe and his associates, complicates its implementation."

"If that's true, there's not much, if anything, I can do about that."

"Nicholas, I thought we had an agreement concerning honesty."

"Meaning . . .?"

"Dino was convinced you were somewhere near Salem, but, as you have probably confirmed, he is easily duped, his reasoning often muddled. I believe he is wrong. I believe you are here. Where else would you be but near your family? I'm looking across the campground at a vehicle resembling a motor home, but the darkened windows and an extra antenna or two contradicts that assumption. My thinking places you inside along with your friend Jethroe, and likely some federal agents. Also, I'm sure a few police of one form or another are strategically placed outside."

"Obviously you have evaluated the situation as you see it. Do you have a proposal?"

"Contrary to your assertions, I believe you have a major influence on their plans. I'm sure, since Victor and Emily are your parents, the agent in charge will consider that and consult you before embarking on a course of action. And, yes, I do have a proposition for you. I think we should consider a trade."

"A trade? If that were possible . . . Ernesto, what do you want?"

"You. You come and join me in Nightmare's . . . oh, I do love that name . . . you and I link up in Nightmare's motor home and Victor and your mother reunite in your, ah, control center. Your objective is satisfied—your parents are free and out of harm's way—and you and I can chat about Maria, um, your Julia. I'm sure you have many questions about her and her life that I might resolve. I'll talk with my associate, Sergio, and guarantee you all safe passage across the center of the campground. You think about it and call me back in five." He closed the cell phone.

"Ernesto," said Victor, "I won't go. I won't put my son in danger in exchange for my safety."

"That's very noble, but the decision is out of your hands. Consider your wife."

"Emily is safe. I saw two men rescue her just after you extracted your thugs from my trailer."

"Ah . . . good. One less innocent to fret over. You are going, Victor."

"Damn you."

"I've been damned for some time now." The Wolf slid the window open. "Sergio. Come."

The older of the bodyguards walked to the side of the motor home, leaned close.

"Sergio, I am going to tell you something and you must not react; you must remain calm."

"I'm a Sphinx."

"The campground is infested with FBI and police."

Sergio's eyes widened. He smoothed his gray handlebar mustache. "How many?"

"Too many. The vehicle directly across the campground is their control center . . . don't look now."

"Dino fucked up?"

"Big time." Lupo flicked a thumb toward the FBI van. "Nicholas Storey is in there. I've suggested a trade . . . Victor for him. I'm sure they will accept my offer. Tell Jack. I want them to cross the campground without interference."

The big man nodded.

"And . . . Sergio, Maria's package is, or will soon be, in FBI hands."

"Yeah. I figured."

"Considering our situation here, I think the time has come to implement our alternate plan, the one we have talked about for years."

Sergio rubbed the back of his neck. "SBC?"

"Yes."

What's SBC? Victor wondered. An alternate to what?

Sergio straightened his back, sighed. "It's that bad?"

"It is."

"No way out?"

"I can't think of one."

Sergio looked into Ernesto's eyes, compressed his lips. "We knew it would come to this."

The two men went silent. Victor scanned their faces for clues. They were planning something. Did they need Nicholas to implement it? Could he warn him?

"Sergio, we been together for, what . . . fifty years?"

"Fifty-two. Since we were kids on the streets."

"You are like a brother . . . family."

Sergio rubbed his craggy face. "Ernesto, you *are* my family."
After a long moment, he shrugged, placed his palm flat on the
window screen. "Arrivederci, Ernesto."

Lupo mirrored Sergio's hand from the inside with his.
"Arrivederci, my friend. We have to tell Dom to do what we do."

Sergio frowned, sucked a breath, released it slowly. "Yeah. That
makes sense. Best for him." He turned away. Head down, he
shuffled toward his associate.

11:55 AM Saturday
23 May 2009

Storey handed the phone to Dave. "Lupo hung up. He wants me to call back in five minutes."

"We know," said Holiday. "We were listening."

"What do you think of the exchange?"

"Well, it trashes our deception concerning your whereabouts."

"Which is probably irrelevant now," said Jethroe.

"It gets Victor out," said Holiday. "You're more capable of neutralizing Lupo than Victor is."

"If it comes to that," said Jethroe. "I think Lupo is stalling. He wants more time."

"I agree," said Olivia.

Holiday turned toward her. "More time? To what purpose?"

"To formulate an escape plan?"

"Or simply delay the inevitable," said Jethroe. "We're dealing with a big ego."

"We could wire Mr. Storey for sound," said Dave. "Lupo thinks we're already listening. Maybe he wouldn't check."

"Do it," Storey said.

"Unbutton your shirt." Dave opened a drawer, came up with a miniature microphone attached to a short wire. "I'll just tape this to your belly."

"You're sure about this?" said Holiday.

"No question," Storey pulled his shirt open, raised his tee.

"Look," said Holiday, pointing at his monitor. "He's talking with one of his men. Dave, I can't make out what they're saying."

"The motor home is dead. They're too far from the other mikes."

Storey buttoned his shirt. "It's time I called Lupo."

Dave gave him the phone. Storey keyed the number, pushed enter.

"Nicholas. You're right on schedule. I assume you agree to my proposal?"

"Ernesto, how do I know my father will be safe crossing the space between our vehicles . . . what do I call it? No man's land?"

"Relax, Nicholas. We are not at war. I have made my companions aware of the presence of law enforcement, and I have specifically told them to allow you and Victor to exchange positions without incident. They know that any untoward action on their part would undoubtedly be fatal. You and Victor are perfectly safe."

"How do you propose we do this?"

"Simple. You walk to the door of the Nightmare motor home, enter, and Victor will step out and walk to your vehicle. Victor tells me your mother has been moved to safety. That simplifies our exchange."

"You're right about the fatal part. Should something even *seem* to go wrong . . ."

"Ah. I doubt you have forgotten your father's safety, and, I'm sure you want to hear what I have to say concerning your Julia."

"I'm signing off now." Storey terminated the call, gave the phone to Dave. He looked at Holiday, patted his jacket pocket. "I have my cell phone. Call me if necessary." He opened the door, stepped out. Olivia followed him.

"Liv, what are you doing?"

She put her arms around his waist, her head on his chest. "Be sure you come back to me."

They embraced for a long moment. Storey pushed her to arms' length, hands on her shoulders. "Count on it, Liv."

As he approached Lupo's guards, the one with the handlebar mustache moved toward him, said, "Mr. Storey. I'm Sergio, his friend."

Storey did not break stride. He assumed Sergio's greeting was a not-so-veiled threat. "I'm here for my father, Sergio."

A few steps brought him to the door of the motor home. He pulled it open. Victor stood at the top of the entry stairs.

"Nicholas, this is not right. They're—"

Storey grabbed the front of his father's shirt, pulled him outside.

"Nicholas—"

"Dad, just go." He pushed him toward the FBI vehicle. "Sergio, my father is leaving."

Storey climbed the entry steps and shut the door. Lupo, in the dinette facing him, motioned to the opposing seat. "Nicholas. Welcome. Please join me."

Storey slid into the booth, placed his hands on the table, interlaced his fingers, his focus on Lupo's face. He tilted his head toward the outside. "I heard your exchange with Dino and your men when you arrived. You claim you had no part in Julia's murder or the kidnapping of my parents?"

"I do."

"That it was a plot by your nephew, Dino?"

"Correct."

"That you came here to stop him?"

"Yes. And I did."

"Why didn't you release my parents immediately?"

"Nicholas, our discussion is not going well. Victor and Emily are free, safe in the hands of the authorities and—"

"Now you have me."

Lupo slid back in his seat, frowned. "And, I am sure, as we speak, that your friend Jethroe is arranging for Victor to be taken to a doctor or emergency room to treat his injury. Your mother will most likely accompany him to provide sympathy and affection. All will be right in their world soon, as it will be in yours in time. If I had not intervened . . . well, it could have been ugly, possibly disastrous if you had launched a rescue attempt."

"Perhaps."

"I'm confident a mission to liberate your parents was considered."

Storey studied Lupo's face, wondering what the little man wanted from him. Probably best to be straight with him. "We had a rescue plan in motion when you drove up in your tanks."

"So my arrival was timed perfectly. Tanks? Oh, you refer to the large vans. My intention was to provide enough seating capacity to transport my nephew and his two-timing associates away from here and—"

"Exterminate them? Like Dino?"

Lupo sighed. "Nicholas, you must stop finishing my sentences. Extinguish them? No. Like Dino? No . . . Danny was not going to kill him. The point is moot. I'm confident that Dino, Danny, and Angelo have been detained by the authorities that surround us now."

"At the very least, Dino will have to answer to murder and kidnapping charges."

"Undoubtedly."

"Ernesto, what do you want from me?"

"I like you, Nicholas. No mincing words. You jump directly to the issue. First, I need to clarify your status here. Nicholas, you are free to go anytime you like. However, I hope you will stay long enough for us to chat. There are so many things we can talk about."

"Really?"

"Did you know that Maria . . . your Julia, called me nearly ever month since her parents' unfortunate death?"

Lupo. Storey wondered if the monthly phone calls to L described in the diaries were to Lupo. "I didn't know you existed until a few hours ago. Why would she want to talk with someone who killed her parents?"

"That has never been proven."

"My friend, Mike Swanson, says that fact and proof don't always live together."

"Let's not waste our time jousting with semantics and fine points of law."

"Okay." Storey crossed his arms over his chest, pushed back in his seat, thinking about the phone calls. Why would she contact Lupo regularly? "Did you talk about her father's package—the evidence he was prepared to give to the FBI?"

"Alleged evidence, Nicholas. There is no proof that such a package exists or ever existed—nothing except Maria's claim that she had it. If there was such a parcel, it was most likely consumed by the fire that killed her parents."

"So, you did talk about the *alleged* evidence?"

"Yes, particularly the first month, or two."

"She contacted you?"

"Yes. Maria disappeared after the fire. I suspected she survived or was not in the house when it blew. I presumed I would never hear from her, which was fine with me; I had no quarrel with her. Her first contact surprised me."

"That was when she told you about, um . . . *alleged* she had her father's bundle of evidence."

"Yes, and that it was in a safe place, that it would be sent to the FBI if something happened to her, or if she did not communicate with her gatekeeper every month."

"Gatekeeper?"

"That is the term she used. Someone, she claimed, who had access to the package and instructions as to its disposal."

"What did you do then?"

"Maria made a proposal, which I readily agreed to."

"An agreement? Enlighten me."

"Nicholas, do you play chess?"

"Occasionally."

"Then you are familiar with 'stalemate?'"

"Umm . . . Stalemate . . . if it's impossible for one of the players to move without placing his king in check. No one wins or loses. It's a draw."

"That describes her proposal quite adequately. Maria believed she would be in serious trouble if she released the so-called evidence, and, by her reasoning, so would I. She said if she did not make a monthly call to her gatekeeper, the package would appear on the FBI's doorstep. If the evidence remained hidden, both of us could live more or less unencumbered—a stalemate, but in this case we both won."

Storey took a moment to digest Lupo's assertion. His focus drifted outside to Sergio who was standing arms folded over his chest, staring back, telegraphing his implicit threat. Storey returned his concentration to Lupo. So far, Lupo's story aligned with the journals.   The L person in the diaries was probably not Lupo. Perhaps her gatekeeper?

"If you did not believe the evidence existed, why did you agree to Maria's conditions?"

"Maria was asking me to guarantee her safety and leave her free to pursue her life—if she did not release the information. I had no quarrel with her. If, as she claimed, an assortment of ledgers, video and audio tapes existed . . . or if there were none . . ." Lupo raised his hands, shrugged. "I had nothing to lose either way."

"Maria's fear leaps from the pages of her diaries. She was afraid for her life. Why?"

Lupo lifted a shoulder. "Perhaps a stressful situation coupled to a bundle of paranoia?"

Storey thought that was unlikely.   "The woman I knew was unflappable, very organized."

"And quite talented."

"Ernesto, her art was . . . is admired by many."

"Oh, I'm not thinking of her artistic skills, but her flair for deception. My Maria . . . your Julia was a con artist."

Storey's squinted as he absorbed Lupo's comment. "You said Maria called you regularly. What did you talk about?"

"Early on, she was obsessed with her safety. Her paranoia was palpable. She called me after—she claimed it was after she had assured her gatekeeper person that she was alive and well. I think she wanted to make certain I knew she still had the evidence. I tried to assure her that I intended her no harm; that our agreement was still in effect. I encouraged her to continue phoning me. It was a way I could verify she was okay."

"Did you try to find her?"

"Yes. I had her phone calls traced. Caller ID is a wonderful invention. She made most of her contacts from public phones in congested urban areas. Sometimes she would make her call from smaller communities or isolated locations. On those occasions, I contacted private investigators nearby and sent descriptions and photos of her."

"I'd wager they found nothing."

"I received a positive identification on three occasions and sent Sergio to find her, but she had left the area or was simply passing through. I concluded that she made her calls as she was leaving for a new location or, most probably, was in transit. We did establish that she was living in a small trailer and drove a large SUV, a Suburban."

Storey felt his pulse quicken, his jaw tighten. "She was living in a trailer and had an old Suburban when I met her."

"Maria was, by then, Julia. She had many aliases. We discussed you at length, particularly after she discovered she was pregnant with your child. It motivated her to propose extending our, ah, 'hold harmless agreement', to include you, your family and friends. I accepted of course."

"She confided in you?"

Lupo shifted in his seat and looked outside toward Sergio before he reengaged Storey's stare. "Yes, your Julia and I were quite chummy by then. I think I was the only contact with her old life. She was conflicted. She did not want to give up her nomadic lifestyle and did not want to raise a child on her own, but her Catholic upbringing stood in the way of her getting an abortion."

"So, I was a convenient way out? Her letters to me—ones that I discovered recently—had a different slant."

"Nicholas, you are the most innocent in this affair."

"Most naïve is a better fit."

"Don't be too hard on yourself. You are a decent, honest man. You are not conditioned to accommodate Maria's level of duplicity and amoral character."

"You are saying it was just a game to her." Storey's pulse pounded in his temples.

"Not entirely, but, yes. She was planning to leave you, go back with Lawrence."

"Larry Lawrence?"

"Yes. And, for the record, I urged her to divorce him before she married you."

Storey pushed upright, his palms on the edge of the tabletop. "She was married to him?"

"Yes, but under another name. Annie Johnson, I think." Lupo cocked his head, his brow furrowed. "You didn't know? I thought you would have discovered that when you read her journals."

"We only scanned a few pages."

Lupo raised his palms in a surrender gesture. "Nicholas, I swear by all that is sacred, I thought you knew. I'm sorry."

Storey realized he had been thinking of Maria and Julia as separate personalities. Maria was a character from the pages of the diaries. Julia was his wife, Eric's mother. She was real. Or was she? What part of their life together had been genuine?

He felt the adrenaline surge as his annoyance bloomed to anger, his heart hammering his ribs, his hands quivering. Why had he not probed deeper? Why had he not challenged her?

"Nicholas?"

Storey stood, paced in the small aisle, trying for calm. A few circuits and he felt some control return.

"Nicholas, you're angry."

Storey looked down at Lupo. "You think?"

"Deception by a loved one is difficult at best."

"Enough about Julia . . . Maria . . . Diane, Annie—whoever." Storey stopped pacing, sat. "Ernesto, what do you want from me?"

Lupo stared at Storey for a long moment. He placed his hands on the table, stared at them as if seeing them for the first time. "Nicholas, I need your assistance to get away from here. I have never asked for help before. I'm not sure how to proceed." He raised his gaze, looked at Storey.

"Why should I help?"

"I came here to rescue your parents from a very dangerous situation. I did that. That has to be worth some consideration. I had a tacit agreement with Victor that would have worked if you and your friends had not been here."

"I'm not sure I have any sway over your situation."

"I ask only that you try." Lupo's voice was muted.

Storey fixated on him, pulled his cell from his jacket pocket, punched a number. "Doc, Ernesto wants to talk with you."

"We just heard back from Manassas."

"Your friend, Martinez?"

Lupo twitched, slumped.

"Yeah. He's handling the Lupo investigation."

"I remember."

"He's received a map and instructions showing how to recover Maria's father's evidence. He's on his way to get it."

"That was fast."

"It was faxed directly to his office. The stuff is hidden in an old fruit cellar somewhere up in the Catskills."

"Wow." Just like the diaries said.

Lupo looked up at Storey. "The evidence?"

Storey drew a deep breath, nodded.

"Let me talk." Lupo held out his hand.

"Doc, here's Ernesto." Storey gave the phone to Lupo.

"Ernesto Lupo here. Give me a moment." Lupo held the instrument against his chest. He waved his free hand toward the door. "Go, Nicholas."

"But—"

"Nicholas. Just go. Go back to your associates. Thank you for trying."

"Ernesto, I—"

"Damn it, Nicholas, get out of here. Your friends are waiting."

"Okay." Storey lingered for a few seconds. "Thank you, Ernesto."

Lupo shrugged.

Storey turned and left the motor home. He shut the door behind him, looked at Sergio. "Ernesto kicked me out."

Sergio nodded. "I heard." He waved for Storey to cross the campground.

"Have a nice day," Storey said.

Sergio did not respond.

Storey walked slowly across the open space to the control center. Before he rounded the corner of the vehicle, he stopped and looked back. He felt a strange connection with the three men, Sergio, Jack, and Fredo, who stood watching him: He owed them, and Ernesto, for saving his parents from an almost certain death. He knew their incentives were not altruistic; that their actions were self-serving. But, each of them, in their own fashion, had displayed a bit of humanity. He raised his arm, extended a palm toward them. Sergio returned the gesture.

The man they called Dom sat in the canvas chair, unmoving, staring at the FBI vehicle—a park bench statue. Storey wondered if he was studying them, or if he was even aware of the events surrounding him. Dino's three co-conspirators lay face down on the ground, their hands behind their heads.

Storey turned, walked toward Olivia standing by the control center entry. They embraced. He wiped a tear from her eye. "Liv, it's over."

12:30 PM Saturday
23 May 2009

Storey embraced his mother and father, one in each arm, his eyes wet. "Dad, you should be in an emergency room."

"When I know you're safe," Victor patted his son's arm, raised his bandaged hand. "I'm fine. Holiday had one of his agents give me a new bandage."

"Mom," Storey said. "Can't you—"

"Nicholas, you know how he is. Once he makes up his mind . . ."

Storey hugged her again. "Mom, I'm so glad you're okay. Did they hurt you, or do anything . . ."

"Nicholas," said Emily, "stop worrying. Dino terrified me, but Vito and Bart treated me like I was their mother. I heard them talking when they thought I was napping. They were going to call The Wolf; said he would stop Dino. Maybe they're crooks, but they were nice to me."

Storey smiled, patted her cheek. He wondered if she understood Dino planned to kill them. "Mom, you can find pearls in a pigsty."

Emily touched Storey's cheek, ran a thumb over his upper lip. "Nicholas, what happened to your mustache?"

"I had to shave it off."

"Oh my. You looked so dignified."

"Nick," said Doc, "I have to interrupt. You need to move to the front of the bus. We need space to work the equipment in the back. Actually, I'd prefer you all got out and away from here . . . we've got to corral these guys now."

Holiday watched the group sidle toward the driver's compartment, then said, "At least, get down on the floor."

"After all this." Victor held up his bandaged hand. "I'm gonna watch. Ringside seat."

Holiday sighed.

Through the side window, they focused on Dino's motor home and the men outside. Jethroe sidestepped, held out an ear bud for Storey. He and Olivia exchanged spaces.

"Doc has made a deal with Lupo," said Jethroe, "Jack, Fredo, and the guys spread-eagle on the ground will walk over and surrender to the marshals at the north end of the campground. Lupo and Sergio will collect Dom and follow later. Lupo convinced Doc that Dom would respond to him and Sergio, but would likely go ballistic if a uniform approached him, particularly if handcuffs were involved."

"Doc trusts them?" Storey said as he adjusted his earpiece.

"The Sheriff's SWAT team has set up crossfire with automatic weapons. Any monkey business would be suicide."

Holiday activated the control center's exterior speakers. "This is the FBI. You are surrounded. Don't move."

Fredo's chin dropped, his eyes bugged. Trembling, he raised his hands. The men on the ground pressed their heads and elbows tighter into the dirt.

"Each of you has at least two automatic rifles dedicated to your demise. Drop your weapons and kick them away."

Sergio and Jack, with thumb and forefinger, pulled pistols from their shoulder holsters, let them fall, and kicked them aside.

Holiday's voice boomed again. "Good. Now, Vito, Bart and Gavino, stand up, hands behind your head."

The men complied.

"Okay. One at a time, walk toward the officers to your left. Gavino, you first. Good. Now Vito. Bart. Fredo, you're next." Holiday paused until the deputies had handcuffed them all. "Okay, Jack. Your turn. Put your hands behind your head."

"Doc's taking no chances with the big guy," Jethroe whispered.

Holiday waited until Jack was escorted away. "Okay, Ernesto. You can come out now."

The motor home door opened and Lupo stepped out, leaning on his cane.

"Weapons on the ground, Ernesto."

Lupo shrugged, reached into his jacket pocket with his free hand, dumped his firearm and knife, shuffled toward Dom. He stood in front of him and dropped to one knee, his back toward the control center. He turned to Sergio, motioned him to help. Sergio knelt, one hand on Dom's knee. Both men talked softly to the man. After a long moment, Dom smiled, nodded. Lupo and Sergio leaned closer and patted Dom's shoulders.

Lupo struggled to stand upright. Sergio rose, towering over Lupo, obscuring Storey's view of Dom for a brief moment.

Sergio and Lupo whipped around, each firing a handgun toward the control center vehicle.

The SWAT team's return fire was immediate.

Lupo, forced backward by the impact, fell like a bag of laundry.

Sergio put a hand to his chest. His knees folded. He toppled forward, stiff as a tree.

Dom leaped from his chair. He pointed a pistol toward the control center, fired.

Storey flinched, brought his arm up to shield his face as the tempered glass exploded. The window gone, the nearly simultaneous rattle of automatic weapons was earsplitting. Storey saw Dom's arms flail, his weapon fly up and out of his hand as he folded sideways.

The Center was quiet. The few seconds of silence played out for Storey in ultraslow motion. He saw the SWAT team, weapons ready, moving toward the three bodies, prodding them, checking for pulse, lowering their weapons. Roe's "Is everyone okay?" was like a tape on a too slow setting. Storey studied the nuggets of glass that covered the table and floor—the remains of the window. He turned toward Olivia. "He shot the win . . ." She looked at him, her eyes wide, her jaw slack. Her knees buckled. Storey grabbed her. "Liv, what . . .?" He felt something warm on his hand. He looked at it. "Oh God! Liv's been shot."

3:30 PM Saturday
23 May 2009

The surgery waiting room of the Bend, Oregon, trauma center was spartan, not well lighted. Storey paced. Victor and Emily sat on a couch, Emily absently turning the pages of a *People* magazine. Victor, newly bandaged left hand cradled in the palm of his right, stared at the floor. Jethroe straddled the back of a chair.

Storey looked at his watch, did not stop moving. "It's been over an hour."

"Sixty-seven minutes," said Jethroe.

"What's taking so long?"

"You want them to do their job right. Right?"

"Of course, but—"

"Any sooner, I'd worry."

"I keep thinking if you hadn't brought me the earpiece, we wouldn't have exchanged positions. I could've taken the bullet, not Liv."

Jethroe traced his old scar, ear to chin. "Nick, she'll be fine."

"If I hadn't asked her to—"

"It's not your fault, Nick."

"She didn't have to be there."

"She wanted to be there."

"But, what if I—"

"What if Holiday hadn't had the helicopter on standby?" Jethroe crossed his arms over his chest. "What if he hadn't insisted a medic be part of the team? What if the trauma center wasn't close by? What if—"

"Okay, okay. It just seems like a long time since they took her into surgery."

"Any sooner, I'd worry."

"You said that already."

Jethroe spread his hands, palm up, shrugged.

"Nicholas, you should call Olivia's mother again," Emily said.

"Mom, I've left two messages on Corine's answering machine. She's probably shopping or doing something with Sarah. Maybe they went to a movie. She'll call my cell when she comes home."

"Sometimes it's hours before I notice I have a message waiting."

"Mom . . . when we know something, I'll call again. Okay?"

He resumed pacing, his hands clasped behind his back. He hoped Corine would not call until he knew more. Without some positive information, he was afraid she would panic. How would he deal with that, and over the telephone? Would she blame him? The wound, although bleeding a lot, had not seemed critical, and was not near any major organs. Olivia would come through this. He rubbed his face with his hands. Yeah, well, Dr. Storey, you know that how? Think about something else.

Okay. Jethroe has arranged for a car to take Corine and Sarah to the Salem Airport and fly them to Bend—in his jet. Corine will be pleased. Sarah will be excited. Jethroe has booked a suite of rooms in a nearby hotel for them, and Mom and Dad, and me. I probably won't use the room much, but it is a place to crash for a couple of hours.

God, I'm blessed with good friends. Friends? They're family. Make a note. I need to be more appreciative. He'll probably karate chop me, but I'm going to give him a hug before he flies back to Salem with his jet.

The door opened. A small man in surgical scrubs entered. "Are you Olivia Barton's family?"

"As close as you can get just now," said Jethroe.

"I'm Dr. Mason, her surgeon."

"How is she?" Storey said.

"She's in recovery. We found the bullet. Small caliber. A .22, or a .25. I'm guessing. Lodged under the left clavicle. Scraped the bone, just missed the lung. Clean wound. Bled a bit. Transfusing her now. She'll be up and about in a couple of days, playing tennis in six weeks, I'd wager."

"Can we see her?" Storey said.

"She'll be in recovery, oh, an hour . . . two, tops. Then to intensive overnight. Best one, no more than two, go in for five or ten. She'll sleep most of the night. I'll see her in the AM. She'll be more alert then."

"I'm staying," said Storey. "Can I hang out in her room tonight?"

"Uh . . . Perhaps. The nurses are usually accommodating."

"She gets a private room tomorrow," said Jethroe.

Mason raised an eyebrow. "I don't know if a single is available. I'm only the surgeon. I don't make those decisions."

"Take me to the decision maker," Jethroe said.

The doctor opened the door. "Follow me."

*****

Storey and his mother followed the nurse into Olivia's ICU room.

"I'd like to stay," Storey said.

"There's a chair." She pointed. "The nurse may ask you to leave if they're doing a procedure. Call me if you need anything. Just ask for Carmella."

He looked at Olivia, the IV, the heart and blood pressure monitors, the catheter bag. She was pale, but breathing regularly, apparently asleep. He touched her hand.

Her eyes fluttered open.

"It's Nick," he said.

She blinked, her eyes drifted shut. "I love Nick," she murmured.

Tears streamed from Storey's eyes.

Emily patted his arm. "I'll be in the waiting room."

1:15 AM Tuesday
26 May 2009

Storey sat in a chair in Olivia's hospital room watching her dangling her feet over the side of the bed, adjusting her sling and gently rubbing her shoulder. "Does it hurt?"

"A bit."

"Did you take your pain pills?"

"They make me sleepy."

"What can I do?"

"Go get a breath of air?"

Storey chuckled. "I'm glad you're feeling better."

Jethroe walked into the room with Holiday in his wake. "Look who I found lost in the hall."

Storey jumped up. "Doc, good to see you." Holiday looked worn-down: three-day beard, bloodshot eyes, rumpled hair, shoulders slumped.

Holiday turned to Olivia. "Jethroe tells me you're going home."

"So they say. I'm ready. Just waiting for the paperwork."

"Oh. That I'm familiar with."

"Thanks for the roses."

"The least I could do. I feel responsible. I should have insisted that you . . . that all of you leave the bus before I started the round-up."

"As I remember," Storey said, "you wanted us to leave."

"Yeah, and you told us to drop to the floor." Olivia shrugged, winced, put a hand to her shoulder. "Don't beat yourself up. Leave the second-guessing for the bosses and chiefs who weren't there."

"You could've been killed."

"I wasn't."

Victor and Emily sauntered in, followed by Corine and a girl child, her strawberry blonde curls bouncing with each step. Storey eyes flicked from Corine to Olivia. He thought five years had enhanced the mother-daughter look-alike; a touch of make-up and a rinse to tint her gray streaked brown hair, and Corine, tall, wiry, in her mid-fifties, could pass for Olivia's twin. He remembered Corine as down-to-earth, sometimes curt, even abrasive, and occasionally detached, impersonal. She liked to be in charge.

He dropped his focus to the youngster. She resembled Olivia, except for the eye and hair color.

"Mom, this is Doc Holiday . . . Doc, my mother, Corine Barton. And, my daughter, Sarah."

"Doc?" said Corine. "Are you a doctor? I don't remember seeing you."

Holiday smiled. "No. I'm Dale. FBI. People have called me Doc for so long I've almost forgotten my real name.

"Sarah. Such pretty hair." Holiday folded his long legs, sat on his haunches in front of her. "I have a daughter. She's five. How old are you?"

Sarah held her grandmother's hand, leaned into her, looked at Olivia.

"It's okay, Sarah. Doc is our friend."

Sarah grinned. "My birthday is in July.' She held up a hand, fingers splayed. "I'll be five."

Holiday straightened, chuckled. "I thought you were much older."

Sarah shook her head vigorously. "Nope."

Olivia patted the bed next to her. Sarah tried to climb up. "Mommy, It's too high."

Corine lifted her.

"Grams says no hugs. Does it hurt where the bad man shot you?"

Olivia stroked Sarah's hair with her left hand. "It will be well soon."

Storey's breath caught as he watched Sarah. What was it about her?

"Doc," said Jethroe, "everyone is here. Tell us what you found on the video tapes of the, uh, shootout."

"Sarah, come with grandma. We'll get that fudge bar you wanted."

Sarah slid from the bed. "Okay, Mommy?"

"I'll join you," said Emily.

Storey couldn't pull his eyes from Sarah as she skipped from the room holding hands with the two women, her reddish blonde curls luminous in the sunlit background of the hallway windows. What was it about her?

"Okay, Doc. Elucidate," said Jethroe.

"Yeah. Well . . . Lupo didn't lose his gun when I told him to drop his weapons. We found a potato peeler with a big black handle, and Dino's stiletto. Apparently, he put the pistol in his inside jacket pocket. We couldn't tell for sure from the blow-up of the video, but it's the only thing that makes sense."

"Dom used Dino's small pistol to shoot Olivia?" said Jethroe.

"Yeah."

"Lucky it wasn't one of the bigger guns," Storey said.

"We're getting ahead of the story," said Holiday. "We magnified the video at the time Lupo and Sergio were talking to Dom."

"When they were on their knees with their backs toward us?" Storey said.

"Ah, yeah. Lupo and Sergio had pressed very close together to block our view, but the blow-up told us enough. Remember Lupo had Dino's cohorts throw their weapons toward the chair Dom was sitting on?"

"Yes," said Jethroe.

Storey nodded.

"Well, when Lupo turned it around for Dom to sit, it was placed directly over the guns. In the video, we could see Sergio lean forward slightly . . . twice. Evidently, that was when he picked up the Glocks, one for him and one for Lupo."

"And Lupo slipped Dino's pistol to Dom." said Jethroe. "They weren't soothing Dom, they were telling him to shoot at the bus. Did you amplify the sound and pick up anything?"

"We did, but not much. A word here and there . . . if you read between the lines there's enough to suggest that they set Dom up to get shot. Sergio's and Lupo's final words to each other were crystal."

Storey and Jethroe stared at Holiday. "Well?" they chorused.

"Arrivederci."

Storey's jaw dropped.

Jethroe nodded. "Makes sense," he said. "SBC."

"Yeah, they were shooting in the air, well over the top of the bus," said Holiday.

"SBC?" Victor said. "What's SBC?"

"Suicide by cop," said Olivia. "Not uncommon."

Victor stroked his face, his mouth agape. "They planned it," he whispered.

"Evidently," said Holiday. "Dom thought the attack was real, so he shot directly at us."

"Doc, I mean they planned it—Ernesto and Sergio. I heard them talking . . . when I was in the motor home with Ernesto. Ernesto said Maria's evidence was on the way to the FBI; that there was no way out; that it was time for their alternate plan—SBC. They included Dom, said it was best for him. I didn't understand, but now I get it. With both of them gone, there would be no one to care for him."

"You could be right," said Holiday.

"As you know, I spent some time with Dino and Dom," said Victor. "Dom responded to one-liners. I doubt he would have understood anything beyond 'shoot at them.'"

"There's nothing in the video or audio to disprove your theory," said Holiday.

"Have you come up with anything that would lead us to Dino's contact in Salem?" said Olivia.

"Dino has lawyered up. He's not talking, but Fredo, the guy who called Lupo, can't stop. He claims he was sitting outside the motor home and the window was open and he heard Dino making the arrangements. He said his connection was a guy called Cad, short for cadaver."

"You're kidding."

Holiday shrugged. "That's what he said—he didn't know his real name. We pushed him, but he stuck with it. He described the guy as tall, very thin, with gray skin and hair. He could be an albino. Fredo said he met him once a few years ago: says he operates out of Portland."

"Imported muscle?" said Jethroe.

Holiday shook his head. "No. Fredo says he's a private detective they'd used before. Claims Dino paid him to find Julia and follow her around for a while; that he wanted Cad to arrange a hit on Julia. Fredo claims that Cad found a guy that had worked with Nick who agreed to do the job."

"Fredo knows all this from listening to Dino?" said Olivia.

Holiday nodded.

"Did Fredo give you any names?"

"No. Except for Cad, Fredo swears he didn't hear any other names. We pushed him hard about that. I believe him."

"Fredo's testimony is hearsay and probably won't mean much in court, but it's a starting point," said Olivia. "We can sift through the PI license records for a thin guy with a pale complexion. You can bet the farm that Cad won't talk or have any records. We might get lucky and find something."

An aide entered pushing a wheelchair. "Ms. Barton. You're cleared to leave."

"I'm ready," said Olivia.

"There's a van out front," said Jethroe. "The jet is waiting at the airport. Victor's vehicle is on the way home. Nick, I can take over as co-pilot and have Randy fly your Skylark back to Salem and secure it in your hangar. I presume you want to accompany us in the jet with Olivia."

Storey nodded. "Thanks."

"Doc, It's been a pleasure to work with you again," said Jethroe. They shook hands. "Call me if you need anything."

"Ditto, said Holiday. "Olivia, I'm so relieved to see you up and about."

"I'll be fine."

"Okay," said Jethroe. "Let's get the hell outta here."

3:15 PM Tuesday
26 May 2009

The ramp of the Lear unfolded. Storey and Olivia met Jethroe as he exited the flight deck.

"Did you arrange a ride for me?" said Olivia.

Jethroe pointed to a black Mercedes rolling across the tarmac. "Just tell Karen where, and she'll take you. She'll wait and bring you to Nick's place after you've squashed the warrants for Nick's arrest."

"Do you have your laptop with you?" Storey said.

"Yeah. Why?"

"Do you have the security camera memory stick?"

"No, but I loaded it into the computer memory. You want to see the video again?"

"Yeah."

"Nick wants to review it before I leave for the precinct," said Olivia.

Jethroe shrugged. "Okay." He looked at Storey. "Something we missed?"

"Maybe."

Corine and Sarah made their way toward the exit, followed by Emily and Victor. Jethroe lifted Sarah into his arms. "Would you like to fly again sometime?" She lit up with a wide smile and hugged him. "Careful on the stairs," he said, lowered her to the floor.

Swanson and Donna exited the van. "Welcome back," Donna said, embraced her parents, patted Sarah's head. "Climb aboard. Hope you're all hungry. Jethroe's caterer is setting up a barbeque and a bunch of goodies for us at Nick's place."

"Hi, Sis," Storey said from the top of the ladder. "Where's Eric . . . and Lee?"

"Your place. With Suzume."

"Ah, Suzume.   An anchor in the midst of chaos. How are the boys?"

"Fine. Playing with Legos when Mike and I left."

"You *and* Mike?"   Storey said, looked at Swanson, grinned. "It's about time."

"Amen," said Jethroe.

"Mike," Storey said, waved Swanson toward the jet, "we're going to review the security camera video. I think you should join us. You can ride with Jethroe and me after."

Swanson embraced Donna, kissed her cheek. "Catch you later," he said, leaped up the stairs into the plane. He stopped, stared at Storey. "What happened to your mustache?"

"Shaved it off."

"I can see that. Why?"

"Had to. When I left Barry's office—"

"Hey," said Jethroe, "you want to see this video clip or hold a wake for Nick's lip hair?"

"It's weird. He looks naked."

"Get used to it." Jethroe placed his computer on the foldout table near the front of the jet, activated it, adjusted its position so all could see. "Okay. Nick, it's your party. Where should we start?"

"Near the beginning where the guy is walking toward the camera with the ladder. Before he painted the lens."

Jethroe tapped a few keys. "Here?"

"A few frames more; when he's closer . . . there. Stop. Can you magnify his waist area?"

Jethroe's fingers flew across the keyboard. The picture zoomed in on the man's midriff.

"Can you blow it up a little more? Ah. Good." Storey leaned closer to the screen. "It's Oscar Loukas."

"How do you know?"

"See the silver rectangle, the belt buckle,"

"Yeah."

"Look close. See the red L inside the black O?"

Jethroe bent forward, squinted. "It's grainy, but, yeah, now that you point it out, I can see it."

"He wears that buckle as if it's part of him. It's the same as the logo on his truck."

"What made you think of Loukas?"

"At the hospital, Holiday said Fredo claimed Cad's wire tap guy worked with me. It nagged at me during our flight." Storey tapped his temple. "Suddenly the light comes on. Loukas. Had to be Loukas. He drove away from McGuire's in a tan Camry. I saw the same car parked by the side of the road when I checked on the Bird Wednesday night. If I'd had my head screwed on right, I would've recognized it sooner."

"So, Loukas is our lock picker," said Swanson.

"My money is on him as the guy who planted the bugs in my house and office. He's good at what he does, and surveillance equipment is only a mini-step away from installing security systems. It fits with his 'Watch your back, this isn't over,' threats. He said it twice. Once when I terminated his contracts and again after I fired Orland."

"May I take the computer to the station with me?" said Olivia.

"Your techs have the DVD's. They give the complete picture."

"This will be quicker. They can validate from the raw recording later, maybe enhance the image, and get a better picture."

Jethroe pulled a thumb drive from the computer case. "I'll record the segment. You can take it. There's private stuff on here I'd rather not expose to your captain." He punched a few keys. A moment later he handed her the miniature drive. "It's all yours."

Storey followed Olivia as they descended the stairs and stepped onto the tarmac.

"Promise you'll take it easy," Storey said. "Don't want you to pop a stitch or something."

She pulled his head down, kissed his cheek. "I'll come to your place after."

"Doctor Mason said you should rest."

She put her fingers over his mouth. "I'll be fine."

Karen, petite, with short curly blonde hair, wearing the ubiquitous Security Associates blue business suit, exited the Mercedes and held the rear door open.

Olivia opened the front passenger door. "Karen, If you don't mind I'd rather ride up front with you. Suspects ride in the back."

5:45 PM Tuesday
26 May 2009

The rattle of pots and pans echoed from the kitchen as Jethroe's caterers prepared dinner. From the fireplace hearth in his living room, Storey surveyed the assembly before him. Everyone important in his life was here: Sarah cross-legged on the floor with her picture books; Swanson and Donna on the short couch; Jethroe perched sidesaddle on the arm; Corine, Emily, Victor and Valerie on the long leg of the L-shaped couch. An occasional shriek from Eric and Lee playing with Suzume floated down the hall from the back bedroom. Olivia had just arrived.

She set her latte on the coffee table amidst the array of peanuts, fruit, vegetables, dip, cheese and crackers. "Okay," she said, "you want to hear my story. What I tell you shouldn't leave this room." She took a moment and made eye contact with everyone.

"About six months ago I was, as the old saying goes, fat, dumb and happy working with my partner, Neil Walker. I had applied for a transfer to teach at the academy, and I thought the summons to Captain Burke's office was about that, but, long story short, he said I was being assigned to partner with Oliphant."

"Why?" Swanson asked.

"He didn't say, but he assured me the assignment with Sam would last no longer than a year, and that my academy teaching application was still on the board."

"How generous of him," said Swanson. "A year with Oliphant. Bummer."

"Well, working with Sam was, to be kind, stressful. He's a loner, hates to work with female detectives, and thinks he's always right."

Olivia winced, paused to reposition her sling shoulder strap.

"Would you like to sit?" said Valerie.

"No, I'm good."

"Burke bypassed the chain of command," said Swanson, "did your Lieutenant know what was going down?"

"If Rivers knew, he didn't tell me. Captain Burke called me into his office about once a week to see 'how it was going; did I notice anything unusual.' After a few of his friendly chats, I asked him what he wanted from me. He stammered around for a bit, and finally said that Sam's case closure percentage was very high, but the conviction rate was low."

"Cherry-pick the evidence against a suspect; ignore, or bury the rest," said Swanson.

"Right. Many of Oliphant's indictments fell apart if the defense attorney was lucky, or smart enough to dig out all the facts."

"So," Swanson continued, "Burke was asking you to rat out a fellow officer. That's a good way to become a pariah in the Department—wherever you're assigned."

"Yeah. I said I wouldn't do it, to find some other way."

"Why didn't he turn it over to internal affairs and let them investigate?"

"Mike, I'm guessing he didn't want them digging around in his department. That can be very disruptive."

"So, what happened?"

"Burke issued an order for detectives working a case to submit individual reports."

"No collaboration?"

"That was the idea." Olivia sipped her latté. "There was a lot of grousing, but it wasn't a problem with most partners. And, my visits with Burke stopped."

"How did you get assigned to Julia's case?"

"Our names were at the top of the assignment board. Sam and I were next up for any case that came along."

"Dumb luck," said Swanson.

"Yeah. Just another of life's imponderables."

"Oliphant was after Nick for Rainey's *and* Julia's demise," Said Jethroe. "How did you get the warrants withdrawn?"

"Okay, Rainey first.   I called Renee Walker, the Arson investigator,.   She said the clock on the wall over Rainey's safe stopped at 6:24, well within the Coroner's estimate of time of death. The clock on his desk quit at 6:29.   That set the time of Rainey's death within a few minutes.   We were lucky Rainey didn't have digitals. Mike, Renee said you were familiar with the investigation. You may know more than I do."

"Perhaps."   Swanson glanced at Victor.   "We can discuss that later."

"When Rainey died, Nick was with me at Wiley's in Albany. The bartender can verify that we were there.   She recognized Nick from the 6:00 news."

"So," said Swanson, "that gets Nick off the hook for Rainey. "What about Julia?"

"The photos on Nick's camera chip were date and time stamped. They placed him a good distance across town from the Mall when Julia was killed."

"The time and date could be reset," said Swanson.   "The time stamp on a digital might not hold up as evidence,"

"That was Oliphant's position, but one of the photos shows a bank clock in the background that agreed with the camera within a minute or two, and Lars Swenson can establish when Nick was at the Harrison job site; . . . and, Red McGuire and some of the men who were in his bar can place Nick at McGuire's near the time Julia was killed. Nick's afternoon is well documented."

"How can you prove Nick took the pictures?" said Jethroe.

"Nick had Lars take photos of him on the Harrison site pointing out—"

""I wanted to document the mess I found," said Storey.   "If Orland wanted to challenge my firing him, the pictures would be proof he was not doing his job."

"I had Valerie mark the chip so she could verify it was from the camera Nick gave her to make prints. I copied the photos onto three thumb drives. I put one in an envelope and put it in Sam's inbox, and mailed one to Valerie."

Valerie nodded. "I got it in Monday's mail."

Olivia turned toward Storey. "I logged the camera chip into the evidence locker, and I included the third drive as part of my report that I filed before we flew to the coast."

"How did they get a warrant if Burke or Oliphant was aware of the photos?" Swanson asked.

"They hadn't seen them or read my report. Burke was out of town for a couple of days, then the weekend. Sam probably doesn't know how, or didn't want to plug the memory stick into a computer. More to the point, I think, it was from me, a female. To be fair, due to Burke's separate report policy, Sam didn't have access to my documentation."

Olivia took a swallow of her latté. "Mike, to answer your original question: after Burke read my report, he ignored Sam's objection and cancelled the warrant. Sam wanted to question Nick. He said Nick could have hired someone to kill Julia."

"Gotta give Sam some credit. He's hangs on till the bitter end," said Swanson.

"I told them about Holiday's recordings that show Dino arranged for Julia's killing. We'll probably get them later, but Burke believed me." She saluted Storey with her cup. "Nick, you're no longer a fugitive."

"Bob Abrams tells me that Oliphant and your forensics people were in the garage last Friday," said Jethroe. "Bob gave them the original discs from the security camera. Have they come up with anything?"

"If they have they're not sharing it yet, but I know they're working it. Captain Burke called Norma, our computer whiz, to show her your cut of the security video . . . and the belt buckle blow-up. I've worked with Norma before. She'll put it together."

"What will happen now?"

"The Captain put me on medical leave. He asked me to brief my ex partner, Neil, and give him all the reports."

"What about Oliphant?" said Swanson.

"I don't know. Burke asked me to leave and shut the door. When I left the premises Sam was still in Captain Burke's office."

6:45 PM Tuesday
26 May 2009

A pair of jays flitted through the shadows in the forest of trees on the steep slope behind Storey's house, their squawking echoing in the evening silence. There was no wind. Swanson sat in a chair on the patio staring into the tall firs, absently swirling cognac in a snifter. The female jay settled on the far end of the deck railing. The male made several raucous fly-bys before she abandoned her perch and rejoined him. They zoomed up over the house and disappeared.

Storey opened the slider and came onto the deck. He leaned on the railing facing Swanson. "We're having dessert."

Swanson raised the glass to his nose, inhaled the cognac's bouquet, took a sip. He didn't want to engage anyone in conversation. "I'll join you in a bit."

"We're having Mom's peach cobbler."

"Smells great, but I'll pass for now."

Storey shrugged. "Your loss."

Swanson tipped the large glass, drained it. He rose and followed Storey back inside where he poured another slug of cognac. "Nick, we'll be in the den," he said, motioned for Victor to join him.

In the den, Swanson dropped onto the couch, pointed to the chair opposite.

Victor sat. "What's up, Mike?"

"I got a call from Renee Walker today," Swanson said.

"The Arson Squad's chief investigator of Rainey's office fire?"

"That's the one."

"What did she want?"

Swanson sipped his cognac. "Maybe you should tell me,"

Victor pushed back, ran the fingers of his good hand through his hair. He sucked a big breath, let it out slowly. "I thought the stuff in his safe burned up."

"Scorched the edges. The records are basically intact, but yours were mailed to the frauds investigators some time ago."

"They have Rainey's copies of my accounts from the early days?"

"And copies of some contracts with your subcontractors."

"That was a long time ago, Mike."

"There is no statute of limitations for tax fraud."

"Rainey probably mailed them when Nick cancelled the insurance."

"No. They had them before Nick and Rainey had their encounter."

"The little prick could've sent them earlier. He was convinced Nicholas was going to cancel."

"Victor, it doesn't matter."

"I suppose. What do I do now?"

"I'm not sure. I have to talk with the ADA, probably the IRS. Get their perspective."

"You think they'll prosecute?"

"Maybe. Unless we negotiate a plea. I think there's a more immediate concern."

"Which is?"

"Telling Nick. He's the CEO now. He'll have to deal with the collateral damage to the company."

Victor grimaced. "After he kills me, you mean."

"I'm sure he'll be upset."

"That's a bit of an understatement. I promised Valerie I'd tell Nicholas when we returned from our trip. I even rehearsed my speech. The kidnapping and Olivia getting shot derailed the whole thing."

"That's all water under the bridge, Victor."

"You think I should tell him now?"

"The sooner the better. That's my advice as a friend, and as your lawyer. By the way, you should've told me long ago."

"To what end?"

"We could've stopped Rainey; put him in jail."

"And ruined the reputation of some good people." Victor shrugged. "Didn't figure it was my decision to make." He stood, paced. "Okay. Ask Nicholas to come in here."

"You want me present?"

"Umm . . . Yeah. He'll undoubtedly have lots of questions. You'll have to explain the legal ramifications." Victor sighed. "And, if you're here, he might not kill me."

Swanson gave him a feeble smile. "I'll go get him."

Storey stared through the den window. Victor and Swanson sat on the sofa watching. Occasionally Storey turned and looked at Victor and shook his head. After a few moments he filled his lungs, exhaled slowly, and sat in the chair opposite the couch.

"Okay, tell me if I got this straight. You would find a willing subcontractor or two . . . or a dozen, and get them to agree to kickback some of what you paid them—tax free income. Probably you shared the spoils with Mr. Sub and you both got tax-free money. You covered it with a contract for the full amount on Storey Construction's books, and the sub got a contract for the lesser amount for his records. Unless there's a simultaneous audit of you and Mr. Sub, it's almost impossible to trace."

Victor looked directly at his son. "That's the essence of it."

Valerie's words before his last meeting with Rainey echoed in Storey's head; *Victor, and George have a long history . . . things you don't know, perhaps have no need to.* Who else was aware of the situation? Was he the last to know? "Rainey was blackmailing you . . . us?" he said.

"Yes," said Victor.

Storey rubbed the back of his neck. "George had access to accounting records as part of his insurance underwriting. He reviewed your books *and* the subcontractors'. He found the discrepancy in the contracts . . . right?"

"And held us all hostage."

"How long?"

"Several years."

"His blackmail was inflated rates?"

"And, a yearly consulting fee."

"Why? Dad, why did you do it? It's not who you are . . . who I thought you were. The man I thought I knew wouldn't even consider. . ." He looked at Swanson. "Mike?"

"Tax fraud," said Swanson.

"I could give you a bunch of reasons," said Victor. "Probably none that you'll agree with. Just starting out, cash was somewhere between scarce and nonexistent. It was a way of generating operating capital for all the up-front overhead expenses. Rent, gas for the trucks and equipment, money to buy equipment and tools, insurance—well, you know—those costs that won't wait until the customer pays."

"Sounds like a convenient excuse. Yeah, Dad, I do know. That's what banks are for . . . business loans," Storey said. "You get a contract and use it for collateral for a loan to cover temporary negative cash flow."

"Yeah, that works *if* you have a good credit rating. Thirty-some years ago, I didn't. It wouldn't have helped much. Interest rates were ridiculous and inflation devoured everything. Bid a job and by the time you needed supplies or materials, the price escalation ate up the profits."

"There had to be a better way. And don't tell me everyone was doing it."

Victor shrugged. "Well, it was not uncommon. Son, you weren't there. You came on the scene after we had a good track record, and enough cash and credit to carry us through lean times."

"Apparently I took over a business built on fraud and deceit."

Victor sighed, looked away. "That's a bit over the top."

"How would you describe it?"

"A kick start? Priming the pump?" Victor threw his hands up. "Okay. It was illegal. Nicholas, if the company had folded then, we wouldn't be sending those nice checks to the Governor and the Feds every three months. And, we probably wouldn't be living in nice homes and enjoying a reasonable level of financial security."

Storey rolled his eyes. "I can't believe you just said that. The end justifies the means? That flies in the face of everything you taught me. What happened to 'the only real thing you have is your integrity?' I thought it was engraved on the inside of your forehead."

Victor rose, moved to the window, and looked out. He placed his good hand in a pants pocket, his bandaged fist on his chest, and rocked toe to heel for a long moment. "You're right, Nicholas. I'm sorry."

"You're sorry . . . *you're sorry*! That's all you have to say?"

Shoulders slumped, Victor turned and faced his son. "Nicholas, you take people at face value and that's good—and bad. People make mistakes, don't always tell the truth, keep secrets, and sometimes do unethical things—things they may regret—but most of us do the best we can with what we have at the time. Son, you need a healthy dose of real-world reality to temper your idealism."

Storey waved an arm. "The reality is; Valerie knew . . . didn't she?"

Victor nodded. "Don't blame her. Valerie has been on my ass for months to tell you . . . particularly since we put the wheels in motion for you to take over as CEO. I've been trying to find a way. Just couldn't get it together. I took the trip to nowhere to get some alone time; to wrap my mind around it."

"And you left me with half a deck to deal with Rainey. Val should have told me."

"She wanted to. I said I would when I got back from my trip—and before you had to meet with Rainey—but Dino and his gang of misfits showed up." Victor returned to the couch.

"Mike," Storey said, "how will this affect the company finances? Is the company liable?"

"It's certainly possible. Not sure until I get into the details with the ADA or the IRS. At this point I only have the heads-up from Renee Walker, the arson squad investigator."

"How about our ability to bid jobs? Won't our capability to post a bond be limited? That would put serious restrictions on the type of work we can bid or take on."

"We just don't know yet." Swanson took a gulp of cognac. "I suppose a tax lien, if it comes to that, could affect the amount of bond the insurance company would authorize, but you aren't there yet."

Storey slid back in the chair. "I'm sure our insurers won't cough up a dime if illegal acts are involved—including tax fraud."

"True."

Storey laced his fingers behind his neck. "The grapevine will spread the word to everyone in the state within a week."

"I'll talk to Renee," said Swanson. "See what they found. Maybe it's not as bad as it seems. I'll get my law partner involved. Stacy specializes in this sort of stuff. We might be able to fix it without going public."

"Mike, this is bound to leak out. There's no way to stop it."

Storey walked to the window, focused on a squirrel climbing the walnut tree in the side yard. The company reputation was flushed down the toilet. All the years of fair dealing wouldn't matter. His father was a crook.

He turned toward Victor. "Are there any other hidden time bombs?"

"None that I know of."

"Does Mom know?'

"I told her while we were on our trip."

"Donna?"

"No."

"Jethroe?"

"No."

"How about you, Mike?"

"Not until Renee called me, and Victor verified it."

"Dad, is anyone else involved?"

"Just the subcontractors."

"Okay, I've heard enough. Dad, you created this mess, you can fix it . . . or not. I should never have opted for the CEO position. When I worked the job sites, I felt I belonged, that I was contributing."

"Nicholas, you were, are invaluable."

"Well, suddenly, I don't care anymore."

"Don't say that."

"I'm going to pour myself a stiff drink and go outside and think about this. Shit, I don't need to think about it. My resignation letter will be on Val's desk in the morning."

"Nicholas. We, I need you. At least stay and run the field operations. You love being hands-on at the job sites."

"What is it about 'I don't care anymore' don't you understand?"

"Nicholas, I know you're angry. You have every right, but don't do this."

"Dad, I think you should leave by the time I finish my drink," Storey marched out the door, slammed it behind him.

Two weeks later
10:00 AM Tuesday
8 June 2009

They met in Swanson's office around the conference room table, Storey, Jethroe and Swanson drinking coffee, Olivia sipping a latte.

"I see you've dumped your sling," said Jethroe. "Can you use your right arm now?"

"Enough to write and use my computer keyboard. Can't drive yet. Mom or Nick take me wherever I need to go. Today, my partner, Neil, drove me to the station and then here."

"You've been assigned to partner with Neil again?"

"Yeah. Technically, I'm still on medical leave, but I go in every couple of days for an update."

"Hopefully, you can share with us," said Swanson.

"I can."

"What happened to Oliphant?" Jethroe said.

"He retired."

"The grapevine says it wasn't voluntary," Swanson said. "They couldn't afford to expose any dirty blue linen. What's he doing now?"

"He's working for a PI."

"Ah . . . digging up dirt on people. Tailing errant spouses and such. He's found his calling."

"So, what else is new?" said Jethroe.

"You know that Loukas and Bowie have been arrested for Julia's murder."

"Yeah. Aggravated murder. Murder for hire. Could mean the death penalty," said Swanson. "How did you put it together?"

"Forensics found a footprint in the mud outside the gate that matched Oscar's boot—"

"Can't go anywhere in Oregon during the rainy season and not leave a trail," said Jethroe.

Olivia smiled. "And, a small swatch of cloth that was snagged in the chain link fence matched a shirt they found in his house. Add in the belt buckle in the security camera video, and a fifty thousand dollar deposit in his savings account and we have a good case.

"They found Bowie's fingerprints in the T Bird. He'd wiped the door handles and steering wheel clean but he missed a couple under the dash, probably left there when he hot-wired the car. A neighbor saw him park the T-bird in his garage early Wednesday morning."

"How did he know it was Nick's T-Bird?" said Swanson.

"*She* saw the 57 TBRD vanity license plate. Thanks again to the Oregon mists, Forensics found a tire track in his garage that matched the left front tire. The blood on the headlight rim matched Julia's type and DNA."

"Our lab confirmed that," said Jethroe.

"We found twenty-five thousand in cash stashed in a metal box behind a loose panel in Bowie's garage. He's toast."

"He sold out cheap," said Swanson. "It's a universal rule. The guy doing the dirty work gets paid the least."

"Bowie has always been the doer. He's got two felony assault convictions and two dismissed for lack of evidence."

"Does Loukas have a record?" said Storey.

"Before he moved to Salem from the LA area he was investigated for grand theft but wasn't charged. They suspected, but never proved, that he programmed a back door to bypass the security systems he installed."

"I'm convinced he tried to frame me for Julia *and* Rainey's death," said Storey.

"And came close to succeeding," said Jethroe. "Think about it. It took some elaborate planning and timing to know where and when Julia would be, steal the T bird, run her over, and return the car to the garage. I agree with you, Nick: he planted the bugs in your house and office. That's how he knew her plans. Had to be Loukas. Bowie doesn't have the smarts."

"I believe that he got someone to make the Stevens phone call to get me out of the office when Julia was killed, and, if he did mess with the security system at Dad's house that would explain how he could have lifted my gun, used it to shoot up Rainey's wall, and return it with the three bullets missing."

"All the pieces fit," said Olivia, "But we'll probably never prove any of it unless one of them cops to it."

"It's moot now," said Swanson. "After they're convicted, and I'm sure they will be, they're facing life with a minimum of 30 years, most likely life without parole."

"What about Dino?" said Storey. "He's the source of it all."

"The feds have a long list of charges against him," said Olivia. "Whether they defer to us or pursue theirs is still up in the air. Whatever comes down, at best, he'll never see the light of day without bars obstructing his view."

They sat silent for a long moment.

"Sometimes I think I could have prevented Julia's death," said Storey.

"What?" said Swanson.

"You're kidding," said Jethroe.

Storey held his hands up in defense. "I know, I know, it's silly. But if I'd listened to Oscar, given him another chance rather that terminate his contracts, maybe—"

"That's really dumb," said Jethroe. "Dino would have found someone else if Cad's operative hadn't heard Loukas moaning about you at McGuire's."

"Logically, you're right. I've told myself that a hundred times, but it still bugs me."

Jethroe shook his head, pushed his chair back, stood. "I need some fresh air. Let's walk over to Annie's and have a cup of real coffee, maybe a doughnut, or two. I can't take another swallow of Swanson's swill.

Three Months later
4:30 PM Tuesday
25 August 2009

Storey swung his sledgehammer, breaking the last stud in the wall separating the bathtub and toilet. With a few thrusts of his pry bar, the tub slid from its supports. He pulled it alongside the other fixtures in the center of the room: a toilet, two sinks, a fiberglass shower enclosure, and the remains of the vanity. Tomorrow a pair of carpenters would arrive to assist with the remodel and he would have help carrying the heavy pieces to the dumpster in the driveway.

He sat on a sawhorse, wiped his sweaty forehead on a sleeve, and surveyed the room. He had pulled the drywall from the walls and ceiling and removed the partition separating the master bedroom from the bathroom. He nodded, satisfied with the results of his work; a clear space thirty by fourteen feet opened into what had been Julia's two-story studio at the far end.

Her art supplies had gone to the college along with some of her paintings; the remainder Storey placed on consignment with the gallery in Portland, except for a seashore painting and a portrait of Eric. High in the garage attic they awaited the day he might want them. The proceeds from the gallery sales were committed to a trust for Eric's education.

A Goodwill crew had taken Julia's clothing and personal items and all the furniture from the study and bedroom, including the bed.

Jethroe had performed an extensive search for Julia's next of kin. She had no living relative. As were her parents, she was an only child. There had been no service, just a memorial at her gallery, organized by her artist friends. Her ashes were tucked away in the back of a cabinet in the family room. Storey had sequestered her diaries in a drawer of his desk in the den.

He had studied her writings from her teenage years up to the time of their marriage. The personalities he found there seemed unreal. He thought Lupo's evaluation of Julia and her aliases was right on—she had only partially completed the transition from adolescence to adulthood. Rather than growing and resolving conflicts, she had moved to each new identity carrying the same obsessions and insecurity with her.

He pushed up from the sawhorse and shed his dust-laden boots at the door leading into the hallway. In the kitchen, he pulled a Killian from the fridge, made his way through the family room and onto the back deck. He flopped into a chair, put his feet on the rail, and looked up the slope at the tall firs, their branches swaying with the breeze—the view he would see from his new second floor bedroom suite. He lifted his bottle in salute, took a sip. Now that he had completed demolition of the old and was ready to build anew, he felt as if fresh, clean blood surged through him.

"Hello . . . Nick?"

"Jethroe, I'm here . . . on the deck."

Jethroe and Swanson stepped through the partially open slider.

"So this is what you do when you're not working on my new house," said Swanson.

"Hi, guys."

"There was no one at my . . . Donna's and my new place."

"We poured the footings and stem walls this morning. The framing crew will be there in a couple of days. Sorry if concrete doesn't set up on your schedule."

"It's just that we got a 90-day escrow on Donna's house. You think we'll be able to move in by then?"

"Wow," said Storey. "You're really into *your* new life. You run off to Vegas and come home married to my sister, jump headfirst into fatherhood, and now you're like a kid in a toy store about your new house. What happened to the august bachelor we all know and admire?"

"I've let too many good things slide. No more."

"How's my sis doing?"

"We're great. Valerie has her helping with the accounting at Storey Construction."

"I heard. She's good at that. And Lee?"

"He's a neat little guy. We do all kinds of stuff. He loves to ride in the Corvette with the top down."

"How about a beer?" Storey said.

"Thought you'd never ask," said Swanson.

In the family room, Swanson and Jethroe sat on bar stools, Storey in his lounge chair, each with a Killian red.

"Is Olivia happy with her new assignment at the Academy?" said Jethroe.

"Very," Storey said. "Regular hours, challenging work, and no emergency call-outs."

They were silent for a few moments.

"You should grow it back," said Swanson.

"What?" said Storey.

"Your mustache."

"It's not part of the new me."

"There's a new you?"

"I'm trying to shed all the Julia stuff. I started growing it when I met her."

"You look like a college kid that needs a nose wipe."

"At least it's different. Is there anything new on the Rainey fire investigation?"

"You should grow a new one. . . . The last I heard the coroner said Rainey died from a ruptured aortic aneurysm. He was surprised it hadn't burst sooner."

"Rainey was a walking time bomb with a short fuse," said Jethroe.

"Renee Walker said they came up with a scenario that fits with the bullets they found imbedded in the wall. If Rainey were standing against the wall, two slugs would have missed his ears by one or two inches, the third just below his crotch. The pattern was precise. The guy is good with a gun.   The lab found powder residue on the shoulders of Rainey's jacket and on the front of his pants.   It's reasonable to assume the perp stood Rainey against the wall and used him for target practice—perhaps trying to scare him, or . . . well, who knows why.

"Renee thinks Rainey expired on the spot and the intruder dragged him out to the back hallway and left him there.   Marks on the carpet support her hypothesis, and Rainey's shirt and jacket were high up on the back of his neck."

"Any suspects?" said Jethroe.

"Renee thinks it was one of Rainey's victims.   If it was, she's sure he burned his file or took it with him.   There are no clues or evidence to work with except for Nick's fingerprints on the lamp, and that's been explained."

"They can't prove it was Loukas?" Storey said.

"Unless something new develops—oh, not all the files were tax or business related.   Some were photos or videos of guys in sexually explicit situations—of both persuasions."

"Brother Harold played around with cameras and electronic stuff," Jethroe said.

"Exactly. Renee got a search warrant for their residence, but it had been cleaned out. Harold is in the wind. One interesting thing. They found recording equipment identical to the one you found in the lamp in your den."

"Harold was trying to find something to blackmail me with?"

Swanson shrugged. "Could be."

"He's a creepy sonofabitch," Storey said.

"Apparently he's a smart creepy sonofabitch," said Jethroe. "My bet is that Harold is living the good life in the Caymans or some other haven where they stashed their spoils. This whole thing with Rainey is really ironic. If the arsonist had held off for a while, Rainey's aneurysm would have done him in, and Harold would likely have cleaned out the safe and then gone poof. Everybody would have been off the hook."

"I'm thinking that's a safe bet," said Swanson.

"What's happening with Victor and the tax police?" said Jethroe.

"I talked with Stacy, yesterday. I'm letting her handle it. The convolutions and contradictions of the tax codes are not my thing. She said the copies of the old records are not clear.   She showed me a copy of a fuzzy and hard-to-read contract. Without Rainey's or someone's testimony to verify their authenticity, a case can be made that they are forgeries."

"Meaning they won't hold up in court?" said Jethroe.

"Possible . . . unless the originals from the subcontractors can be found. So far, of those still in business, none have kept records older than ten years."

Storey took a pull on his beer. "How much do the back taxes add up to?"

"Annette is still working on it, but she says it's not a big number."

"We can hope," Storey said.

"Interest and penalties add up big time," said Swanson, "but Annette thinks the shaky evidence will force the tax gurus to make a deal."

"Will Dad get jail time?"

Swanson shrugged. "I think it's unlikely, but as I said, I find the tax codes so byzantine that my opinion isn't worth much." He moved to a chair opposite Storey. "Enough with the tax and Rainey bullshit. Now that you've trashed your bedroom, what's next?"

"Well. I plan to add a second story directly above . . . make that the master bedroom and bath. I gutted the existing master and bath. I'll convert that space to two bedrooms and a bath. Then I'll tear out the wall between the den and the small bedroom. That'll be a library or more office space. The studio will be a game room."

Jethroe smiled, raised an eyebrow. "With a pool table?"

"I'll bet you know just the place to get one."

"I do. It'll be my house warming gift."

They all laughed.

"Hmm," said Jethroe. "That'll make two new bedrooms, one for Eric, one for Sarah, and one for guests . . . and an office for Olivia? Her new assignment should allow more time for her writing."

"Don't get ahead of yourself, Roe. I've been thinking about this remodel for a long time."

"If the shoe fits . . ."

"It's too soon. There are still Julia issues I have to resolve to get my head straight, and Eric is just beginning to understand that she's not coming back. I need to spend more time with him. He likes the park. He really goes for the pony rides. Just watching him is a pleasure."

"How's he handling it?" said Jethroe.

"He talks about her less and less. Sometimes he wonders what she'll bring him when she returns from her trip. But, I think he's coming around. Our cat Goldie died a few weeks ago and we buried her on the hill out back. Yesterday he asked me if mommy was dead could we put her in the ground next to Goldie."

"Kids," said Jethroe, shaking his head. "They have a way of simplifying things."

"And you? Are you dealing with it?" said Swanson.

"I've been studying Julia's diaries hoping if I understand her life before we met I can come to terms with what happened between us. I feel angry and really stupid that I allowed her to draw me into her intrigue."

"Don't beat yourself up. She sucked us all in," said Jethroe.

"That may be, Roe, but you didn't live with it everyday. I should have known something was not right."

"If you're standing in a swamp and the crocs are circling, it's hard to plan next week's barbeque."

"Thanks for trying, Roe. I had plenty of time to think, but I buried myself in work, and, to use your analogy, I ignored the crocs—hoped the problem would resolve itself."

They sat silent for a few moments, sipping their beers.

"As I read the early diaries, when she was herself, Maria, then Dianne, Annie and Cheri, I felt sorry for her," Storey said. "Her parent's murder was tragic, left her with no one. Even though she had her father's evidence package, she was deathly afraid of Lupo, and saw his shadow behind every bush."

"Mucho paranoia," said Swanson.

"Yeah, but in spite of that, she called him often."

"Her only connection to her past," said Jethroe. "From what I heard of your conversation with Lupo in Dino's motor home, Lupo became a surrogate father of sorts, someone she could talk to, someone familiar with her former life."

"Larry Lawrence was another beachcomber type," said Storey. "They roamed the beaches in Florida for a while. When he took off for California, she changed identities again and followed him. On the way west, they got married in Reno. They wandered the southern beaches in winter, moved north in summer, selling paintings or doing odd jobs. Lawrence would disappear for months at a time and leave her to fend for herself."

"Let me guess," said Swanson. "You walked into her life during one of Larry's ah . . . vacations."

"Yeah. You know the story. I met her on the beach at Newport, bought the painting that used to hang there." Storey pointed to a blank space on the west wall. "Her diaries said she wanted a chance for a normal life. That was after she was pregnant."

"Was pregnancy part of her plan for 'a real life'?" Jethroe made quote marks with his fingers.

"The diaries are vague. I could read them either way. It's clear that she used it to pull me closer."

"To reel you in." said Swanson. "She knew you wouldn't let your kid grow up as a beach bum."

"We were good for a couple of years before she spent more time on her inspiration trips than she did at home. The last year or so she was seeing Lawrence as part of her trips—drifting back to her old life."

"You got that from her journals?" said Jethroe.

Storey straightened his back, clasped his hands together. "Her scribbles said she intended to leave me and Eric, to just disappear. During her last few months she deliberately picked fights, or did things to whip up trouble. She had a detail plan and schedule sketched out in her diary."

"She planned when to stir the pot?" said Swanson.

"Yeah, and when she would disappear. She marked the first of September as F day."

"F day?"

"Freedom day, the day she would take command of her life. She had lived most of her life since high school as a free spirit, answering to no one—having no commitments. She felt suffocated, swept away by everyday routine and the constant demands on her time."

"So," said Jethroe, "she couldn't tolerate the normal life she thought she wanted."

"Apparently."

"Why didn't she just write you a Dear John and disappear?"

"Roe, Julia was a schemer. I didn't realize to what extent until I read the diaries. She wanted to make me so angry with her that I wouldn't try to find her."

"Did she want money? A divorce?"

"She didn't care about money. He father left her a trust. After Eric was born, she had Barry add Eric as a beneficiary and me as the trustee until he turns 21. The final accounting was just completed last month. It adds up to something just north of two million."

"Wow," said Jethroe. "A millionaire beach bum."

"Yeah. Weird. She rarely tapped the trust."

"How about husband Larry?" said Swanson.

"I don't think he knew she had money. Her will mentions him; gave him a thousand dollars. I've been wondering about the bigamy aspect. Could he contest it?"

"She recognized him with the thousand bucks," said Swanson. "The issue is moot. And she married Lawrence . . . and you, under an alias. I'm not sure what all that means."

"We're good. Barry filed a name change for her. Legally she was Julia Dee Williams when we married."

"That had to be Barry's input."

"Yeah. She came to him wanting to protect Eric, well, then he was her unborn. Swore him to secrecy. Poor guy had to abide by the attorney client thing until she died. How do you do it—hold onto all the confidential stuff? It would drive me bonkers."

Swanson shrugged. "Part of the job."

"She took good care of Eric financially," said Jethroe.

Storey nodded, took a pull of Killian's.

"So," said Swanson, "back to my question. How are you coping?"

"I'm past feeling angry and frustrated for letting myself be snookered . . . well, most of the time. I'm erasing her from my life as fast and as best I can." Storey waved an arm. "I've nearly cleared the house of her presence. I'm feeling better, sleeping better."

"And, you've got Eric," said Jethroe.

"Yeah. And I'm holding him close."

5:05 PM Tuesday
25 August 2009

Corine breezed into the room, followed by Olivia and Sarah.

Jethroe and Swanson jumped to their feet. Storey rolled out of his lounger.

"Corine. Nice to see you," said Swanson. "Hi, Liv."

Jethroe patted Sarah's head. "How's my favorite Sarah?"

"You have more Sarahs?"

"Oh, yes. But you're my favorite of all."

A shaft of light illuminating Sarah's red-blonde hair reminded Storey of the day in Olivia's hospital room. Then, he had been mystified by his reaction; now he was confident he understood why.

"Nicholas, we need to talk with you," Corine said.

"We were just leaving," said Jethroe.

He and Swanson deposited their empty bottles on the counter. "Hi and bye, Liv," said Swanson. "Goodbye Sarah."

When the door closed behind them, Olivia pulled Sarah in front of her and drew her close. She looked down at her daughter and up at Storey.

"Nick, I . . . well, I . . . there's something . . ." Olivia looked at her mother.

Corine crossed her arms over her chest. "Olivia Ann Barton, if you don't tell him, I will. There's no good time or easy way."

"What are you two talking about? Storey said. Is there something I need to know?" *She's finally going to tell me. Past due, and I'm ready.* He placed his empty on the counter with the others. "What is it, Liv?"

Corine cocked her head, swung it toward Storey and back to Olivia.

Olivia squatted, her eyes at Sarah's level. "Sarah, I want you to go outside on the back deck with Grans. Okay?" She looked up at her mother. "Grans will read to you from the new book we got yesterday. It's on the coffee table,"

Sarah nodded , her strawberry-blonde curls bouncing.

Storey smiled, no longer uncertain about Olivia's message.

Sarah ran and got the book. "Gran. *The Lost Thing*. It needs a place to live." She grabbed her grandmother's hand and pulled her toward the door. "Read me *The Lost Thing*."

"Olivia—"

"Just go, Mom. I'll come get you later."

"You promised—"

"Mom, go."

Corine blew air through her compressed lips, allowed Sarah to pull her outside.

"This is beginning to sound ominous," Storey said.

Olivia took his hand, kissed his cheek. "Let's sit on the couch."

She disengaged and stared across the room, hands folded in her lap. After a long moment, her eyes found his. "Nick, we need to talk about us . . . about Sarah."

Storey put an arm along the back of the sofa, ankle on his knee. "Okay." He felt gooseflesh creep up his arms.

"Nick . . . Sarah . . . I . . . Oh, hell." She wiped her eyes with the back of her hands. "I've rehearsed this so many times."

Storey gripped her shoulder. "Just say it, Liv."

She pulled his hand to her lap, held it in between hers, refocused. "Nick . . . Sarah is your daughter." She blinked, but the tears escaped. "Damn. I don't want to be a blubbering female."

Storey placed both feet on the floor, crossed his hands over his stomach, and rested his head on the back of the couch. "People think Big Andy is—"

"No way."

Storey rolled his head, looked at her. "You lived with him."

"I stayed in his house for a while . . . Andy is a friend from high school. Until Sarah was born he looked after me as if he were my big brother; then I moved back home with Mom. I wasn't about to impose on him any more, especially caring for a newborn."

"Why didn't you go home from the get-go?"

Olivia looked at Storey, wiped her eyes on a tissue from a back pocket of her jeans. "I did for the first few weeks, but, you know my mother, she—"

"She ragged at you for having a baby, um . . . she probably said, 'out of wedlock'."

"Exactly. I didn't need that, and her well-intended advice."

They were silent for a moment.

"You're still living with her," Storey said. "Something must've changed."

"When she held Sarah for the first time, she cried—insisted we come live with her. As if someone threw a switch, all her judgmental garbage evaporated. We have our moments, but generally, it's good."

"Rumor has it that Andy deserted you."

"I know. I've given up trying to dispel that impression, but gossip has a life of its own. Andy tells me to forget it. He says he doesn't care; people who count know the truth. He comes by every couple of months to see Sarah. They have a great time. The only problem is, Sarah wants to get tattoos like her Uncle Andy."

Storey chuckled. "A five year old girl covered with tattoos. Wow."

Olivia looked at him, her brow furrowed. "Nick you seem so . . . well, calm."

"What did you expect?"

"I thought you would be angry, throw things, storm out of the room—something."

"I was furious when I first figured it out . . . mad that you hadn't told me, righteously outraged that I missed so much of Sarah's growing up."

Olivia's chin dropped, her eyes widened. "Nick . . . you knew?"

"Suspected. I wasn't positive, but it was enough to drive me crazy."

"How long? Since when?"

"Since the day you left the hospital in Bend, well, maybe a few days later."

"How did you know . . . what made you suspicious?"

"Sarah's hair."

"Her hair?"

"Yeah. I felt a bump in my gut when Sarah skipped into your hospital room. It bothered me for days before it hit me. The light was just right; lit up her hair like a halo. Sarah's a reddish-blonde. My sister's hair was the same color when she was a kid. I pulled photos of my mother when she was a kid. Same color.

"Then when our mothers started their buddy-buddy thing, I was with Sarah a lot. I soon realized that she's got my mother's square chin and that she moves like a Storey."

Olivia nodded.

"We hit it off right from the start. She jabbers on about anything, everything . . . answer one question and she has two more."

"Tell me about it. By the way, she told me . . . she called them your visits."

"She's always after me to read to her. She carries a book with her like some kids hang onto a blanket or a stuffed animal."

"After all that, you didn't feel you had to clue me in that you knew?"

"Well, I wasn't sure, and I figured you would tell me sooner or later—when you were ready. And, like I said, at first I was mad at you." He touched her shoulder. "Just for the record, I did throw stuff."

Olivia chuckled through her tears. "I feel better already. You were . . . um, distant for a while. I thought you were just having trouble assimilating the Julia thing."

"That, too."

They looked at each other for a moment. "Nick, I . . ."

Storey embraced her. They kissed. They parted, stood, embraced again.

"Nick."

"Liv."

"We should tell Sarah now."

"Our daughter Sarah?'

"Yes, our daughter Sarah Ann."

"Sarah Ann. Her grandmothers' middle names."
"You approve?"
"Perfect."

*****

Sarah pushed closer to her mother. "Nicklas is *my* daddy? He's Eric's daddy."

Olivia lifted Sarah into her arms. "I know it's confusing, but it's true. Eric is your brother."

"Laura has a brother. His name is Paul." Sarah looked from Olivia to Storey and back several times. "They live in the same house with their mommy and daddy. Are we going to live in the same house? I like this house. I can hide under trees on the hill."

"Sarah, would you like your daddy to hold you?"

Sarah held out her arms. Storey took her gingerly. He could not stop the tears. Sarah wiped them with her fingers.

"Are you sad?" She touched his nose, stroked his face. She turned toward Corine. "Grams, Nicklas is my daddy."

Six Months later
4:30 PM Tuesday
13 November 2009

Storey stood in front of the fireplace at the family's Newport condominium tearing pages from Julia's diaries and tossing them into the flames. He glanced at Olivia watching him from the couch. For a month, they had been living together in his Salem home with Sarah and Eric. The house remodel was complete except for some painting touch-up, master bedroom closet shelves, and bookcases in Olivia's office space.

Sarah loved having a little brother to care for. Eric was not yet sure he liked to share, but thrived on the attention from his grandmothers, who argued over whose turn it was to babysit Sarah, Eric, and their cousin, Lee, while their parents were at work.

Storey turned his gaze to Eric playing with Legos near the sliding glass door leading to the small deck overlooking the beach and Sarah paging through a book alongside her mother on the couch. Life was good and about to get better.

He had rejoined Storey Construction as Field Operations manager. He loved being on a job site again. Regular hours provided more time to be with Olivia, Sarah, and Eric. Valerie had taken the CEO role; Donna was acting as financial director.

Storey had reconciled with his father, now fully retired. Victor had paid the back taxes and some penalties. He would not disclose the amount. He was on probation for two years on the condition he do 300 hours of community service each year. Storey chuckled, thinking of the irony. His father was coaching little league pitching, one of his favorite activities.

Storey still felt the occasional twinge of remorse for being so righteous about his father's tax manipulations. He wondered what he himself would have done if his chosen profession had suddenly ejected him; what short cuts would he have found acceptable if he were without funds to support a wife, a daughter, and another child soon to be born. Jethroe was right again; it was not his place to judge, but to provide support. How many times over the years of their friendship had Roe been the agent to crystallize his thoughts?

Olivia was ready to get married, as was he, but he had delayed until he was sure Eric did not think Julia would reappear. Now, occupied with his new sister and Cousin Lee, Eric rarely mentioned Julia.

Storey accepted that Julia's life had been tragic, shaped by circumstances beyond her control, but thought it essential to have a clean slate—to be free of the last remnants of Julia before he and Olivia made it official. The house remodel and disposal of her paintings and personal effects had accomplished that for him, except for the diaries and Julia's ashes.

His cell phone vibrated. He looked at the screen. Jethroe. "Hey, Roe. It's been a while."

"Lots of new clients. Had to find some new people and arrange for their training. Just checking in. Went by your house. No one home. You're at the beach?"

"Yeah. With Olivia and the kids."

"Couple of things. I talked with Holiday. Julia's evidence package has broken the whole case wide open. They found where the dead bodies were buried . . . for real. They got the bad guys on the run—the whole organization. Dino is singing his fat head off and I think they put him in witness protection."

"You think?"

"Yeah. When I asked for details, Doc clammed up, changed the subject."

"Meaning we'll probably never hear of Dino again."

"Fair bet."

"Well, I won't lose any sleep over it."

"Good. Wanted to give you the news and tell you I'll be out of town for a week or so."

"More clients?"

"No. Pool tournament in Seattle."

"Good luck."

"No luck involved, my friend. See you later." Jethroe terminated the call.

Storey turned the phone off, put it back in his pocket.

"Roe?" said Olivia.

"Yeah." He summarized the call, resumed ripping pages from a notebook and feeding the fire.

"Nick?"

"Liv?"

"I take it that you've rejected that publisher's offer."

"To buy the journals?"

"Yes."

"Yeah."

"It was a lot of money."

"Liv, some things are not for sale." He grabbed another notebook. "Here. Help me get rid of these."

She rose from her seat, hugged him. "I love you, Nicholas Storey."

A few moments and the fire was roaring. They stepped back, held hands waiting for the fire to abate.

Storey grabbed the poker, stirred the ashes. "That's that." he said. He removed the silver-gray urn from a top shelf of the bookcase. "I'm going down the beach a quarter-mile or so." He pointed south.

*****

Olivia adjusted the tripod of the telescope she had moved from the living room to the deck, focused the instrument on Nicholas walking in the sand near the upper wash of the surf. He stopped, studied the shoreline, looked inland, walked farther south, repeated his examination. He turned toward the setting sun.

After a few long moments, he removed the urn's cap, threw it far out over the waves. He waited for a swell to recede, followed it. Just as another began its rush he swung the urn in a high arc. A spiral of gray-white powder spewed forth and drifted out to sea on the wind. He raced back to the dry sand above the fingers of the tidal surge. He chased the outgoing surf again and swung the urn once more, but little ash was expelled. He grabbed the vessel with both hands and shook a few bits free. He raced inland but the breaker caught him, burying his feet to the ankle.

Now Olivia understood the strange remark Nicholas had made during their drive from Salem to the condo. *The end is at the beginning.* He had spread Julia's ashes at the place he met her.

She refocused the scope, her hands quivering. Nicholas dumped handfuls of sand into the urn. He waited for a wave to retreat and, holding the urn with both hands, ran toward the ocean spinning around like a discus thrower at a track and field event. The urn sailed in a high arc, slowly tumbling, out and beyond the breakers.

57TBRD